1636

THE ATLANTIC ENCOUNTER

THE RING OF FIRE SERIES

1632 by Eric Flint
1633 by Eric Flint & David Weber
1634: The Baltic War by Eric Flint & David Weber
1634: The Galileo Affair by Eric Flint & Andrew Dennis
1634: The Bavarian Crisis by Eric Flint & Virginia DeMarce
1634: The Ram Rebellion by Eric Flint & Virginia DeMarce et al.
1635: The Cannon Law by Eric Flint & Andrew Dennis
1635: The Dreeson Incident by Eric Flint & Virginia DeMarce
1635: The Eastern Front by Eric Flint
1635: The Papal Stakes by Eric Flint & Charles E. Gannon
1636: The Saxon Uprising by Eric Flint
1636: The Kremlin Games by Eric Flint, Gorg Huff & Paula Goodlett
1636: The Devil's Opera by Eric Flint & David Carrico
1636: Commander Cantrell in the West Indies by
Eric Flint & Charles E. Gannon
1636: The Viennese Waltz by Eric Flint, Gorg Huff & Paula Goodlett
1636: The Cardinal Virtues by Eric Flint & Walter Hunt
1635: A Parcel of Rogues by Eric Flint & Andrew Dennis
1636: The Ottoman Onslaught by Eric Flint
1636: Mission to the Mughals by Eric Flint & Griffin Barber
1636: The Vatican Sanction by Eric Flint & Charles E. Gannon
1637: The Volga Rules by Eric Flint, Gorg Huff & Paula Goodlett
1637: The Polish Maelstrom by Eric Flint
1636: The China Venture by Eric Flint & Iver P. Cooper
1636: The Atlantic Encounter by Eric Flint & Walter Hunt

1635: The Tangled Web by Virginia DeMarce
1635: The Wars for the Rhine by Anette Pedersen
1636: Seas of Fortune by Iver P. Cooper
1636: The Chronicles of Dr. Gribbleflotz by Kerryn Offord & Rick Boatright
1636: Flight of the Nightingale by David Carrico

Time Spike by Eric Flint & Marilyn Kosmatka
The Alexander Inheritance by Eric Flint, Gorg Huff & Paula Goodlett

Grantville Gazette volumes I-V, ed. by Eric Flint
Grantville Gazette VI-VII, ed. by Eric Flint & Paula Goodlett
Grantville Gazette VIII, ed. by Eric Flint & Walt Boyes
Ring of Fire I-IV, ed. by Eric Flint

**To purchase any of these titles in e-book form,
please go to www.baen.com.**

1636

THE ATLANTIC
ENCOUNTER

ERIC FLINT
WALTER H. HUNT

1636: THE ATLANTIC ENCOUNTER

A Baen Books Original

Baen Publishing Enterprises
P.O. Box 1403
Riverdale, NY 10471
www.baen.com

ISBN: 978-1-9821-2475-5

Cover art by Tom Kidd
Maps by Michael Knopp

First printing, August 2020

Distributed by Simon & Schuster
1230 Avenue of the Americas
New York, NY 10020

Library of Congress Cataloging-in-Publication Data

Names: Flint, Eric, author. | Hunt, Walter H., author.
Title: 1636: the Atlantic encounter / Eric Flint & Walter H. Hunt.
Other titles: Sixteen hundred thirty-six
Description: Riverdale, NY : Baen, 2020. | Series: Ring of fire
Identifiers: LCCN 2020021158 | ISBN 9781982124755 (hardcover)
Subjects: GSAFD: Alternative histories (Fiction) | Science fiction.
Classification: LCC PS3556.L548 A6186688 2020 | DDC 813/.54—dc23
LC record available at https://lccn.loc.gov/2020021158

Pages by Joy Freeman (www.pagesbyjoy.com)
Printed in the United States of America
10 9 8 7 6 5 4 3 2 1

To our wives, Lucille and Lisa,

and also to the many health care workers

who work so diligently and selflessly for all of us.

Contents

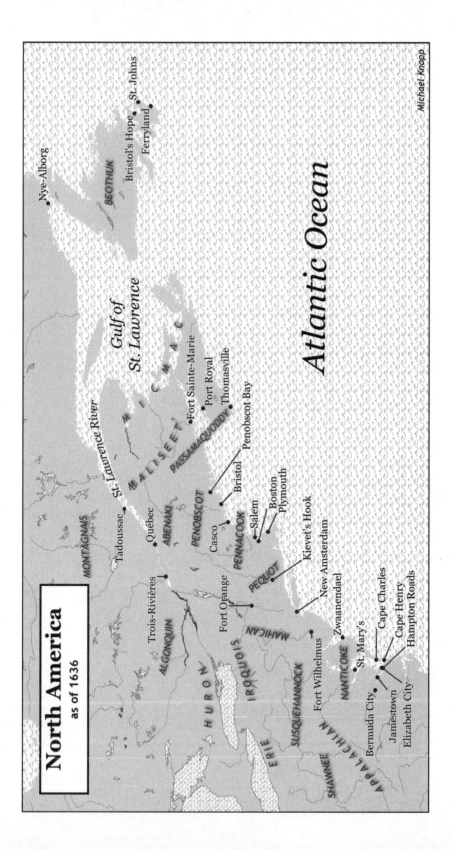

North America
as of 1636

Atlantic Ocean

Gulf of
St. Lawrence

St. Lawrence River

Michael Knopp

Nye-Alborg

BEOTHUK

Bristol's Hope • St. Johns
Ferryland

MI'CMAC

MONTAGNAIS

Tadoussac
Québec

MALISEET

Fort Sainte-Marie
Port Royal
Thomasville

PASSAMAQUODDY

Penobscot Bay

ABENAKI

PENOBSCOT

Bristol

Casco

Trois-Rivières

ALGONQUIN

PENNACOOK

Salem
Boston
Plymouth

Kievet's Hook

HURON

IROQUOIS

Fort Orange

MAHICAN

PEQUOT

New Amsterdam

ERIE

SUSQUEHANNOCK

Fort Wilhelmus

Zwaanendael

NANTICOKE

St. Mary's

APPALACHIAN

SHAWNEE

Bermuda City
Jamestown
Elizabeth City

Cape Charles
Cape Henry
Hampton Roads

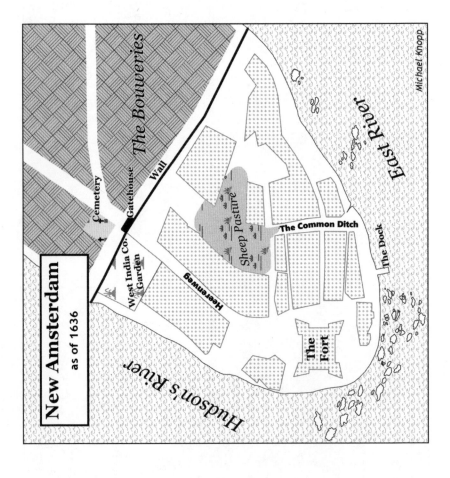

New Amsterdam
as of 1636

The Bouweries

Cemetery

Gatehouse

Wall

West India CO
Garden

Heerenweg

Sheep Pasture

The Common Ditch

The Dock

The Fort

East River

Hudson's River

Michael Knopp

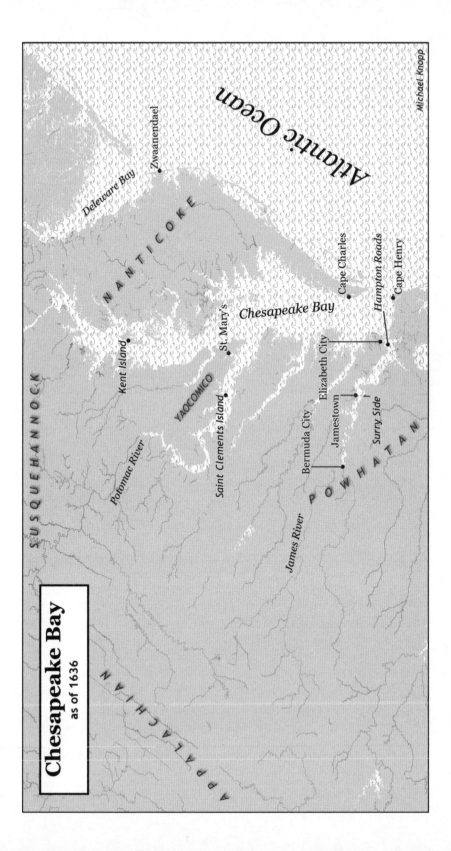

Chesapeake Bay
as of 1636

Atlantic Ocean

Chesapeake Bay

Deleware Bay

Zwaanendael

NANTICOKE

SUSQUEHANNOCK

Kent Island

St. Mary's

YAOCOMICO

Saint Clements Island

Potomac River

APPALACHIAN

James River

POWHATAN

Bermuda City

Jamestown

Surry Side

Elizabeth City

Cape Charles

Hampton Roads

Cape Henry

Michael Knopp

Prologue

October 1635

Bamberg, capital of the State of Thuringia-Franconia
United States of Europe

"Come in," Ed Piazza said, in response to a knock on his office door. His secretary stuck her head into the room.

"Leopold Cavriani is here, Mr. President," she said.

"Send him in, please." Ed pushed aside the papers he'd been looking at, opened one of the desk's drawers and pulled out a file folder. Then, with a peculiar expression on his face—part interest, part exasperation—he handed it to Estuban Miro.

The new chief of intelligence for the president of the State of Thuringia-Franconia half rose from his chair across the desk to accept the folder. It was rather on the thick side. "What's this?" he asked.

"One of the more—ah, adventurous—projects left to us by our departed former prime minister."

Miro raised an eyebrow and resumed his seat. Given that the former official in question, Mike Stearns, was not known to be risk-averse—to put it mildly—this promised to be interesting.

A man was ushered into the room. Estuban recognized him, although they'd never spoken to one another at any length. He was Leopold Cavriani, a close associate of Piazza and the person generally considered in charge of the far-flung and extended Cavriani family's commercial enterprises.

The association in question was a rather gray and shadowy

1

business. Piazza used Cavriani as an informal go-between and facilitator as well as a confidant.

The president waited until Cavriani had taken a seat before proceeding. "You can find all the details in the folder, Estuban. For the moment, let me summarize the matter." He leaned back in his chair. "A little over a year ago, we were approached by a Dutchman named Jan van der Glinde."

Miro cocked his side slightly. "*We . . . meaning . . . ?*"

"Not me, initially. I only found out about this when Mike Stearns handed the matter over to me along with"—again, his expression indicated interest and, this time, more than a little exasperation—"about eight jillion others."

Miro nodded his understanding. The United States of Europe had a parliamentary system; under it, the opposition party formed a shadow cabinet when it was out of power, so that it would be ready to take charge of government should political fortunes turn in its favor. In this instance, though, there was a peculiar twist. The man who would normally be the recognized head of the opposition, Mike Stearns, was now a general in Gustav Adolf's forces fighting in Poland. Given that it was impractical for him to play any direct role in the affairs of the Fourth of July Party, leadership of the opposition had fallen partly to Stearns' wife Rebecca and partly to Ed Piazza.

The division of labor between the two was subtle and complex—and on Piazza's part, sometimes of questionable legality. Being the chief executive of the USE's most populous and wealthiest state, Piazza was in position to form what amounted to a shadow *government*, not simply a shadow cabinet.

Ed Piazza, a high school principal in his former life, was somewhat uncomfortable in that role. Certainly much more so than Mike Stearns would have been. But he'd taken it on nonetheless, because the policies and political tactics being followed by those currently in charge of the USE, especially the Swedish chancellor Oxenstierna, were of dubious legality themselves. The new nation was coming perilously close to open civil war.

Piazza cleared his throat and continued. "Van der Glinde initially approached Francisco Nasi, who passed the matter on to Mike." Nasi had been Stearns' chief of intelligence. For all intents and purposes, Estuban Miro had succeeded to his position—except that he reported to Piazza instead of Stearns.

"Van der Glinde came here from New Amsterdam—what

up-time, in a different world, would become New York City. He claimed to represent the colonial authorities. It's hard to judge the truth of it, but Nasi did a little digging and discovered that this guy was also serving as an intermediary for Kiliaen van Rensselaer."

For the first time since he'd entered, Cavriani spoke up. "Rensselaer is the greatest *patroon* of the Dutch colony, though he resides in Amsterdam. He's involved in a number of New World projects. Some have worked out; some..." he made a gesture as if to say, *you pay your money and you take your chances.*

That was enough to jog Miro's memory. "His wealth derives from the jewel and precious metal trade, as I recall."

"That's right," said Piazza.

Estuban's mind was moving ahead. "So he wanted assistance from the USE to fend off the French. King Charles' cession of all English rights to the New World didn't *theoretically* affect Dutch holdings, but..." He shrugged. "If Richelieu establishes French dominance in North America, the Dutch holdings will most likely fall sooner or later."

"Right again. Nasi said that Van der Glinde was very dramatic about it. 'Save our neck from the French wolf,' the Dutchman told him. Of course, there wasn't much we could do at the time.

"But given that hostilities with France had still not officially ended, Mike decided it would be worth sending an expedition across the Atlantic to see what trouble they might be able to stir up for the French."

"What sort of expedition?"

"Nothing overtly military. Even if it was a good idea—and I'm pretty sure that no one thought it would be—we don't have the forces for such a purpose anyway. Mike told Francisco to see about sending a single ship.

"With radio capability, we could at least stay informed of what the French were up to over there. In the end, we put an up-timer named Gordon Chehab in charge. Francisco decided that having a small dirigible aboard would give the expedition some mobility, so he chose Chehab, who had experience piloting balloons."

Estuban nodded. "As it happens, I know Chehab. I knew he was considering building an airship—a dirigible, not a balloon, precisely. I assumed that he planned to go into competition with my own ships." He made a small approving noise, too soft to be a grunt. "It seems his security is good."

Piazza now swiveled in his chair to regard Cavriani. "And that explains *your* presence. Since we're now at peace with France, we can hardly send an expedition with the overt intent of causing them political trouble."

Cavriani smiled, almost seraphically. "Yes. 'Trade missions' are handy things, aren't they?"

Piazza spoke. "I asked Leopold to do us the favor instead of one of the Abrabanels because he's a little further under the radar and he has no obvious and direct ties to the USE. Given the change in political circumstances, Chehab's expedition will be under the auspices of the State of Thuringia-Franconia. You'll serve as our liaison, Estuban."

"I take it Prime Minister Wettin has no knowledge of the affair."

Piazza smiled. "Not unless Mike told him as part of his briefing when he left office. And if I know Mike—which I do—he would have seen no reason to do so." Piously, he added, "There's never been anything *official* about the whole business, you understand."

"Naturally not." Estuban had no objection to official piety, when the circumstances warranted it. "A Dutch *patroon*, purely in his capacity as a private citizen, made inquiries through the intermediary of another private person, which in the end led to no official action. Chehab's expedition is itself a private enterprise, under the auspices"—here he nodded at Cavriani—"of yet another private citizen. Not that the cardinal won't see through that, of course."

"Of course," Piazza agreed.

"Our sole interest," Estuban continued, "is in the possible commercial benefits which might accrue to the State of Thuringia-Franconia, as well as, of course"—his own tone got noticeably pious—"the well-being of citizens of the province, engaged in lawful business."

"Precisely."

The room fell silent for a moment. Then Piazza cleared his throat and said: "And don't bother telling me the whole damn thing is probably a wild goose chase. I know that. Leopold knows that. Nasi knew it too. Hell, Mike just about said as much."

There was another brief silence. "Then why did he authorize—no, let's say, set the thing in motion?" Miro asked.

Piazza chuckled. "He said, 'What the hell, now and then a wild goose gets caught, doesn't it?' Though it might get kinda rough on Gordon Chehab."

Part One

April 1636

The ever-hooded, tragic-gestured sea

—Wallace Stevens,
"The Idea of Order at Key West"

Chapter 1

Hamburg
United States of Europe

The first look Gordon Chehab ever had of the ship that would take him across the ocean was on a blustery day from across the harbor. He had come all the way from Grantville, part by stage and part by riverboat down the Elbe; he had taken his time—which was part and parcel of the way people got around in the year of grace 1636. It was the present day for him, and for all the rest of the inhabitants of the small town in West Virginia that had been carried back to this time by the Ring of Fire. But rough travel was nothing new for Gordon; he'd hitchhiked his way across the United States several times when he was younger.

The ship didn't have a name at the time he first saw her. She sat high in the water, unladen; carpenters and riggers were hard at work.

He walked along the broad dock, his duffel slung over his shoulder, but before he reached the ship's anchorage he heard his name being called from the quarterdeck.

"Chehab?"

He shielded his eyes against the afternoon sun. "That's me."

"Was told you'd be coming," the man said in Amideutsch, though it was with a round Dutch accent. "Thought you might come in yesterday."

"Not much chance of that. I made the best time I could."

The man grunted. "No rush, I suppose. We'll not be weighing anchor for some weeks." He turned aside and spat over the side of the rail. "Care to come aboard?"

"It's why I'm here."

The man gestured to the gangplank. Gordon walked up as one of the riggers walked down. The man who'd spoken to him was waiting at the top, and firmly grasped his hand.

"Maartens," he said. "Claes Maartens. I'm to be the sailing master for this expedition."

"Gordon Chehab. You work for the Cavrianis?"

The man looked about, as if it were a scrap of information not to be overheard. "*Ja*," he said quietly. "Though, as they say, not *officially.*"

Gordon didn't answer. From the time at which he'd been approached by Francisco Nasi until now, the entire expedition had been a matter of secrecy. At the outset, he'd been told the expedition would be undertaken by the government of the United States of Europe; but since mid-1635 that government had been in the hands of Wilhelm Wettin rather than Mike Stearns. And, by extension, Don Francisco was now a private citizen.

So, very quietly, the expedition's auspices had been taken over by the provincial government of the State of Thuringia-Franconia. Gordon now reported to President Ed Piazza's head of intelligence Estuban Miro, usually through the intermediary of Leopold Cavriani. The expedition was now officially a trade mission for the SoTF, rather than for the USE. Apparently Prime Minister Wettin hadn't been informed of the project, either, which made Gordon feel a little exposed.

It's an off-budget program, the spymaster had told him at their first interview. *Wettin doesn't know about it—I'm not sure that the Emperor really knows about it either.* His briefing from the President of Thuringia-Franconia, Ed Piazza, confirmed that.

If caught or killed, Gordon thought, *the President will disavow all knowledge of your actions. Good luck, Jim.*

"Yes," he said. "I suppose we do."

Maartens gave him a place in the captain's cabin to temporarily stow his gear. No one was sleeping aboard the partially refit ship: there was a boardinghouse where the craftsmen were staying. He then gave Gordon a thorough tour of the ship he would call home for most of the next year.

"She's a beauty, I'll say that," Maartens said. "Used to weather, from what I see." The tour had started amidships. As he spoke, Maartens placed one of his beefy hands on the main mast. "We took off her lines, the shipwright and myself, and we realized that she was probably set to handle most of what the Atlantic can throw at us."

"*Most?*"

"There are storms that no one can handle." Maartens made a gesture. "'Twould be bad luck to speak of that. But properly ballasted, she should do well. I'd rather be on her deck than up in that airship of yours."

"Then it's arrived."

"*Ja*. It's ashore, a great heap of canvas, all of its rigging, and that basket or whatever it is. We'll rig that like a lifeboat. The rest of it, we'll store in part of the lower hold which we'll rat-proof as you specified. I have to tell you, though, I don't see how that could ever fly, whether or not the rats gnaw holes in it."

"It flies," Gordon said. "That's my department. It's why I'm here."

Maartens looked at him sidelong. "Some up-timer thing, I'll wager."

"I first flew in a balloon up-time," Gordon answered. "This is a little more sophisticated than that: it's a dirigible. But the technology isn't all that complicated in any case—but back to the ship."

Maartens patted the great mast with his hand. "The original shipwright knew what he was doing: it'll stand up to heavy weather. The ship has three masts, as you can see, fore"—he pointed forward, then behind—"and mizzen. We're going to rig her fore and aft rather than square, which I'm not sure I hold with—I think that's going to cause us more trouble, but it means we need fewer crew. Wrong kind of weather, though..." He looked skyward, as if the bright sunny day would darken and prove him right. Then, shrugged. "*Ach*. But with the ripstops in the sails, and the extra reefing sails...As long as the crew is trained properly, she'll handle all right."

Gordon nodded, not sure what to make of what he'd been told. Sailors had their own language, and he'd not learned it quite yet.

Maartens led him aft, talking all the way. "She's designed to be fairly shallow draft, in case we want to take her upriver or into some coastal waters. But you pay for that, you do—in stiff weather she'll take on water. Sailors have a saying," he added, poking Gordon with a sharp elbow, "'sailing with your own coffin.'" He chuckled. "But God willing we'll be spared that."

The ship had been originally built for and used in the Baltic Sea. It had been acquired for this expedition, and from what Maartens told Gordon, it had been structurally intact but had "been through some heavy seas"—by which Gordon came to understand that those heavy seas had beaten the living crap out of it.

Cavriani had probably gotten a good deal, Gordon thought. To some extent that was a blessing in disguise. Though Maartens complained about the extent to which the rigging was a ruin, it meant that the riggers and carpenters could rework her from start to finish without having to engage in a struggle with seventeenth-century shipwrights.

She had originally been square-rigged. Gordon had needed to have that explained to him, because the sails didn't *look* square. Maartens explained in a voice with scarcely leashed patience that the term referred to the rigging, not necessarily the sail itself. Square rigging was suitable for the type of ship, but sails with that sort of rigging—at least given seventeenth-century materials— tended to be baggy. It meant that, even though it was stable in rough seas, the ship had to catch the wind at least three points behind in order to properly fill. But it was stable, less likely to capsize in rough seas.

The disadvantage for square-rigged ships was the amount of crew required to handle them. By rigging the ship fore and aft only, a quarter to a third the number of men would be required, though they'd have to be more skilled as the maneuvers were a bit more complex. But fewer crew meant fewer people who might be working against their interests.

There was still daylight when Maartens finished showing him around the ship, but that was hardly surprising: at fifty-three degrees north. Days in Hamburg were long, even in April. Maartens showed him everything: the masts and ropes, the decks and holds, the spars and ... a number of other nautical things that Gordon couldn't remember.

You're the airship guy, he kept reminding himself. He'd done a little sailing, but on a fairly calm lake on a fairly nice day—not across the Atlantic Ocean in a seventeenth-century sailing ship. It struck him as a bit crazy, but the idea that his home town had been transported back to the Thirty Years' War was like a plot from a fantasy novel as it was. He knew he'd have to trust his life and the mission to men like Maartens.

The Dutch sailing master seemed pleased with the ongoing work, with one singular exception.

"I know you up-timers have a lot to say about ship design," he told Gordon as they stood on the quarterdeck. "Some of the old salts in Hamburg harbor can't say enough about what they think will happen to this ship when she launches. But I trust what I've been told." He laid his hand on the ship's wheel, which was smooth and polished wood, quite different from the weathered walls nearby. "But this—*ach*, it'll take some getting used to."

"The wheel? Why?" he asked. "How did you *plan* to steer her?"

"Why, with a whipstaff, of course. I know your Admiral Simpson *insists* on this contraption, but it's..." He took hold of one of the handles and pulled the wheel slightly counterclockwise. "It's just *foreign*, you know."

"I don't know of any other way to steer a ship."

"Really." Maartens looked at him, half-amused and half-scowling. "Well, a whipstaff is how *sailors* control their ship. It's simple—you want to go to starboard, you pull the staff to port and push down. This—you turn the same direction you want the tiller to go? Madness."

"Makes sense to me."

"Not surprised," Maartens said. "But Miro insisted on it. *More control*, he said. True, you couldn't move more than five or six points of sail with a whipstaff, but at least you knew what you were doing."

"By pushing the tiller the opposite way."

"Aye, that's right."

Gordon decided that it was better not to argue the point.

Almost nothing was decided that first day—as Maartens had pointed out, the ship wasn't due to be launched for at least a few weeks. But Miro had given Gordon considerable leeway for the mission: where they were to go, who would be included, and so forth. Sitting on his bed in the rooming house overlooking the Speicherstadt of Hamburg as the late-setting sun cast its last rays between the warehouses, Gordon resolved one thing: the name of the ship.

When he was just a kid in Grantville, he had seen—repeated over and over on television—the disaster that had claimed a space shuttle as it launched from Florida. It was a horrible sight, but not long afterward the president—President Reagan—had given a speech that had stuck with him. In the face of the tragedy, the speech had praised the astronauts who had died that day. *The future doesn't belong to the fainthearted,* he'd said. *It belongs to the brave.* That line had stuck with him, along with the more famous one about slipping the surly bonds of Earth to touch the face of God.

That vessel—that ship—had never reached its destination. But the ship for which it had been named, on which Gordon had done a history paper later on, was famous: it had sailed for two years, opening up the world of the sea for nineteenth-century science. It was a worthy name, and Gordon wanted to adopt it.

In a few weeks, *Challenger* would slip the surly bonds of the Old World and journey to the new, and he and the others aboard would try to be worthy of its name.

Chapter 2

Even from the top of the gangplank, Gordon could see how much Pete had grown. Four years ago, when the Ring of Fire had taken them all back to the seventeenth century, his oldest younger brother had been lanky and a bit soft, avoiding the beer gut by twenty-two-year-old metabolism and lots of baseball. Now—

Well, now he was a soldier. In fatigues with a sergeant's stripes on his sleeve, there was nothing soft about him.

"Big bro," Pete said, coming up to meet him.

"Peter." Gordon shook his brother's hand, and then found himself taken up in a bear hug. "Great to see you."

"Same here." Peter Chehab let go and stepped back. "You look good. Mom and Dad wanted me to say hi."

"And Penny?"

Pete looked away across the harbor. "Yeah," he said after a moment. "I'm sure she'd say hi too."

"You didn't see her?"

"She was on call. I was only in Grantville for a few hours."

Pete's wife, Penny, was a nurse—one of the relatively few up-timers with medical training, like himself; she would likely be busy all the time. But Penny was his *wife*, and he had a little baby daughter ... which was why he was married in the first place.

But that was a conversation for another time.

"Thanks. I've been meaning to write, but ... you know, time gets away."

13

Pete laughed. "Every time someone from Grantville says something like that it makes me laugh. 'Time gets away.' *Right.* So...what's the deep dark secret project? Dad said you were working for the Man."

It was Gordon's turn to laugh. "Let me buy you a drink and tell you all about it."

Hamburg was full of pubs, especially since it was in use as the anchorage for some of the USE Navy. There were a few places down by the docks that the crew frequented; instead, after Pete's gear was stowed, they walked into the Altstadt and found a quieter place where they wouldn't be easily overheard.

Gordon gestured to a table. No one took particular notice— there were only a few patrons in the gloomy room. The brothers sat at an unoccupied table.

At Gordon's gesture a pitcher of beer and two ceramic mugs arrived, along with a wedge of cheese and plates of *Labskaus*, a sort of local stew that reminded him of their grandmother's shepherd's pie—except that this had beets in it.

Pete needed no encouragement; he dug right in.

"The lieutenant had a saying, which sounds even better in German," Pete said between bites. "'When in doubt, eat. If there is nothing to eat, sleep.' Never quite know where your next meal is coming from."

"How are things down in—wherever you were last posted?"

"Suhl." Pete stopped eating for a moment. "Not too bad, after the Ram Rebellion was over. For a while, though, things got pretty hairy."

"And what about back home? Penny, and my little niece?"

"I hear she's growing up fast. But she's only a year and a half old, big bro."

"And you didn't have time to see her when you were last in Grantville."

Pete set his fork beside his plate and looked up at Gordon. "I don't know when this became a conversation about me."

"It isn't. But given why I arranged for you to come up here, it might be."

"All right, Gord. Let's have it. What's the big dark secret project? What are you doing out here—with such tight-ass security?"

Gordon took a sip from his own mug. The beer was thin

and hoppy, not really to his taste, but there was no pop and you couldn't drink the water.

"Do you remember when I hitchhiked across the country, the summer after I graduated from high school?"

"Remember? How could I forget? I wanted to come with you."

"I know you did. But you were only sixteen and still in school."

"It didn't matter." Pete smiled. "I didn't know at the time how much it didn't matter."

"Well, they didn't know when I'd get back if ever, and it was important to Mom and Dad that you finished school. They had hopes for you, Pete—that you'd find something you wanted to do, or that some scout would like the look of your fastball—"

"You mean, so I could get out of Grantville and out into the real world."

"I don't think they would have put it that way, especially Mom."

"This is old ground, big bro. Grantville was a dead end until the Ring picked it up and dropped it into the middle of a bloody war. Then things started looking up.

"I hated that summer. David and Terri and Luke marked your trip with little pins in an AAA map tacked onto a corkboard in the family room, every time you called home. And instead of being on the road with my big brother I was stuck back there. I thought about just running away, but I didn't for some reason."

"Because I talked you out of it," Gordon said. "More than once."

"So why are we talking about the summer of '94, anyway?"

"When I left Grantville it wasn't to *go* anywhere." Gordon leaned back in his chair, mug in hand. "It was to get as far away as I could. Not from you, or Mom and Dad, or my other brothers and sister—just to get away from Grantville. I don't think I even knew how small it was when I left, but I sure as hell did before I'd thumbed as far as Cincinnati."

He took a sip of his beer. "I tried to hide my 'hillbilly' accent, y'know. That's what they called me. Asked me where my banjo was. All that crap."

"Banjo?"

"Well, they could tell I couldn't dance." Mugs clicked together and both brothers drank.

"So my eyes were opened," Gordon said. "I mean, when we were growing up we always heard about how Dad was from 'away,' from Wheeling, the big city. But Wheeling was nothing."

"And Grantville was less than nothing," Pete said.

"Right. The last one in our family to get out and see the world was Grampa Charlie, and that was to go to Korea. Guess *he* learned to duck."

"He was at the Inchon landing." Pete raised his mug again and took a long drink.

"Do you remember the night I called you from El Paso? I was working as a dishwasher at a hotel chain. I'd been on the road a couple of months—you'd started your junior year at the high school."

"I remember how pissed off I was that night."

"Bro, you were pissed off the whole of your *junior year*. You told me that Mr. Piazza said you were going to wind up in the state prison if you kept it up, and—"

"And you asked me what kind of trouble I was getting into, and I told you nothing that really mattered. It was just evil ways. 'You got to change your evil ways, baby,'" Pete sang, off-key like every other male member of his family, and they laughed again. Then Pete said, "So what does this have to do with—"

"I'm getting to that. Don't rush me."

"You're just like Grampa Charlie. Never just give the facts, got to have a whole damn *story* to go with it."

"I'm buying. You get the story."

"Fine, whatever. Go ahead."

"I told you that the only chance we have for happiness in this world is to hold on to some kind of dream, Pete. I didn't know what mine was at the time."

"I didn't either. I mean, when I was thirteen I wanted to strike out Barry Bonds and win the World Series. But at sixteen..."

"Well, bro, on that trip that summer I found out what my dream was. I wanted to *fly*."

"Meaning?"

"I could've wound up anywhere, Pete. A buddy from that hotel in El Paso got a job offer from his cousin in Denver and invited me to go with him. There was a long-haul trucker who would've taken me all the way to L.A. if I bought him enough coffee. And there was this sweet young thing from Portland, Oregon, who had a motherly streak and wanted to take me home.

"But I stopped in Albuquerque, New Mexico. A dozen years and one Ring of Fire later, I'm still not sure why I wound up there, but my timing and the universe's timing somehow lined up. During the first week in October, 1994, quite by accident, I found myself in the middle of the International Balloon Fiesta. And I knew that I wanted to fly."

"In a balloon?"

"Damn straight. I went back in '96 before I went to EMT training, and again in '99. I had tickets and a place to stay in 2000...but I got me a German vacation instead."

Pete thought about that for a minute, and then his eyebrows went straight up.

"Do you mean to tell me that you're building a—a..."

"The correct term is 'dirigible,' my man. And that is *exactly* what we're building. And when it's done, I'm going to get to fly it."

"In the war zone?"

"No way," Gordon said, and lowered his voice. "Not in Poland. In *America*."

Pete didn't say anything for a while. Gordon pushed the last bits of the *Labskaus* around on his plate.

"So you're building the Goodyear Blimp."

"Not exactly. It's a dirigible, but it doesn't have much of a frame other than a keel and a nose cone to keep the bag from deforming. It couldn't carry the weight, particularly since we don't have any aluminum. It would have to be made of wood, and we just don't have enough lift."

"Couldn't you salvage some—"

"Yeah. As if. After almost four years, Pete, all the salvaging that's going to happen has already happened. No, it's a big airbag with a long boat-shaped thing underneath connected by catenaries. It'll be stored aboard *Challenger*—"

"That's the name of the ship?"

"Yeah." Gordon sipped at his beer. "Thought you'd like that."

"You did a paper on that old ship, the one that went around the world. Still, seems like a bad luck charm to name it for the one shuttle that didn't make it."

"Let's not focus on that. As I say, it'll be stored aboard ship, and we'll launch it from shore."

"So you're not planning to go across the Atlantic in a balloon."

"Hell, no." Gordon sat up straight. "Depending on the weight it carries, I'm not expecting much more than a hundred miles' range. It gets lofted, flies inland, then comes back to the starting place. It's not the *Hindenburg*."

"Didn't that one turn out badly too?"

"Well, yes. But this is a hot-air ship, not a hydrogen one."

Pete let his brother look off into the distance for a few seconds, then said, "So how do I fit into all of this?"

"Well, it's like this, little bro. The expedition for this jaunt is pretty small, especially aboard the balloon when we go inland. There's going to be a doctor in the crew, and I can help out as a combat medic. I'm the linguist and the director of tourism: my German's good and my French is pretty solid, and after a little while in this area my Dutch isn't so bad either. But if everything I hear is true, there'll be times when talking isn't going to work."

"You mean...shooting instead."

"And not necessarily asking questions later."

"I have a previous commitment, Gord. I'm in the Army, you know. There's a war going on with the Poles and now the Bavarians."

"All taken care of," Gordon said. "If you're willing. Detached service. There's no one I'd rather have at my back. We'd be away for at least a year. No mail, no visits home: no chance to keep in touch except by radio, and not very often...I realize that it means leaving Penny and Karen behind..."

"That's less of a deal than it might be."

"You're sure."

"Yes. This has become a conversation about me again."

"We might as well get it out in the open, little bro. I shouldn't take you that far away from your family."

The last comment was met with a stony silence.

Gordon wanted to ask further, but his brother didn't seem interested in pursuing it: Pete gave him back the stare he used when he was getting ready to strike someone out.

"All right," Gordon said at last, and looked into his mostly empty mug, as if there might be an answer in there.

"So you want to take me up in a balloon. A—a dirigible."

"Yep. And on the ground, too. Think of it as a replacement for the trip I couldn't take you on when you were sixteen."

"Even if it means being away...from home...for a while, it probably beats getting shot at down south."

"You may get shot at in America, Pete."

"So where are we going, exactly?"

"Newfoundland, at least, to check out the Danish settlement

there. New England coast, possibly New Amsterdam. See what the French are doing. It was originally a scouting mission for Francisco Nasi, but he's been succeeded by Estuban Miro. Officially, it's now a trade mission for the State of Thuringia-Franconia." Gordon smiled. "Think of it as the best detention you'll ever serve for Mr. Piazza."

"The, uh, President." This time Pete looked into his mug for several moments. "And if I say no?"

Gordon Chehab was about to reply, but stopped suddenly, perplexed.

"I—I'm not sure. I mean, you know what's here now, and it's being kept quiet...I just assume—"

"You assumed I'd say yes."

"I guess I did."

"I'll have to think about it."

"Fair enough," Gordon said after a moment. "We're not due to sail until—"

"Okay, I've thought long enough," Pete said. "Count me in. On one condition."

"Which is?"

"We don't go back to West Virginia."

Chapter 3

Stephane Hoff lifted his pen, dipped it into the inkwell and poised it over the paper; but before he could even write the customary polite salutation, he leaned his head back on the chair and set it aside with a sigh.

Working for Monsieur Servien was never easy. He was demanding, precise and—as Hoff had learned quickly—astute enough to see through the words and determine if anything of consequence was actually being said.

Other than false information, the provision of which was out of the question if one wanted to continue living (let alone be paid), there was nothing that the intendant despised more than information free of content.

The up-timers had an expression for that—*as they had for everything else*, Hoff mused to himself. Monsieur Servien had a very accurate "bullshit detector." Therefore, rhetorical flourishes aside, it was critically necessary that reports be thorough, factual and—most important—actually contain useful intelligence.

Otherwise, Hoff thought, *I don't get paid.*

He sat up straight, wiped the excess ink off his quill and dipped it again, and began to write, tucking his left hand under the table by old habit.

Most esteemed Monsieur,

In accordance with your direction and advice, I have been observing the ship under renovation in Hamburg harbor. She is a former Baltic trading vessel, roughly one hundred fifty tons, under the command of a Dutch sailing master named Claes Maartens. The ship is to be named Challenger—

He paused for a moment, trying to come up with a solid French equivalent.

—which name seems to hold special significance for up-timers; Le Défi might be a suitable translation. There are two Americans associated with the vessel—one who has been on hand for some time named Gordon Chehab, and another who arrived just this week, his brother Peter. I am sure that they have been charged with some special mission, since they have discussed matters privately away from the ship—I regret that I was unable to overhear the import of their conversation.

The younger brother is a soldier of some sort; the elder is not—though I am as yet unaware of his area of specialty, since he does not appear to have the habits and skills of a seaman. It is possible that he will command the expedition.

Hoff paused again, scratching his ear with his quill. What could he say about the older brother? What was he doing there? Up-timers, other than a few who remained in Grantville, didn't usually involve themselves with any sort of project without deliberate purpose.

He dipped the pen in ink again and continued to write.

I do note, however, that the sailing master is on cordial terms with shipfitters and chandlers and has little trouble obtaining supplies and assistance in port. Not only is his patron's credit good, but his ready access suggests that this project is important to someone of wealth or influence or both.

That really said very little, and upon reflection sounded like a thinly concealed justification for continuing to keep him here in Hamburg; but Hoff let it go. Either this was important to Servien—and thus *Monsieur le Cardinal*—or it was not. There wasn't much that Hoff could do about it.

Something was going on with this *Challenger*; but he was at a loss just yet to determine what it was.

> *The refitting operation is still several weeks from completion, but what little I have been able to learn suggests that the vessel will be prepared to clear out of port sometime in early November. Its destination is unknown, but I will bend all of my effort to obtain that information as soon as possible.*
>
> *I believe that this matter is of continuing interest, and request additional time to supplement your knowledge on the subject and accordingly remain*
>
> > *Your obedient servant,*
> > *S. Hoff*

It proved more and more difficult to see what was actually going on aboard the ship as it came closer to being seaworthy. Stephane realized that in order to further inform Servien it would be necessary to get aboard: and that meant only one thing.

There wasn't much opportunity to learn to sail at home in his native Alsace, but there was one thing he had learned there as well as in Paris, where he'd spent time—and that was to climb. He was agile and...*compact*, which was a polite way of saying *short*, and heights didn't bother him at all.

There was a certain amount of risk in the venture. He'd been shadowing the two Americans—he'd even followed them to a place in the Altstadt where they'd gone for a private meeting—and if they recognized him, things might go badly.

But he needed to get closer.

So, on a brisk, windy afternoon, he positioned himself out in the open on the dock and looked up at the topmast, where one of the riggers was fighting the breeze. It didn't take long to be noticed.

"Hey, short stuff," said a voice from the deck.

Stephane feigned indifference, looking up only after a few moments. "Are you talking to me?"

"Shortest thing dockside," the man said. It was the Dutch sailing master, Maartens. "Long way up," he said, gesturing upward.

"Doesn't look too far to me," Stephane said.

"Aye, you'd know how far it was if you fell from that height, *niet waar*?" The sailing master laughed along with a few of the other sailors nearby.

"Guess I don't have to worry about that. I never fall."

"Eh? That's a pretty brave statement for a little man. I think maybe"—he looked at his companions—"I think maybe you'll have to put your money where your mouth is."

"You want to make a bet?"

"Sure, sure. What's it worth to you?"

Stephane put his hands on his hips and craned his neck to look at the mast, as if he was trying to estimate its height. "If I make it to the top without missing a step, you take me on for your crew."

"And if you don't?"

"Then you fish me out of the water and you have a good laugh."

"Or mop what's left of you off the deck."

"Not so funny, I'll guess," Stephane said.

"No. Not so funny. All right, little man, you're on. Let's see you climb this mast without putting a foot false."

"And if I make it, you'll sign me on?"

"We'll see, we'll see," Maartens said.

It wasn't quite the endorsement he wanted, but it was a start. Stephane nodded and came up the gangplank to the deck. He could already hear the other sailors sniggering; the younger American, who had been bent over a sawhorse working, stood up straight, curious; Stephane avoided making eye contact.

Compared to the sort of climbing he'd been doing since he was small, the mast was a breeze. There were places to put his feet all the way up, though he would have been able to make it even without—it just made it easier and faster.

Ten minutes later he was standing next to the topman, with as good a view of Hamburg Harbor as anyone could want.

Half an hour after *that* he was signed on as a junior member of *Challenger's* crew, and was put immediately to work—fifteen feet away from the Americans he was trying to watch.

✧   ✧   ✧

Gordon and Pete were on deck watching boats in the harbor when an argument began amidships. One party was Maartens; the other was a pair of crewmen, who were speaking in rapid Dutch in a voice full of snarl but short of shout. One of the men was pointing overboard toward the dock at a collection of boxes and two large trunks.

Next to them stood two women: one was younger, from her stance and attire a servant of some sort, and the other, a woman nearer their age, was looking up defiantly at the main deck of *Challenger*, arms crossed over her chest, her face full of anger.

"Someone you know?" Pete asked.

"Not yet," Gordon said. "But I have the feeling I'm about to." He walked toward the argument, wondering what it was about.

Maartens had an unfolded sheet in his hand and he shook it at the two men—big, burly Dutchmen who clearly hadn't finished having their say.

"—you can load it on the deck, you blighted *klootog*," Maartens was saying to one of them, "or you can go serve on another ship."

"She won't let us," the man answered. "Not until she comes aboard."

"Then let her come aboard."

"A woman on a sailing ship?" he said. "That's courting disaster and you know it."

"Superstition," Maartens said, glancing at Gordon as he approached, Pete trailing. "Nonsense."

"What seems to be the problem?" Gordon asked, though he suspected he already knew the answer.

"*Ach*, nothing that matters, Chehab," Maartens said. "These two oafs don't want to let them aboard." He gestured vaguely toward the dock. The men stalked away, pushing past Gordon and Pete; Maartens scowled at their backs with a look that said, *this is not over.*

"Because they don't want a woman on the deck."

"Something like that."

"I assume that *you* have no problem with the presence of a woman aboard."

"Coming aboard? No, of course not."

Gordon sensed that there was more—something Maartens was not saying. The sailing master glanced at the paper in his hand; Gordon looked at it too. After a few moments he shrugged and handed it over.

Gordon looked at the paper—a letter from their original patron—then at Maartens, then at the two women on the dock.

"You understand," Maartens said, "that I take a more reasonable line on such matters than my crew; they are not as enlightened about *modern* attitudes. As for the others..." he spread his hands, as if he was powerless to change minds.

Enlightened was not an adjective that Gordon associated with the sailing master, but it was a mildly clever way of sidestepping the issue.

"You don't like the idea that our patron has added this..." Gordon looked at the letter again. "Ingrid Skoglund to this mission—to *Challenger*'s passenger list." He read through the rest of the letter: this was to be their doctor—not quite the person Gordon had expected, but he wouldn't turn her away.

Maartens didn't answer.

"I realize you're not thrilled with *me*," Gordon said quietly. "But based on what's written here, she's as valuable to the expedition as I am. I'm a medic; she's a *doctor*, trained in Grantville. I can patch up someone who gets a cut; maybe put in a few stitches. If we're in Virginia and someone breaks a leg, she can take care of it. Without her, that man's a cripple, or worse. She's—"

"A woman," Maartens said.

"Sure looks that way," Pete said.

Gordon glanced over his shoulder, then looked back at Maartens. "She's a trained professional. And a woman, yes. And you don't like that."

"I don't think I have much choice. But it's not sitting at all well with the crew. As for me..."

"You're *enlightened*," Gordon said.

"*Ja.* I have enough other things to get used to... I can get used to a woman doctor. But the others..."

"This is your crew," Gordon said. "If there's something they need to get used to, you'd better get them used to it."

"Or else?"

"Or else I go find another sailing master."

Anger flared in Maartens' eyes, as if to say, *you wouldn't dare.* But it was clear that he believed—that he knew for certain—that even if Gordon wasn't ready to supplant him, their patron would not hesitate.

"But I don't want to even consider it," Gordon continued. "I want to meet this doctor, and get her gear aboard *Challenger*. The crew is going to have to deal with it."

A few minutes and some angry conversation in Dutch later, the cargo and effects on the docks were being hauled aboard, and Ingrid Skoglund and the other woman had come up the gangplank to stand facing the sailing master and the two up-timers. After making sure they were safely aboard and their trunks and boxes were safely stowed, Maartens made an excuse and walked aft, leaving Gordon and Pete with the new arrivals.

"I'm Gordon Chehab," Gordon said. "This is my brother Pete. You must be Ingrid Skoglund."

"Yes," she said. "You are up-timers, I can see."

"How can you tell?" Pete asked.

"It's obvious, to someone who has spent time around you." She shrugged slightly. "But it is difficult to explain in precise terms."

They were speaking in English: the letter, and a very slight accent, identified her as Swedish, but she was completely fluent. She was also what Grandpa Charlie would have called *handsome*: not quite pretty, but strong and healthy, height a little above average, with blue eyes and an oval face framed by curls tucked into her modest bonnet.

Gordon smiled. "I guess you're right. I didn't think about it."

Skoglund stepped forward and took him by the elbow, leading him a few feet away, away from the servant woman and Pete. "I think I may owe you thanks for helping with a difficult situation," she said. "Clearly not everyone is happy with my presence."

"I did what I thought was right."

"Yes. Of course. But I want to make one thing clear," she said. "In your time women are considered equal to men—I have read a great deal about the future time—yet there are some things about it that I do *not* like."

"No doubt."

She frowned at Gordon, but again looked him directly in the eye. "My appreciation is limited to these words. I do not feel myself obliged to offer you any *favors* in return for your good will—and that goes for Sofia as well." She nodded toward the servant woman, who was standing nervously next to Pete.

Gordon couldn't answer at first, and then had to force himself not to laugh. "You think I...you expected me to—"

"I have neither brother nor father here to protect me. I just wanted to be clear."

"Yeah," Gordon said. "Clear. It never even crossed my mind, Doctor. And Pete is married and it probably never crossed his mind either. You have my word."

She nodded, and let her stern face relax into a smile. "Ingrid," she said.

"Ingrid," Gordon said. He extended his hand; she took it, though she did not remove her glove.

The beginning of a wonderful relationship, he thought.

Chapter 4

Work continued on *Challenger*, almost exclusively by people who weren't named Chehab. Gordon was what Maartens charitably called "not handy"—he didn't have a good feel for the ship at the outset, whether it was barely avoiding being clocked by a swinging boom, or losing his balance on the gangways between decks, or tripping over the rigging. His most useful preoccupation was learning to read the down-time charts and to tie the knots that every able seaman knew. Pete, by comparison, turned out to have learned carpentry from somewhere, and soon was in thick with the laborers working on the decks. Ingrid and her assistant, Sofia, kept to themselves: clearly Maartens had spoken with the crew and warned what might happen if they succumbed to either superstition or their natural inclinations, while the two women had no interest in ship-fitting once their berths were arranged and their cargo was brought aboard.

Neither of the brothers had any inclination to go aloft, where more nimble and agile men and boys scrambled and climbed, heedless of the distance they might fall if they should put a foot wrong. Pete had witnessed an amazing display by a little Alsatian who signed on with the crew after going up the mainmast in record time; it was one of the first times either of them had seen the sailing master look impressed.

✧　　✧　　✧

A few weeks after Pete, the radio and its operator arrived and came aboard *Challenger*. The equipment was bulky and primitive; Gordon had seen some ham radio setups before the Ring of Fire, but they were usually just plugged into the wall. There was no AC power outlet anywhere aboard ship—he was pretty sure of that—and that meant that the radio had to carry its own power supply. That took up most of the space, and weight, and it set Maartens to further grumbling.

As for the operator—a down-timer named Ulrich Jaeschke, a quiet and unassuming man who looked as out of place aboard a sailing vessel as Gordon himself—the Dutch sailing master ignored him entirely, just as he ignored the up-timer landsmen. Jaeschke was assigned a berth with the able seamen, who kept their distance from someone with a skill they didn't completely understand.

Gordon began to feel as if he were being watched whenever he was aboard *Challenger*—which was more and more as time went on.

The spring days had been short, a race against the sun, but they became progressively longer, making Gordon eager to get underway. One particularly wearying day he was especially tired and decided to get a little rest before the evening dinner bell. He shared the small aft cabin with Pete; the ladies had been assigned the second cabin in the fore of the ship and Maartens, of course, commanded the first, and had more or less defied the brothers (or anyone else) to take it away from him. As it turned out, though, their quarters were remarkably snug, proof against the winds that blew in from Helgoland Bight.

Pete was already there, whittling away at a piece of wood as he sat on his hammock.

"You look a little worried, big bro. Anything bothering you?"

"No, nothing."

"You lie very badly, which must've hurt you in the army. Out with it." Pete stopped whittling to admire his work. "What's wrong?"

"I don't know." Gordon shrugged out of his coat and hung it on a peg, then rolled into his hammock—a maneuver that he did now without thinking, but had taken him a few days to learn properly. "Just a feeling."

"What sort of 'feeling'?"

"Like I'm being watched. Spied on, really."

"Well, you *do* stick out. You're taller than half the crew—"

"Pete—"

"Not taller than *me*, of course. But taller than half these mal-nourished down-timers. And you're older than most of them—"

"*Pete*—"

"And uglier, of course—"

Gordon rolled out of his bunk and grabbed Pete's side rope, threatening to dump his little brother on the deck.

"Pete," he said, "I am totally serious. You know we're trying to keep this project quiet. If someone's spying on it—spying on *us*—we have to find out who it is."

"And do what? Throw him overboard?"

"You're the man of action, little bro. I'm not sure what to do."

"All right, all right. Let me do a little looking around." Pete went back to his whittling. "Do you suspect anyone, Sherlock?"

"I don't think so. Maartens just took on some new crew for the shakedown—a few able seamen that can take her downriver and out into open sea and back. Maybe it's one of them."

"It's early in the season as it is," Maartens said, squinting at the cloud-filled sky. "All of these changes have taken longer than needed."

"That's what will keep us safe on the open ocean."

Maartens spat over the side. "You up-timers love to tempt fate, don't you?" He looked at Gordon. "Nothing keeps us 'safe,' Chehab. *Safer, ja*, I would say that. But the ocean is always there to swallow us.

"It will take us two or three days in the shakedown, and then we should be about ready for launch. That will have to be soon enough."

"Why so long to shake down *Challenger*?"

"Want to make sure everything is seaworthy. I'm not going to try and cross the Atlantic without a few days in calmer waters."

"Suppose everything is all shipshape. Is there any reason to come back to dock?"

"I hadn't planned to have everything stowed aboard before shakedown. We'd have to come back for supplies."

"What if that were done in advance?"

"It isn't how we've always done things."

"How is that different from most of the rest of this mission? Is any of the rest of this like the way you've always done things?"

Maartens scowled and folded his arms across his chest. "*Nein*, it is not. But there is some reason for this, eh?"

"Of course."

"And you will tell me why?"

"When we are under way."

"*Ja*. 'Operational security.' This is some deep, dark plot of... our patron, is it not?"

"No," Gordon said. "I'm just making stuff up."

On a chilly, clear spring day, *Challenger*'s sails filled with the brisk wind and she made her way down the Elbe and into the channel and open ocean.

It was here, Gordon thought, that he would find out if this mission was at all practical: not due to its planning, or its goals—but if he would show any propensity for seasickness. He wasn't worried too much about the adventure... Pete was by his side, and the New World lay ahead: America, but not the one they'd grown up in. That world was never going to happen, at least in that form, at least in this version of history.

Good riddance, he thought. *I get to fly.*

As for Stephane Hoff, he soon realized that what had been mooted as a shakedown was nothing less than the beginning of the voyage itself. A few days after leaving port, with *la Manche* behind and open ocean ahead, he understood that by getting aboard *Challenger* he was going to get a firsthand look at the expedition.

But unless he could somehow make use of the radio, he might have no way of reporting it.

Chapter 5

The North Atlantic

There was much to be said for the element of surprise, but there was also much to be said for a sailor's innate conservatism.

Gordon Chehab had no familiarity with the open sea, but he had a plan for the journey: to sail from Europe to America, taking what the map showed to be the shortest possible route, crossing the Atlantic to Newfoundland and then making their way down the coast to the English-speaking colonies in New England, to New Amsterdam, and then south to Maryland and Virginia—then, when they'd learned as much as they could, back to Europe.

It made sense on the map.

It did not make initial sense to Claes Maartens, who would not have chosen to go that way at all.

"The north coast is a dangerous place, Chehab," Maartens told him on the night they passed the Channel Islands, only a few dozen miles from true open ocean. "That's not how *sailors* cross the Atlantic."

"How would you do it?"

"Well." The Dutch sailing master's face brightened, as if he might now have an opportunity to affect the direction *Challenger* would be going. "The best way is to follow the trade winds, the northeast winds, and make for the Caribbean."

"The *Caribbean*? I don't want us to—"

"It's not necessary to follow them *all the way*, Chehab," he said. "It depends on just where the edge of the trade-wind zone lies. Somewhere south of Gibraltar we could cut west, perhaps bear for Bermuda or Virginia. We'd have to navigate around the Sargasso; the winds are unpredictable and we might become becalmed, but..."

"And if we made directly for Newfoundland? What then?"

"I...if we crossed out of the trade winds and bore north, we would be in the variables. The wind could come from any quarter, though we would benefit from the fore-and-aft rigging, if we weren't swamped by the waves."

"Sailing with our own coffin. I remember."

"*Ja*," Maartens said. "It might be a longer trip, but if we could raise the east coast of Newfoundland—" He jabbed a thumb at the chart, then carefully traced the rough coast of Labrador with his index finger. "The charts say that the current is favorable along the lee of this coast...but it's a bad wager, Chehab. I'd rather head for Virginia or the Bahama Islands and beat our way up the coast."

"But if we made for the Maritimes—for Newfoundland—we could make it."

"Tacking all the way," Maartens said.

"You know how to do that," Gordon said, and got the scowl he expected.

"I'd like us to take the southern route."

"It's not as important as going north."

"We can still go south first."

Gordon took several moments before replying. He saw some glimmer of hope in Maartens' face; the Dutchman had clearly wanted to convince him of the folly of sailing the northern route across the Atlantic.

"We'll do the tacking thing," Gordon said at last. "We go north."

Ingrid Skoglund and her maidservant, Sofia, had settled into a regular routine aboard ship. Maartens had faced down the most recalcitrant of his crew—he'd even let go a couple of them back in Hamburg: older men who couldn't get used to women aboard; but he treated the Swedish doctor and her companion in the same way he treated the radio and its operator—as installed equipment that he didn't understand and didn't care to learn.

They took their meals with the sailing master or, when weather permitted, on the quarterdeck away from most of the crew; Maartens allowed this violation of his privacy merely (as he said) for convenience—but whenever they were with him, and whenever he encountered them as they walked around the ship...which, to Gordon, seemed remarkably frequent...he was scrupulously courteous. Sofia rarely spoke; Ingrid was particular in her formality, meeting Maartens' eye but restricting their conversations to as few words as possible. Maartens seemed more gruff with his crew after such encounters, as if he had postponed his normal peevishness to take it out on others.

On a sunny but brisk afternoon, Gordon finally decided that it was time to get to know the doctor. He'd kept his distance for the first few weeks, and Pete seemed to have no real interest in following up; he'd snorted with laughter when Gordon had told him of her insistence that she owed him no *favors*...he'd wanted to throw his kid brother into the harbor, but had decided to ignore it instead.

The two women had found a seat on some securely lashed crates amidships, where they were mostly out of the wind. As Gordon approached, the servant girl said something to Ingrid that he didn't catch, rose and with a slight bow to Gordon walked aft toward the pilot house, out of earshot but not out of sight.

"I hope I'm not interrupting," Gordon said. "May I join you?"

"If you wish."

Gordon settled himself on the crates, but at a respectful distance. For what it was worth, Ingrid seemed standoffish, but not upset or threatened.

"I'd like to know a little more about you," he said. "Since we are going to be working together."

"What would you like to know?"

"Where you're from, how you came to be a doctor, that sort of thing. I was not expecting that we would have a..."

"A Swede?"

Gordon smiled, and to his surprise Ingrid did as well. "No. I didn't expect a Swede. Though I don't have, well, any *problem* with Swedes. I just assumed that...someone other than a Swede would have an easier time on a ship full of...non-Swedes."

Ingrid smiled again; the sun peeked from behind a cloud and lit up her face. The breeze blew a few strands of hair from under her hat; she reached up and tucked them back into place. "I told our patron that I might not be best suited for this expedition, but he insisted. To be honest, I was hoping he would agree; certainly Sofia would rather be on dry land. We shall both have to make the best of it."

"As will we. I don't know what to expect; the New World—well, it's where I'm from, sort of, though it's a time I've only read about and as far as I can tell most of *that* is exaggeration."

"You shall have to use your own eyes—and your own judgment."

"I was expecting to do that in any case."

They sat a few moments in silence, then Gordon added, "Doctor—Ingrid—you are too clever by half."

"Why do you say that?"

"When I sat down a few minutes ago I told you I wanted to know more about you, and you have succeeded in completely diverting the conversation. This is part of your bedside manner, I suppose."

He saw anger in her eyes for a moment, then they softened. He thought about what he had just said and realized that it could have been misinterpreted—*damn American idiom, she thinks you're coming on to her*, Gordon thought. *Damn, damn, damn.*

"You mean...the way I attend patients."

"Yes," he said quickly. "Yes, that's exactly what I meant. I'm sorry, your English is excellent, and I used an idiomatic expression. When I was learning French I had no end of trouble with them."

"Language is elusive," Ingrid said. "Speaking a foreign tongue is sometimes like riding a wild horse. It can toss you over and knock you senseless. Or worse."

"Or worse," Gordon repeated. He placed his hands on his thighs and looked at them, then up at Inge. "Now. Tell me about yourself."

"On a single condition."

"Which is?"

"You tell me about *yourself*."

"Agreed. So—who is Ingrid Skoglund?"

"A good question," she said. "The answer is simple: I am a doctor, trained in your hospital in Grantville. I was born and grew up in Jansköping, where I learned the skills of a midwife." She folded her hands in her lap and looked down at them, as if they belonged to someone else. "I think...I think that I might have been content to remain there and bring new lives into the world. My father was a doctor; he had no son, so he taught me much of what he knew."

"So what changed?"

"What has *not*?" She laughed. "*You* have changed everything. You up-timers have turned the world on its head. New knowledge. New ways of killing people." Her face became solemn. "We knew of the war, and our king's desire to change the balance between the powers. But when the Ring of Fire altered things, my father decided to travel to your wondrous home city to see what he could learn. He chose to take me with him."

She looked away from Gordon then, letting the stiff breeze blow more stray curls into her face. It was clear that this was something emotional for her, though he wasn't sure why.

"There was so much to learn," she said, without looking back. "So many books, so many papers, so many new techniques. He took it all in like a drunkard who could not help himself.

"He died in Grantville," she said at last, turning to face Gordon. "He was simply too old—his heart was weak, and I could not save him. Even Doctor Nichols could not save him. It was just as it was when my mother died: my father could not save her either.

"I was ready to journey back to Jansköping. I was going to return home and..."

Again she looked away, letting her thoughts be dispersed by the sea breeze. Gordon waited for her to continue; when she said nothing, he said, "That was never going to happen."

"A consideration of what *might have been* is a subject every up-timer should understand, Min Herre Chehab—"

"*Gordon.* Else I'll be obliged to call you *Frau Doktor Skoglund* every three minutes."

"Gordon." She pronounced it clipped and short-voweled; he decided at that moment that he liked the sound of his name on her lips. "Very well. I do not think about what might have been, as it has no meaning now. But I do confess that I am still surprised at what happened...how I have reached this point."

Gordon did not answer, but waited for Ingrid to continue.

"When my father died," she said, "I assumed that I would be dismissed—I was no more than a Swedish midwife, after all, and not the renowned Doctor Hjalmar Skoglund. Everything I had ever known, everything that the world had taught me, assured me that the only way I had been able to learn the medical arts was because of my father's indulgence.

"It was all gone: it was as if it had never been—except for the kindness and generosity of Doctor James Nichols. I could never imagine that anyone would have extended himself, especially a—a—"

"A man from the future," Gordon finished her sentence; he wasn't sure what word she was going to use to finish that sentence—something to describe his skin color, presumably—but decided that he didn't want to hear it.

"...Yes," she said, smiling. "A *man from the future*. He told me that he admired my talents and my intelligence and that... ahem." She placed a hand on her chest and said in a faux deep voice, "'There are damn few doctors worth the title, girl, and we can't afford to lose you.'"

It was actually a very decent impression of Nichols' voice; Gordon couldn't help but smile.

"You mock me, Min Herre... Gordon." But her heart wasn't in it: she was smiling as she spoke.

"I do no such thing. Dr. Nichols is a wonderful man. Thank God he was in Grantville for Rita Stearns' wedding when the Ring of Fire happened."

"Our God is mighty and wise," Ingrid said. "And Dr. Nichols is wise as well. He arranged for me to study a year in Salerno." When Gordon did not seem to understand, she added, "The *Schola Medica Salernitana*. I did not know that there *were* women doctors, but in Salerno I learned from the best of them. There was so much to learn and so little time..."

"And you were a drunkard as well, like your father."

"Yes," she agreed. "But I was better prepared for it. I learned everything I could, and then returned to Grantville. I even have a fair copy of the *Trotula Major*—it is in my cabin if you would like to see it."

A doctor's version of the etchings? Gordon thought and almost said—but obviously she meant nothing else by her words; the *Trotula Major* was obviously a big deal, whatever it was.

"Impressive," he said at last.

"You appreciate scholarship," she said. "Or so it seems."

"What about Sofia?" Gordon asked.

Ingrid looked at her servant, who had continued to look out to sea, only glancing occasionally to see if her mistress required her assistance.

"She is devoted to me, because I saved her life. She was with us in Grantville—it was a wonder to her, as it was to all of us—and when I went to Salerno she naturally came with me. There she became very ill and I nursed her back to health."

Ingrid looked away before Sofia returned her attention to the doctor—as if she did not want her to be disturbed, or perhaps did not want this conversation to end.

"I believe I have fulfilled my obligation, Gordon. You must now tell me about yourself."

The matter-of-fact turn caught Gordon by surprise for just a moment; but he recovered. "I don't think I have too much to tell. I'm just a regular guy—I was born in '76—1976—and was twenty-four at the time of the Ring of Fire. I hadn't decided what I was going to do with myself; I was more concerned about Pete: he was always getting into trouble, and I think I hadn't been as good a brother as I might have been—"

Ingrid put up her hand. "I believe I asked you to tell me about yourself, not your brother. I feel that I understand *him* quite well."

"Really. I'm not sure I do."

"Oh, you dissemble with me. Your brother is young and assertive, a typical soldier from any age: he believes himself invincible and attractive to every woman at every moment. He is married, and yet his eyes follow Sofia—and me—whenever we come into view."

"I'll kill him," Gordon said.

"I do not feel threatened," Ingrid said. "I will let you know if that changes."

"For sure."

"In any case, your brother is not of interest. As for you...you call yourself a 'regular guy': but every up-timer is from a place we can scarcely imagine. What you must think about our time..."

"I talked about this with Pete—I know, I know," Gordon said, holding up his hands. "A lot of up-timers think of the seventeenth century as a second chance. But even if it's a second chance for Grantville, the story would have been lots different if a piece of a big city had been thrown back here, or a piece of a big university with lots of professors—"

"I would guess," Ingrid said, "that it would have been a disaster. A big city from your time, from what I have read and heard, would have been full of people who would have been slaughtered by the first troop of cavalry that rode through. As for a university full of professors: if they were anything like the universities of today, they would never be prepared for this time.

"I am inclined to believe that the Lord of Hosts chose the exact place to bring back to us: a small, remote town with good people."

"We're not all good people, Ingrid."

"Enough of you are," she said, and smiled again. It was as if the sun had peeked out from behind one of the clouds above.

He told her about growing up in Grantville, about his family, about his home and his travels after high school...and about the balloon festival in Albuquerque that made him want to fly. She listened with close attention—but he wasn't sure whether she truly understood.

It was going to be interesting when she first went up...he wondered what her reaction would be.

Finally he decided he had talked enough, and that Sofia had looked out at the ocean enough. He stood and offered a polite bow, then walked away, trying to decide what he was going to do with Pete when he found him.

Chapter 6

Paris, France

If Étienne Servien had learned only one thing in the service of the crown, it was that men were subject to many perils, and that many of them ultimately proved fatal.

It seemed trite to think of men's lives that way, like playing cards discarded on a table, like coins spent in the market, like wooden soldiers in the hands of a child: but it was nothing if not apt. To the great gamblers, and the great generals, most men were *exactly* that: elements of a wager, resources to be put at risk, pieces on a battlefield...better that they not put a face on such things, placing their sentimentality or mercy in the path of their duty and desire.

Far better not to think about it at all.

Servien picked up the letter from his escritoire and walked to the window. There was a bench seat there, giving him a fine view across the broad avenue to the street below, where there were people he would never know, engaged in pursuits that some great gambler or great general—or, quite possibly, his proximate employer, the Great Cardinal—might even now be directing, obstructing or abetting. The sun rose, the sun set: and life went on.

He unfolded the letter, and in the slanting light of the afternoon sun, reread the beginning of the text.

Most esteemed Monsieur,

In accordance with your direction and advice, I have been observing the ship under renovation in Hamburg Harbor. She is a former Baltic trading vessel, roughly one hundred fifty tons, under the command of a Dutch sailing master named Claes Maartens. The ship is to be named Challenger, *which name seems to hold special significance for up-timers;* Le Défi *might be a suitable translation. There are two Americans associated with the vessel—one who has been on hand for some time named Gordon Chehab, and another who arrived just this week—his brother Peter. I am sure that they have been charged with some special mission, since they have discussed matters privately away from the ship—I regret that I was unable to overhear the import of their conversation.*

The younger brother is a soldier of some sort; the elder is not—though I am as yet unaware of his area of specialty, since he does not appear to have the habits and skills of a seaman. It is possible that he will command the expedition.

Essentially knowing himself to be a pawn in someone else's hand, Servien felt a sympathy for his agent, the Alsatian Stephane Hoff. He had been plucked from the streets of Paris, trained and refined from the raw material that Servien had found: the dross separated and discarded, the gold burnished.

With an indication that there was some project underway in Hamburg, he had suggested to Cardinal Richelieu that it might be worth placing a set of eyes and ears to learn what it was about. His Eminence had given it scarcely a moment's thought and waved his consent, as if it was of no consequence.

As if it was indeed a chess piece or a wooden soldier. Which—to Richelieu, at least—it was.

There had been a handful of letters. They were carefully written, as if Stephane believed that Servien could see through any dissembling, or that he would not be compensated if the information was insufficient. Falsehood, Servien would not tolerate: but the cardinal, and thus the cardinal's servants, were generous when it came to intelligence—particularly when there might be danger involved. True, Stephane had not exactly volunteered to be an agent; true, the assignment to Hamburg might be less preferable than one in his adopted city of Paris, the center of the universe as far as Servien was concerned—but still, Stephane was useful, and capable, and might be suitable for greater and more responsible tasks.

He set the letter aside. It had been three, almost four weeks since it had arrived, and there was no message since. He had perhaps been captured, or even killed. There were so many perils...and so many of them fatal.

He knew what Père Joseph, Cardinal Tremblay, was likely to say: *What can you expect? He has no loyalty except that which you buy.*

He thought he knew what His Eminence was likely to say: *The man was of no consequence. A street-beggar converted into a spy? I have paid to teach him his letters, to educate him with skills that would serve me well—and now he has gone. Find another, and perhaps I shall open my purse again.*

No loyalty, Servien heard again in his mind. *Of no consequence.*

Stephane was gone: no trace of him was left behind. The up-timer ship *Challenger* was gone as well, cleared from Hamburg Harbor a little after Stephane's last letter, bound for God only knew what destination. The Baltic, perhaps, to aid somehow in the war effort. The Mediterranean, to interfere with the mess in Italy. Or Spain. Or England, or Scotland, or...

Two up-timers: a fine sailing-ship, a special mission, possibly some manner of *Grantvillieur* technology aboard.

It was far short of the fount of information Servien had hoped to provide.

When the summons did come, Servien anticipated his master's disappointment at the best, and his anger at the worst: not over Stephane, he supposed, but at the lack of up-to-date information on this up-timer expedition. Cardinal Richelieu was unhappy with intelligence that was out of date or unimportant, and God help the messenger if it was wrong.

As a good servant, however, and as an intendant who had kept his head—and his position—for some time, he was a keen observer. Thus, when he was bid to come to Richelieu's reception room, he took note of every detail that might provide him with information as to the current circumstance, and to his master's state of mind.

To his surprise, in the grand—and as yet incomplete—hall that led to Richelieu's public chambers, he noted the presence of a young, well-dressed nobleman, leaning against a pillar, clearly bored and somewhat out of sorts.

"Ah," he said at Servien's approach. "If it is not our good Cardinal's carrion bird."

Servien did not choose to respond, but wondered to himself why the man was there. The man was a dandy, and conducted the life of a bon vivant, a ladies' man; his name was de la Marche—Phillippe de la Marche—a younger son of a wealthy blue blood, too youthful for politics and too undisciplined for the Church. He even had a nickname, perhaps one that he had arranged to be bestowed: *Le crève-coeur*—Heartbreaker.

"Tell me," de la Marche said, standing straight and ambling directly for him, "what is on your Master's mind?"

"I do not take your meaning, Monsieur." Servien changed his pace and direction slightly, so that he could reach Richelieu's chamber quickly and more directly.

De la Marche was a step ahead, and positioned himself so that Servien would have to go right past him.

"Of course you *take my meaning*," he repeated. "You understand me very well, little man. Very well indeed."

Servien sighed. He looked up the hall and noted a red-tabarded member of the Cardinal's Guard, the handpicked soldiers directly answerable to Richelieu; after a moment he caught the man's eye. He made a gesture—passing his right hand over his right ear, and returned it to his side.

De la Marche took no notice. "I wish to know why my friend and patron has been summoned to the ... Illustrious Presence."

"I am sure I do not know."

"I am sure you *do*. You know everything that goes on in that room." He pointed behind him. "My patron may be his nephew, but he is not fond of being suddenly summoned by the red robe. I should like to know why."

Nephew, Servien thought. But the only nephew the cardinal might summon ... would be Jean: Jean Armand de Maillé-Brézé—whom he had appointed, at age seventeen, to be *grand-maître de la navigation.*

The Admiral of France. The *soi-disant* Admiral of France.

Servien caught the guardsman's eye again, then returned his attention to the young nobleman before him. The guardsman began to walk slowly toward where they stood.

"Whatever my master's plans might be, Monsieur, and whatever I may know about them—I know that he does not like to be kept waiting."

"He shall *have* to wait until I am done with you."

"Are you threatening me, Monsieur?"

"I do not *threaten* my inferiors," he answered. "I command them to speak. So—speak, so that I may be better informed."

"And if I choose to remain silent?"

De la Marche had apparently not even considered the possibility. Like all bullies, he did not know how to react when his intended victim was not intimidated.

Servien was in the employ of Armand-Jean du Plessis, Cardinal-Duke de Richelieu, first minister of France. He understood intimidation very well—and understood that it did not emerge from the mouth of a young, arrogant fop, or from the point of his sword, should it come to that.

"Then I shall extract my information by unpleasant means."

"The cardinal would not wish to be disturbed either by improper sound or unseemly violence, Monsieur. And while he would, of course, hold his nephew blameless, he would find some way to cause you to regret your precipitate action."

"Are you threatening *me*?"

"No," Servien said. "Not at all." He looked past de la Marche at the cardinal's guardsman standing a few feet away, his hand resting lightly on the hilt of his sword. "I do not threaten my inferiors."

Before the young man could frame a reply, Servien stepped past him and rapped at the door. From within he heard the word "Come," and he opened it and closed it behind him.

"Forgive my tardiness, Your Eminence," he said; Richelieu stood bent over a large table, looking at a map that was held down with several knickknacks and items from the cardinal's broad desk. "I was delayed by annoyances."

Richelieu looked at him. "Is that young fool still loitering about?"

"I regret to say that he is, Monsieur."

"While I understand the sort of companion that my nephew attracts, I do not generally approve. Fortunately"— the cardinal permitted himself a small smile, which did not cause Servien to relax in the least—"he appears to suffer from *mal de mer* whenever he is aboard a sailing ship, so there is no chance for Jean to appoint him a captain by mistake."

"I am gratified to hear it."

Servien walked to where Richelieu stood, taking a brief glance at the map. It was a copy of the New World chart devised by the Englishman John Smith.

"Eminence?" he said after a moment.

"I hear that your young Alsatian has vanished," Richelieu said without preamble. "A shame."

"I did not know that Your Eminence was so well informed."

"After all these years? Come now, Servien, my best and most faithful servant. That I am *aware* of something should be your default assumption."

"Of course. Forgive me."

"I absolve you of your ignorance. Now, to the matter at hand. I have reviewed the copies of your correspondence with your young spy. Quite informative; quite informative indeed. I would say that you made an excellent investment in him."

"Thank you, Monsieur."

"And, indeed..." Richelieu spread his hands across the map, then traced the long, sinuous coastline with his index finger. "If he has found a way to survive and return to us with further information, I would be prepared to reward him quite well. It seems that our up-timer friends are heavily invested in some scheme, and he was quite close to it."

"But we... did not learn of its import."

"Actually," the cardinal said, "we do have some idea of it. It was sighted on two occasions after it set sail from Hamburg; once from the south coast of England, and once from Normandy. It sailed west—and out to sea."

Servien looked at the map, then back at Richelieu.

"To the New World, you believe."

"Yes, to the New World. The sparrow returns to its nest: the up-timers return to America."

"This is not the America they knew."

"No. Indeed it is not. This is a wild land of savages, an untamed wilderness. An inhospitable place..."

"Which largely belongs to the French crown now."

Richelieu turned and walked to the hearth, where there was a carefully banked fire. The day outside was pleasant, but Richelieu's receiving chamber was chilly; there was a draft from somewhere, perhaps owing to the continuing construction of the *Palais-Cardinal*. He extended his long hands toward the fireplace, then settled himself into an armchair; he waved Servien to another nearby.

"There is a peculiar class of plants, Servien; I have read of them—they apparently exist in profusion in the New World, in that untamed wilderness that His Christian Majesty now owns. They are called in Latin *Dionaea muscipula*; English governors a century up-time from this year of grace dubbed them 'Venus flytrap.' Do you know of them?"

Servien shook his head. "I do not, Eminence."

"I shall have to arrange to have one or more of them in my garden, when time allows." Richelieu placed his hands together in front of him, palms up, slightly cupped. "These remarkable plants have pairs of wide, stiff leaves with tiny hairs on them. They remain dormant and quiet until an insect lands on them and then walks...ever so carefully...across the leaves and touches one and then another of the hairs. Then, and only then, the leaves snap shut—" he clapped his hands together so suddenly that Servien started in his seat.

Richelieu smiled.

"I beg your pardon, Eminence," Servien said. "Please continue."

"Once the leaves are shut, Servien, the plant *consumes* the tiny insect. It is carnivorous, you see—a plant that eats tiny animals, such as insects." He let his hands relax again, resting them on his knees.

"Remarkable."

"Yes. I should like to have one of them to study—in any case, France is much like that singular growth. We have laid open and in wait for a few years; our title to the former English colonies is unchallenged, and our ownership of the lands shown on that map is unimpeded, except for a single Dutch colony. Along with our established domain to the north and west, it gives France a huge swath of territory to settle, to develop, to *exploit*. With the peace, we finally have an opportunity to undertake this venture."

"I see."

"Clearly the Americans see this as well. Just as we are the plant, they are the insect. The departure of this up-timer-crewed ship for the New World is the trigger that moves us to action. Your spy told us enough to convince me that this is the time."

"You intend to deploy our fleet to the New World?"

"I would not say our entire *fleet*, Servien. That would be peremptory—and incautious. Even though we are at peace, we cannot assume that situation will prevail forever. But we have resources to deploy and someone to command them."

"Our *grand-maître*."

"Quite." Richelieu placed his hands together again, palm up. "And this little expedition...which does not know that *we* know...might well be caught in the trap."

This time, when the cardinal clapped his hands together, Servien did not bat an eyelash.

Chapter 7

The North Atlantic

A thousand years before Gordon was born, and more than six hundred years before the date on the calendar, people had made the crossing that *Challenger* was undertaking now. Their boats were even shallower draft and their instruments were far more primitive. They had not possessed an ephemeris or twentieth-century maps.

Gordon also knew that they didn't have helmets with big horns, either: that was just in the movies and the comic books. But horny helmets or no, the Vikings had followed the stepping stones across the ocean until they reached North America. Despite Maartens' skepticism, he intended that his expedition should do so as well.

It was a decision that he would think about long afterward.

In open ocean, *Challenger* enjoyed a few days of calm seas, which were pleasant enough that Gordon and Pete spent more time on deck. Maartens was not as happy about them, though; the ship made little headway, as he ordered changes of heading to try and proceed. It wasn't as if there was insufficient wind: the sails looked full to Gordon.

"It's not the wind," Maartens said. "It's *this*." He pointed to the sailing chart tacked to the table in the pilot house. The map of the

Atlantic, direct from a twentieth-century book, showed a tinted oval path that followed the North Atlantic coast and extended arms northeast to the British Isles and eastward toward Africa. "It's more powerful than the following wind, and it's costing us time."

"You mean the Gulf Stream," Gordon said.

Maartens scowled at him. "Is *that* what it is. I imagine that it will make the return trip faster."

"It always did. That's how they found it," Gordon answered. "I think Benjamin Franklin first mapped it."

"Who?"

"A famous American." *Who might never be born*, Gordon thought. "We have to get north of it."

"The further north we go, the worse the storms," Maartens said. "You want this ship to be trapped in ice, Chehab."

"It's quite a way to the Arctic Circle."

"The what?"

Gordon looked down at the chart. "In order to avoid the Gulf Stream, we will need to sail north—but not as far as the polar ice cap. We need to sail toward *this*"—he pointed to the area northeast of Labrador and west of Greenland—"and then work our way down the coast."

"It would be easier to sail south of this Gulf Stream, then head west and let it take us *up* the coast."

"But we're not doing that."

"Because you have this great desire to see Newfoundland first."

"Because," Gordon said, standing up straight, "the purpose of this mission is not simply to reach North America, but to learn as much as possible about the situation there. And, incidentally, to avoid being killed or captured in the process.

"If we went to Virginia first, there is some chance we might find that the French are *already there*. If I were Cardinal Richelieu, I'd try to exercise my claim there rather than in Newfoundland—it's more temperate, it's more fertile, and it has a valuable cash crop."

"Tobacco."

"That's right. King Charles' father hated tobacco, but King Charles was taxing it—and requiring every hogshead of the stuff to be carried in English hulls, to be stored in English custom-houses, and subject to English tax. When he sold off his colonies, he sold off a lucrative income stream. The Virginians are probably thrilled, but they're also probably defenseless."

"You really think that the French have taken Virginia?"

"I don't know. That's why we're going to North America. But if they have, we'll probably be welcomed as a prize of war. I'm not eager to spend any time in a French prison; are you?"

Maartens grumbled a reply but it was clear to Gordon that he hadn't thought much about it at all.

"If they *have* taken over Virginia," Gordon continued, "we'll know about it in advance. And the Gulf Stream will help bring us home. *Begrepen*? Understood?"

Maartens was a burly, well-built man; he angered easily—particularly at his own crew. Gordon stood two or three inches taller, but was perhaps forty pounds lighter. The Dutch sailing master was also steadier on his feet on a sailing vessel.

Gordon wondered if the sailing master's temper was going to get the best of him, and if the approach he'd just taken with the man had been enough to set him off.

"This was what Miro advised, *ja*?"

"Cavriani, actually. He has some cousins involved in the Danish venture in Newfoundland, and yes, he thinks—so does Miro—that Virginia's the first target of French expansion. And he doesn't want us in some French jail either."

"I'd rather have heard that from *him*."

Maartens crossed his arms over his chest, as if that settled the matter—but Gordon had a good comeback.

"That can be arranged," Gordon said. "You can hear it directly. It'll be a good test of the radio."

Though the route had been previously discussed, Gordon wanted to avoid dissent—having Maartens as an ally was important, and he wasn't about to risk having him as an enemy. Accordingly, he paid a visit to the structure that had been built amidships to hold the radio equipment. It was small, barely big enough for two people (who weren't too tall); it was sturdy, covered with a solid roof that held a large, irregular canvas tied down and covering *something*—the crew avoided it, as if it was going to jump out and bite them. A thick, rubber-coated cable emerged from the canvas and connected to the antenna, strung across the masts and crosstrees. Another cable extended over the side and into the water, where it attached to a hardwood plank sheathed in copper—the ground for the antenna. Though the down-timers didn't truly believe it, a lightning strike on the mast, the highest spot for a hundred miles in any direction, wouldn't harm the ship a bit: it would discharge harmlessly in the ocean as long as the radio was offline. A knife switch in the radio cabin connected and disconnected the radio to the antenna.

As the day was cool and fair, the door to the shack was open and Gordon could see Ulrich Jaeschke, the radio operator, sitting by the receiver with his long legs stretched out toward the doorway. When he saw Gordon approaching he sat up, but Gordon waved him off.

"I think we're going to have to put you to work, Herr Jaeschke," he said. "We should see if you can actually reach the mainland with this."

"*Ja*, of course we can, Herr Chehab," the young Magdeburger said, his English tinged with the clipped *plattdeutsch* accent common to the northern part of the Germanies. He slapped the ceiling with the flat of his hand. "Just have to connect the radio to the antenna."

"The lads are afraid of the wires. They don't think that it's safe to touch the wires."

"What, do they think it will bite them?"

"Or electrocute them."

"There's no *juice* in the antenna if I'm not transmitting. It's just like flypaper—except for radio waves. Even if I am, up on the mast there's nothing to ground to, and so nothing to fear. At most it might tingle if they grab it."

"Try telling *them* that. They mostly think it's magic, and that you're some sort of magician."

"And so I am," Jaeschke said. "Two years ago I was at a brickworks, sweating out an honest day's pay—and now here I am, doing magic on a sailing ship. You up-timers have changed everything."

"You're complaining?"

"*Nein*, not a bit. I've baked enough bricks to last a lifetime, Herr Chehab. I don't care if I never see another."

"Fair enough. What do you need to get ready?"

"Nothing, really." He rested his hand on the big knife switch. "I'll warm up the set."

Jaeschke was right about the crew's aversion to the antenna. It was held off from the mast by ceramic insulators. There were two wires running down from the top of the mast to each side, forming a giant upside down "V." The diagonals ended well above the ship's rail with large insulators attaching to the ropes that anchored them. The main armature was nearly a hundred feet long, hooked to posts along the mainmast, with the side lengths extending along the sails.

After a fair amount of cursing and ordering by Maartens, *Challenger* turned into the wind, keeping the ship relatively motionless. Jaeschke stepped back inside his sanctum, where the dials and instruments were already glowing.

Maartens, for his part, leaned against the taffrail and squinted at the sky, which had gone from mostly sunny to mildly cloudy in a matter of minutes.

"I don't like this, Chehab," he said, spitting over the side. "Not at all."

"You wanted to make sure our patron agreed with the course," Gordon said. "We can ask him."

"On a clear day. But I'm not happy with the look of those clouds."

"What's wrong?"

Maartens looked Gordon up and down, as if measuring him. "Remember our little talk about safety on open ocean, up-timer? I told you that anything your technology brings to the table makes us safer, but there's no way to be completely *safe*. I'm not happy to be lying hove to in mid ocean with a storm coming. Anything can happen out here."

"I appreciate your wisdom."

"And you ignore it."

Gordon walked away from Maartens, who remained at the rail, looking up at the sky. He could faintly hear the crackling noise of the radio, though the door to the shack was closed.

"You wanted guidance," Gordon said. "Jaeschke will get in contact; you'll get your guidance; then we'll follow the course."

The sun was behind a cloud, so much of the radio shack was in shadow.

Gordon looked up at the sky. The wind was picking up, and things looked darker than they had just a few minutes ago.

There was a loud crackle from inside the equipment shack; Gordon looked toward it.

Then he heard the rumble of far-off thunder.

"I think the storm is here," Gordon said.

"What?"

Gordon could feel the first hint of rain on his face. "Weather," he said. "It's coming." He took two steps toward the shack and saw a huge arc of lightning erupt from a cloud in the distance.

The sky had darkened quite a bit in the last few minutes. The crew was beginning to batten things down on the main deck. Maartens turned to look at Gordon, then glanced up at the mainmast.

Another crash of lightning came out of the sky. Several seconds later—Gordon counted, as every mountain boy learned to do—a loud rumble of thunder echoed across the ship.

"Crap. He's got to disconnect."

Maartens grabbed Gordon by the shoulder. "If the lightning hits the mast, your wires will run right down into the sea, *net wahr*?"

"Not if the damn radio is still in circuit! I've got to tell Jaeschke to hang up."

He shrugged loose from Maartens and began to run, but the first rain on the deck, which was tilting slightly as the wind pushed at the ship, got the better of him: his feet slipped out from under and he landed on his backside.

Maartens caught up with him. "Damn landsman, you're the least handy man I've ever seen. What needs to be done?"

"The radio. It has to be disconnected or—"

"Or?"

Gordon hauled himself to his feet. "Or else. I've got to get to the shack." He made his way a few steps aft, trying to keep his balance; but then there was someone there before him: the Alsatian, Hoff.

"I'll take care of it," Hoff said, and began nimbly making his way past, using toeholds and hand braces without looking. The rain was coming down now in big fat droplets; fifteen feet above the deck the lightning came down again; Gordon thought it was closer this time, lighting up the entire scene with a bright glow for a moment—and then again a moment later. A loud roll of thunder followed.

Well if this isn't just crazy, Gordon thought, as he tried to follow. He heard another crackle coming from the radio in the shack. Why hadn't Jaeschke disconnected the switch? Granted, the shack had no window, but he still should have been able to hear the thunder.

He was probably too preoccupied with the radio. If he was having trouble, and given his relative lack of experience... Thankfully, Hoff had reached the door of the shack and was yanking at it.

Oh, Christ. Somehow the door had gotten stuck. The Alsatian turned toward Gordon, alarm in his face: the down-timer didn't know what might happen, but knew that if an up-timer wanted the radio turned off, it was time to turn it off.

With a fierce yank, Hoff was able to pull it open. Gordon heard a few words: "Jaeschke, you need—"

But he was interrupted by a brilliant flash and a sound that Gordon would remember for the rest of his life: a crack that transformed itself suddenly into a ringing like the sound of the world's biggest hammer striking the world's biggest bell. There was an explosion in the shack and then the smell and sound of fire.

When Stephane's senses returned, the first thing that swam into view was a kindly woman's face, framed by bright light. His first thought was that he had died on the deck, and that this was Heaven and that he was looking up at an angel.

But he did not think he was likely to end up there: even if his deeds hadn't betrayed him, he was hardly in a state of grace—and there were too many things in pain to suggest that he had given up his body just yet.

Slowly he began to be aware that he was being spoken to. He swallowed, closed his eyes and opened them again, and tried to sit up—but someone gently pushed him back down into his hammock.

He closed his eyes again and listened to the voice—a woman's voice, which wasn't making much sense just yet. He could hear the rain pelting down, but there was no thunder—

There had been thunder all right: it was moments after a flash of lightning that had come out of the sky and jumped from the tip of the mast to the wire at the top of the shack, and then there had been an explosion and he'd grit his teeth and clenched his hands around the door post as it blew off its hinges—

It was the last thing he remembered, before waking here.

"—seems finally to have relaxed," the female voice said. "He should be able to sleep more easily," she added.

"It's a wonder he's alive at all."

"You would know better than I, Gordon," she said. "I suppose that you up-timers understand all about lightning."

"Enough to stay away from it."

"Stephane did something brave—and foolish. We could have had two casualties instead of one."

Stephane opened his eyes at the mention of his name. "One?" he croaked, scarcely able to form the word.

Gordon Chehab came into view. He looked concerned. "How are you doing?" he said.

"Thirsty."

"Sure." He brought a small ceramic bowl to Stephane's lips, and helped him to drink a small amount of something—watered wine, from the taste of it. He swallowed a few times, managed to keep from coughing, and moved his head aside.

"Thank you."

"You may have saved the ship," Chehab said.

"But not..." the cough came then, and it took a moment to continue. "But not everyone on it."

"No." Chehab set the bowl aside. "The lightning strike grounded on the radio shack. The...operator was inside. The radio was destroyed. There was a fire..."

Stephane closed his eyes again. He'd not spoken to the radio operator, only nodding in passing; he had seemed a nice enough sort, a down-timer who had been canny enough to get a new skill.

And the radio was gone. Even if he'd figured out how to send a message, that was no longer possible.

"Poor guy." Stephane wasn't sure if he was talking about Jaeschke, the radio operator, or himself.

He realized for the first time that he would have to get away from *Challenger* somehow, somewhere in the New World; there were French colonies, and he would have to reach them.

Poor guy, he thought, and let himself drift with the sound of the rain.

Part Two

May 1636

The grinding waters and the gasping wind

—Wallace Stevens,
"The Idea of Order at Key West"

Chapter 8

Thomasville, Newfoundland

Gordon wasn't sure what he expected to see when *Challenger* came in sight of land. He had a notion that the New World would look like an untamed wilderness, with settlements clinging to the coasts—the slightest breeze capable of dropping them into the sea, palisades facing inland against attacks from hostile Indians. Movie stuff, or what boys read in their adventure books.

But the sight that greeted him from the foredeck of *Challenger* was nothing like that. The hills were bare, stripped of trees and vegetation; inland of a fortified settlement, he could see smokestacks. It was a scene from Dickens—the Industrial Revolution come to roost on Newfoundland.

Pete came up to stand beside him. "Wow. Doesn't look like 1636 to me."

"It's 1636, all right. According to what I've been told, they started with a map of mineral deposits. They're taking coal and iron ore out of the ground and making pig iron. It looks like Cavriani's cousins made a smart investment."

"Why haven't the French grabbed this place?"

"They tried, last year. But the Danes drove them off. Rumor is the Danes used a submarine to do it."

"*Submarine?*" Pete shook his head. "That sounds like bullshit got loose from the pen."

Gorgon shrugged. "I'm not vouching for it. I'm just telling you what I heard. But whether the submarine part is accurate or not, what does seem clearly established is that the French found this place a tough nut to crack. Which means they'll probably be probing somewhere else next."

Pete gestured toward the harbor, now coming into view. There were two ships anchored there—one of which was clearly well armed.

"I'd guess that's true. But those ships can't just rot in the harbor. Sooner or later they'll be somewhere else, and..."

"And they're going to need friends. And that, bro, is why we're here."

"Oh, is it?"

The two brothers turned to face Ingrid, who had come up to stand beside them.

"I understood that our purpose in the New World was to gather intelligence, Gordon," she said. She looked across the bay at the settlement and frowned. "And we have the first of it, don't we? What sort of place is this, in the New World?"

"It's a colony," Pete said. He gestured toward the hills and smokestacks. "It's freakin' Pittsburgh." When Ingrid frowned, he continued, "It's amazing, really, how much they've built in just a few years. It took them decades to screw up the Alleghenies, but they're well on their way to do it to Newfoundland already."

"I would have thought that you would find this a pleasing sight," she said. "This is what the future looks like, doesn't it?"

"Not all of it." Pete looked at her. "Do you think we like industrial wasteland? We left that behind. West Virginia was full of stuff like this—coal mines that stripped the tops off mountains and poisoned rivers."

"And here we go again," Gordon said, "except it's in New-foundland."

"I wonder who it is that is apparently so fond of your sort of technology. I'm sure they revel in this display—of *modernity*." She turned on her heel and walked away.

"Sail ho!"

Maartens snapped his spyglass shut and turned from the taffrail to where Gordon and Paul stood. He looked aloft. "What flag does she fly?"

"Danish Hudson Company's house flag," came the answer.

Maartens said, "How's your Danish, Chehab?"

"Not great. But since Ingrid—Doctor Skoglund—is Swedish, she could probably translate. Well enough, anyway."

Maartens looked at the sky as if he were imploring Heaven—the idea of consulting a female doctor to speak for his ship had clearly never even crossed his mind.

"Perfect. Could not be better: may be a hostile ship, and no one speaks the cursed language." He opened the glass again. "She's got the wind at her back—she's reaching on us."

"So—*is* she hostile?"

Maartens grunted. "She hasn't fired on us yet, if that's any indication. She's a cattle ship, so she won't have many guns anyway. But given the wind, she's got to have come out of the port there. Our courses will cross within a half hour unless I change our point of sail."

"Maybe we should see what she wants."

Challenger's sailing master let the rudder drift so that the ship made no headway. The Danish ship continued to approach, hailed *Challenger* and came alongside.

An officer and three soldiers climbed over the rail of the Danish vessel and *Challenger*'s rail and onto her main deck. They looked as all soldiers do: self-important and fearless, anxious to exert their authority.

"Captain," the officer said in good German, touching the rim of his helmet. "What ship is this, and why are you in our waters?"

Maartens shrugged. "I'm the sailing master, not the captain. You have boarded the *Challenger*. We are on a trading mission for the State of Thuringia-Franconia. I had not realized that I was in anyone's waters." He looked up at the mainmast of the Danish ship. "What is more, I hadn't realized that Denmark had any claims here: doesn't all of the New World belong to the French?"

The officer scowled. "Not all. That is Thomasville," he said, waving toward the distant shore. "It is granted to the Danish Hudson's Bay Company."

"And you are...Swedes?"

"Americans," Gordon volunteered, stepping forward. Maartens looked annoyed at the interruption, but shrugged.

"*Amerikaner?*" the officer said. He turned slightly and shouted something toward the Danish ship. "Our captain will want to talk to you, I think."

"Who is your captain?"

"Lars Johanssen," the man said. "This is the ship *Kristina*, a vessel of the Danish Hudson's Bay Company."

"Never heard of him," Maartens said.

The officer was clearly unhappy with the comment, but shrugged. "You will come with me, American."

Gordon glanced at Maartens, then at Pete. "Let's go, bro."

"Just you," the officer said, putting his hand out as Pete took a step forward.

"A custom of my country," Gordon said. "We use the buddy system. Wherever I go, he goes."

"I don't—"

"Your Captain Johanssen wants to talk to me, does he? Well, we make it a habit of only boarding foreign vessels in pairs."

The officer looked from Maartens to Gordon and back—then he nodded. "All right. Come with me."

Kristina was a smaller vessel than *Challenger*, ninety or a hundred tons compared to a hundred and fifty. It looked like cramped quarters and smelled faintly of cattle. The captain of *Kristina* met them on the quarterdeck, where he stood surveying his ship and his new guests.

"Captain Johanssen," Gordon said.

"Yes. And you are?"

"Gordon Chehab," Gordon said.

"Peter Chehab."

"Brothers, eh? Yes," Johanssen continued. "You look like it. Well. What brings you to Thomasville?"

"That takes some explaining," Gordon said. "And I don't want to tell the story more than once. Do you...speak for your settlement?"

Johanssen seemed surprised by the question. He tensed and looked as if he were framing an angry reply. He looked from Gordon to Pete, who appeared relaxed and ready, like a boxer looking for the right opening.

"*I* am asking the questions here."

Gordon didn't respond at once, which made Johanssen seem even more angry.

"I could simply impound your ship for violation of our coastal waters."

"You're welcome to try," Gordon said.

Johanssen swept his gaze across *Challenger*. To most observers—up-time or down-time—it looked pretty much like any other ship of the era; but an experienced sailor would see the subtle changes that were evidence of up-time modification.

A superstitious—or cautious—down-timer wouldn't want to be caught by any up-time surprises.

"I'll take you ashore to talk with Sir Thomas Roe. Your timing is very good, *Amerikaner*. A few weeks from now he'd have cleared out for Hudson's Bay."

Dockside, Gordon expected to hear mostly Danish, but there was quite a mix of languages: English, German, even some French. The town, which was called Thomasville, had been here less than two years; the buildings were all new, with none of the weather-beaten look of every harbor in Europe.

Feels like a movie set, he thought.

Captain Johanssen and his men escorted Gordon and Peter along the dock, directing them toward a building with a clock tower, set back from the wharf.

"Sir Thomas should be at the *Rådhus*," Johanssen told them. "He will be less patient with you if you are not forthcoming with answers."

Pete leaned close to Gordon. "So, how's your Danish?"

"I know enough to get slapped," Gordon answered quietly. "But Roe is an Englishman. I'll try to let him do the talking. From what I understand, a couple of Dutch frigates got away from the battle that destroyed the fleet, and a couple of years ago they were raiding all along the coast."

"Is that still happening?"

"I don't know. Or, rather, neither did Estuban Miro nor Leopold Cavriani, my contacts in the President's office. Even if they're gone, I'd be just as happy if Roe didn't find out we have a Dutch sailing master. Admiral van Tromp has supposedly gathered all of the Dutch fleet he could find in Caribbean waters. if these two ships' captains have any sense, they'd have obeyed the order to join him. But ships' captains don't always show sense."

Gordon said the last sentence just loud enough for Captain Johanssen to give him another angry scowl. It made Gordon smile.

At the *Rådhus*, there was plenty of bustle. Cavriani's intel on Thomasville was that it had originally been intended as merely a stopover point for an expedition to Hudson's Bay—the Danes had been primarily interested in mining and extraction. But it seemed to Gordon as he stood at the top step and looked out across the town that the people there were intending to stay—and prosper.

The idea of a mining town was nothing new for a West Virginia boy, but the notion that it might be prosperous was a little unusual. But these down-timers had something that the West Virginians never had: advance knowledge of what to look for, and where to look for it. And it would be theirs to keep—unless the French came and took it all away.

In a spartan receiving room inside the *Rådhus*, they were at last presented to Captain Thomas Roe. After Johanssen had escorted them into the room, he departed, leaving the two Americans with Roe. He directed them to seats, taking the most comfortable one for himself.

"Lars tells me you weren't very eager to talk to him," Roe said. "He's a good man, but takes offense easily—you must be very sure of yourselves."

"I don't know what you mean," Gordon said.

"Aye, of course you don't. So tell me—what brings *Americans* to Newfoundland? You're not here for the fishing, I assume. Are you looking for work?"

"No," Gordon said. "We have steady work. We're here to get the lay of the land."

"Why?"

"Knowledge is power, Sir Thomas," Gordon said. "Our employer wants to know how things stand for the various settlements in the New World. We're on a...trading expedition."

"*Trading*, is it. And what have you learned so far?"

"This is our first landfall. We knew you were here—but you've progressed quite a bit."

"Thank you, I suppose. The miners and the smelters are kept busy. May I ask—who is your employer?"

Gordon looked at Pete for a moment, then back at Roe. "It's a trading expedition, sir. We work for ourselves."

"A fine answer, but it falls short of the truth."

"I don't think we like being called liars," Pete said quietly.

"I'm sure you don't. I would not consider doing so. But you should be aware that some of the costs of undertaking the Danish Hudson's Bay Company have been underwritten by Saul and Ruben Abrabanel."

"I am aware of that," said Gordon.

"They are relatives of... the USE's gray eminence, Don Francisco Nasi. I'm sure they'd not want their gentle cousin to interfere in a legitimate business venture."

"He is in retirement."

"That surprises me."

"We are a republic, sir," Gordon said. "Governments come and go. Mike Stearns is no longer Prime Minister, and Don Francisco is no longer—"

"Do not insult me by suggesting that he no longer has influence. But I take your meaning: this expedition... has no official sanction by the USE, then."

"We are a trading expedition for the State of Thuringia-Franconia. We have no intention of interfering with your business or other ventures here. In fact, there's only one group whose possible interference should be of concern."

"The French."

"Sure enough. This settlement would be an attractive target for France, I should think. It's a good thing that we're not at war with them. And neither are you."

"That's true... for the moment. But they claim all of North America because of the transaction between their king and your king."

Roe frowned when Gordon said *your king*, but didn't say anything. It was clear that he knew that Gordon was talking about Charles of England, not Christian of Denmark.

"They haven't troubled themselves with it thus far."

"Their eyes have been elsewhere, Sir Thomas. But sooner or later that will change and Thomasville will become a target."

"We can defend ourselves," Roe said. "Let them try."

"Be careful what you wish for," Pete said.

Roe looked from Gordon to his brother. "Why do you say that?"

"Because you're *vulnerable*," Pete said. "Even if you think you aren't. This isn't the easiest place to take, but it can be taken—or destroyed. You're isolated and you don't have many friends."

"Are you threatening me? Or this settlement?"

"No," Gordon said. "Certainly not." He looked at Pete, who was looking at Roe as if he was sighting down the barrel of a rifle. "We're not threatening you. The *king of France* is threatening you."

Roe leaned back in his chair, as if considering the matter for a moment, then stood up and walked to a heavy escritoire at the side of the room. He reached into his vest and withdrew a key, with which he unlocked the drawer; opening it, he took out a packet and brought it back to where he had been sitting.

"I received this letter from Saul Abrabanel two months ago, Mr. Chehab. He informed me..." Roe sat in his chair once more, holding the envelope in his hands. "He informed me that he had heard from his cousin that an expedition was being equipped to...trade...in the New World, and it would likely make an appearance here at Thomasville. I have delayed my departure for Hudson's Bay so that I might be present when you arrived."

"I repeat," Gordon said, "we are not your enemy."

"I do not think you are. I merely wanted to see for myself what sort of men would be involved in this venture. You apparently have drawn the interest of the cardinal."

"Richelieu?" Pete asked.

Roe gave Pete a look that seemed to mean, *do you know any other Cardinal worth mentioning?*

Gordon said, "I was not aware that *Monsieur le Cardinal* knew anything of our project."

"Of *course* he does," Roe said, slapping the packet against his thigh. "If there is one rule you should always observe, *min Herrer*, it is that *Monsieur le Cardinal* knows a great deal about *everything*. He does not presently have the resources to intercept and sink your fine ship, but he might place obstacles in your way. Where are you bound next?"

Gordon looked at Pete, then back at the captain. "Massachusetts Bay."

"I wish you good luck with them. They are an unpleasant

sort, easily taking offense. But they hate the French, particularly because of their view of the Catholic faith."

"And you, Captain. Do you hate the French as well?"

"I don't hate anybody. But I do pick my battles. What about you?"

"We're new here," Pete interjected. "Ask us in a few years."

Outside in the hall, Lars Johanssen, who had been doing his best to listen without being noticed, wondered quizzically what all the laughter was about.

Chapter 9

They got the Cook's tour.

In the two and a half years the Danes had been in New-foundland, they'd done a great deal, establishing a thriving colony that could keep itself fed while exploiting the mineral resources of the island. The Abrabanel brothers had prepared Roe and his men very well, providing them with up-time maps of mineral resources—iron, nickel, copper, even a few veins of gold in the north at Baie Verte.

"But it's still *vulnerable*," Gordon told Roe. "The French will get up here sooner or later, and miners with shovels won't do much against infantry."

"The French can't be everywhere at once."

"No," Gordon answered. "They can't. That's partly why they're not here."

"So what does the USE want from us?"

"I don't speak for the USE. To be honest, I don't even speak for the State of Thuringia-Franconia, the sponsor of our trade mission. But I *do* believe that the most desirable outcome is what-ever will inconvenience *le Cardinal* the most: unify his enemies against him. Scattered through North America there are plenty of settlements, and groups, that aren't at all interested in serving the king of France. They're even less interested in being told to get off his land, since some of them have no place else to go.

"Richelieu has a very simple plan: *divide and conquer*. If he can keep the various settlements and colonies apart, he can attack them in detail without sparing too many resources from Europe."

"You want us all to work together."

You think? Gordon thought. "I believe that we both believe that to be for the best, sir."

"And you will make that happen?"

"Yes."

"Aye, and good luck with that," Roe said. "The Puritans in Massachusetts Bay have made common cause with the Plymouth settlers, but they don't really like them. And they're constantly banishing members of their sect who don't speak, or dress, or think the right way. If they see any threat at all from the French, I think they'll expect God's holy fire to come down and smite all the Papists for miles around. I would not expect much coopera-tion from *them*."

"At the moment," Gordon said carefully, "I'm only asking for cooperation from *you*."

"I don't think just writing them a letter is going to do much good, but I don't know what else I can do."

"Perhaps a ... personal envoy?"

"You mean like an ambassador? There aren't too many people who I both trust personally and would have confidence..."

Roe's expression was one of concern, but then it brightened.

"I know just the man."

"Oh?"

"I'll send Thomas James. He helped organize this colony, and would be ... diplomatic enough to deal with the damn Puritans."

Gordon paused and looked carefully at Roe. The man was an old salt of sorts—clearly somewhat refined, but still a little rough around the edges. He spoke plainly and forcefully, and from what Gordon had been able to see, was listened to by everyone.

There was something more to his choice than merely finding the right man for the job.

"Please tell me more about this Captain James."

"He's my second here at Thomasville," Roe said. "He ... we both served His Majesty King Charles in the past, exploring in Hudson's Bay, looking for the Northwest Passage."

"Which doesn't exist."

"Well, aye, of course it *doesn't*, but this was five or six years ago before you up-timers came and gave us all a hint of our future. Let us speak the truth, *Minheer* Chehab," he said. "The world has been changed in ways that have nothing directly to do with the Ring of Fire—by what I have been told, in your time line I shall have been dead more than a year by the year of grace 1636, as should our friend in New France, Captain Champlain. And yet here I am, and there *he* is.

"When I was sailing in the northern latitudes years ago, and when James undertook his 'strange and perilous voyage'"—and here his voice took on something of a sneer—"we thought well that there was a way to get to the South Sea by sailing through there. All we found was ice and rocks and the evidence of those who had been there before us. But it wasn't until you up-timers came and *told* us that we were convinced that the passage wasn't to be found."

"You said that Thomas James is your 'second.' I...have the feeling that you don't think too highly of him."

"He's able enough as an administrator," Roe said. "He's been able to keep the ore miners and the sheep herders and the cod fishermen at peace with each other.

"But he has the habit of putting on airs. An *educated* man, a man of singular refinements is our Captain James. While I endured privations in the north, those years ago, I could not get just compensation for my expense—while he returned to a hero's welcome, writing of the perils and dangers that he met at every turn. Yet how many of those dangers were due to his own failings and mistakes? Yet since he was so fair-spoken, his hearing at court was gentle and welcoming.

"I've read of my own death in this other world you come from. It was in penury, sir, while James went on to die comfortably at his own home, his legacy and fame secure."

"That was a world where you had not brought about all of *this*," Gordon said, sweeping his hand to take in the view from the hill above the town—the smelters, the pastures, the busy docks and the sea beyond. "This is a different world, sir. And a different Sir Thomas Roe."

"His Majesty's choice to give English claims over to the French, to keep his crown and I suppose his head, has made bedfellows of Thomas James and myself." He shrugged. "It seems clear that each of us has brought his own skills to this venture.

"He might view a diplomatic mission as a sort of challenge, a matter that would take up his abilities and his 'refinements' in the service of our colony and our new royal patron."

And, Gordon thought, *maybe get him out of your hair.* "I'd welcome the chance to meet Captain James," he said.

Roe's description was an accurate one. James was very much a "strange bedfellow," and was eager for the chance to travel.

"I have heard much of your up-time city," James told Gordon as they sat in the *Rådhus* watching the afternoon shadows lengthen. "It is a place of wonders, I have been told, with carriages that move of themselves, and machines that speak at a distance."

Gordon nodded; in the four and a half years since the Ring of Fire, he had become accustomed to the wide-eyed amazement of down-timers to the wonderful world of Grantville—the place that he had escaped from up-time, and that Pete had called *less than nothing* months ago when they sat in the tavern discussing the mission.

"This ship of yours, the *Challenger*...is it full of wonders as well?"

"I wouldn't say that. We're...out of touch with Europe, and we're not transporting anything we can drive. But we have a few tricks up our sleeve."

James took a moment to think through the expression, and seemed to understand it. "Sir Thomas has suggested that I might be of use to our settlement if I accompanied you. I must tell you that I am eager to be quit of this place—I am constantly called upon to settle petty disputes, and it is simply not the same as being on the open sea."

"I thought you found that somewhat...perilous."

"Ah, well. Yes. One wants one's own adventures to be compelling reading."

"So it wasn't quite as dangerous as you let on."

"Oh, it was *dangerous*: there are islets of ice big enough up there to crush a ship, and waves tall enough to drown it; there are other perils as well. Do you know of the voyage of Jens Munk?"

"I'm afraid I don't."

"He was sent out by our good king of Denmark fifteen years

ago to explore Hudson's Bay. He took it far less seriously, and what wind and wave didn't kill, cold and privation did...only three of the expedition made it back home.

"But that being said, I would be a poor explorer indeed if I had not provided for remedies to the many perils we faced. I was congratulated, and rightly so, for my service to the crown."

"I'm sure we'd be glad to have a man of your accomplishments aboard *Challenger*, Captain James."

The well-spoken captain seemed to breathe a quiet sigh of relief when Gordon said this, as if it might have been some sort of test that he'd had to pass.

"Yes," he said. "I daresay you would."

In the light of the morning *Challenger* prepared to weigh anchor; Thomas James was rowed out to the ship and welcomed aboard, and though he seemed less than pleased with his accommodations in a crowded forecabin, he did not trouble Maartens with a complaint.

Maartens, for his part, did not seem happy when Gordon found him on deck, staring up at the top of the mainmast.

"Something wrong?"

"We're short a topman," he said. "Brave sod to jump overboard and swim to shore in the dark, in *this* water."

"Someone deserted? Who was it?"

"The Alsatian. Hoff."

"I thought he was still confined to his bed."

"So did our doctor," Maartens said. "She went down to check on her little patient and couldn't find him in his hammock; *Challenger* is a fine vessel, but too small to get lost in. We searched her from orlop to topmast and there's no sign of him."

Gordon didn't know quite what to say, so he waited for Maartens to continue.

"He's capable enough to get himself a position—he speaks good German and French and English, and is a very able seaman. Can't fault the man for his bravery, either." Maartens let his gaze travel amidships, where a keen eye could see that there'd been some kind of mishap. "But he may find this is a different world. I turned out the watch, and no one's missing valuables—or I'd take a party ashore and find the little bastard."

"One less mouth to feed."

"Aye," Maartens said, spitting overboard. "But you've brought another aboard. So I suppose it's a wash."

He turned away from Gordon and walked toward the afterdeck, shouting orders to make sail.

The journey across the Ocean Sea had been adventure enough for a lifetime. But it was clear that the ship would be headed south from Thomasville, to other settlements where it might be more difficult to disguise his accent. Stephane had much to report, particularly now that *Challenger* was no longer able to contact Europe by radio—and if there was a better choice than simply going over the side of the ship while it rode at anchor he would have taken it. But from what he had heard, the Danish town had a good mix of people from various nationalities; the other alternative, to wait until *Challenger* reached New Amsterdam, meant that Monsieur Servien would almost certainly have written him off.

Which, he reflected, *might have happened already.*

Still, if he could find a way to send a message back home (or, if the Lord God and all the saints were kind, to find a way back home himself), he might continue his mission—and thus continue in the employ of the cardinal's agent. The best way to do that, he determined, would be to reach New France.

So, with the moon low on the horizon and most of the ship's company asleep, he found his way aft. On a place along the rail hidden by a stack of wooden crates, out of sight of the watch, he let himself carefully down into the water.

The harbor water was *cold*.

Stephane had expected it to be cold, but this was icy. There was something metallic and unpleasant about it, too, reminding him rather of a part of a river in Alsace that was below a dyeworks. The ocean was wide and deep, but that was beyond the immediate harbor: most of whatever was being dumped into the water was remaining close to shore.

He'd swum in that river, but he was only a child at the time, too young to know when something would make him sick, too young to be bothered with cold or whatever came out of the dyeworks. Now he was older, and he wasn't sure whether he was still young enough to be not bothered. He swam through the muck as quickly as he could, holding his breath against the smell. He could feel the coldness of the water draining his strength, and wondered if he'd make it to shore at all.

But at last he fetched up on the beach, well outside of the town of Thomasville. The night air was chill and there was a faint breeze. It was quiet and peaceful—there were no stone ramparts, no night watch past a few men on the wooden palisade, walking back and forth on the platform—really no more than a formality. It was no old-world city, that was for sure.

He wondered what they might think of a soaking-wet Alsatian—*a Frenchman*, they would think—wandering around at night outside their little Danish town. Was he a spy, or a one-man invading army, or just a deserter who decided to go for a swim in the harbor that they were filling with whatever was left over from their smokestacks?

They wouldn't think of it, because it would never occur to them to look. They weren't expecting an attack, even from natives—assuming there were any in residence on this island.

Thomasville was certainly *not* Paris.

He climbed the palisade as easily as he had gone up the mainmast the first day in Hamburg. There were two guards nearby, one leaning on his polearm, the other filling his pipe. The natives would have had no problem making their way into the settlement.

They didn't see or hear him come up, and didn't notice when he went down the other side. Thomasville slept, its narrow little streets in shadow. There was no watch there: no one noticed when he found a set of clothing hanging on a wash line that fit well enough. He left his sodden sailor's garments behind: by morning he would be a hod-carrier, a fishmonger, a journeyman carpenter—or whatever other role came to hand.

But whatever he was to the citizens of Thomasville, he was still Servien's man...and a *spy*.

He smelled fresh-baked bread, which made him hungry, but he'd have to leave that problem for the morning. The smell also brought memories—of Paris, to be sure, but even more of his native Alsace. For the first time since he'd come into the cardinal's service, Stephane felt a little homesick.

Chapter 10

Paris was a long way from hilly Alsace where he had grown up, but it called to him from his youth. Youngest of eight children, there was nothing on the family farm to keep him there—not working in the vineyards nor cultivating hops (his papa used to say, "wine and beer—everyone drinks at least one") nor herding goats. He was not made out to be a monk, and there was no money to do much else. So, when he was seventeen, he left home and set out for the city.

Nothing motivates quite like privation. Paris had lots of hungry, desperate people in the spring of 1634, and a country boy from Alsace was more than likely going to become a victim, prey rather than predator. But Stephane had learned a few things as the youngest of eight: when to be seen and when to be silent; how to avoid a beating if there was one to be given out, whether at fault or not; and how to make sure there was always a portion for him for dinner.

He was agile; he was nimble; he knew how to hide, and soon to steal and to deceive. There were plenty of small-time gangs in the rabbit-warren streets of Paris who welcomed someone like that. One of them, a one-eyed rag pedlar named Marcel, took him in and within a week had him out on the street doing odd jobs, with the victims mostly men and women much like himself—except that they were unsuspecting and easy prey.

Marcel himself was only incidentally a rag pedlar. After the sun went down, he and his little band retired to a bolt-hole not far from the sprawling marketplace at Les Halles and divided the spoils of the day. To his credit, Marcel took a large share, but allowed his operatives to keep a fair amount for themselves; and no one, no matter how poor their take, went hungry or cold. He inspired loyalty among his boys—and got it: Marcel was careful, paying the needed bribes, protecting them all from the constabulary, never aiming too high to attract the attention of the mighty, nor troubling the poorest who would have nothing to lose by turning them in.

It was, as Marcel pointed out, a good and healthy relationship. The rag pedlar made sure to light the occasional candle to the Blessed Virgin to thank Her for his good fortune, their little hideaway an island of calm in a sea of want.

It was easy now, at two years' remove, to look upon that time with fondness; Marcel's 'family' only stole from those who were already well enough off to afford it. For a time, Stephane even thought that he might graduate to some legitimate profession, as a few of the other 'boys' had done. But even if that hadn't happened, it was a comfortable enough life, better than anything that had awaited him in Alsace.

It all came to an end one warm summer evening.

Stephane was just coming from his usual place near the Pont Royal, where he entertained passersby with sleight of hand and juggling tricks, while his partners worked the crowd and slit the convenient purse. They'd split up: they always did, taking care as they made their way back to the safe house. Flushed with success he'd allowed himself a stop at a pastry cart in Les Halles, where he'd bought a sou's worth of fruit-filled tart; he still remembered its sweetness, of *confit* and honey, how it had smelled so wonderful and tasted so delicious. Marcel would not mind a sou spent thus, especially with the number of sous he was bringing home.

But he never brought them home. As he made his way through the covered markets, following one of a dozen paths that would lead him there, he smelled fire—and heard shouts and cries.

At first he thought it might be just spilled cooking grease, the sort of small fire that happened all the time in the markets; but as he came closer he saw that it was larger, hotter, and more out of control.

From twenty yards away he knew that the fire was more than just a cook fire, and that the place where his 'family' had lived was in the midst of it. Ten yards closer, and he noticed—with the keen senses he'd developed from the Paris streets—that there was a great number of constables moving around in the crowd, which was mostly trying to get away from the fire.

He had turned away then, knowing that there was no place for him to go home to.

At the time, he thought he'd done a good job of mixing with the people trying to get away from Les Halles, just another poor Parisian sod in the crowd. There was nothing that would have—or should have—distinguished him. He had never attracted attention—never stepped outside the bounds that Marcel had set, never done anything that set him apart, made him a person of interest.

Except that someone had been interested in him.

He did not make it out of Les Halles that day. He knew every path through the marketplace, but so did the constables. They found him, seized him against his protests of innocence, and brought him to the Prison de l'Abbaye, the new one next to Saint-Germain-des-Prés; without explanation they tossed him into a crowded, dark cell at the rear of the second floor. The slamming of the iron-bound door and the turning of the key in the lock closed the door on the life he had known since coming to Paris.

They left him in that cell with a half-dozen others, all of whom protested their innocence frequently and loudly enough that one of the keepers came into the cell and laid about him with a truncheon. Stephane had found a corner to the left of the cell entrance, where he feigned sleep, and only got a sharp poke in the chest—he reacted with a *whoof* and collapsed to the floor clutching his midsection and was afterward left alone. It was no worse than anything his older brothers had dealt out as he was growing up, and much less severe than the beating some of his cellmates received, the guard taking obvious delight in dealing it out.

He found a way not to be seen, not to be noticed, not to be bothered. He wondered at the time if that meant that he'd be left to rot in the Prison de l'Abbaye for whatever crime they decided he'd committed. Sleight of hand and juggling, or even the occasional cutpursing, didn't usually send you *there*. But there he was.

Two days after landing in the cell, two sunsets and sunrises later, they came for him. The guards that took him out didn't seem to know his name: they picked him out as the youngest and the smallest man in the cell. He was beckoned to follow—not picked up and roughly handled: it was just, "*Eh, le mec, vous là-bas, venez avec nous.*"

He went with them. It was not as if he were given a choice, but there was some illusion of courtesy, some vague notion that they were instructed to treat him gently. When in a situation like that one, it was best to cling to whatever there was, no matter how thin the reed might be.

They took him to a room on the third floor, one much more clean and neat than the place they'd left him. There was a table and two chairs, a bottle of wine, two cups, and a loaf of bread on the table, along with a leather pouch and a pipe with a long, carved stem. He wasn't sure whether he was supposed to eat and drink: after two days of the brownish slop that was all they'd been fed, the idea of a cup of wine and bread was almost too much for him. He was never sure afterward what kept him from it—perhaps natural streetwise suspicion.

He left it alone, instead pacing out the dimensions of the room, glancing out the tall, barred window at the city beyond, wondering what was going to happen next.

They didn't make him wait long: a single toll of a nearby church bell—fifteen minutes at the most—and the door swung open again to reveal a middle-aged man, conservatively dressed in dark hues. What Stephane noticed first was the man's hands: long-fingered, a scholar's hands, with the faintest ink-stain where the pen would be held, and no rings or adornment whatsoever. In fact, he had no badge or mark of office at all; it was as if he designed to blend into the background—much like Stephane preferred for himself.

The second thing he noticed was the eyes: deep set, around a small nose; dark and piercing, as if they took in every detail.

"Ah," the man said, gesturing to the table. "I see you have not partaken of refreshments." He turned to the guard who had opened the door for him. "Leave us, *s'il vous plait,*" he said.

"But, Monsieur—"

The man held up one of those long-fingered hands. "*Leave us,*" he repeated. "Do not make me repeat myself."

The guard withdrew quickly, dismissed like a misbehaving hound. Stephane heard the door being secured.

"Now," the gentleman said. "Let us sit and enjoy this fine wine. Alsatian," he added, picking up the bottle and examining the label.

Stephane's heart skipped a beat. He felt suddenly unmasked, exposed, as if this man knew exactly who he was.

"Excuse me, Monsieur, but I..."

"Sit," he said, gesturing to a chair. Stephane felt that he had no other choice. The wine bottle was opened, and wine was poured into the two cups. "*Salut,*" the man added, and drank first; Stephane followed, taking a careful sip. He was not at all surprised to find that it was excellent.

"You can enjoy *petun* as well, if you wish."

Stephane did not answer; he was surprised to see the New World herb on the table—there was a rule against it in prison, though many of the guards and prisoners used it nonetheless.

"I would like to put you at your ease, Stephane," the man said at once, completing the task of unmasking him. "Yes," he continued, "I know your name—it was easy enough to obtain. And yes, I know your profession."

Stephane did not answer; there was nothing he could say.

"I assume that you are bursting with questions. All young men are; the ones that learn to ask the *right* question, at the *right* time, have a chance to become middle-aged men...and sometimes, if they are even more careful, to become old men. Perhaps I am mistaken, but I think you have a good chance to become middle-aged, Stephane."

"Assuming, that is, that you ask the right question."

"I'm not sure what that might be, Monsieur."

"Do not hesitate, Stephane. Begin with the most obvious."

"As you wish," Stephane answered. "Why am I here?"

"Excellent," the man answered. "That is truly excellent. A less wise man might have asked who I am. The effrontery—in case it was later determined that I was well known, and to ask my identity would be an affront to my notoriety. No, you have begun with the most obvious.

"You are *here*, young Stephane, because you were picked up on suspicion."

"Suspicion of what?"

The man made an offhand gesture with one hand. "Does it really matter? The Prefect of Police is really quite competent in following orders. Suspicion it is, and let us let it go at that. Truly, of all of Marcel's little band of thieves and confidence artists, you were the one of greatest interest."

"Marcel?"

"Do not dissemble with me. Your mentor. Your—keeper. Your father, I venture to say."

"My father is in Alsace."

"A turn of phrase. He is—or, should I say, *was*"—Stephane's heart sank: if the man were telling the truth, it confirmed what he already feared—"your protector here in Paris. As I say, of all of his former wards, you are the most interesting."

"Marcel. Is he—"

"Sadly, yes, he is dead. The wheel of fortune turns, young Stephane. Perhaps it is fortunate that you stopped on your way home, *non*?"

Stephane remembered feeling sick for a few moments, as if he were going to vomit up the wine and the last few days' gruel. The gentleman sitting opposite, speaking of Marcel's death in polite, casual tones, was suddenly repellent.

He stood up from his chair and went to the window, turning his back on his drinking companion.

"Who are you, then?" he asked, not turning.

"I am your new employer, Stephane," the man said. "Unless you would prefer to continue to rot in this prison. It would be a waste of your obvious talents, but...*c'est la vie*, I suppose."

"But who *are you*?" He turned, his face hot, but his eyes dry and filled with anger. "Or is that not the *right question* now, Monsieur? Who are you that wishes to employ me?"

"Now it comes to this question," the man said. "Very good. Now that we understand each other—"

"We do not," Stephane interrupted. "Even so."

"As you wish. My name...is unimportant: but if you must have it, my name is Servien. Étienne Servien. I suspect you have not heard of me. But you will know the name of the man whom I serve."

"Speak it and I shall tell you," Stephane answered.

"Of course," Servien had said. "His name is Richelieu. The Cardinal-Duke de Richelieu."

✧   ✧   ✧

He had learned his letters from his mother, who was a strong believer in such things; but he knew very little more. Servien demanded that he be able to read and write well enough to correspond: he told Stephane that he could be taught such things, and would prefer that he learn than he try to train a highly literate dullard to be clever and observant as he believed Stephane to be. Of course, no highly literate dullards had been deposited in the Prison de l'Abbaye, at the mercy of Monsieur Servien.

As far as he knew.

For all of the summer, and fall, and into the winter, he devoted himself to studies under the tutelage of a stern Dominican priest, Père Montségur, at a monastery outside of Paris. Stephane was his only student; the priest always carried a wooden dowel, ten inches long, as if he was constantly searching for some carpentry project that needed his attention: but its real use was to correct Stephane's penmanship, or use of the *accent grave*, or anything else that annoyed the good Père—by a sharp rap on the knuckles of his non-writing hand and a stern *faîtes attention!* Because of this, he developed the habit of placing his left hand beneath the table as he wrote. Père Montségur used the dowel on his left shoulder instead—and Stephane always made sure to wince, even though it scarcely hurt at all.

The abbey was no haven of ascetics. Père Montségur was a younger son of a nobleman in the country, and was thus accustomed to finer things—and saw no reason why his pupil should not enjoy them as well. There was fresh fruit, and olives, and cheese, and bread baked every morning, and *vin ordinaire* better than the best he'd ever had. He learned his lessons well—not just the writing, but tests of observation and memory...and learning all that could be learned about the great wonder of the age—the phenomenon known as the Ring of Fire.

No one could say for certain what it was that brought the up-timers to Thuringia in the fall of 1631, three years before Stephane's first encounter with Monsieur Servien. The Church was decidedly silent on the subject—Père Montségur would only say that he had not been given any particular doctrinal guidance on it. There was a bishop in the new town responsible for the souls of those devoted to the Church Universal, and as his Holiness was satisfied with that the Père would be satisfied as well.

✧   ✧   ✧

There was always this to be said in favor of Stephane's new life. His mother would have strongly disapproved of his former career as a thief, had she ever found out. His new profession as a spy in the service of France's ruler...that might be another matter entirely.

A pity, of course, that she'd never find that out either.

Chapter 11

In the morning Stephane found a sunny place on the dock to idle, waiting for an opportunity to present itself. Thomasville was an active port—there was a lot going on, between fishing and mining...it was just a matter of finding a way off the island.

Learning to wait was a part of one's nature as a spy. There was always something to wait for: means, motive, opportunity...it was something else Père Montségur had taught him: it was not merely what you *did*, but also when you did it that mattered. It made him wonder at the time when the good Père had been in the business, and made him smile now to think of it. No doubt before the war—it was never discussed. Paris had been a hotbed of intrigue long before *le Cardinal* had become the master chef of that particular dish.

Late in the morning, the opportunity presented itself. Two fairly grimy men were walking along the dock near where he stood, speaking a combination of English and Danish. They were not happy.

"...That *skiderik* Jens *promised* us twice what he paid. You know that, Ole. I'm not going back to Cape Breton to shovel coal for him—not now, not ever."

"A man has to eat, Karol."

"Eat?" The first man stopped and poked the other in the chest. "*Eat?* This is a boom town, you lackwit. There's more chance to earn your daily meal here than anywhere in the New World. It's all here, if you're willing to work."

"And the wages—"

"They *have* to be better than what Jens is paying."

"I don't know..."

"That's the problem with you, Ole," he said, as they continued to walk past where Stephane was standing. "You *don't know.* You don't know anything. How to earn a day's wage, how to make love to a woman, how to..." his voice trailed off as they continued down the dock.

Cape Breton, Stephane thought. *Off this island.*

They had been talking about shoveling coal in Cape Breton, which he knew was also on an island, but one that was closer to the mainland. It might be possible to make one's way across from there to Québec. How far could it be?

After Ole and Karol were well out of sight, Stephane walked briskly down the dock, looking for wherever they had come from. He had his answer quickly: a large, deep-draft vessel was offloading a cargo of coal into a series of wagons; a number of dirty, burly men were working at the pile with shovels. He couldn't tell, but could guess, that the two men passing him had been here a few minutes earlier with the rest.

He stood there long enough to be noticed.

"What are you looking at, then?" the foreman asked him, shouting from the dockside, where he was attending to one of the carts.

"Just admiring the work," Stephane said. "You look to be a few men short."

"They come and go," the man said. "What's it to you?"

"I might be looking for work," Stephane answered.

"You?" The foreman, who was a substantial man with arms and legs thick as tree trunks, gave out a laugh. "This is no work for a scrawny mama's boy. You don't look strong enough to lift a shovel."

"You just want to keep all the pretty girls for yourself and your men."

"Pretty girls? There aren't but a few, and they're all native girls. If that's what's drawing you here, *ung mand*, you should look elsewhere...you sound French. Are you from that settlement up the river?"

Stephane shrugged. He didn't care what conclusion the foreman reached.

The man gestured at the tender; there were a pair of shovels stuck into the pile of coal, as if they'd been left behind.

✧　　　✧　　　✧

A quality that Monsieur Servien had always admired in Stephane was the tendency for people to underestimate him. Stephane was slight of build but had a strong back and arms—and was used to working; unlike many of his companions in Paris, he was no layabout, and he knew that the only way to get off this island was to convince the laborers that he was one of them.

He worked steadily through the morning and afternoon, shoveling coal into the sluice, a long trough that extended from the coal pile on the tender down to the cart on the dock. It was strenuous, but steady; he tried to make his movements efficient, not picking up too much with each shovelful, while the burlier Danes bragged and tried to show their strength by taking larger quantities and throwing them harder and further down the trough. By early afternoon they were stopping frequently when they were winded.

Stephane took his share of ribbing from the bigger men; but he simply ignored them and focused on the work: bend, lift, toss; bend, lift, toss. He thought about Marcel, about Servien, and about the hills of Alsace . . . with an occasional thought about Ingrid Skoglund, the angel who might well have saved his life in the storm.

By the time the men trooped off the tender at sundown, tired and dirty, they had stopped making fun of the little Frenchman. Jens, the foreman, paid each of them their wage. Each of the Danes complained about the amount; Jens smiled through the whole transaction—they could take his money or they could turn their backs, and they decided—for today at least—to take his money.

Stephane received his money last. It was less than the others had been paid for a long, hard day's work, and Jens seemed to smirk even more when he handed over the pittance.

"Is there a problem?" the foreman asked.

He could see that the other men were watching for his reaction. "Did you find fault with my work?"

"You did well—for a beginner," he answered. "It's an acquired skill. You would not want me to pay you the same as I pay those who have worked at this task for a long time?"

"No, of course not."

"Well, then—"

"I would expect you to pay them *more*," Stephane said. "Not just more than you pay me—more than you are paying *them*."

"What do you mean?"

"I mean what I say," Stephane said. He took the few coins and pocketed them, laid his shovel on the coal pile, and walked away from the foreman.

The evening was spent in a dockside bar. The other men welcomed him—his little display had earned their respect.

"We're shipping out tomorrow," Gustav said as he set down his mug. "You work hard, *Französ*." He gave Stephane a hard slap on the back. "I like that."

"Honest day's work," Stephane said when he recovered from the slap. "Back to Cape Breton?"

"*Ja*, that's right. Takes two days to get there, then two days loading up the tender, then back here. Round and round." He swirled a finger in the air. "Boring work, but it buys the beer."

"It doesn't seem so bad."

"It's crap," one of the others said: Lukas, Stephane remembered. "But it's better than marching in formation, eh, Gustav?"

"A *lot* better," the big man agreed. "I was with the Saxon infantry at Breitenfeld. We all ran away, away, rather than be run over by the cavalry. Rather be shoveling coal, eh, *Französ*?" That was what they all called him: 'Frenchy,' in German. It was good enough—someone had asked again, during the afternoon, if he was from the French settlement, and he'd answered with another shrug.

"Getting killed on the battlefield isn't what it used to be," Stephane said, and sipped on his beer. It wasn't particularly tasty, but it helped drive out the coal dust.

"I'd rather be working the coal tender than going down in the mines," Lukas said. "But that doesn't make it *good*."

"You ask too much of life," Gustav said. "You should take it as it comes, like *Französ* here. I don't know why I drink with you at all."

"Because you don't like drinking alone," Lukas answered, and they all laughed.

Two mornings later, the tender was empty of coal. Crates of supplies had been loaded on board, wrapped in canvas to keep coal dust from settling on them; and it put back out to sea. Stephane wondered to himself what Père Montségur—or, indeed, Monsieur Servien—might have to say about what he'd seen.

Chapter 12

Paris, France

Servien walked along the broad corridor toward the great salon that his master planned someday to make into a theater. He would have scoffed at the idea of a theater in the *Palais-Cardinal*, a needless extravagance even for a patron of the theater such as Richelieu—except that up-timer history *said* that it had been built, and that Lemercier had done it in grand style.

At the entrance to the room he passed a servant, nervously shifting from foot to foot. Inside, standing and admiring one of the newer frescoes, he could see a handsome young nobleman, his back turned toward the door.

Servien stepped forward and cleared his throat. The sound echoed in the room, and the man turned to face him. He was clutching a letter in his hand, the seal broken.

He saw Servien and his face darkened.

"Ah, my uncle's most trusted servant. Tell me, where is your master?"

"He is concerned with other business, Monsieur *Grand-Maître*. I was asked to attend you."

"I should like to speak with him about—about this." He brandished the letter as if it were a weapon.

"It would be my honor to bring back any message—"

"No." The man tucked the letter inside his coat. "No, I wish to speak with him personally. Retire, and bring back my uncle."

Servien sighed—not too loudly, he hoped: there was no need to offend the highborn young man. He would have liked nothing more than to do as he was bid: to retire from the salon and fetch the cardinal to speak with his nephew, Jean Armand de Maillé-Brézé, his sister's son, the new Grand Admiral of France.

Servien even knew the content of the letter. *It is the king's will that you shall undertake a mission to our new lands in North America and enforce our writ...*

"I beg your pardon, Monsieur," Servien said patiently. "His Eminence is abroad in the city in his carriage, and cannot presently attend you."

"He is abroad—then I shall wait."

"I do not know his commitments, Monsieur. And I know that your time is valuable."

Maillé-Brézé beckoned him closer. Their discussion in this large room had taken the form of an exchange of players upon a stage: every word had echoed off the polished floors and the cornices of the ceiling.

Servien approached until they were close together.

"Do you know the contents of my uncle's letter to me? Of the Royal commission that accompanied it?"

"I have been informed, Monsieur. His Eminence confided his plans to me so that I might attend you. He felt that it was a great honor bestowed upon you, an opportunity to add luster to your honored name."

"A great ... an opportunity to—he is sending *two ships* thousands of miles from France," Maillé-Brézé spat out. "To go to *Virginia*, of all places. I see no honor in treating with savages. I should likely be gone from court for more than a year, perhaps two."

"There are men other than savages in Virginia, Monsieur. His Christian Majesty has new subjects in that land that must be brought to heel."

"Charming." Maillé-Brézé turned away, then rounded on Servien once more. "My uncle chose to have me honored as *grand-maître de la navigation* not to round up recalcitrant subjects half a world away, but to command His Christian Majesty's fleets at war."

"We are no longer at war, Monsieur," Servien said mildly.

Maillé-Brézé looked exasperated, in that extravagant manner

that came easily to young men. "We will be again, soon enough! Unless you're fool enough to think the current peace with the USE will last."

Servien made no reply. Truth be told, he suspected the same himself.

Maillé-Brézé brought himself very erect. "So—clearly you can see that my duty lies here, not in—in Virginia."

"I would concur, Monsieur, except that it is not my decision to make. I humbly ask your pardon, but in truth, it is not *yours* either: it is the king's, and by the letter you have received he has made it, and made his will very clear. To ignore it... or defy it... ill becomes a loyal servant of the crown."

Like Champlain, Servien thought. Who, if given two well-armed ships like the ones given to Maillé-Brézé, would do exactly as he was ordered without question.

"You suggest that I contemplate treason? I should strike you."

"I make no such suggestion," Servien said. "I do no more than observe that we are all obliged to do the king's will, particularly when he expresses his desire so clearly."

"All except my uncle. What is it that he says? 'I cover it all with my red robe.' He does as he pleases. This—" he withdrew the letter once more. "This letter is *his* doing. He arranged for my appointment as *grand-maître*, and now he arranges for me to be away from court. It is all part of some grand intrigue."

"Once again I beg your pardon," Servien said, accompanying his words with a polite bow, "but I detect in Monsieur's remarks an intimation that he does not consider this task an important one."

"How perceptive of you, Servien. Uncle has always spoken highly of your intelligence and insight," he sneered.

"I shall thank His Eminence for his compliment," Servien answered, trying his best to sound guileless. "But if I may assure you, Monsieur, that this mission is of *prime* importance to the crown. It is no mere errand to be given to a lad of no consequence." Maillé-Brézé bristled at the word "lad," and Servien continued, "His Eminence asked specifically that you be designated to lead the expedition. Virginia is a former English colony—"

"I know what it is," Maillé-Brézé interrupted.

"A *former English colony*," Servien repeated, "which is settled on land which now of right belongs to the kingdom of France.

Its inhabitants must be convinced that the right and proper course for them is to submit to our king's will. It shall be done by negotiation if possible, and by force if necessary.

"I can assure you that it was your uncle's intent that you be the one to gain stature and honor in this undertaking. No offense or insult was intended—indeed, quite the opposite—the man who subdues the Atlantic plantations for His Christian Majesty will be elevated in stature among all of the luminaries of the court."

Whether Maillé-Brézé had simply accepted the inevitable, or had decided that it was time to end the interview, was unclear to Servien; without any further word, the nobleman turned away and walked toward the door, beckoning to his servant and leaving Servien standing alone in the middle of the great hall.

After Maillé-Brézé was gone a panel in a nearby wall swung open, revealing a concealed doorway. Out of the darkness emerged the gray-robed monk Father Joseph, the *in pectore* Cardinal Tremblay, Cardinal Richelieu's confessor. He had a wry smile on his face.

"Walk with me," Joseph said, and they took their leave of the salon and strolled along a wide corridor toward the receiving rooms at the front of the palais.

"That was well done," the monk said.

"You were listening to the conversation."

Joseph shrugged.

"I do not think he was fond of my flattery," Servien said. "He assumed I was merely being a sycophant."

"Were you?"

"Not entirely. He has been charged with an important task— and if he succeeds, His Eminence will surely heap further honors upon him."

"And if he fails..."

"If Maillé-Brézé succeeds, it will benefit France, it will benefit Cardinal Richelieu, and it will even benefit Maillé-Brézé. But if he somehow manages to bungle the assignment, Father, the cardinal will be able to lay it at the feet of the young man's inexperience or impetuosity."

"It is a perfect double-edged sword," Joseph said. "A master-stroke, don't you think?"

Servien stopped walking and turned to face the monk, who stopped as well, tucking his bony hands into his sleeves.

"This was your idea."

"I fail to see why it is important whether it originated with me," Joseph said. "But even if it did...if the cardinal wishes his nephew to gain honor in the court in this way, I am not one to object. If he is the right man for the job—"

"On which subject I am hardly certain. But pray continue."

"If he is, then his skill in executing it far outweighs his present petulance. But who would be sent instead? Few at court—including His Majesty—know anything at all about Virginia or the rest of the Atlantic colonies in the New World."

"What if he refuses to go?"

"Refuse a direct order from his sovereign? Perish the thought. Indeed, my friend Servien, banish it from your mind. He is the son of a marquis, the nephew of our Cardinal, and the brother-in-law of the First Prince of the Blood. The chance of him actually refusing to do as he is commanded is as remote as a journey to the moon."

Servien considered reminding Father Joseph that, yes indeed, the up-timers had in fact journeyed to the moon; but that was a feat unlikely to be repeated in this year of grace 1636.

Still, the idea that Maillé-Brézé might refuse to undertake the mission had never occurred to His Eminence—or to Servien. There should be no need to play to Maillé-Brézé's pride or vanity at all, not when a command in the king's name was given.

But he was a nobleman—and such was the way with which those of gentle birth needed to be treated. Cardinal Richelieu was a past master at the art.

And, indeed, so was Servien.

Chapter 13

Nye-Alborg
Labrador

Stephane found it easy to tell where the Danes had settled along
the shore of the Saint-Lawrence: instead of the thick covering of
tall pines, there was scarcely a tree to be seen inland to where
the hills began. It was like that on both sides of the river that
emptied into the gulf, but the crew of the coal-hauler paid it no
mind, nor did they seem to notice the murky water of the river
or the acrid smell of coal dust that pervaded the settlement of
Nye-Alborg.

If Thomasville was not Paris, Nye-Alborg was even less so.
It was a new settlement, a town that had clearly grown from
nothing. The buildings along the wharf had scarcely been able to
take on the grim soiling that coal smoke left behind. The dock
fittings were bright and new and there was more building going
on up the hill.

The coal tender tied up at the dock while Jens stood on the
foredeck shouting to shore in Danish. The crew lounged about,
showing no particular interest in unloading the cargo that had
been transported back to the mainland settlement.

"What's he doing?" he asked Gustav. The big man had taken a
liking to him during the transit—they'd swapped obscene jokes in
French and German, and told stories of their lives before coming

to Newfoundland. Gustav bragged about his time as a soldier; Stephane told whatever lies came to hand.

"There'll be a crew to unload the boat."

"We don't do it?"

"You're damned right we don't, *Französ*. We're in charge of putting the coal on the boat, and taking it off the boat. I'm not a stevedore."

"I'm surprised."

"Why?"

"I would have thought that Jens wouldn't want to pay someone else."

Gustav grunted. "Eh, you're right that he pinches every coin until it screams. But no matter how little he pays us, he pays the idlers on the dock even less."

Jens had accurately figured out the mentality of his employees. By not forcing them to do extra work, by paying them more than the tiny wage given to men even further down the chain, and by letting them run free—as long as they returned to the coal tender to take care of the next shipment—they stayed with him. Regardless of their complaints, Gustav and the others knew that they were in a good spot. There were plenty of others waiting to take their jobs, just as Stephane himself had done when Karol had walked off the job in Thomasville. There would be other things for Karol to do, but from what Stephane had heard, the pay scale wasn't that good. After hearing the description, he'd rather shovel coal than work in a smelter, which sounded like some intermediate circle of Hell.

There was a rooming house not far from the wharf, at which Gustav, Lukas and the others were regular guests. As they walked up the steps from the cobbled street, the smell of fresh bread overlaid that of fish and filth and coal smoke, and Stephane and the others found themselves in a brightly painted common room.

A heavyset woman in an apron and cap, wiping her hands on a towel, looked up and smiled, then gave some sort of greeting in Danish. The other men replied, then Gustav elbowed Stephane and said, "This is the Goodwife Lykke, our hostess." He added, in a whisper, "That's not her real name, but that's of no matter."

"A pleasure to make your acquaintance," Stephane said in French, bowing. Mistress Lykke might or might not have understood, but she seemed charmed. She beckoned them through the common room and to a narrow hallway, where there were several rooms whose doors were slightly ajar. Gustav steered Stephane to the far one, pushed the door open, and beckoned to a pair of narrow beds, stacked one on top of the other. The room was scarcely wider, with just enough room for a small table with a ewer and bowl, and a corner to stash their duffel bags.

"Up top for you, little *Französ*," he said, and sat down on the bottom. Stephane shrugged and pulled himself up to the top. The mattresses were thin, but comfortable; all in all, this would be as snug a place as he'd slept in since before he was sent to Hamburg.

He lay back on the bed. "Why does it matter that her name isn't Lykke?"

"It means 'happy.' She's a happy woman—here in the New World. The story I hear is that it wasn't so back in Denmark: too many children, some brute of a husband...someone paid her way. I don't know who, or how, but she made it work—and someone set her up here."

"And now we pay her most of our money for—"

"A clean room and a few good meals, and some left over to keep us occupied until it's time to go back." He stood up and rattled the edge of Stephane's bed. "Come on, *Französ*," he said, chuckling. "Let's go get occupied."

Stephane had no intention of staying in Nye-Alborg: he wasn't going to make the return trip—it was just a waypoint to New France upriver. But while he was there, he took advantage of the opportunity to look around—when he wasn't otherwise... occupied.

The town was really a wonder. Nye-Alborg lay at the mouth of a river; along with the coal tenders, there were a dozen or more fishing boats that left the dock early in the morning and came back each evening weighed down with the biggest and heaviest catches of fish that Stephane had ever seen: the stalls at Les Halles never had such a variety and quantity as what they brought ashore. Even the smaller boats, called by the Danish word *kano*—a solid log that had been hollowed out, Indian-style—brought back impressive hauls.

And that seemed as nothing when compared to the wild game that the hunters brought down from the forests. The Danish Hudson's Bay Company had attracted men from a variety of professions, both from Europe and from the Americas; in the three years since the company had been operating in the New World, the rapidly growing colony had gathered up English, French, Germans, Poles, Dutch and practically every other nationality, employing them to feed the growing settlements.

In the morning after they arrived, while most of his comrades were still sleeping off the effects of their late-night carousing, Stephane walked the dock and heard a dozen languages and what could not be communicated in words was accomplished in gestures. There were no idle hands in sight—everywhere there was buying and selling, sawing and hammering, lifting and shoving and sweeping and dragging...it was a company town, with inflated prices but lots of things for sale.

As for the coal, it came from inland and was brought to the wharf directly on a track, modeled on what the Danish colonists had seen in the up-timer-occupied parts of Germany. Stephane walked along the rail line, built from hardwood slats with hammered metal bracings: it ran, flat and straight, up into the hills. Beside the rails were two dirt tracks, wide enough for a man to walk a horse or a donkey.

"That's right," Jens told him when they met on the dock that afternoon. "When they first started taking the coal out they had these heavy carts—but they were always breaking down or turning over, and it takes a bloody great monster of a horse to haul a full load. So last year they built this, and now we move three tenders full of coal a week to Thomasville. Keeps the miners busy—keeps us busy—and it keeps the smelters running back on the island."

"How far does it go?"

"Why do you want to know?"

"Just curious," he said. "I'm interested."

"There's more to you than shows, little man," the overseer said.

You have no idea, Stephane thought. "Does that mean you pay me more?"

"I don't pay for curiosity," he answered. "I pay for steady work. I didn't think you'd earn your pay"—which, Stephane considered, was less than he was paying the rest of them—"but you've done well. Stay with me, and I'll take good care of you."

"I can just imagine."

✧   ✧   ✧

There were two idle days at Goodwife Lykke's boarding house. There were two free-spending nights at Nye-Alborg's alehouses; the town had several, each catering to a set of professions. The coal shovelers shared with the coopers and wheelwrights and blacksmiths, and stayed away from the fishermen and the game hunters. The professional classes kept to themselves, an arrangement that satisfied both groups.

On the morning of the third day, the carts began to arrive on the rail track. With the sun only just above the horizon, the attention of the people of the town was taken by the screeching of flanged wheels on the rails. The hungover coal shovelers pulled themselves out of their bunks and began the backbreaking work of moving the coal from the carts into the now-empty tender. It was the same as what they'd done at Thomasville, but in reverse—the rail track ended on an elevated platform, and the designer of the carts had constructed an ingenious system whereby a wooden panel on the side could be unbolted, allowing the cart to be emptied down a sluice into the waiting tender. The shovelers had to keep up with what poured in, filling the boat with what was provided.

They worked all day. Moving coal from the carts into the tender was easier in some ways because of the sluice, but they had to keep up with the flow of carts to keep them from backing up. They took short breaks in shifts—and the coal kept coming and coming.

By evening, when the tender was full and the carts stopped coming, the crew made its way back to Goodwife Lykke's. Some of the crew, including Stephane's roommate Gustav, went out for a last turn through the ordinaries of Nye-Alborg. Stephane made sure he ate his fill but retired early, which made him the butt of some jokes from his crewmates. With no snoring man sleeping on the lower bunk, he was able to get himself to sleep.

With the moon up in the sky, though, and his fellows still not returned, Stephane took his bag and crept out of the rooming house. Before leaving, he set a small portion of his wage on the corner of the common-room table—an offering to Goodwife Lykke for her comfortable beds and fresh-baked bread.

Making his way down the dock without being seen was child's play for one of Marcel's protégés, and finding an empty *kano* and taking it out into the river without being caught was just as easy.

He had one tense moment when one of the nearby taverns rang its closing bell, but within a few minutes he was away and free, making his way up the great river. It was a simple matter, he thought, to make his way a few miles upriver to Québec, where the French governor would give him every assistance.

In a drenching rain two nights later, the simple matter looked a lot less simple.

"If you survive this," he told himself and the night and the rain and anyone else who might have been listening, "consider yourself blessed by the Virgin and all the saints."

He had settled under the cover of a tarpaulin that he'd found in the *kano*, and he had been rowing his way upstream against a surprisingly strong current, waiting for Québec to come into view. It had not providentially done so—not on the night he had stolen it, nor the next day, nor this day; and night was coming on fast enough that he knew he would have to find a place to tether the boat so he could get some rest.

New France—which was all of the land hereabout, by arrangement of *le Cardinal*—was huge; it was desolate; and even this late in spring it was cold. Desolate and cold he could handle: he had no need for anyone else, and living on the streets in Paris (and elsewhere, in his new profession) had taught him to be indifferent to the cold.

It was the *huge* that was daunting. He knew that Québec was upriver from the mouth of the Saint Lawrence; there was a French settlement there...but where in hell was it?

He had been following the river and staying close to the north bank. The *kano* had quickly carried him out of sight of Nye-Alborg; west of the settlement the land was rough and untenanted, and there was nothing like a road near the shore, so he had no real fear of being followed.

Now, as night fell early, he maneuvered into shallow water, where he could tie up the boat to some sturdy tree roots. The tree canopy near the shore afforded him some shelter from the rain.

Someone had stored a packet of dried meat and a waterskin aboard the *kano*. But there was little left two days into his extended voyage; he made a meal of what he had, offering a prayer to the Virgin as he did so, and then settled back, wrapped in the tarpaulin, and fell quickly asleep.

Chapter 14

On the St. Lawrence River

Stephane had no idea what woke him. The rain had stopped, but the gentle lapping of the river against the side of the *kano*—which had helped put him to sleep in the first place—remained constant. The animal noises were just the same; there was a heavy cloud cover, giving no sign of either moon or stars...but something was just *different*, some change in the quiet.

He was unarmed, but for a small hatchet that had also been stowed aboard the boat, and the long oar—hardly a useful weapon for someone his size. He slid his hand along the bottom of the boat and grasped the hilt of the hatchet, and then scanned the shore for some sign of enemies.

It should have been completely still; but he heard the faintest sound—perhaps a footfall in the underbrush; it could have been an animal, but Stephane was suspicious.

Get out on the river, he thought. *Or does that make me an easier target?*

Not at night, without a moon, he decided.

He reached for the anchor rope—

And suddenly his hand was seized by a pair of strong hands that lifted him almost upright.

"What fish has the river served us, then?" said a voice in clear-accented French.

He struggled but to no avail—the man who had hold of him suddenly grabbed his other hand which held the hatchet, causing it to fall. He heard a small splash, and his heart sank.

In dim light he could scarcely make out the figure of the man holding him. He appeared to be a native.

His French was perfect, though. "*Il est muet.* Does he speak? Who are you, little man?"

"I should ask the same of you," Stephane said as calmly as he could manage. "Am I in New France?"

The man laughed, and lifted Stephane bodily from the canoe and set him on the riverbank.

"Now, now, this is all New France, *non*? Are you a Frenchman?"

"I demand to know who seizes me in this way," Stephane answered. "I am on the king's business."

"The king—a drowned rat on the river is on the king's *business*, is he indeed. Does the king's servant come with a fine reward for his capture?"

"I am sure."

The man laughed again and let go of Stephane's arms. "Well then, Monsieur, we should get to know each other better. Tell me who you are."

"As I said before, I am a servant of the king, on my way to Québec. If you will assist me I shall see that you are rewarded."

"Québec is your destination, hm? In a flat-bottom dugout *canoe*? You are days away from the *habitation*, Monsieur. You would surely be drowned or flooded long before you reached Québec."

"*Days*—how far away is it?"

"A hundred leagues from here. Perhaps more. You would say...three hundred, or three hundred and fifty miles."

Huge, Stephane thought. The enormity of it struck him like a blow; he tried to think of what to say, and couldn't come up with anything.

Il est muet.

"The woods are full of...predators," the man said. "Come and sit, little man. We will have a smoke and decide what to do."

In the small amount of illumination afforded by the lighting of the pipe, Stephane could see that he was in the presence of a native. The man was dressed for the outdoors, but in European-style breeches and a heavy coat, though he was obviously darker skinned and wore his hair in a greased queue.

As he passed the pipe to Stephane, he said, "I am called Savignon. I was upon a time a friend to Brûlé, but we parted ways when he chose the English king over the French one. Now I am in the service of the Sieur de Champlain."

Other than Champlain, Stephane didn't recognize any of the names. "The Captain of New France?"

"The same, and a friend to my people—what is left of them, in any case. Now then: who are you?"

"My name is Stephane Hoff," Stephane said. "I am on a particular mission for the king of France. I am sure that the Sieur de Champlain will welcome me."

"You are a long way from your king, Monsieur Hoff," Savignon said. "And Champlain makes his own decisions about who he *welcomes*. From what I understand, he has been treated with indifference by that king, and by the minister who serves him."

Stephane inhaled deeply from the pipe, and was able to let the smoke out with only a small amount of coughing. It was strong tobacco; he wondered how Savignon had come by it.

"You speak of the cardinal," he managed at last.

"Yes. The red-robed cardinal. Are you perhaps *his* agent? Then the captain is unlikely to welcome you at all."

"Not exactly."

"If there were enough light to look into your eyes," Savignon said, "I might see the truth of it. But, no matter: I will leave it to the captain to decide what to do."

"Then you will take me to him?"

"Why not? It will be an interesting diversion. You can tell me all about your mission."

Stephane did not answer that remark, since he was not particularly interested in doing anything of the sort. Instead, he replied, "Tell me, Savignon. How do you come to have such excellent command of French?"

"Ah, I can thank Étienne Brûlé for that. Did you know him? He was a *coureur de bois*, as I am—a woodsman, you might say, who was employed by the captain to learn the ways and language of the native tribes. When I was young, he brought me to Québec to live, so that I might learn French ways; I have been a..."

"Go-between?"

"Just so. A go-between. Brûlé...he made a poor choice a few years ago, when the English privateers took Québec away from

France with his help. The captain turned his back on him, and some of my fellow Hurons felt themselves betrayed. They caught him and did what honor demanded."

"Did they kill him?"

"In the end, yes," Savignon said, taking a long pull on his pipe. "But only after their sport. And then, when he was dead, they ate him."

"*Ate...*"

"You seem shocked, Monsieur Hoff. I can only say...welcome to the New World."

In the daylight Stephane got a better look at the native *coureur de bois*. Savignon was tall and stocky, handsome in a foreign way with a prominent nose and a square jaw, covered with a close-cut beard. His eyes were piercing and gray, and he seemed to notice everything.

He was also tireless, as Stephane learned.

When they rose in the morning fog, the rain had cleared. Savignon took his own hatchet—Stephane's was apparently lost for good—and fashioned a functional oar and handed it to Stephane, while he took the primary one for himself. They pushed the canoe out into the river and began to make their way upstream. From the time they began to row, Savignon scarcely paused.

"How long will it take us to reach Québec?" Stephane asked in the midmorning.

"Québec?" Savignon laughed. "We would be rowing for days. I do not intend to escort you to Québec, Monsieur."

"But that is where I must go."

"No doubt," Savignon answered. "But the river is a strong rival, the further upstream we go. No, we will travel to Tadoussac, and you can find a sailing vessel to take you the rest of the way."

"This is a busy place?"

"Oh, *oui*, for many years. When the French first came here it was a place where the Montagnais and other natives could trade furs with Europeans. The Sieur de Champlain conducted there a *tabagie*, a great meeting, when he came to New France." He let his oar trail in the water. "It was one of the ways that the native peoples learned that he would listen to them—and listen to the land."

"I'm not sure I understand what that means."

Savignon looked out across the wide river. "I have walked many paths in this country, Monsieur," he said. "I have stood on the shore of the Great Sea, and I have seen the headwaters of the lakes in Huronia. I have met men who listen to the land... and many others who simply will not.

"Consider the men who settle in the east—the English. They believe they can coerce the land to listen to them, by cutting all of the forests and killing all of the game. As for their attitude toward those who already lived on the land they now occupy... but for the help of those natives they would have perished in the starving winter. Still they have contempt for the native peoples."

"The Sieur de Champlain does not? I thought he was at war with them."

Savignon took up his oar and began to paddle once more. "Some warriors' blood ran hot. They heard a story that the Sieur de Champlain had laid down with sickness in his bones and would not rise again."

"I had not heard that the Sieur de Champlain was sick."

"He was not. But they *thought* he was. They learned otherwise."

Stephane did not respond, wondering where all of this was leading. "So we are making for Tadoussac," he said.

"*Oui*," Savignon said. "It is very busy. Your king has encouraged merchants and settlers to make their way to America, and many of them have come here. Perhaps they will go to other places when New France spreads across all of the land. In the meanwhile... you should have no trouble making your way to Québec from there."

Chapter 15

Québec
New France

Three decades earlier, Savignon told Stephane, Champlain had drawn a map of Tadoussac harbor in meticulous detail. He'd taken the soundings himself from the lead aboard his ship, *Bonne-Renommée*, and found that at the mouth of the Saguenay River, there were places nearly two hundred fifty fathoms deep— *une profondeur incroyable*, as he'd later written. Icy-cold water from the north flowed at Tadoussac from the Saguenay into the Saint Lawrence—Stephane knew that had he somehow wound up overboard, he would have died within minutes. His Alsatian hardiness would not have helped him a whit.

It was Tadoussac where the deep-water ships came to anchor, and where native tribes came with fur pelts to trade. Savignon knew many people, white and native, and was soon able to put him in contact with the captain of a small shallop bound for Québec. No appeal to patriotism could obtain him a berth: it took, instead, the payment of some of his carefully hoarded *louis d'argent* that had come with him from France and had survived his many adventures since.

It took three days to travel upriver, the boat anchoring at some settlement or other each night. The captain was in no hurry to reach Québec. He did not seem in any hurry to do much of anything. Stephane could barely conceal his irritation at this indolence—and insolence; so that by the time they finally reached the Île d'Orléans, both men were eager to be rid of the other.

Québec was located on the brow of a hill overlooking the river. It was not an imposing settlement; it looked less finished than the Danish one on the coast. Savignon had told Stephane the story of how the French had actually been ejected from the place only a few years ago, just before the Ring of Fire, by a privateering expedition led by Englishmen; it was certain *that* would not be repeated, at least at the behest of their current king.

Upon his entry into the town—unremarked and unchallenged— he inquired after Champlain, and learned that he resided in his own *habitation*, but that he was unlikely to be found at home in the daytime.

He found the place easily enough; indeed, it would have been hard to miss it. At his knock, a native servant answered, but refused Stephane entry, indicating that he should return later in the day when the master was to be at home.

"Your hospitality leaves something to be desired," Stephane told the man.

"I do as I am bid, Monsieur," the Indian said. "The captain does not permit any stranger within his house when he is not home."

"I am sent by the king of France, and by his minister."

"I am the servant of the Sieur de Champlain," the man answered.

Stephane could not immediately frame a reply—surely the man must see the difference between a king and a captain!

"I demand that you accommodate me. I am sent by the Sieur's sovereign—and therefore *your* sovereign. You will admit me, for he commands that the Sieur aid me in my mission. I demand it in the name of King Louis and the Cardinal-Duke de Richelieu."

The name of the cardinal seemed to ring out into silence, almost as if everyone in earshot had stopped to hear it. The servant did not reply, but glanced over Stephane's shoulder, as if there was someone standing behind.

Stephane turned, and found someone there: an older man with a military bearing standing, arms crossed.

"The cardinal demands, does he?" he said. "Well, then, come inside my house and we shall see what you have to say."

✧　　✧　　✧

Long before Stephane departed for Hamburg, Monsieur Servien had taken particular care to inform him about Samuel de Champlain, the captain-general of New France. It had allowed Stephane to form a mental picture of the man.

It had never crossed his mind that he might come face to face with him until he chose to abandon *Challenger* in Thomasville harbor a few weeks earlier. It had also never occurred to Stephane that the description, such as it was, would be so completely at odds with the man himself.

"He is a curious case," Monsieur Servien had told him. "Champlain was one of the first of our countrymen ever to venture into the interior of New France for His Majesty. He was well known, and well beloved, of our King Henri the Fourth of glorious memory."

"Henri *the Fourth*?" Stephane had said, incredulous. To imagine someone alive who had served a king now twenty-five years dead, murdered before Stephane was even born, was beyond conception, a fact which had made Servien laugh.

"Young men cannot imagine a world in which they have not lived," Servien had said. "Don't fear, young Stephane. The world got on quite well without you.

"But to Champlain. His first ventures into the New World were in the last century, and he visited New France for the first time more than thirty years ago. He has survived rivalries at court, changes in loyalties, conquest by the English, and even the enmity of the Queen Mother when she was regent. He even survived his own death."

Stephane did not quite understand what Servien had meant by that, and it clearly showed on his face.

"As you are aware, Stephane," Servien explained, "the up-timers have provided us with considerable information about the strange and wondrous world in which they lived before the Ring of Fire transported them into our midst. According to their great compendium, their *Encyclopédie*, Monsieur Champlain was to have suffered an apoplectic attack sometime in the autumn of 1635 and returned to dust on Christmas Day. But—miracle of miracles! He did not. Instead, he is alive and well, and his presence... his influence must be taken into account in any consideration of the New World to which His Majesty now lays claim."

"I don't understand. Is he a... hindrance? Could His Majesty not simply recall and replace him?"

"It is more complicated than that."

"I daresay it is," Stephane said. "Perhaps Monsieur could explain more clearly."

"Champlain is a romantic fool," Servien said. "He honors the traditions and the customs of the savage natives, and has always enjoyed their trust. He—personally—is held in awe by them. It is not an exaggeration: last fall, when rumors of his death circulated among the Five Nations, a war party made an attempt to take the settlement at Trois-Rivières. An informant passed this intelligence on to Champlain, who was there to thwart it. Thus, he enjoys the confidence of our king."

"What does Cardinal Richelieu think of him, if I may be so bold as to ask?"

"He believes that Monsieur Champlain is an obstacle to the greater glory of an expanded New France. He believes that Champlain will do what *he* thinks best, and his actions may not be in harmony with the cardinal's superior wisdom.

"And he believes, young Stephane, that it would have been better for all concerned if Champlain had simply suffered his attack and gone to God on Christmas Day last, as the up-timer histories assured that he would."

Samuel de Champlain did not appear to Stephane to be any sort of fool, romantic or otherwise. He was of above-average height, with no stoop of old age. Stephane, remembering Monsieur Servien's comment about Henri IV, had expected him to be ancient beyond understanding. But while it had gone gray and silver, he still had all his hair and, seemingly, most of his teeth. He presented an imposing figure, sitting at ease in his armchair while Stephane stood before him, knowing that he had achieved his goal by reaching him but now completely unsure what might happen next.

"Courtesy demands," Champlain said after a long pause, "that I welcome you as a countryman and a servant of our king. Yet it also demands of you that you show me the respect that I am due. So tell me, young man. Why does Cardinal Richelieu choose to send me a *spy*?"

"I . . . do not think that he intended to *send* me to you, Monsieur Captain. I have simply arrived here, and I need, and request, your help."

"You said that. A few moments ago it emerged as a demand. It pleases me that you have rephrased it as a request."

"I did not know how I might be received."

"Your illustrious master did not fully describe my character, my inclinations?" Champlain made a gesture in the air, expressive and yet dismissive. "He is disappointed that I am yet here."

"In New France?"

"Aboveground," Champlain said. He stood up slowly and walked to the window of his *habitation*, as it was called. From the window one could see the neat lanes and small houses of the settlement of Québec. He placed his hands on the sill and looked out, and without turning around said, "He promised me that there would be an entire continent open to settlement by France, yet there is still much to be done—in Virginia, and elsewhere. He wants other, younger men to do it."

"I cannot speak of the cardinal's intentions, Monsieur."

"No, no." Champlain turned. "Of course you cannot. None of us can. But we must all dance to his tune. So. Tell me what help you so urgently require, young man. What crisis threatens that has brought you so far?"

He returned to his seat and, for the first time, gestured Stephane to another chair.

"Surely Monsieur has heard of the Ring of Fire."

"Yes, of course. The miracle which has brought men from the future to our world of today, a few years past."

"I was given the task of reporting—"

"Ah, now we discuss the spying."

"As you wish: *spying* on an expedition sent by the people of the future to the New World. I had not intended it, but I accompanied them on their ship as far as Thomasville, the Danish settlement at the mouth of the *Saint-Laurent*."

"What sort of ship is this—some wonder from the future?"

"No, it is a sailing ship, though it has a number of improvements. It is steered with a wheel, and not a whipstaff, and they have devices that help them determine their position. Their ship is not a ship of war, but rather an explorer; they are seeking intelligence to bring back to their masters, just as I am hoping to send word back to *my* masters regarding what I have seen. They have not heard from me since we departed the Germanies, and I am desirous of composing a letter that can be taken back. Or, if circumstance allows it, to find passage back to France to report."

"To the cardinal."

"To Monsieur Servien, my employer."

Champlain crossed his arms across his chest and frowned. "*That* one. Have a care, young man: he is a snake, and utterly loyal to Cardinal Richelieu. To him, everyone is no more than a chess piece, to be maneuvered and sacrificed. I hope he pays you well, and I pray that you have an opportunity to make something of your gains."

As he spoke, Stephane felt a chill... though it might have been no more than a strong breeze through an open window.

This man truly is no fool, Stephane thought. *Romantic or otherwise.*

"I would not presume to understand what Monsieur Servien intends," Stephane answered. "But even though it is only to further his own ends, he has provided me with opportunities that I would never have had otherwise. If I am inclined to be loyal to him because of that, then so be it."

"Of course," Champlain said. "I perform my duties out of loyalty as well—to the kingdom of France."

"I am from Alsace," Stephane answered. "I am employed by a servant of your king—but I am not His Majesty's subject. I have no great love for any other sovereign, however, especially the foolish one who surrendered all of his claims to this continent for thirty pieces of silver. Our *Comte* owes his allegiance to the Hapsburg dynasty, but that is so far away from everyday life in our land that no one even takes notice."

"Is your loyalty then for sale?"

"I suppose it is. But at the moment the proprietor is Monsieur Servien."

Champlain thought for several seconds, then seemed to come to a conclusion.

"Very well, Monsieur," he said. "I shall assist you. But first— tell me more about this ship."

Chapter 16

Land of the Five Nations

Samuel de Champlain had been an artist and cartographer during his earliest travels, and he amazed Stephane with his skill.
Even with somewhat diminished eyesight, and a slight palsy that
made his drawing hand shake, he was able to render an accurate
depiction of *Challenger*, as well as the features in Thomasville
and Nye-Alborg that Stephane was able to describe. He also did
a quick sketch of Stephane himself, which he scarcely recognized.
The last few months had aged him ... or perhaps more accurately
weathered him. After looking at the picture for a few minutes
he tried to find words to describe it and thus describe himself,
but found himself wanting.

Il ist muet.

The great captain made arrangements for his letter, with
the drawings of *Challenger* and the Danish settlements, to be
conveyed overseas by a courier, traveling aboard an ocean-going
vessel departing from Tadoussac. (Though, thanks be to God
and the blessed saints, not the ship that had brought him to
Québec.) Stephane repented of his earlier manner: the lessons of
the cardinal and his subordinate suggested that it was fear, not
trust, that compelled loyalty and cooperation ... but he still felt
himself bound by the duty of service that had brought him so

far into this new world. Perhaps there would be a role for both Champlain and himself to play—the old and respected captain who had known Henri IV, and the spy from Alsace with his life still before him.

Champlain also made arrangements for Stephane's departure from New France. He had close and friendly relations with the natives on the other side of the *Saint-Laurent*. It took time to arrange a meeting with them, but four days after his arrival in Québec they departed by *bateau*—a version of the *kano* that had brought him partway upriver, with somewhat more refinement and stability—and made their way to a settlement of Mohawks a few miles inland from their coastal landing point. The chief spoke no French, but there was a young warrior who did, and Champlain conducted an interview with him partially in his language and partially in theirs. The young man, adorned with European attire as well as his native clothing, seemed to be eager to offer assistance. From the glances of the various natives in the village, though, Stephane felt that he was being measured up for the next night's dinner.

"Do not fear them," Champlain had told him at the end of the interview. "They are eager to frighten you—they have asked me what species of hare you might be."

"I hesitate to ask your answer."

"I told them that you are from the fiercest part of my kingdom— that you are a man of the mountains, but you are equally comfortable in the places of stone, by which I take them to mean the cities. Almost none of them have ever truly seen a city, but they have heard wondrous tales of Paris."

"All of which are true."

"Substantially," Champlain agreed. "The important ones. I told them that they should fear a French hare more than an English wolf, and that you possess depths of which they are unaware."

"How do I know that I will not be turning on a spit by nightfall, being basted like a roast fowl?"

"I have received assurance that they will not harm or molest you in any way due to their personal loyalty to me and to our monarch."

"Our king has little to do with it, I suspect."

"You may believe what you wish, Monsieur Hoff. But they have made this promise, and they will keep it."

"I wish that your man Savignon could accompany me, at least while traveling with these people."

"He has...other duties elsewhere. You may speak with the voice of the cardinal, young sir, but my resources are sparing. You shall have to be brave all on your own."

The captain of New France left him in the company of the Mohawks, who showed his person the utmost respect. Still, particularly once Champlain had departed, Stephane found himself the subject of scrutiny that made him extremely uncomfortable.

I am a French hare, he kept telling himself. *Fear me, you savages.*

Stephane and a group of a dozen Mohawks left from the village and traveled overland, making a steady pace along forest tracks that Stephane could not even discern. They carried their boats with them: they called them by the French word *canoe*, similar to the Danish *kano*. They were wooden, covered with birch bark and pitched to make them watertight. By late afternoon they reached the shore of a lake which they called *Caniaderi Guarunte*, meaning "the lake in between"; and which, his French-speaking guide told him, had been named by the French after the great captain himself: Lake Champlain. Three canoes pushed off into the lake, and they were soon moving southward across it—an idyllic scene, except that the Indians were armed.

It was a fair statement to say that he was nervous.

In the boat in which he rode, a Mohawk sat ahead of him, paddling almost languidly. Another sat beside him and yet another, also paddling, sat behind. They were all nearly expressionless, like wooden statues, looking straight ahead as they moved across the lake.

It was unnerving; Stephane assumed that was their intention. He concentrated on the beautiful scenery—the deep blue of the sky, the trees in their thousands on the banks of the lake and up the steep hills—and on the mission, and on the assurance that Champlain had given him about these particular natives.

They will convey you to the Dutch trading post at Fort Orange in safety.

Clearly, they responded to authority when it was backed by power—the ability to affect, and in some cases end, their lives. Champlain had told him of the rumor, based on up-time books, that he had suffered an attack of apoplexy: it had put the entire Five Nations, a confederation of tribes, on the road to war the previous autumn. Only an armed response led by Champlain himself had stopped the attack, much to the surprise of the attackers.

Champlain was amused, or Stephane might think bemused, by the fact that he had not had that attack of apoplexy. But for the moment, it kept natives like these Mohawks loyal, or at least biddable.

As Stephane sat in the canoe contemplating this, the Mohawk beside him turned and let his face relax into a fierce grin.

"The great captain made us promise that we would get you safely to your destination," he said in competent French. "A pity."

"Why a pity?"

"It is a measure of a man to see how bravely he dies," the Indian said.

Stephane did not reply for a moment, wondering what lay behind the grin.

"You would not go back upon your word."

"Do you fear that I would, pale one?" the Indian asked. "We are far from the great captain now."

"Is your word worth so little that you would break it on a whim?"

"You are brave enough to ask that question. Are you brave enough to hear the answer?"

The question hung in the air; the Mohawk sitting behind let his paddle drift in the water, as if awaiting Stephane's response.

"If your word has any value, warrior," Stephane said carefully, "it is meaningful whether you are in the presence of the great captain or not. Those you swear by watch everything you do, just as the God to which I bow can see all of my actions. You break your word at peril from heaven. I trust that you believe that as well."

The savage looked at the sky, then along the lakeshore, as if he might be imploring his barbarian gods in some way. Then he returned his glance to Stephane.

"We do not break our word," he said. "But we would still want to see what you are truly made of."

Yes, Stephane thought. *I am certain that you do.*

✧ ✧ ✧

It was a fine land, this huge wilderness that now belonged to His Majesty of France. Stephane supposed that the continent of Europe must have looked this way, long and long ago—verdant forests filled with broad, tall trees, wildlife of all sorts unaccustomed enough to man to not run away at his approach, scarcely any evidence of civilization. How long ago did France, or the Germanies, or Alsace look like this?

Before the Romans, certainly.

The Mohawks knew all of the lakes and rivers and all of the paths through the wilderness. They followed marks and signs that were indiscernible to his eyes. But for his guides he would never have made his way south—in fact, he might well have had to demonstrate his bravery as they made him die.

There was only one more tense moment as they traveled south. After they disembarked from the canoes at the south end of the great lake, they followed yet another unrecognizable trail, and they came upon another set of Indians. There was a brief exchange of conversation, all in the native tongue; both groups, his own guides and the others, gestured toward him during the intercourse; but apparently there was no change of loyalties and they were allowed to pass.

He did his best to conceal his relief.

Chapter 17

Atlantic Coast
North America

Maartens took his time sailing *Challenger* south from New-foundland. Gordon would have liked to see the pace pick up, but the Dutch sailing master insisted that there were all sorts of dangers—shoals and rocks and other things—along the coast.

They had some of the soundings maps for the Maine shore, but not enough of them to satisfy Maartens. Instead, he relied on John Smith's map from 1614 which, in Gordon's eyes, was more a work of art than a navigational tool. The weather was about what could be expected: brisk in the daytime, chilly at night, the strong breeze blowing off Georges Bank. When it rained, it rained in sheets; their oilskins could hardly keep up with it. When it was sunny it seemed as if the sun was a remote thing, far away in the sky, not really imparting warmth to go with the daylight.

For all that, it was better than some of the weather they'd seen crossing the Atlantic. There had been times when Gordon wondered if, for all of his up-time knowledge, and the importance of the mission, he would wind up at the bottom of the sea like relics from the *Titanic* never to be seen on national television. The storm that had destroyed the radio hadn't even been the worst of it, but it was the one he remembered the most. He knew he would remember that one the rest of his life. Losing the radio was a heavy enough burden, but what really weighed on Gordon was the death of Jaeschke. The young radio operator would still be alive if Gordon had thought more quickly, or if the door hadn't been stuck, or if...

If, if, if. It made him want to be alone, even if the weather was rotten. Ingrid, and even Pete, seemed to realize that, and kept their distance while he stood at the rail and looked out over the ocean as it pitched and rolled beneath *Challenger's* hull.

There were only a few settlements to be seen. After they cleared the land that Gordon's map showed as Nova Scotia, *Challenger* made sail westward toward the Maine coast. The day after, during a drenching rain, Gordon thought he could make out a fleur-de-lys on a banner hanging limply from a stockade...and wondered if the French invasion had already begun.

Three days from Thomasville the ship anchored in a rocky cove at the mouth of Penobscot Bay. It was out of the wind, at least. Maartens made some vague comment about scraping the hull, or straightening the sails or something. It permitted crew and passengers to go ashore.

"We should unload the dirigible," Pete said, looking out across the water.

"Why?"

"So we can get it aloft." He stood up and balanced on the rock he'd been sitting on, his feet rocking back and forth. "That's why we have it, right?"

"It's here for exploration." Gordon pulled his jacket a little tighter. "Not much to explore around here: rocks and trees, maybe a few Indians..."

"I wasn't thinking about what's here. I was thinking about *Boston.*"

"That's a few hundred miles away."

"That far? We're in Maine, aren't we? The states are little out here, Gord. Little tiny states. They're close together."

"It's a couple of hundred miles, Pete. We're not going to unload the dirigible here, or launch it from here."

"And you're not going to fly it over Boston," Thomas James said, walking from the woods toward the rocks. He had Ingrid Skoglund on his arm; Sofia trailed a few steps behind, looking around her with an expression that was a mix of wonder and fright.

Pete turned to face him. "Oh, yeah? Why not?"

"Because," James said, disengaging himself from the doctor and stepping up to face the brothers, "you do not wish to anger those people."

"I'd be more afraid of flying it over Thomasville," Pete said. "Those dudes are *serious*."

"I am not sure what you mean by that," James said. "But those...the Danes are a very *rational* people. If you flew your dirigible in the Newfoundland sky, I am sure that Sir Thomas would think carefully before he took any action." James frowned. "I am not sure how vulnerable it would be—is it fragile?"

"Somewhat," Gordon said.

"But if he was not sure, he would assume nothing. As for the Puritans...what did you have in mind?"

"Yes, Pete," Gordon said. "What *did* you have in mind?"

"I'd think it would impress the hell out of them," Pete said. "Imagine, there you are plowing the fields in your Pilgrim hat and you look up and see a lighter-than-air ship cruising above you."

"It'll *scare* the hell out of them. And they're not Pilgrims, they're *Puritans*."

"Same diff."

"No, *not* the same diff. Pilgrims are in Plymouth, and even if they're allies, they're different cultures. These people, the ones in Massachusetts Bay, are *Puritans*—they're not trying to get away from England, they're trying to reform its worship."

"So no Pilgrim hats."

"No," James said. "But they are not people you want to frighten, Chehab. They will draw the wrong conclusions."

"That we're the enemy?" Gordon asked.

"They have plenty of enemies, some of their own making, and they seem to have no trouble gathering more of them. If you approached them with hostility then they might or might not ultimately become your friends. But if you take on attributes that would make them believe that you emerged from Satan's realm...they will *never* be your friends."

"I don't get it."

"My brother is slow," Gordon said. "Wouldn't you say, Ingrid?"

"He is slow in some matters," she said, "and quick in others."

"I'm not sure I like hearing that," Pete said, frowning.

"That is why *you* are not in charge of this expedition," Ingrid said. "I think that I am inclined to agree with Captain James. I know very little of this group, these New Englanders, but I know a great deal about zealots. They know no bounds to their passion, and admit no reason into their counsels unless it agrees with their doctrines."

"So..." Pete shrugged. "So we've got to tiptoe around them."

"I think we have no other choice," Gordon agreed. "We want to gather intelligence in the New World, Pete. We're not here to show off."

Gordon's expectations regarding Massachusetts Bay Colony were colored, as always, by what he'd been taught at school. In this case it wasn't much. He assumed that there was one little settlement, ten to fifteen years old, full of religious dissenters who came to the New World to get away from authority.

He couldn't have been more wrong. There hadn't been much to see along the Maine coast—a few little fishing settlements, a few Indian encampments (the natives were wary; their canoes stayed well clear of *Challenger*)—but as they came in sight of Cape Ann it was obvious that there were several little towns along the coast.

"What do you know about the colony?" he asked James, as they watched the sun set over the dense inland woods.

"Some of what the good doctor said is true: the men of Massachusetts have chosen to separate themselves from the mother country because they cannot tolerate the Church of England," the English captain said. "They are not as extreme as their cousins to the south. Some of the Massachusetts settlers returned home in 1633 when the English King disposed of his claims; but most have stayed. As for the men of Plymouth... they remain, having no desire to return—or no alternative. But the many Massachusetts towns outnumber them."

"Are either of them friendly?"

"As if *any* of them are friendly with any of the others." James snorted. "From what I have heard, and read, the first Massachusetts expedition separated into two settlements almost upon arrival, with Governor Winthrop establishing Boston on the peninsula, and his deputy, Dudley, locating upriver at Newtown. But there were already Englishmen where he purposed to settle: right here"—he gestured toward the promontory of Cape Ann, dwindling in the distance—"but *those* Puritans would not unite with those of a different covenant."

"They wouldn't let him land?"

"They turned him away. And when he arrived at Shawmut—what the natives called it—there were already the Dorchester settlers at Mattapan and some others scattered all around. I daresay they had to be more accepting than the Salem men had been."

"I thought it was all empty."

"Is that what your up-timer book told you?"

"It didn't tell me near enough," Gordon said. "All I know is that there should be a good-sized town at Boston, and the governor is some guy named Vane."

"I believe that is in error," James said. "Winthrop is still governor—or was in the spring, when we last had intelligence of the place up in Newfoundland."

As they crossed the bay toward Boston they could see the smoke from chimneys, and through a spyglass Gordon picked out a few more substantial buildings, including what looked to be some sort of factory.

"That's an ironworks," Maartens said, reclaiming his instrument and squinting through it. "And hard at work, too."

"Where'd they get iron?" Gordon asked. "I didn't know there was any in this area."

"It's bog iron," Maartens answered. "They pull bog ore out of yon swamps and smelt it. I didn't know they'd started doing it."

"It's got to be poor quality."

"If that's all they've got, for now," the Dutchman said, "but they'll make do. It's probably too much work to bring it from inland—and there aren't real mountains to speak of until you're practically in New France. But I imagine they've got enough to give them something to make plowshares out of."

"And are they planning on beating them into swords?" Gordon said.

"That depends a lot on what happens in the coming year, I'd guess," Maartens said.

Pete couldn't resist trying again. As *Challenger* drew close to Boston, he found Gordon on deck inspecting the stowed dirigible, and poked him in the ribs.

"Don't you have something better to do?"

"That's a pretty damn stupid question. You know I don't have anything to do until we make landfall. I've been thinking about the dirigible again."

"What about it?"

"I still think we should go aloft."

Gordon stood up straight. He and Pete were about the same height, but he was stocky where Pete was wiry—the virtues of army life for his younger brother made the difference.

"I think we've already had this conversation."

"No, you let Ingrid tell you what to do."

"She has a pretty sensible approach, and she's right—they are zealots, and there's really no sense in scaring the crap out of people we're trying to befriend." Gordon leaned against the bundled dirigible, which was taller than he was. "I don't want to see the French wipe these guys out. Neither the Puritans nor the Pilgrims can go home because England doesn't want any of them back. And King Charles won't lift a finger to save them."

"So *we're* going to protect them against the French?"

"I don't know. Maybe. But I think we've got some time, because Virginia's probably at the top of their list. They'll get to New England eventually, though." Gordon sighed and cracked his knuckles; one, two, three.

Pete lost the argument again—or, rather, he didn't put a dent in Gordon's approach. Rather than anchor out at the tip of Cape Cod and deploy the dirigible—which they'd dubbed *John Wayne*—*Challenger* sailed through the beautiful sun-dappled afternoon and made for Boston's island-studded outer harbor.

Boston was the biggest settlement they had seen in the New World. Neither Gordon nor Pete had ever been to up-time Boston, and in any case the town was even a completely different shape than it had become by the year 2000, at least according to the maps that Gordon had in hand. There were two prominent hills to either side of the town and an imposing, taller hill behind; the town itself was perched on a peninsula, what James had referred to by the native name "Shawmut." The modern map made Boston out to be fairly flat, so there'd been some serious landscaping in the intervening few centuries.

They had a copy of the Bonner map from 1722 that showed the town's general layout; but even that was misleading, as it looked as if the Mill Dam hadn't been built yet—though there was a sort of causeway where it would be. The hill to port was crowned by a fort and the one to starboard by a windmill, steadily creaking in the breeze. The hill behind, which was composed of three peaks, had a tall pole on the top.

The arrival of an unknown ship in Boston Harbor clearly attracted attention. Through his spyglass, Gordon could see that from the tower on top of the hill with the flag someone was watching them approach.

By the time *Challenger* had laid alongside the wharf that jutted furthest out into the harbor, a small crowd of people had assembled. They were modestly dressed—no "Pilgrim hats," as Gordon had said, but their clothes seemed muted, their faces expectant and somewhat solemn.

"Some welcoming committee," Pete said, looking over the taffrail as *Challenger* tied up.

"They don't look happy to see us," James said. "Dudley should be among them—he's the military leader—but I don't see him."

"Dudley?"

"The deputy governor." James frowned. "There's someone else giving orders, though..."

Gordon looked into the crowd and noticed a small group making its way toward the front. They were armed with pikes or muskets, great long things a few years out of date, four feet long and more, and they wore metal corselets and helmets, which reflected the early-summer sunlight.

"Pete," he said quietly, "make sure you're primed and your powder is dry."

"Expecting trouble?"

"Don't know. But it doesn't hurt to take precautions."

Gordon walked down the gangplank to a murmur of voices. With his up-time-styled clothing and neatly trimmed hair and beard, he must've looked a sight to these Puritans. Gordon resisted the urge to chuckle as he thought of the great scene from *Close Encounters of the Third Kind*, one of his favorite movies growing up.

All trace of humor disappeared when two of the armed men reached the front of the crowd. They held their muskets in their hands and each had a slow match in a holster at his side.

Another man, obviously a captain of some sort, stepped out to stand between them.

"Who are you, stranger?" he said. "Your flag is not one I know."

He didn't look interested in chitchat.

"My name is Gordon Chehab," Gordon said. "I am leading a trade mission from the State of Thuringia-Franconia, a part of the United States of Europe. Is this how you greet all your visitors?"

"Questions are mine to ask," the man snapped back. "These are dangerous times. 'United States of Europe'... then you are a Swede."

"Not exactly. I'm an American."

"'American'?"

"I'm from Grantville. You know, Ring of Fire. Just arrived a few years ago."

The mention of the words "Ring of Fire" caused murmurs throughout the crowd, until the captain turned and cast an unfriendly glare, bringing the people to silence once more.

"'Tis said," the captain said, "that you come from the time to come. We find this strains our belief. God is mighty and His works are wonders, but we wonder if this Ring of Fire is not a work of the Devil."

"It's not."

"Indeed."

"I am not the Devil's servant," Gordon said. "No horns, no tail." He smiled, but there were no smiles in return.

Gordon's mouth suddenly tasted of shoe leather. If it was possible for him to kick himself, he would have done so.

"The Devil's servants sometimes wear fair guises," the captain said. "But it is not up to me to decide. What is your business here in Boston?"

"I had hoped to speak with your governor about what is happening and what is to come. But I come in peace."

The man seemed to size him up in great detail, as if determining if his ball cap concealed horns and his trousers hid a tail.

"I will bring you to Governor Winthrop," he said. "A guard will be posted at your ship until your fate is decided. You will come with me." He turned, as if expecting to be instantly obeyed.

"Do you mind if I ask your name?"

"No," the man said, turning back. "I am John Endecott."

That was a name that Gordon knew very well. In a few months, if the up-time history was still any guide, John Endecott was going to start a bloody war with the Pequots.

Chapter 18

Boston

Gordon did not want to go alone into town—he thought about giving the line he'd used in Newfoundland, that they only traveled in pairs—but Endecott left no choice; the troop formed up around him and they marched away from the wharf.

Boston was like a rural German town, but even more so. Most of the houses were no more than log structures with clay chinking in between to keep out the drafts; they were covered with thatched roofs. He could see people looking out through the windows, furtively, as if they didn't want to get caught doing it.

The one thing that had always spooked him a little bit about down-time was that, unlike modern day where people walked along the street trying their best not to mind other people's business, everyone in the current era seemed to be watching everyone else—maybe to see what they were doing, how they were dressed, or whether the other guy's next move was to reach for a sword or a pistol or something.

And here in Boston, it was like that but doubled and tripled—as if everyone made it their business to watch everyone else. Endecott was particular about this task. No one seemed to want to look him in the eye as the little troop passed up the street from the dock.

There were no pilgrim hats at all. The Puritans dressed plainly, that was for sure. Unlike in Germany, where every burgher was trying to outdo every other one with ruffles and slashes and color and all, these people dressed plainly to a fault.

All except perhaps the hats. Gordon was planning on having a good laugh with Pete about that—but not when he was surrounded by armed men who didn't seem to know how to crack a smile.

The street from the dock went up a hill. At the top on the left was a church—white painted, with a steeple but no cross on top, unlike practically every church he'd seen in Europe.

In front of the church some poor sod was locked up in a pillory—he was on the short side, and could barely stand upright with his neck and hands caught in the holes. There was a wooden sign hanging from his neck labeled BLASPHEMER. It looked as if some of the locals had been using him for target practice with their overripe fruit.

"Does it bother you, stranger?" Endecott said. "He is a sinner and deserves his punishment."

"It seems a little harsh."

"A day or two in the bilboes is nothing compared to the eternal punishment the Supreme Judge will render that one if he continues to sin," Endecott said. "But even if the Lord shows mercy to him for his crimes, only by harsh punishment will he learn to correct his ways. Do you..." Endecott thought for a moment and then said, "Do you Americans have a different way of punishing errant children? Surely you must thrash them if they are indolent or disobedient or unruly."

"Adults and children should get different treatment," Gordon said. "Don't you think?"

"Of course," Endecott said. "Children are not punished in public. Their fathers take care of it in the privacy of the home."

I'll bet he makes sure of that, Gordon thought.

The little group turned and followed a broad avenue that led to the edge of the built-up area. Shortly, they reached a handsome house fronting a farm.

Endecott walked up to the door of the house and knocked; he entered and left Gordon to cool his heels for several minutes.

Finally he returned and beckoned to Gordon.

"The governor will see you," Endecott said. "And you will mind your tongue, stranger."

Gordon took his hat off and ran a hand through his hair.

No horns, he thought, but decided not to share the joke with the scowling Captain Endecott.

"I will do my best," Gordon said, and stepped into the house.

A clerk directed him along a narrow hall and into a study, where a well-dressed man rose to face him. The study was spare, even by seventeenth-century standards: there were perhaps a hundred books, a framed print of the Smith map of New England, and a few other items that showed the man was a scholar. There were two chairs in the room; Governor Winthrop gestured Gordon to the other, and returned to his own seat.

Gordon had just a moment to size up the governor of Massachusetts. Winthrop was tall and broad-shouldered; even sitting he seemed to dominate the room. He had a carefully trimmed beard and moustache, and his hair and his clothing were dressed in modest Puritan fashion. He seemed to give complete attention to every aspect of his visitor before speaking.

"I understand," Winthrop said at last, "that you have come from this new nation at the heart of the Old World. Brother Endecott rode all the way from Salem to Boston to confront you."

"We come in peace, sir," Gordon said. "We do not seek a confrontation. The only people showing weapons were the men at the dock."

"A fair point. But we are on our own here, stranger. It may be fairly said that we have no friends."

Imagine that, Gordon thought, but didn't say it aloud.

"My deputy, Brother Dudley, is not here at the moment; he is on his way to our settlements on the Connecticut River to consult with them. Endecott—with my permission—took charge of your reception, in case it was hostile.

"So," Winthrop said. "You come in peace. Tell me what you want of me."

"This is a...trade mission, Governor."

"It is rather more than that, I think."

"I make no such claims, sir, and am not trying to represent *Challenger*'s mission as anything other than what it seems. We are here only to communicate with you and introduce ourselves."

"You have come a long way to do that."

"Your colony is not the only place we are visiting."

"This is not an explicit embassy, then. Nor, obviously, an attempt at conquest. Your new kingdom: whom do you count an enemy, and whom a friend? Is our former King Charles in either camp?"

"Our relations with him have not been friendly, although we are no longer at war," Gordon answered. "As you may know, he ordered our embassy held hostage in the Tower of London until we succeeded in..." He was about to say "springing them" but then, figuring the colloquialism would be unknown in this day and age, settled for "liberating them by force of arms. The United States of Europe is allied with the kingdom of Sweden, and through the Union of Kalmar with the kingdom of Denmark. We have also fought the kingdom of France, though we are no longer at war with them either. But we are worried about the disposal of English claims here in North America. We have no desire to see France—or any European power, for that matter—establish a monopoly and stranglehold over the colonies in North America."

"You no less than ourselves. I am left the governor of a stranded colony; and I do not know what this status means."

"I can imagine. Actually, I'm...surprised to find you as the governor of the colony."

"Why is that?"

"Well, historically...that is, in the past of the future from which I come..."

"Your Ring of Fire presents some complexity, does it not?" Winthrop said, chuckling. "Your history does not have me in office at this time? Who *should* be governor of our colony?"

"Well, sir, it's not quite like that. Your deputy Thomas Dudley should have just been replaced by a man named Vane."

"Harry Vane?"

"Yes. Sir Henry. The younger one, I think. I'd have to look it up."

"That pup is not fit to govern here, and even if the situation were different—even if our king had not abandoned us—I could not conceive it happening. Your histories must be quite fanciful."

"Yes, sir," Gordon said, not sure how to reply.

"Well," Winthrop answered. "We live in a different world, all because of your arrival. Brother Endecott is very suspicious of you, young man, and of your Ring of Fire. I have thought about it, and read of it, and prayed, and I still do not understand it. Do you have any better explanation?"

"For the Ring of Fire? No, Governor Winthrop, I surely do

not. It caught all of us by surprise, and we've been trying to sort it out ever since."

"With some success, I daresay."

"American ingenuity, sir, and a will to live."

"We may be needing some of that ingenuity, Master Chehab. When we first settled here we found ourselves surrounded by enemies—harsh winters and dangerous, Godless natives. To these we can now add the French, who claim what our king once claimed. We received a letter—"

He turned and began sorting through a series of papers stacked neatly on the side of his escritoire. "Here it is. In the late fall of 1633, most of three years ago. It invalidated our patent, saying that our land was now subject to the king of France as King Charles had disposed of his rights and claims to all holdings in the New World on the first of August."

He brandished the letter, and Gordon saw anger in Winthrop's eyes. "It was not an *invitation* to return to England: no, indeed. The canting archbishop did not want Dissenters to resume their residence in England—neither Separatist nor Nonconformist, Calvinist or Antinomian. We were directed to go seek our way in the world with no alternative—and no right of return. It has led us to make common cause with our brothers in Plymouth. There have been disputes in the past, but we have no choice other than to take them by the hand.

"We are not the only ones, sir. The Calverts are under threat in Maryland, and though they are Papists I fear for them as fellow Englishmen. As for the Virginia planters, I understand that their work of a generation is to be surrendered at the point of a gun, if the French are able to concentrate their forces.

"The French eye has not yet been turned on us, though natives in their pay have already provoked our settlers along the Connecticut River—both from Massachusetts Bay and Plymouth. And as for the natives we would like to consider friends, or at least friendly, they have shown themselves to be untrustworthy at best and savage and ruthless at worst. Our own outlying towns are not safe. It is a dire situation, and I do not see it getting better."

Winthrop was very much like Gordon had expected. He had left England behind—and as he said, there was no England to which he could return. What was more, he earnestly believed that Massachusetts Bay was the place that God had selected as the promised land for Puritans. The idea that it would be taken away appalled him.

"I cannot offer you direct military aid," Gordon told Winthrop. "It's not our mission."

"Then I must ask again: why are you here?"

"*Challenger* is a trading vessel—"

"We can leave off the dissembling, sir. I think we both understand what you *must* say. Tell me what you truly seek."

Gordon thought for a moment. "All right. *Challenger* is on a scouting mission, Governor. I'm trying to see the lay of the land—what's really happening, where everything stands. When we've learned all we can, we'll return and make a report."

"When will that be?"

"I...don't know. Maybe in the fall. We weren't given a specific return date, and things are somewhat in flux at the moment."

If I still had a radio... Gordon thought, and then he thought, *yeah, or a 747, or an internet connection, or a whole lot of other things that I'll never see again.*

"My employer," Gordon said carefully, "believes that the only way to stop the French is to forge an alliance among all of their opponents. What little I know of your settlements..."

"From your future vantage point, you mean. The one in which Harry Vane is the governor."

"What little I know," he repeated, "tells me that as much as you would like to consider yourself the new Jerusalem, the shining city on a hill, you'll be no match for French regular troops—or even well-armed *couriers de bois* and Indian allies. You need friends, sir."

"As I said, we have already made alliance with our...brethren to the south. The Old Colony. Plymouth." He said it this time with a hint of distaste, though far less than he had seemed to show for Archbishop Laud or the king of England. "They have a representative here in Boston; he will want to speak with you. But you suggest a friendship, perhaps, with your people."

"We would welcome the opportunity. There are things we can do for you."

"Other than fight our enemies."

"For now."

Winthrop waited for a moment before nodding. "I expect that will have to do."

Chapter 19

"Looks like you passed the test," Pete said as Gordon ascended *Challenger*'s gangplank. The troop of soldiers stood on the dock, watching his steps, then were dismissed other than two men who remained on guard, looking vigilant and suspicious.

"Yeah." Gordon sat on a trunk next to the bundled dirigible. He took his ball cap off and wiped his brow; the day had turned warm—though he felt he was sweating more than just because of the weather. "They know they're on their own—they've kissed and made up with Plymouth, but they're not sure whether they're screwed yet."

"Are they?"

"I don't know." He put his cap back on. "The actions of King Charles have left them to go their own way, which they were more or less prepared to do in the first place. I get the impression that they've almost stopped arguing with each other. Almost."

"You mean, these guys and the Pilgrim hat guys."

"I wish it was that simple."

Pete slumped into a seat next to him. "What do you mean? I assumed that every different group of Pilgrims—Puritans—whatever the hell they all are—" Pete made a brushing-off gesture; one of the soldiers on the dock tensed, and he turned it into a friendly wave. "I thought they all went off and made their own colonies. Connecticut and Rhode Island and Vermont and all."

"None of those places exist yet, little bro. Especially not Vermont—that didn't exist until the American Revolution. There are basically two colonies here: Massachusetts Bay and Plymouth. Plymouth is older, smaller and more intense. Massachusetts Bay is all over the place, with a bunch of little settlements—here, up the coast, inland. Both of the colonies put down trading posts on the Connecticut River and up in Maine, and both have friends and enemies among the Indians."

"Is Massachusetts friends or enemies with the casino guys? I can't remember that tribe's name."

"The Pequots. I'm not sure. Governor Winthrop explained it to me, and as far as I can tell, they're upset because some Englishmen were killed on the Connecticut a couple of years ago in some sort of reprisal for something the Dutch did."

"That doesn't make any sense."

"The natives claim that they can't tell the English and Dutch apart."

"'They all look alike to us'?"

"That's about the argument, yes. And until the Pequot chiefs give up the killers, Massachusetts is not interested in taking sides with them against another group of Indians—the Narragansetts." Gordon held his hand up. "And before you start referring to them as the 'beer guys,' let me just tell you that there's an ongoing rivalry between *all* the Indian tribes in this part of the world.

"They all get along, sort of; they're linked by custom and marriage and old habits and old grudges, and the English and Dutch and the French have been mixing into it and messing everything up for half a century, regardless of the Ring of Fire. It comes down to land, and guns, and wealth—mostly furs, from what I understand.

"And it comes down to—" Gordon lowered his voice. "It comes down to religion too. The English colonists, mostly the Plymouth ones but these guys here as well, think that they're here to make Christians of the heathens. What's more, any land that isn't being actively worked, such as these enormous forests full of animals with furs, is obviously being ignored—so they claim it for their own. They cut down the trees, plant crops, let their cows and pigs and whatever else roam around. The natives hate that."

"I bet."

"They also hate the idea that their land, which they've been occupying for hundreds of years, is being taken over by people who have a fundamentally different idea of what it's for. And they hate the idea that their society, which works for them, screams 'Satan' to the good Christians of these two fine colonies. They keep coming out on the short end of every transaction."

"You know," Pete said, "based on what you say, this is a situation that is beyond us. This isn't really about the French claims on English colonies at all. We should cut our losses and leave."

"I wish it was that easy."

"It *is* that easy, big bro. You wave to the nice little zealots on shore"—he waved again, making the same soldier scowl up, hand on his musket—"and you say sorry, we've got nothing, bye bye. Y'all come visit us if you're ever in Magdeburg."

"We might be condemning them to death."

"*We?* History is condemning them to death, Gord, if they don't change their attitudes. Not you. Not me. *Them.*"

Thomas James had been to Boston before, as a trader from Thomasville. He had more freedom of movement in the town, as he was not under immediate suspicion as an up-timer (and as a representative of whatever other category into which the Puritans had filed them). He returned from ashore just as the sun was at the horizon, and sought out Gordon on the aft deck.

Gordon was settled in an out-of-the-way place out of the wind, with a book in his lap. The Englishman's shadow lay across Gordon's daylight, and he looked up.

"It's you," he said. "I thought it was Pete, come to give me a hard time." He snapped the book shut; it was a history book, one of a small cache that had been lent to the expedition.

"Your brother is very determined in some matters," James said, finding himself a seat. "It is always a problem with the young."

"Hey, *I'm* young."

"Yes, of course, but there is a world of difference between the two of you, Chehab. Your brother is impulsive, quick to anger, settled in his opinions—especially when he has just decided them. A valuable man in a fight, I don't doubt. But you would do well to be selective in taking his counsel—or possibly avoid it altogether."

"Is there something I can do for you, Captain James?"

"I was able to renew a few old acquaintances while ashore. The men of Boston are very worried—not just about the French, but about a number of other matters. This business with the Pequots divides them, and it is not at all clear where Governor Winthrop is likely to stand. Some of his advisors in the Court of Assistants are all for blood revenge against the Pequots for their attack on John Stone, while others—a minority, I should say—see no reason to risk life and limb by going to war over someone who they really didn't like in the first place."

"Tell me more," Gordon said. *Tell me something I understand,* he thought. He knew that John Stone was the English ship's captain whom the Pequots had killed in revenge for something the Dutch had done, but wasn't sure of the political situation. James clearly had a good feel for it, and was either being intentionally vague, or simply didn't know the extent of Gordon's ignorance.

James cocked his head at Gordon, perhaps trying to figure that out.

"You understand the basis of the problem, I assume. Three years ago the Pequot sachems on the Connecticut River decided that they'd had enough of mistreatment, and massacred some poor sods from the Narragansetts who were on their way to Kievet's Hook, the Dutch trading house upriver. The Dutch kidnapped the chief sachem of the Pequot, a savage named Tatobem, who was two years younger than God at the time." James laughed at his own turn of phrase. "They demanded a hefty ransom, and when the Pequots paid it, they sent him back—as a corpse."

"Does this say something about the Dutch? How was that *possibly* a good idea?"

"Chehab, you apparently come from a more enlightened age, or at least a gentler one. You express outrage at the way the Dutch treated an Indian dignitary—yet all Europeans do much the same. They think less of the Indians: they are either children in need of a firm parent, or lazy and indolent and in need of a whipping. They are a breed that has given up their right to the land because of *vacuum domicilium*—that any lands not actually being worked should belong to anyone, and why shouldn't it be some European?

"The Dutch are more mercenary than most, and yes, the killing of Tatobem in particular was a vicious act. However, as you up-timers like to say, I do not think any of his murderers or any of the officials back in New Amsterdam are . . . 'losing any sleep over it.'"

The sun was behind the trees now; Thomas James sat framed by the sunset, his face traced with shadow.

"I guess you aren't either," Gordon said at last.

"Are *you*?"

"Do you know where it leads, Captain? Do you know what happens in the up-time history"—he slapped the cover of the book he held with the palm of his other hand—"forty or so years from now? There's a huge, nasty, bloody war. Practically every tribe in New England goes to war seeking to drive the English colonists into the sea. Towns are burned to the ground. There are massacres and atrocities and in the end whatever trust existed between natives and Europeans is destroyed forever."

"I'm not surprised," James said mildly. "It happened in Virginia in 1622; you know that, I assume? When the great chief of the Indians died, his younger brother plotted and carried out a massacre there and killed a third of the whites. There is no trust between the races in Virginia. Why New England should be any different escapes me, Chehab. If anything, I would think these people would be even more intractable."

"Things have changed since 1622."

"I daresay. There has been a great event—the Ring of Fire. You may have heard about it in your remote village."

"Your sarcasm is comforting."

James leaned forward, elbows on knees. He scratched his beard, then hawked and spat. "You will not change their hearts or their minds, Chehab."

Chapter 20

On the morning tide, a small ship, perhaps half the size of *Challenger*, arrived at the dock. Gordon came out on deck, where Pete was watching the proceedings.

The most important passenger, whose effects and luggage were being unloaded, was a tall, distinguished-looking man past middle age with the hint of a moustache and a bare chin; his manner was imperious, as if he was accustomed to having his orders followed. From time to time he looked up at *Challenger*; the two brothers looked back. No greetings were exchanged.

"Who is that, do you suppose?" Pete asked.

Gordon gestured toward the other ship's mainmast, which flew a white banner with a pair of pine trees and an Indian, with some indecipherable words coming out of his mouth. There was no Cross of Saint George to be seen.

"Massachusetts banner," Gordon said. "This is someone important. My money's on Thomas Dudley."

Though they were likely too far away for his words to carry to the deck of the smaller ship, the man chose just that moment to glance in their direction. Pete gave the man a friendly wave and a big-toothed grin.

"Howdy," Pete said.

On Gordon's second journey into Puritan Boston he was not alone, but was at the head of a delegation: Pete and Thomas James,

133

Ingrid Skoglund and her maid, and two members of the crew. They were escorted by Massachusetts soldiers, but it seemed less like a police cordon or a press gang than when he had been taken to see Winthrop the previous day. James had made sure to equip Pete and Gordon with proper hats similar to the one he wore: brushed felt, clashing only slightly with their up-time clothing.

The street was crowded, since a number of others were walking toward the head of the street that led from the dock. Some of them wore clothing with gold threads—the better sort of folks. Their destination was clearly the same: the meeting house, which had its doors thrown wide.

Pete elbowed Gordon as they passed the church he'd seen the previous day. The stocks were vacant this time, though they had not been cleaned; the BLASPHEMER sign lay in the dust, unattended.

"Yeah," Gordon said. "It won't be empty for long."

As they approached the meeting house, the locals' attention became focused squarely on the group from *Challenger*. There were two men in corselets and helmets, muskets in hand, at the doors; a young, stout man in fine clothing stepped between them and into their path.

"This is a meeting only for the men of the colony," he said pointedly, staring at Ingrid Skoglund.

She gave him back a cold stare. That caused murmurs among the crowd—which, Gordon noted, had a number of women in it. He supposed that Ingrid was supposed to cast her eyes downward, but she was having none of it.

"You can keep out any women you like—*from the colony*," Gordon said. "Doctor Skoglund is not a woman of Massachusetts Bay."

"That much seems obvious."

Before Ingrid could reply, Pete said, "Do you have a name we can call you, big man, or should we just make one up?"

"My name is Simon Bradstreet," the man said. "Magistrate and Assistant to the governor. You would be wise to hold your tongue, up-timer, and show respect."

"Let me write that one down," Pete answered. "Look, pal, we—"

"I do not answer to 'pal,' or to 'big man,'" Bradstreet answered, hands on hips. "What is more, I—"

"—think we should leave this to Governor Winthrop to decide," Gordon interrupted. "Master Bradstreet, my brother does not mean to give offense." *Well, he does, but let's not get into that,* he thought.

"But Doctor Skoglund is a member of our expedition, and shall be treated as such. You may keep your own customs and traditions, but do not presume to dictate ours. I do not think that this decision should be made peremptorily, or in the street. If the decision lies with another, I beg your indulgence to consult with him. And if it is yours to make, and you turn her away, you turn us all away."

The audience had become quiet; even Pete had decided not to insert some comment. Bradstreet stood for several moments, his hands on his hips, his brow furrowed.

"I will inquire the wisdom of others," he said at last. "Remain here."

He turned and went into the meeting house. Murmuring began again; Gordon got the impression that this Bradstreet fellow was not someone who was accustomed to backing down.

"This is not auspicious," Ingrid said quietly. Sofia whispered something to her in Swedish that Gordon didn't make out. "Yes, I know," she answered in English. "But we must persevere."

"We all go in," Gordon said. "Or we all go back to *Challenger*."

"Surely your mission has greater weight than defending my position or honor."

"This isn't about your position, much less your honor. It's about whether we're going to be treated properly—all of us. You know, we respect your ways, you respect our ways. That sort of thing."

"They are armed," Ingrid said, "and we are not."

"Don't bet on that," Pete said, smiling.

She looked at him. "Are you expecting trouble? Isn't that... a trifle provocative?"

"You don't bring a knife to a gun fight," Pete said. "And you don't bring a slow match musket to a pistol fight." He stretched his shoulders out under the fancy long coat he was wearing—which, Gordon noted, was a little out of keeping with the warm late-spring day.

"You were expecting—"

"Happiness and smiles. Rainbows and unicorns. Sweetness and light," Pete said. "No, ma'am. Not expecting nuthin'... but my big bro told me to keep my powder dry. So let's not make any assumptions, or get the zealots' knickers in a twist."

Ingrid frowned, as if she was trying to untangle the knot of slang Pete had just thrown at her. Gordon wanted very much to slap his brother in the head, but he also couldn't help but admire his turns of phrase.

Bradstreet emerged from within the meeting house.

"You are to be admitted," he said, looking unhappy about the matter. "*All* of you. But," he added, before standing aside, "you will not speak until you are addressed. Is that understood?"

"Of course," Gordon said, looking at the others in his group. "After you, Magistrate."

The inside of the building was plain and unadorned, as they expected, and it was filled with people. Other than Ingrid and Sofia, the gathering was exclusively male. From the rear of the hall, where they entered, to the front, every seat in every pew was taken—and there was an upper story with a balcony, also filled with onlookers. At the far end, instead of a lectern, there was a little platform with benches on which a group of people sat facing the audience—stern men, a dozen or more, with Governor John Winthrop in the center. A pair of benches had been provided a little in front of the foremost pew; Bradstreet gestured to them, and then returned to a place on the platform.

"You indicated that you wished to speak," Winthrop said. "Unless there be further objection"—he paused and looked about—"we will hear what you have to say."

Gordon stood again and walked in front of the platform. He'd thought about what he was going to say, but wasn't sure how it would come out.

"King Charles has sold all of his lands in the New World to France. So far, the French have made no effort to enforce their authority here in New England. So far, all they have done is clash with the Danes in the north. But we do not think that situation can last much longer. Unless you are willing to submit to French rule—"

A little hubbub swept the room. The most frequently muttered imprecation seemed to be *papists*. Not *damned papists*, though; these people took the prohibition of blasphemy very seriously.

Gordon paused to let it die down, before continuing. "You need to find allies—and find them everywhere you can. My nation is no longer at war with France, but we do not think that state of affairs will last for more than a few years. I am not in position to offer you a military pact at this moment, but the possibility exists for the future and I would ask you to take it under consideration. In the meantime..."

He took a deep breath. The rest of what he had to say was not likely to be met with much favor. "In the meantime, I strongly urge you to do all you can to avoid hostilities with the natives. Whether or not there is the possibility of forming an alliance with the tribes—"

Another little hubbub swept the room. Gorgon couldn't make out the words but the underlying sentiment was clear enough. *This man is a blithering fool* was the gist of it.

But he soldiered on. "You still do not want the natives to become allies of the French—and you can be sure the French will be striving to make them such. There is nothing you can do to prevent the French from offering gifts and blandishments to the tribes, but you can do all in your power to keep the natives from becoming your enemies even before the French begin their machinations."

He was tempted to go on, but this was not a receptive audience. The longer he preached to them, the more likely they were to simply dig in their heels. He'd made his points; let them ponder the matter for a while. In any event, he had come to the conclusion that whatever might or might not develop, the Puritans and Pilgrims were clearly going to be the laggards straggling behind—if they ever joined at all.

So, he sat down. Winthrop was lost in thoughts for several moments, while the audience in the meeting house once again took to conversation. Finally he rapped them to silence once more.

"We will consider all you have proposed," he said at last.

And that was that.

After they left and were well away from any unfriendly ears, Pete made his own consideration clear. "What a bunch of useless assholes. Can we get out of here already?"

"Yes," said Gordon. "Let's try the Dutch in New Amsterdam."

Brest
Brittany, France

The port of Brest lay on either side of the river. It was dominated by the extended fortifications and naval wharves that *le Cardinal* had ordered to be built beginning five years ago.

On the naval dock, in the shadow of the great tower that Sourdéac had built a generation earlier, the *grand-maître de la navigation* and his father, the Marquis de Brézé and Marshal of France, looked out across the *goulet* that separated the harbor from the wider roadstead beyond.

"The wind is fresh," Urbain de Maillé-Brézé said. "With up-time navigation you should have a fair sail."

"I still feel as if…what do the up-timers say? I am *being played*."

"Serving the will of His Majesty is not *being played*, Armand," the Marquis answered. "This *is* an important mission."

"I am at His Majesty's service, of course. But I fail to see its importance, Father. Why waste resources and manpower and *time* on a place so far away?"

"I think I can answer that," his father said. He looked away from his son and held his hand over his eyes against the glimmer of the sun on the water.

"Yes?"

"You cannot see it, my son. But it is there. Beyond the *goulet*, beyond the Brest Roadstead, beyond the outer islands…beyond the ocean—there is the *future*."

"I don't understand."

"Have you read up-timer history, Armand? I have, and Cardinal Richelieu certainly has. In the time line from which the up-timers came, the power and the wealth of the world shifted westward to the Western Hemisphere. One of the most powerful and most wealthy places was Virginia. His Eminence recognized the potential, and it is the essential reason why France has acquired those vast territories."

"Surely the king of England must have known this as well."

"Suffice it to say that the king of England does not impress me as a monarch who takes the long view. He *did* make use of up-time accounts to act preemptively against those who would act against him in the future—the dissenter Puritans, the radicals in their Parliament, and so forth, who would eventually put him to death—but he completely ignored the value of his North American possessions."

"That strikes me as absurd, Father. If these Godforsaken places were destined to be rich, why would he sell all of them for *any* amount of money? And why sell them to France?"

"The cardinal, your uncle, can be very persuasive. What is more, I think that King Charles was thinking more about keeping his head attached to his neck than whether he could reap profits from tobacco."

"When were his enemies scheduled to commit this regicide?"

"1649."

"More than ten years in the future?" Armand de Maillé-Brézé almost broke out in laughter. "Surely with the other steps he had already taken, his path would not lead to the loss of his life, at least not in that way."

"King Charles is obsessive," Urbain said. "And a fool. What England would have become—it will never be. *France* will take its place. France will be the greatest country in this century."

"And, Armand, you will be part of it. Your fleet—"

"Two ships is not a fleet, Father."

"Your ships will carry the banner of France to His Christian Majesty's new possessions. And there is something else, something you have not been told. There is an up-timer ship, and it is somewhere on the coast of the New World, and it may be carrying up-time technology. It might even already be in Virginia. In addition to imposing His Majesty's will upon the colonists, you are also to locate this ship and, if at all possible, capture it."

"What of the up-timers aboard?"

"Your uncle would like them to become...our guests."

"And not drowned in the Ocean Sea, I assume."

"It was not specified," Armand said. "I assume that it would be better for them to survive, but *c'est la guerre* if they do not."

Bamberg, capital of the State of Thuringia-Franconia
United States of Europe

Ed Piazza sighed and leaned back in his chair. "I suppose there's no chance..."

Estuban Miro shrugged. "There is always 'a chance,' Mr. President. Or it might be better to say, there are *too many* chances. There is the chance that the *Challenger* was destroyed at sea in a storm; or ran aground; or was ambushed by pirates. There is the chance that the radio simply malfunctioned. Going a bit further afield, there is the chance—"

Piazza waved his hand in a gesture that was a bit weary. The silence coming from the Atlantic was only one of many problems besetting him at the moment, and not by any means the most pressing. "Never mind. There's no point in speculating. All we really *know* is that we've heard nothing from Gordon Chehab for weeks—long past the point where he should have been able to report, no matter what the conditions for transmission were."

"Yes."

"Though he might be able to contact us from the tower in the Caribbean."

"Ah. That." Muro shifted in his seat. "He could . . . if he knew about it. We decided, for reasons of operational security, not to brief Chehab on it."

"Because—"

"Because, Mr. President, they were equipped with their own radio. There would be no need to travel that far—considerably beyond the expected range of their expedition—to use another."

"Even as a backup?"

"Even so."

There seemed nothing more to say. Or do. Ed could only hope that two more of the few Americans who'd passed through the Ring of Fire into this New World hadn't been lost, as so many had by now.

He picked up another of the many pieces of paper on his desk. "Okay, what's the story with—"

Part Three

July 1636

The outer voice of sky and cloud

—Wallace Stevens,
"The Idea of Order at Key West"

Chapter 21

Fort Orange
On the Hudson River
New Netherlands

Dutch civilization in the New World looked very little more advanced than French civilization. Stephane Hoff arrived alone at Fort Orange; he had no intention of arriving in the company of a band of savages—particularly those known to be in the service of, or at least in alliance with, the French. He inferred that in this anonymous state he made no more impression on the settlement than it impressed him—which was to say, not very much.

Fort Orange squatted on one bank of the great inland river. Its gates were wide open on the morning he walked in from the wilderness; no one took notice of him as he entered the town.

"What's your pleasure?" the publican asked, in heavily accented Dutch.

Stephane gestured to the keg mounted behind the bar. He placed a copper coin in front of the man, and at a scowl added a second one; the other picked up the coins and rapped them on the surface, grunted, and pocketed them. Shortly he was given a stoneware mug, which he carried to a bench seat near a window.

Everybody drinks, as his father had said. It had been part of

Monsieur Servien's training as well; one of the best places to pick up gossip was where it was freely given.

A few minutes after he took his seat, another man not much older than Stephane—dressed much as he was, with slightly more worn clothes and gear—came into the ordinary. The tavern keeper met him with an even deeper scowl, but accepted his payment and provided him with a drink.

The man looked around the room, but no one seemed eager to provide him with a place to sit. There was something about him, something grotesque that Stephane could not quite identify—but at the same time it was unusual enough to make Stephane curious.

He gestured to a seat on an adjoining bench; the man eagerly crossed the room and took the offered place. He took a long drink from his mug, and nodded appreciatively.

"You're new," the man said.

"Just arrived," Stephane said. "I was...up north."

The other looked at him curiously. "Truly."

Stephane wasn't sure what might have aroused suspicion, so he didn't answer, merely taking a drink from his mug.

"I'm Bogaert," the man said. "Harmen van den Bogaert." He extended a hand which Stephane took; he noticed that he had become the focus of attention from everyone in the room.

"Stephane," he said. "Stephane...Burg." *Close enough,* he thought.

The handshake went on a little longer than Stephane might have liked, and he let go of the man's hand.

"You are a trader, I presume," Bogaert said, gesturing toward Stephane's clothing. "Unless I am mistaken."

"I gather that you are as well."

"I am a surgeon by profession, Mynheer...Burg," Bogaert said. "But a few years ago I had the opportunity to travel into the wilderness. His Excellency the governor granted me the honor of serving as an ambassador to the Iroquois, and I journeyed among the natives for some time." He smiled, showing remarkably white teeth.

"How did you find them?"

"Fierce," Bogaert said. "And mercenary. There was a considerable amount of wealth being diverted from Dutch and into French purses—beaver pelts and the proceeds—and those in authority in New Amsterdam, as well as here, were eager to know why."

"Did you learn anything from your embassy, Doctor?"

"A great deal." He smiled again. "It's a very wild land, Myn-heer Burg. Full of wild people. But impressionable, I daresay. All you need to do is . . . suggest something and they'll pick right up on it. No subtlety: no subtlety at all."

Stephane wasn't sure what to make of that comment. *Always listen*, Servien had taught him: *you never know whether someone might drop a gold sovereign.*

"They are . . . quick to anger," Stephane said. "I understand that they recently went to war against France with little if any provocation—surely they would not hesitate to do so against the Dutch as well, either here or in New Amsterdam?"

"If you have any experience in the wilderness, Mynheer Burg," Bogaert said, "you know very well that there is not one tribe but half a dozen, and each has many chiefs, and there are clan loyalties and ancient disputes and alliances. They argue out their differences—sometimes—in one of their great castles, where they have a fire they keep burning."

"The Council Fire," Stephane said. Champlain had described the structure of the Five Nations alliance to him while he was in Québec; there were indeed a wide range of agendas and motivations—what the Mohawks wanted was not always what the Senecas wanted, and the tribes in between might want some third thing.

"Correct. That is where the cool heads of the old chiefs pre-vail. Or not. It was at the Council Fire that the Iroquois chose war last autumn."

After Bogaert said these words, Stephane heard a murmur in the room. It stopped just short of openly hostile, but it was clear to Stephane that Bogaert was getting all sorts of dirty looks from others in the room.

"You seem to have some detractors in this ordinary, friend Bogaert," Stephane said.

"Jealousy is a powerful emotion," Bogaert said, smiling again.

Bogaert gave him some advice on making his way down the river before they parted company, and soon he was out in the town again alone with his thoughts.

It did not last long. As he walked, he noticed that there was an Indian following him; the man did not seem threatening, and was making no attempt to conceal himself, but was definitely shadowing Stephane.

He stopped walking at the corner of a warehouse building and turned to face the native, who met his glance readily.

"Can I help you, friend?" Stephane asked in Dutch.

The native approached, hands held out, palms up, until he was standing in front of Stephane. "I can help *you*," he answered.

"How might that be?"

"You were talking with Bogaert in the ordinary," the man said. "I saw you through the window."

"You know him? Why did you not join us?"

"That is a place for whites," the native answered, and turned his head and spat into the dirt. "I would not sit with that snake in any case, and I offer you friendly advice not to do so either."

"And why would that be?"

"He is unclean," the Indian said. "And as I said, he is a snake—and a liar."

"I found him neither unclean nor untruthful, friend," Stephane said. "But I only just made his acquaintance. As I have just made yours, though you have not given me your name."

"I am called..." he lowered his voice conspiratorially, for no reason Stephane could determine. "Walks-In-Deep-Woods. Bogaert cruelly wronged me. He told me something that I took to be truth, and it was a most cruel falsehood. Now I am exiled from my people."

"What did he tell you?"

"That the great Captain of the Onontio had lain down with sickness in his bones and would not rise up."

"The great Captain...you mean Champlain?"

Walks-In-Deep-Woods looked around suddenly, to see if anyone had heard him say the name; then he placed a finger on his lips and grasped Stephane's elbow, drawing him out of the street. "Do not speak that name, friend! That is bad medicine. That snake Bogaert told me that he had suffered a terrible attack and lay dying."

"How could he know such a thing?"

"You would not believe the tale if I told it to you."

"Let me judge for myself."

Walks-In-Deep-Woods looked at him for several moments, not letting go of Stephane's elbow; Stephane wondered to himself if he was going to have to do something about that.

"It is said that a great city from a faraway place suddenly appeared, bringing wonders, including great books of prophecy about the times to come. Bogaert told me that he had seen one of the books, and it told of the great captain's death. It was to have happened in deep winter, in the year just past.

"Either the prophecy was wrong, or Bogaert was a liar. I know which one *I* believe." He bared his teeth in a disturbing manner.

Stephane shifted slightly and removed his elbow from the Indian's grasp. "And your own misfortune..."

"Is because I spoke of this to my chief, who walked to war with the French. When he found the tale to be untrue, he blamed *me* for the misfortune."

"Why would he do such a thing?" Stephane asked.

"Chiefs do things for their own reasons," Walks-In-Deep-Woods answered. He spat again. "As for Bogaert—I do not know his reasons. I only warn you that he is not to be trusted."

"And what do you want of me?"

"I am a poor exile from my native soil," he answered. "I can barely clothe my nakedness or fill my empty belly."

A beggar, Stephane thought. *Who wants to be paid.* He reached into his wallet and drew out two copper coins, stamped with the form of King Christian—part of his pay from Thomasville. "Here is what I can spare."

"Thank you," the native said, taking the coins from Stephane's hand and bowing. "May the gods of earth and sky smile upon you." His mission accomplished, the man bowed again and backed away, leaving Stephane alone again.

Chapter 22

New Amsterdam
New Netherlands

Pete seemed more surprised by the first view of New Amsterdam than Gordon, and expressed it as they approached from Long Island Sound.

"That's *it*?" he said. "*This* is what's going to become New York?"

"It's never going to be New York, little bro," Gordon said, as the morning fog began to clear and the docks on what the modern times would have called the East River became more visible. "That only would happen if the English had decided to keep their claims in the New World."

"We could change its name."

"Yeah," Gordon said. "We could. But I don't see that happening." He leaned on the rail, squinting across the sun-dappled bay at New Amsterdam, scarcely more than a little hamlet at the southern end of Manhattan Island—no tall buildings, no Statue of Liberty, no big steel bridges connecting it with Long Island or anywhere else.

Of course, everything he knew of New York was from television, lost in a future that would never be. Sitcoms and police dramas—there were probably some episodes on VHS tapes back in Grantville, showing more fragments of a world that *this* world wasn't going to become.

"I expected something a little more grand."

"From what I've read, that's in the near future—in the next ten years in our own time line, New Amsterdam was to have expanded by an order of magnitude. It's really a great place for a city: natural harbor, wide river leading into the interior, nice flat land and good farmland above. No wonder the English wanted it and no doubt why they took it away from the Dutch."

"Didn't the Dutch buy the whole island for, like, twenty-four dollars?"

"More or less. Though that's an exaggeration. It isn't like Peter Minuit just handed some Indian chief a twenty and four ones and got a title deed, like he was buying St. James Place or something. It was a pile of trade goods and weapons and so forth, and the Indians didn't have the same sense of the deal that the Dutch had—"

"'The land doesn't belong to us, we belong to the land.'"

"That's the general idea. But Europeans take a whole different view of the entire thing. That's why they're building a wall across the north side of the settlement—because of the Indians who think they got a raw deal."

"You mean they don't already have a wall?"

"They would have, eventually—it was built in the 1650s in our time line, but events have moved up the timetable. I imagine they'd like to know what's going on beyond it."

"Sounds like a job for the *Duke*."

Gordon smiled; he wanted to get up in the air again.

"We'll have to see what the lay of the land is before we put *John Wayne* in the air," he said. "This is more complicated than the Puritans."

"Oh? Why?"

"Because it's *complicated*," Gordon said. "There may not be too many of these New Netherlanders, but there's no telling which side they're on."

"Not on the French side, though."

"Maybe not down here in New Amsterdam. But upriver, it's not as black and white. They trade with the French, they trade with the Indians that trade with the French. They're looking for an angle—all of them."

In the port of New Amsterdam, *Challenger* was just another ship—with different rigging and an unusual flag, but otherwise not much different from other ships at the dock. Still, it seemed to attract attention, though they were not challenged or confronted as they had been in Thomasville or in Boston.

The view from the dock wasn't much more impressive than the view from the bay. New Amsterdam close up was a messy, disorderly place with muddy streets—no different, really, than any number of European towns. From the deck of *Challenger*, though, Gordon could hear a welter of speech in several languages. Some he recognized, like Dutch and heavily accented English, and others he didn't.

He asked Captain Maartens what he expected, and received a grunt in return.

"I imagine the *schout* will be here any time to see what we're about. We're not carrying any cargo, so he'll demand nothing but a bribe."

"This is a diplomatic mission, Captain," Gordon said. "You shouldn't have to—"

"But we *will*. They expect it. I expect it. Go explore, Chehab. Go do your *diplomatie*, whatever you need to do. We'll likely be here when you get back."

Captain Thomas James, who had been watching the exchange, walked up to join Gordon. "Come," he said. "Let me show you the . . . wonders . . . of New Amsterdam."

Thomas James' sarcasm was unconcealed; his disdain was similarly obvious. He didn't think very much of New Amsterdam or of the Dutch, and he gave Gordon and Pete a history lesson as they walked along the Strand, the street that followed the docks on the east side of Manhattan Island.

"The Dutch Estates General don't know what to make of this place," James said. "The settlement has been here almost fifteen years—and they consider it either the greatest investment of guilders they've ever seen, or the most impressive boondoggle."

"I thought they only paid twenty-four dollars for the whole thing," Pete said.

"Sixty guilders," James said. "Initially. To get the Indians to pull up their tent stakes and leave. But it has cost a hell of a lot more than that to build the fort—which they haven't even finished; to plant the *bouweries*—the farms—and to establish the beaver trade. Every time someone brings in a haul of beaver pelts the High Mightinesses have another bout of believing that the whole thing is going to turn into pure profit."

"Beaver pelts?"

"All the fashion," James said. He took off his own hat and held it up. "Beaver pelt. Smoothed down and brushed. The height of *couture*, as the French would say." He looked Gordon up and down, and then Pete, who scowled at the attention. Pete had a forage cap he'd picked up somewhere; Gordon was wearing a ball cap from John Deere, which looked as if it had seen far better days.

"What?" Pete said.

"Nothing," James said, putting his own hat back on his head and adjusting it minutely. "Beaver pelts. For hats, for cloaks, and coats. But there's more to the beaver trade than that."

"Really?"

"The learned doctors of Amsterdam—and elsewhere—believe that the beaver has great medicinal value as well. The oil from the skin can be taken medicinally for dizziness and dropsy, and the skins are made into slippers to be worn as a cure for gout.

"And then there are the testicles."

"Wait." Pete stopped in his tracks. "*Beaver testicles*? This I have *got* to hear."

"I understand," James said, "that beaver testicles have medicinal value. An extract assists in ..." he hitched up his breeches in a provocative way. Gordon doubled over, laughing.

"It must work for the beavers," Gordon said, when he could catch his breath.

"I'll stick to strippers and porn," Pete said.

The Strand dead-ended in a wide place flanked by a mostly built pentagonal fort. The foundations were of stone, as were the outer walls that faced the ocean; but the interior palisades were no more than strong oak beams with chinking in between. That was the pride of the settlement, according to Thomas James: Fort Amsterdam and the adjoining barracks that held the soldiers deployed at the colony, of which there didn't seem to be too many.

A number of new-looking buildings also fronted the plaza: a bakery, a smithy, and a couple of large warehouse-style structures that could be just about anything.

✧   ✧   ✧

After showing them the key sights and sounds of New Amsterdam, James excused himself.

"Doctor Skoglund wishes to perform some errands in the town," he said.

"And?"

"And," James said, "she asked me to escort her."

"Huh," Pete said. "What prompted her to do that, I wonder?"

"I suspect that she wanted some *mature* company, Chehab," James answered. "You have your own affairs; I am the logical choice."

"I wouldn't say that."

"No," James agreed. "No, you wouldn't. But it is not your decision to make, now is it." He touched his hand to the edge of his fashionable beaver hat, and walked away, back toward *Challenger* and Ingrid Skoglund.

"What do you think of that," Pete said.

"I don't know, little bro. But he's right: Ingrid chooses her own companions."

"Assuming she chose. Because if she didn't, I'll knock his teeth through the back of his head."

"You think she *didn't* choose? She's a force of nature, Pete. I wouldn't worry about that."

Ingrid told herself that she was a realist: that she saw things for what they were, not for the way that she would wish them to be. New Amsterdam, that wished itself to be the great entrepôt of the New World, was a tiny, fairly dirty place, full of pretension and absent the patina of culture that would have made it the rival to the great cities of Europe.

She knew from reading the up-time books, and from what Gordon and Peter Chehab had told her, that New Amsterdam in their time line had become transformed into a city that was incomparable: huge and filled with people of every nation, every skin color, speaking every language. It sprawled from the end of this tiny island onto lands north and east, filling them like water filling a bowl. Millions of people—an inconceivable thought!—in one place, their buildings reaching to the sky, their vehicles clogging the streets, trains passing through deep tunnels and airships passing overhead.

It was a long, long, *long* way from this wretched place. Still, this place was greater than any place they had yet seen in the New World. Perhaps Jamestown would be greater, but there was no way to know yet.

Thomas James walked her along the Strand and into the Market Place, which was teeming with activity this afternoon. There was a remarkable selection: fruits and vegetables, packages of tobacco leaf, sacks of sugar, cakes of indigo—all set out for browsing and buying.

Ingrid was meticulous, but deliberate. She took a certain satisfaction in going slowly and carefully along each aisle, speaking to each tradesman, examining all of the goods that were displayed. Captain James showed extraordinary patience.

At last they were finished with the market. Instead of walking east, she turned her steps north along the Heerenweg, the so-called "Long Highway" that followed the edge of the settled area and passed the burying ground, still lightly populated, but with a number of stone markers for those whose lives had come to an end in the New World.

"There's little past that orchard," James said as they walked along. He was carrying her basket, which he'd insisted upon, and he swept it around. "You have seen all of New Amsterdam that there is to see."

"It extends as far as the new wall, doesn't it?"

"The wall—such as it is—is no more than a boundary line, Doctor," he answered. "This isn't a European city—it's like a park with houses at the bottom end. Can you imagine any of this"—he gestured north; most of New Amsterdam was at their back; they could have been in a Dutch pasture, but for the smell and the sound—"in a proper European city?"

"No," she said. "I suppose I couldn't." She walked a little further and then stopped, noticing an extensive garden plot just past the orchard, extending from the Heerenweg down to the marshy ground at the verge of the great river.

In the summer heat, she could see a number of dark-skinned men working, bent over pulling weeds or straightening the planted rows with long hoes.

"Is that a penance on such a hot day?"

"Penance?"

"A punishment. Did they do something wrong?" She squinted. "Why, they have chains on their ankles."

"That's so they don't run away, I would guess."

"Then they are prisoners?"

"Slaves," James said. He reached into a coat pocket and withdrew his pipe and a tobacco pouch. "They also do not wish to see them rebel."

"I thought human chattel slavery was a feature of Virginia. We didn't see them in Boston."

"Oh, there are slaves in Boston, Doctor. Not very many: they don't adapt well to the climate. But there have been slaves here in New Amsterdam for a dozen years. They're...the more docile ones, not the great brutes that harvest the sugar down in the Carib. These are, dare I say, somewhat domesticated."

"Docile."

"Yes. It's a good business, really."

"It's a despicable business."

"The Holy Bible is full of tales of slavery, Doctor. Don't tell me that your up-timer friends have inculcated their values into you."

"My—" She turned to him, hands on hips. "My *up-timer friends*, as you put it, have nothing to do with my views on the matter. Humans should not be *property*. If they were apprentices or indentures I could understand it—but I presume that these unfortunates are owned for life, without hope of redemption?"

"Compared to their earlier lives—"

"Spare me. They are here against their will."

James packed and lit his pipe. "I should not seek to foment a rebellion, Doctor. I don't think the *schout* would take too kindly to intimations of that sort. They are slaves, and they are *here*. And they were likely sold into bondage by others of their race eager to obtain what they could get. It is no less than disingenuous to fault men for making a profit in a way that so obviously presents itself."

"And you absolve them of moral responsibility."

"Yes." He sucked in and blew out a smoke ring that drifted up a bit and then drifted away on the breeze. "Their morality is that of the marketplace, I'm afraid. Rather than pay for an expensive indenture, and then be required to equip a man at the end with land and tools, they simply buy the services.

"From what I have read of up-time history, it became quite a lucrative business. It looks...unlikely to change."

Chapter 23

Despite limited Dutch, the brothers got on all right with the locals. New Amsterdam was a Babel—even more so, given the events in Europe: Danes and Englishmen and Swedes and even a few Poles had made their way to the New World, settling in the relatively open Dutch colony. New England was, by and large, closed to 'outsiders'; Virginia was no place to be poor, and Maryland was far too small for most of these speculators looking to get ahead and to get away from the restrictive society and the wars in Europe. New Amsterdam was just the ticket.

But for all that it was *small*. Gordon had never been to New York up-time, but he'd looked at enough maps before they left to know that most of what up-timers considered to be "New York City" was the wilderness in this era. The Empire State Building was on Thirty-third Street, right in the middle of downtown New York, and its never-to-be-built future site was most of two miles north of the furthest extent of New Amsterdam—where they had built a makeshift palisade across a part of the island against invaders that no one seemed to think were much of a threat.

"The French?" the blacksmith, a balding, squinting Dutchman had said, spitting in the general direction of his forge. "What do we care about the French? Maybe they'll take care of the fanatics in New England for us."

Gordon and Pete could only shake their heads, wondering whether the Dutch back home saw the threat with the same indifference.

They sat leaning on a fence rail eating slices of brown bread from the local bakery. Suddenly, Pete set down his snack and took a few steps along the muddy lane.

"What's wrong, little bro?"

"Not sure," Pete said without turning around. "I thought I saw something."

"She *was* pretty," Gordon said, taking another bite of his bread. "But I don't think your Dutch is good enough."

"Not that."

"You're right, love is a universal language—"

"*Not that*," he repeated. "I think we're being watched."

"Of course we are. The up-timers are here—the circus has come to town. Seems like everyone is watching us."

"This is different." Pete turned around and walked back to the fence. He didn't pick up his slice of bread; there was a stray dog nearby considering its options. "This is how you felt aboard ship when we were at dock in Hamburg. *Watched*."

"Huh. By who?"

"Don't know. He's faded out of sight again. But I've seen him, just a glimpse, twice. Someone with more than a passing interest."

"What are you going to do about it?"

"I want to do a little recon. But I can't do that and keep an eye on you at the same time."

"I can take care of myself."

"*Sure* you can. Sorry, big bro—I'd be just as happy if you went back to *Challenger* and let me do this on my own."

"That's pretty condescending, Pete," Gordon said, standing up and pulling the sliced bread out of the way of the dog, who looked just about ready to jump for it. "I don't need to be protected."

"The hell you don't. Look." Pete pointed at his big brother. "You're the key man in this operation. Our patron sent *you* here, hired *you* to do this. If anything happens to me, it's sad, but not a tragedy. You'll . . . take care of Penny and Karen, you'll give the news to Mom and Dad. But if anything happens to you the mission's over. So you let me knock around a little bit and see if I can turn up whoever's shadowing us."

"While I go hide aboard ship."

"I wouldn't put it that way, but—yes."

Gordon thought about whether he wanted to press the point. He really didn't feel that he needed Pete to protect him—though he'd specifically invited him along to do just that: to be the one guy Gordon could trust to cover his back.

And he was *right*, which galled him even more.

"Just try not to kill anyone, all right?"

"It's an interesting idea," Pete said.

For a town that was as small as New Amsterdam, Pete found it surprisingly hard to locate his tail. His military training and experience wasn't much use in this sort of work. He knew that he stood out from the crowd, but whoever was following him probably didn't.

New Amsterdam was less impressive than Grantville before the Ring. A nice fort, a few windmills, all kinds of goods on sale and all kinds of languages being spoken—most of which Pete didn't speak.

The most logical thing was to find someplace out in the open, where the person following him would have to be exposed in order to keep close. He walked away from the plaza along a broad street that extended roughly northward; if Gordon or James had been along, they'd probably have been able to tell him some fun fact about it. For Pete's purpose, it was simply a matter of being out in the open.

It took fifteen minutes for him to reach the partially built wall that straddled the island. Where the broad street intersected, there was a large double gate made of stout oak with mortared stone posts and lookout platforms, which were unoccupied at the moment. The gates themselves were open, giving a view of the low-lying farms beyond. Not all of the wall was stone: a hundred yards in either direction it was no more than a wooden palisade. A wagonload of stone had been pulled up near the wall to the west, and two Dutchmen stood smoking their pipes, as if they were in no hurry to put any work into strengthening New Amsterdam's defenses.

No, Pete thought. *They're not worried about the French.*

He walked along the street in front of the wall, exchanging a polite nod with the two stonemasons (*government jobs*, he thought; *must be nice*), and waiting for his tail to appear. It was frustrating—he was sure that he was being followed, but after a while he couldn't trust his own suspicions. A soldier on patrol who thinks he's in someone's scope gets jumpy and starts at everything.

After a few minutes, he noticed a man not too far away. He was short and moved with the sort of nimble grace Pete had come to associate with the crew of *Challenger*—especially the ones who climbed the masts and rigging without safety harnesses or ropes. He clearly wanted to stay out of sight, but the ploy of walking close to the wall—with most of New Amsterdam to the south, dappled by the westering sun—was working against him.

Pete couldn't really turn to see the man's face, but something about his movements—the way he walked, how he held his arms—struck him as familiar.

The little Alsatian, he suddenly thought. *The guy who left the ship in Newfoundland. But ... here?*

Did he want his job back?

Pete was too cynical to believe that. He wasn't sure why the man was here in New Amsterdam, following him—but he didn't believe it was coincidence.

Okay, he thought. *On three.*

One, he said to himself. He reached in a pocket and found his key ring, something he'd carried for years—an eagle medallion that Grampa Charlie had given him while he was in high school. It had the added advantage of being a bottle opener, which came in handy on weekends.

Two, he thought. He made as if to trip on a loose paving stone, and let the key ring fall to the ground. He bent over to pick it up, giving him a clear look at the man following him.

Damn, he thought. *That's who it is. Hobb. Hoff. Something like that.*

Three.

He grabbed the key ring from the ground and began sprinting right at the man, as if he was stealing second off Pudge Rodriguez. *Come on, man, he's going to gun you down with that cannon arm.*

It should have worked. Hobb, or Hoff, or whatever his name was, froze for just a moment when Pete had reached for the key ring, but by the time Pete ran at him he'd taken off as well, dodging onto a side street.

Pete thought his foot speed was pretty good. He was sure he couldn't steal second off Pudge, but he thought he could catch up with the Alsatian topman before he disappeared. By the time he got to the side street, though, the other man was nowhere to be found.

There were no telltale swinging gates, no doors left ajar... and he was in plain sight, while his target had vanished. He spent a little time searching further, but with no luck.

By the time early evening came, it was clearly time for a drink.

Pete looked up from his beer to see a man waiting to speak to him. He was fairly indistinguishable from most of the other inhabitants of New Amsterdam, though the man was politely waiting for him to notice. This was Pete's second pint, and he wondered to himself how long the man had been standing there.

Nah, Pete thought. *It couldn't be that long.* And he was also convinced at that moment that this was not the man whom he'd been looking for all afternoon.

"Yeah? What do you want?"

"Only a few moments of your time, Mynheer," the man said.

At least he speaks English and not just Dutch, Pete thought. "Sure." He gestured to the seat opposite.

The Dutchman sat down. "You are..." he moved it closer so that he could speak softly and be heard over the din of the tavern. "You are from the up-time ship, *ja*?"

"I'm traveling aboard *Challenger*, yes. What's it to you?"

"Ah," he said. "God be thanked. The noble Don Francisco has sent help at last." He looked around furtively, as if afraid of being overheard.

"That's a name you shouldn't toss around lightly, friend." Pete glanced around to see if anyone else had noticed, wondering where Gordon and Captain James had gotten off to.

"Oh, I know, I know. He would not want our enemies to know."

"'Our' enemies?"

"The *French*," the man said, nodding and smiling.

Pete didn't say anything. This was a little out of his department. The French were certainly an enemy, even if hostilities had ceased, but having some random Dutchman throwing Don Francisco's name around was no way to begin a conversation.

"You *know*," the man said. "The French. The wolf at the door. The cardinal," he hissed.

"I know who you're talking about," Pete said. "Maybe you should start at the beginning. Tell me your name and what you're about, and then I can decide what I'm going to do with you."

"*Do* with me?"

When Pete had been on active duty in Suhl and elsewhere, it was sometimes necessary to show a civilian that you meant business. There was a Vietnam vet in his company who had perfected the deadpan look, the one that said, *maybe I'll let you live, and maybe not.*

Pete delivered his best impression of that look to the Dutchman, who looked very uncomfortable.

"My name is Van der Glinde," he said quietly. "Jan van der Glinde. Almost two years ago I was granted an interview by Francisco Nasi, whom I believe to be your patron."

Pete decided this wasn't the time for a long-winded explanation concerning the political changes that had taken place over the past two years, which had resulted in Gordon and him working for Ed Piazza and Estuban Miro instead of Mike Stearns and Francisco Nasi. So he settled for making a slight hand gesture that indicated Van der Glinde should continue.

"I had the honor of speaking with him and presenting our case for assistance here in New Amsterdam."

"Did he promise you anything?"

"He said that he would give the matter his consideration."

Pete shook his head. "That doesn't answer my question. Did he *promise* you anything?"

Van der Glinde hesitated. He appeared to want to say *yes*, but apparently Pete's expression—unchanged and unfriendly— convinced him that he should tell the truth.

"No," he said at last. "But now that you are here..."

Pete waited for the sentence to end. It never quite did.

"I mean to say," Van der Glinde said after a moment, "that I assumed, that I thought..."

"What did you assume?"

"I assumed that you were here to help eliminate the French threat."

"And just how do you suppose we would do that?"

"Well," the Dutchman said. "Well...you are *up-timers*, after all..."

"I don't have a magic wand to solve all your problems. None of us do," Pete said. "So suppose you stop interrupting my ale and tell me just what it is you expect me—or us—to do."

Van der Glinde looked crestfallen.

"Are you the captain of your up-timer expedition?"

"No. That's my big brother. Me, I'm the pissed-off younger brother. I can take you to him, but I'd be surprised if he tells you anything different from what I'm telling you."

Chapter 24

As it turned out, Pete *was* surprised.

Gordon was in *Challenger*'s pilot's cabin looking at sea charts with Maartens when Pete and his Dutchman guest came aboard. The captain made quick work of putting the charts away when they entered.

"Hey," Pete said.

"Someone I should meet?"

"I don't know, big bro. You tell me. I can either leave you two alone or I can toss him into the bay. He, uh, mentioned the name of our patron."

"May I ask *your* name?" Gordon asked Van der Glinde.

"Jan van der Glinde, Mynheer," he answered, doffing his cap. "I have had the pleasure of an interview with your esteemed patron."

"I know," Gordon said.

"You do?" Pete asked.

"How about you hang with us, little bro," Gordon said. "Mr. Van der Glinde—Mynheer Van der Glinde, isn't that the honorific?" The New Amsterdammer nodded approvingly. "He may be able to provide us with valuable information."

"Huh," Pete said, leaning back against one wall. "And if he can't?"

"You can always throw him into the bay." Gordon smiled. "But that probably won't be necessary."

He gestured to a bench, and the two men sat down, while Pete and Maartens remained standing. "Tell us, Mynheer, if you would, what you know of the French designs on New Netherland."

For the next hour Van der Glinde related what he knew about the situation in the back country. As yet there had been no major Indian movement against New Amsterdam, or any indication of trouble up river at Fort Orange; there was still a brisk trade in beaver pelts.

"There's a standing order against trading guns and powder to the Indians," the Dutchman said. "But that's not even honored in the breach. They know that they can ignore the governor without fear of reprisal."

"Why is that?" Pete asked.

"Have you met our esteemed director-general?" Van der Glinde asked, looking from Gordon to Pete. "No, I suppose not. The Honorable Wouter van Twiller is a nephew of our great *patroon* Kiliaen van Rensselaer, and that is the *only* thing that qualifies him for the position. If there is wine to be had, he will drink more than his share. If there is a decision to be made, he will find someone else to make it."

"Does he think that New Amsterdam is in danger?"

"It's probably crossed his mind, yes, but it's not him—or his council, such as it is—that is alarming the citizens, or building the wall at the Kill. It was not the Honorable Wouter van Twiller that sent me to Magdeburg two years ago to make appeal to Don F—to your esteemed patron," he said, noting the frown from Gordon.

"So who sent you?" Pete asked. "If it wasn't the director-general, who did you represent?"

Van der Glinde looked from Pete to Gordon once more. "I . . . was sent particularly by the Honorable Kiliaen van Rensselaer."

"The director-general's uncle, the one you mentioned?"

"Yes," Van der Glinde said. "He sees what is coming, and he has the most to lose. If the French take the colony of the New Netherlands, he will receive nothing in the way of compensation. He is not inclined to let that happen—and is willing to pay well to gain help."

"What sort of help does he want? What does he expect?"

"Up-timer help," the Dutchman said.

"What does that mean?"

Van der Glinde shrugged.

"Five years ago," he said at last, "the world was turned upside down by the coming of you Americans. There had been France, and Spain, England and the Empire, Sweden and Denmark...and then suddenly there *you* were. I have read something of the history that you brought back with you: how the Swedish king was killed in a battle in 1632 and General Wallenstein was murdered a few years later—and how the war dragged on another sixteen years, ravaging all of the Germanies. Spain ended prostrate and only France could be considered to be triumphant.

"You have rewritten history in only a few years. You have changed everything. Four years ago—even three years ago—anyone reading the up-time histories might be able to see the way things were going, and make intelligent choices based on that knowledge. Certainly the English king based all of his future strategy on what he read. But now...so many things have changed, so many winds have blown in new directions, that the up-time histories might as well be stories of another world.

"We think the French wolf will finally begin to turn his attention to the New World, Mynheer Chehab. *My* patron, Mynheer Van Rensselaer, believes that you up-timers have a chance to change the world again."

Gordon leaned forward, elbows on knees, and leaned his chin on his fists.

"That's a very pretty speech, Mynheer Van der Glinde. I hear what you are saying—and it's true: with every year—with every *month*—that distances us from the Ring of Fire, the world that we live in diverges further from the world that might have been had we not come back to change it.

"But everyone else knows that too. We made no effort to keep the future that we knew secret. The cardinal, King Charles, King Philip of Spain—hell, the Sultan of the Ottomans are all aware what history has—*had*—in store. We have so many enemies, so many greedy nations that want what we have—that want what we used to have.

"Didn't our patron tell you, sir, that we have plenty of enemies and plenty of problems of our own? This is far away from the United States of Europe, Mynheer. Thousands of miles, weeks and weeks."

"Then I must ask you a question," Van der Glinde said.

"Please."

"If this is so far away, Mynheer," the Dutchman asked, "then *why are you here*? What can you do? Is this like a bear-baiting, where you place yourselves in front of us and then deny your help, merely to disappoint or enrage us? If so"—he stood up and turned to Pete, spreading his hands wide—"you'd best toss me into the bay and get it over with. I wanted to believe that you were the answer to our pleas."

"We're not here to taunt you," Gordon said. "But our situation has changed in the two years since you spoke to Francisco Nasi. There was another election and Mike Stearns was replaced as prime minister of the USE by Wilhelm Wettin. Nasi is no longer part of the USE government. Before he left, he passed on your request to Ed Piazza, the president of the State of Thuringia-Franconia—that's the most populous province of the USE, if you didn't know already. Ed decided to go ahead with the expedition, but I'm now representing the SoTF as what amounts to a combination trade mission and unofficial diplomatic mission. The truth is, the USE as such is not only not sponsoring this expedition, they probably don't even know about it."

He paused to see if Van der Glinde had absorbed all that. The Dutchman seemed to have followed him pretty well, so Gordon went on.

"A large part of our goal was to see the lay of the land, to understand what was going on in the New World. But it's clear that we can accomplish something more important—to forge friendship, if not alliance, between all of France's enemies here in North America. All of you—the Danes in Newfoundland, the English colonies in Massachusetts and along the Connecticut River as well as the ones in Maryland and Virginia, you here in the New Netherlands, and even the native tribes that are friendly to any of you and hostile to the French—could work together against the threats that exist and the ones that are to come in the future. You outnumber the French here in the New World. You have more guns, more potential soldiers, and you all have something to lose.

"What's more, you need to do this for yourselves and largely by yourselves. The New World is at the end of a logistical tail thousands of miles long. The very thing that has prevented the cardinal from executing his king's warrant across all of North America makes it extremely difficult for anyone in Europe to help you."

Van der Glinde left to go ashore. Gordon and Pete stood at the rail watching the lanterns at the tillers bob as little boats crossed the sound to Manhattan Island, the place that would never become New York.

"I don't think he got the answer he was looking for, big bro," Pete said.

"We couldn't give it to him. He wanted—he *wants*—the magic wand, the magic up-timer technology that makes us invincible. The problem is that it doesn't exist. One good musket ball, one bolt of lightning, one bad case of any number of diseases and we wind up just as dead. We're as vulnerable as anyone born to this time, and every passing year makes it worse."

"I think he knows that, Gord. I don't think he sees us as supermen. I don't think anyone does, not Richelieu, not anyone. They're afraid of how we *think*. American ingenuity, all that. We're all like that guy on TV who could take two pieces of string and a tin can and a pack of matches and build himself a Chevy or whatever."

"MacGyver. I loved that show."

"Yeah, I remember. They think every American they meet is MacGyver. And we *are*, to them."

The lantern was almost out of sight. *Challenger* rode gently at anchor; above, the sky was full of stars.

"If he didn't like our answer," Gordon said at last, "wait until their director-general hears what we have to say."

Chapter 25

For the director-general of New Netherland, Gordon Chehab had set aside a clean and semi-formal suit of clothes. The Germans had an expression—*Kleider machen Leute*—"clothes make the man"—and Cavriani and Miro had suggested in the strongest manner that he should make an effort to impress anyone he met with "the earnest of his mission."

The hardworking Danes and the ascetic Puritans had not needed or wanted to be impressed, but Gordon assumed that the Dutch proprietors in New Amsterdam were more likely to be.

It turned out that he did not need to bother.

"Excuse me?" Gordon said.

"I think you know very well what I mean, Mynheer," the clerk said, smiling in a way that made Gordon's skin crawl. "The governor's time is very valuable."

"I'm sure it is. But so is mine." Gordon looked sideways at Pete, who was standing easy, balanced on the balls of his feet.

The clerk shrugged and began to turn away.

"So . . . when will the governor have time for us?"

"*Wie het weet?*" *Who knows?* "In a day, maybe two. When he tells me he wants to see you, I'll let you know."

"Unless I . . ."

"Pay the slimy bastard," Pete said. "Bribe him."

The clerk frowned. "I don't like your choice of words, *Amerikaner.*"

Pete took a step toward him. "And I don't like your style, Dutchman. In order for us to get an interview with the director-general of New Amsterdam, I have to cross your palm—or you'll keep us iced out here indefinitely. If it's not a bribe you want, what would you like to call it?"

It was clear that the clerk wasn't used to any answer other than yes or no.

"What—" he began.

Pete hadn't raised his hand or changed his expression—he was just standing three or four feet away, doing what he did best—doing what he'd come along to do. He was giving the clerk the cool stare.

The clerk looked at Pete, then beyond him to Gordon. His eyes seemed to plead, as if he didn't know what Pete might do next.

It was Gordon's turn to shrug.

"The director-general—" the clerk began, obviously intimidated, then held up his hand. "I'll check with him."

He disappeared through an inner door, and Gordon and Pete heard the beginning of a muffled conversation in Dutch.

"Not a perfect work of public relations," Gordon said. "But at least you didn't hit him."

"What makes you think I was going to *hit* him?" Pete smiled. "I am a peaceful man."

"You didn't seem so."

"Never let the batter know what pitch you're going to throw, big bro."

"I don't think that clerk knows much about baseball, Pete."

"It's a metaphor."

Gordon smiled. "I know it's a—"

The door opened; the clerk emerged, looking even more intimidated. "The director-general will see you now," he said, and stepped aside.

Gordon and Pete walked toward the inner door. As they stepped into the director-general's office, they heard what sounded like a particularly offensive word in German—which apparently bore a strong cognate in Dutch.

They ignored it.

✦   ✦   ✦

Wouter van Twiller, Director-General of New Amsterdam, was a younger man—a few years older than Gordon. He had been promoted to the position after the Nineteen had recalled Peter Minuit a few years earlier. Pete had wondered aloud, when they were reading over the up-time material on van Twiller, if Minuit had been told that he should have paid only nineteen dollars for Manhattan; but it was pretty clear that the current director-general had obtained his position due to the influence of his uncle.

There was certainly little else to recommend him.

Van Twiller received them in a well-appointed study. He was in a comfortable stuffed armchair—in fact, *stuffed* was a good way to describe how he was placed. He appeared to have missed very few meals; when his substantial girth was combined with his obviously small stature, his appearance was nothing less than comic. Gordon had all he could do to not laugh.

"Well, well, *mijn Herren*," van Twiller said. "I am told that you were...*insistent* in your desire to meet with me."

"Thank you for taking the time for us, Director-General. My name is Gordon Chehab, and this is my brother Peter. We are on an exploratory mission for the State of Thuringia-Franconia— one of the provinces of the United States of Europe—exploring trade and...other possibilities. We have recently arrived aboard *Challenger*."

"I understand that you were asked for help." He smiled—a bit ferally, Gordon thought; his eyes, deep set in his round face, glinted in the gray light of afternoon, streaming in through a window. "A sort of *embassy*, I suppose you might call it."

"An unofficial one."

"What do you have to offer?"

"I am not sure what you mean, Excellency," Gordon said.

Van Twiller smiled again; he had not yet offered the Americans seats, nor did he appear interested in doing so.

"If you have come on your *exploratory mission* to offer us assistance, I would like to know what you care to offer—and I wish to determine what is in it for New Amsterdam—and for me." He reached out of the depths of the armchair and took hold of a tankard, from which he drank.

"I didn't say that we were here to assist you, Excellency," Gordon said. "I am to report back to my patron on the state of the various colonies here in the New World—yours, the English—"

"The English have no colonies in the New World," Van Twiller interrupted. "Their king has sold them all to the French. Sold out: that's how it could be characterized. The meddling Puritans, the Catholics on the Chesapeake, the tobacco growers and the island plantations. All French now—though they don't seem to be in any hurry to enforce their patent."

"So you don't see them as a threat."

"No, of course not. Why should I? We're not English, and New France has no particular quarrel with us. Not to mention that we are thousands of miles across the sea, Mynheer Chabot."

"Chehab."

"I beg your pardon. We are thousands of miles across the sea, and the French king seems somewhat *preoccupied* at the moment, doesn't he? His recent war with the USE went poorly for him, he faces serious unrest at home, and he doesn't have an heir, at least not yet. I don't really think he cares much about New Amsterdam."

Gordon thought, *Your uncle thought there was a threat—two years ago. Just because they haven't gotten around to you yet doesn't mean they don't care.*

Unless Kiliaen van Rensselaer didn't tell his nephew anything. He's half a world away, sitting in his countinghouse in Amsterdam. Why did he arrange to send Van der Glinde to Don Francisco?

"The French are a threat, Excellency. Just because they haven't come calling so far doesn't mean they won't get to it eventually."

"And in the meanwhile...what do you want from me?"

"My instructions are very general, Director-General van Twiller. I am to encourage any of France's enemies or rivals in the New World to make common cause: you, the former English colonies, the natives—"

"Common cause? With the *natives*? With the *Puritans*?" He laughed—a disturbing sort of giggle that made all of his several chins bob up and down. "That is the most absurd thing I've heard this month, if not this year. England, before it sold its rights away, interfered with and hindered us in the name of a conflicting claim. As for the Puritans, they insisted on planting their settlements on land claimed by the Netherlands: they are the stubbornest, most pigheaded folk in Christendom. They made themselves so obnoxious to their king that it is no wonder he cut them adrift.

"They can go straight to *Hell*, Mynheer Chehab, which is where they claim we are all going. I shall not make 'common cause' with any of those mock-pious preeners. And as for the natives: they may be dangerous to soft Virginia planters, but the *burghers* and the *patroons* of New Netherland know how to deal with them. Once the wall on the *kill* is built, there should be no threat from the savages.

"Now," he said at last, taking another healthy drink from his tankard, "was there anything else?"

As he walked along the muddy street, Gordon clenched and unclenched his fists. Pete walked silently beside him, keeping an eye on everyone who passed by.

"He can't really believe that," Gordon said at last.

"Yes, he can. He's a moron."

"The Dutch would never leave a moron as director-general. He's willfully ignorant—he's not stupid."

"No, big bro," Pete said, "he's *both* willfully ignorant and stupid. He thinks that just because the French are far away that they're no threat, and he has no use for anyone who's not Dutch. We just have to find someone here who doesn't agree with him."

Ask, Gordon thought a few hours later, *and it shall be given you*. Waiting at the East River dock was a young ship's mate who escorted them to a smaller ship nearby.

Someone was waiting at the top of the gangplank: a middle-aged man with a carefully trimmed beard and a hawk's nose. He seemed impatient, but greeted them politely when they reached him.

"Mynheer Chehab," the man said. "And Mynheer Chehab. My name is de Vries. Jan de Vries. I understand that you have just had an interview with our"—he paused, looking as if he was about to spit—"director-general."

"You seem to be well informed."

"New Amsterdam is a small town," de Vries answered.

"He wasn't very helpful, Captain de Vries. I assume you know the results of our little chat."

"Not *Captain*," the Dutchman replied. "Commander." He smiled slightly. "They go where I tell them"—he made a gesture—"but they trim the sails. As for Van Twiller, the little *klootoog* wasn't much help, you say."

The expression wasn't one he was familiar with, but Gordon got its meaning. "I cannot say that I am surprised," de Vries added.

"It was worse than not being helpful," Pete said. "He doesn't seem to be much interested in anything other than...consuming."

"That's Van Twiller." A few more Dutch invectives flew past. "Did you offer him anything to consume?"

"That's not why we're here."

"I am curious just why you *are* here," de Vries said. He beckoned to them, and they walked back to the quarterdeck.

Pete leaned against the rail. "Damn," he said. "Everyone is asking us that."

De Vries drew a pipe out of an inner pocket of his captain's coat, followed by a pouch of tobacco. "Then I'm sure that you have a ready answer to that question."

"We're here on an exploratory expedition, Commander," Gordon said. "Our employer sent us to see the lay of the land here in the New World. We have little to offer."

"Other than technology, perhaps."

"I have no technology to *offer*," Gordon said. "The sorts of things you would want—flying machines and armored ships—are not mine to give. I come equipped with something more dangerous, if I can make good use of it."

"And what would that be?" de Vries asked, lighting his pipe.

"Knowledge, Commander. A little insight into what is to come. What happens to all of us—to all of this."

"What *does* happen, Mynheer?"

"I don't know. I can tell you that the future that was going to come about is out of the question now. In the history of my own time, New Amsterdam lasts until 1664 as a Dutch colony, then it's ceded to another European power."

"The French?"

"No," Gordon said. "The English. This was to become one of the greatest cities in the world—New York. A huge place. A rich place. Eventually, an American place. But King Charles sold it away, and unless some English king reconsiders, this might well become a French city."

"I assume that Van Twiller had no interest in this."

"He told me that New Amsterdam had no quarrel with the French, as if Cardinal Richelieu would make some distinction when it came time for him to enforce his king's new patent. He told me that the former English colonies could go to perdition, and he laughed at making any sort of accord with the natives. In short, Commander de Vries, if he speaks for the majority view of most of your fellow New Amsterdammers, he told me that you guys have no friends, and when the French do arrive there'll be no one to come to your aid."

"He doesn't represent a majority view, Mynheer Chehab," de Vries said. "He doesn't represent anyone but a small group of venal men—I don't even think he does what his uncle, the Patroon Van Rensselaer wants him to do. I'm surprised that the Nineteen haven't replaced him already."

"That's good to hear," Gordon said. "Then tell me: I've been doing most of the talking. What's *your* angle?"

"My . . . angle?"

"You brought us aboard your fine ship for a reason. What do you want from me? I've already told you that I have no up-time flash-and-sparkle to offer."

"No," de Vries said, "Apparently you do not. But you *do* have a vision, and you do offer the hope of a powerful alliance. I know something of your United States of Europe, watching your country change the course of the German war. I have even seen one of your airplanes fly over me in the sky: I should like to ride in one someday."

Gordon and Pete exchanged a glance.

"I think you have something to offer New Amsterdam, regardless of the opinions of that idiot Wouter van Twiller. Accordingly, I should like to see what I and the *Staat van Hoorn*"—he gestured to his ship—"can do to further that alliance."

Gordon and his team had practiced the setup procedure plenty of times at the Grantville airfield, but it was the first time it had been done in the New World under time pressure. The dirigible itself was essentially a huge canvas bag reinforced by ripstop seams, which when fully inflated would be an oblong watermelon shape a hundred and fifty feet long and about sixty feet in diameter.

The whole thing weighed more than four hundred and fifty pounds. It was hoisted over the side of *Challenger* and lowered onto a raft, where it was rowed to shore and hauled out by six crewmen, with a bosun there to curse them all the way to watch out for sharp rocks that might tear the cloth. "'Tis all right, they work harder that way, Mynheer," he told Gordon between bouts of cursing. Devout Christians of the time deplored blasphemy, but had no problem with simple profanity.

Once the canvas was laid out flat on shore with the bow pointed upwind, they rigged a line to the fore end of the bag and attached it to an anchor, to guard against a sudden gust pulling the entire affair into the ocean. Then the sailors and cursing bosun returned to *Challenger* and brought back the passenger car, setting it up in the same orientation, and Gordon and Pete got to work mounting the lawnmower engines to the outside, testing the propane tanks, and setting up the fan that would enable the inflation of the canvas envelope.

With the fan in place, Pete started up one of the engines and the blades began to spin, pushing air into the bottom of the sack. Slowly, the great canvas envelope began to fill.

They'd chosen Oyster Island to set up *John Wayne* and get it into the air. It was one of a set of three low-lying islands, surrounded by vast oyster beds, located in the harbor just south of New Amsterdam. For Gordon, however, there was symbolism that none of the spectators could appreciate. Rather than the future Ellis Island or the future Governors Island, the flat, fairly circular spot where they'd decided to set up the dirigible was the future Liberty Island. In the spot where the propane burners were heating up the air was the place where the Statue of Liberty would never stand.

"This is the up-time flash, big bro," Pete said, hands on his hips. "This isn't an airplane, but it's something they've never seen before."

"Bet Van Twiller would like a ride in this," Gordon said.

"Bet he's never going to get it. De Vries, on the other hand..."

"Maybe. I told him we were going to put *John Wayne* aloft, and he got this look in his eyes—as if he already knew what it was good for."

"Which is?" Pete asked, already knowing the answer.

"The purpose we have it along. Recon. Up there we have a better view than anyone on the ground. Tactical advantage, as you put it—we'll see what's coming long before it sees us."

"I'm not sure about de Vries, big bro. Are you sure you want to add him to our merry band?"

"I think he has his own reasons, Pete. We've got to trust someone, sometime, so I choose to trust him. He could be dangerous, but he could also be of enormous help. *Staat van Hoorn* is as close as we might have to a warship on our side."

"I'm going to keep an eye on him, if you don't mind."

"No, little bro," Gordon said. "I don't mind a bit."

Among the many spectators lining the waterfront on Manhattan was a young Alsatian who knew the lines of *Challenger* very well indeed—and even as the lighter-than-air craft *John Wayne* rose into the air, he was planning what he would write in his next letter to his patron far across the ocean.

Part Four

August 1636

The heaving speech of air

—Wallace Stevens,
"The Idea of Order at Key West"

Chapter 26

On the Atlantic Coast
South of New Amsterdam

"It's a whole lot of nothing, big bro."

Pete and Gordon were sitting near the bow of *Challenger* after about a hundred miles' air cruise across the expanse of New Jersey. There had been nothing to see other than Lenape villages and game in the forests—no sign of invaders, foreign or domestic.

Pete was whittling something—it looked like either a bird or a fish: it wasn't clear what would emerge, if anything, when he was finished removing all the parts that didn't belong.

"What, you mean the trip across the Jersey Shore? I don't think we expected—"

"No, not the air trip. The whole damn thing. It's a whole lot of nothing."

"Well." Gordon leaned back against the rail. It was a beautiful summer day; the wind was fresh, the sea placid—it could have been a pleasure sail, except that the seventeenth century was smacking him in the face like the waves that slapped at *Challenger*'s hull. "I'm not sure I'd say that."

"The optimist, as usual. So tell me—we've been in Danish Newfoundland, in Puritan New England, and we've visited the Dutch in New Amsterdam. The Danes think that there's no threat;

the Puritans hate the nonbelievers and the Indians mostly hate the English; and the New Amsterdammers hate everyone."

"Except Jan de Vries."

"Yeah. Except de Vries. So—no help from the industrialists up north, no alliance among the Puritans and the Indians, and the Dutch think they're immune. Meanwhile we're—what? On the way to Virginia to see if the tobacco farmers want to be friends? Or the handful of Catholics in Maryland?" He chipped away at the little piece of wood, trying to decide if it was a wing or a fin.

"I don't know. I didn't know from the beginning and I don't know now. When Ed Piazza sent us on this expedition, he wasn't sure what he expected of it himself. Neither did Estuban Miro or Leopold Cavriani. But we've learned a lot, at least, even though it doesn't seem like we have any allies on the continent. Did Ed expect us to find any? God, I hope not. Better he be surprised at what we learned than disappointed that people aren't lining up to make treaties with the USE.

"What's the worst he can do? Take me off the payroll? Then I'll go back to being a medic, or I'll find a job piloting. And you can go back to your wife and daughter and live happily ever after."

"Whatever," Pete said, seeming to shrug off the comment. "But there aren't many pilot's jobs."

"There's at least one," Gordon said, looking back amidships. "Estuban Miro will find a use for the *Duke* when this is over; he'll need someone to keep her in the air."

"I'm glad to see that you've started to think about what you'll do after the great adventure," Pete said. "We might as well. It'll be over soon."

"What makes you think that?"

"Oh, for Christ's sake, Gordon, I know you don't want to admit it." He set the changeling wooden sculpture down next to him and ran his hands through his hair. "I spent enough years in the army to know when it's time to cut and run. It's just about that time, don't you think? We go to Maryland, and then to Virginia, and then we head home."

"And that's it."

"Yes. That's it. What do you want? What did you expect? Look at who we've met. Of all of them, big bro, have you found anyone who even *looks* like he's going to run outside the rails and change? They're all at each other's throats, or will be. By the time Richelieu decides to bother with France's new spread, it'll be no more than cleanup duty."

"Things change."

"Things might change, big bro. Ring of Fire, butterfly effect, times and tides. But people *don't*. They're all the same, and they're all going to act as they'd be expected to act."

"Is that all?"

"Yeah." He picked up the carving again, looking at it as if he was examining some sort of unknown fossil.

"Well, I'm glad you have this all figured out, Pete. You know, when you get going with a full head of steam, you're hard to stop. But there are times that you are totally, completely, full of crap."

"What?"

"The problem with your whole tortured analysis, little bro, is that even though we haven't changed any hearts or any minds, we have the biggest prize of all: the thing we were mostly sent here to get."

"And that is?"

"Knowledge, Pete. Before this trip, we didn't know squat about what was happening in North America. All we had was what was in a bunch of history books—which was bound to have gotten off, even way off, five years after the Ring of Fire. We have lots of knowledge now. And that's worth a lot more than convincing Puritan John Endecott that he should sit with the Pequots and sing 'Kumbaya.'"

Two days after Gordon and Pete returned with *John Wayne* from exploring the coast and the Delaware Valley, *Challenger* and *Staat van Hoorn* found an anchorage on the coast, opposite Cape May. De Vries had signaled his desire to go ashore at this particular place, and Gordon saw no reason not to accede to his request.

Gordon and Pete took a small landing boat ashore and found de Vries and four of his crew waiting for them. De Vries' face was solemn. He was usually either cheery or sardonic, but rarely showed much in the way of emotion; Gordon was curious, while Pete was guarded—he wasn't sure what to make of the scene.

"There's something you should see, *Amerikaner*," the Dutch captain said as they approached. "Van Twiller knows about this, but doesn't pay it much heed. But it may help explain why Europeans mistrust the natives so much."

He struck off inland, crossing the beach and climbing up the sandbank, then walking into the scrub forest beyond. Gordon fell in beside him, Pete and the other Dutchmen a step behind.

"There's mistrust on both sides," Gordon said.

"*Ja*, no doubt. But there is something you need to remember, up-timer," de Vries said. "When the Dutch have a dispute with the English—or the former English, the Puritans—each knows that the other is dealing with civilized men. We have our wars and our brutalities: we kill each other, sometimes we give no quarter. But that is a matter between soldiers."

"What's your point, Captain?"

"Merely this." De Vries pushed through some underbrush and swept aside some low-hanging branches, so that they could see beyond a line of trees to a cleared land. There was the vaguest outline of a palisade, within which Gordon could clearly see the crooked foundations of several buildings, overgrown and broken; from where they stood, he could make out a half-dozen little crosses, obviously marking graves—and they, too, were overgrown and uncared for.

This had once been some kind of settlement—and it had clearly been abandoned for several years.

"I have heard up-timers speak of the great injustice done to the native peoples in the time to come, how they were cheated and oppressed, killed and herded into—what is the word? *Reservations*. Yes, reservations. Prisons without walls, far from their native lands. All of this and more because they were not *civilized*, because they did not accept the Savior, or simply because they were different.

"But they did *this*, up-timer. Five years ago a group of merchant adventurers—the great patroon Kiliaen van Rensselaer and several others, including my cousin David and Captain Blauvelt of *Staat van Hoorn*—saw great promise for this place, far from New Amsterdam and enough out of the way of Virginia that it could thrive. They built a fort here and transported more than two dozen settlers and called it *Zwaanendael*: Swan's Valley.

"But when we returned a year later with fifty more colonists, we found the fort burned to the ground, the buildings destroyed, the ashes scattered."

There was real anguish in his voice; Gordon could barely look at the Dutchman, and he found that he had nothing to say.

"The settlers gathered up what we could of the remains and buried them there. Later news came of what had happened: a party of Indians had come into the settlement and while they were talking of *friendship* and *trade* they cut down the men where they stood—they even butchered the dogs. Then they burned it all down. They took the shield bearing the Dutch arms and used it to make tobacco pipes.

"The company thought about trying to reestablish the colony," de Vries said, looking away from Gordon. "But this was a place full of death—and Van Rensselaer believed that with the coming of you up-timers there would be changes here in the New World as well. The new settlers were sent to New Netherland, and that was the end of *Zwaanendael*."

"I assume that the settlers did nothing to offend the Indians."

"You take their side? You side with the murderers?"

"No, damn it, I—I'm trying to understand this, Commander. Are you saying that a group of Indians just wandered in one day and began massacring innocent civilians? No provocation, no warning, no hostility until..."

"*Ja*," de Vries said. He poked Gordon in the breastbone with his index finger. "*Ja*, that is exactly what I am saying, up-timer. This is the part of the world you live in that you never seem to understand. I was trying to explain it to you, before. The Indians are not like the Dutch, or the English, or, God in Heaven, like you *Amerikaner*. They are a race apart. Why they choose to do this or that is beyond my understanding: but they *do not think or act like us*.

"It may be that you can make the *Englesen* and the *Daner* and the men of New Amsterdam become friends, if they see a common enemy in the French. But as for the natives...they will never be friends: not as long as they are capable of doing *this*."

"I saw worse in Germany," Pete said. "And there was worse than that before the Ring of Fire. When Tilly's army broke into Magdeburg they butchered somewhere around thirty thousand people. *Civilized* peoples do this sort of thing to each other all the time."

"That is war," de Vries said. "This..." He let the branches go, obscuring the view of *Zwaanendael*. "This was just butchery."

Pete was getting angry. "You want me to describe cases of sheer butchery in Europe? How much time you got, de Vries? It'll take me hours."

De Vries turned away and began walking back toward the beach. The Dutch captain didn't seem inclined to continue the conversation.

Pete shrugged his shoulders and turned to follow. Gordon put his hand on his younger brother's shoulder; Pete turned back to face him.

"I don't understand the point of this demonstration," Gordon said.

"Oh, no?" Pete answered. "I do. He wants you to understand exactly where he stands...where most of them stand. They'd probably all be happy with how things turned out for the Indians up-time. But not satisfied."

"What do you mean?"

"They'd probably only be satisfied if we'd been able to exterminate them entirely. So who exactly are the savages here? You think he'd cheer up any if I told him about Wounded Knee? The Trail of Tears? We could spend all day arguing about who's a savage and who isn't."

Pete turned and walked away, leaving Gordon to follow on his own.

Chapter 27

New Amsterdam

Watching *Challenger* and its great dirigible depart, accompanied by the *Staat van Hoorn*, was a relief for Stephane. He had kept out of sight for a day and a half, remaining as far away from the docks as possible. He found himself a job spreading animal waste at the West India Company garden, along the river next to the Heerenweg. The close encounter with Peter Chehab near the wall on the *kill* that separated New Amsterdam from the *bouweries* had shaken him. He wasn't sure what the American might have done if he had caught him.

What would Stephane have even said to him? *Pardonnez-moi: I am no more than a simple spy. I mean you no harm—I am only here to report your actions and your movements.*

He suspected that would not have been received in a civilized manner.

New Amsterdam was almost too small a place in which to get lost. It was scarcely a square mile in size—though it had grown considerably in the last few years, with immigrants coming in from other settlements and extending the town into the *bouweries* north of the island's tip. Fort Amsterdam and the residences of the governor and the chief minister, along with the great customhouse and the mill, dominated the town. Just north was the great marketplace: not so great by Paris standards, but big enough for the traders with their piles of furs that were the wealth of the colony. Beyond that was the long highway, the *Heerenweg*, that ran straight to and through the wall and beyond to the pastures and gardens beyond.

Stephane had come into the town a few days after *Challenger* arrived, riding on a flat boat carrying pelts from upriver. In the end New Amsterdam was just the same as any town; he had relied on his own skill to see and not be seen and had almost paid for it. But Stephane congratulated himself on disappearing from sight when the up-timer began to sprint toward him. He had no chance against someone who had been at home in the back alleys and across the rooftops of Paris. New Amsterdam was no Paris...but alleys were alleys and roofs were roofs.

And soldiers were not spies. Peter Chehab was an able-bodied young man, but he had not learned from Marcel.

When *Challenger* was over the horizon Stephane relaxed and found himself a perch out of the way on the dock, and thought about his prospects. He also found himself thinking about Marcel for the first time in a few years; he had shunted that all aside almost from the time Servien had made him the offer of employment in the prison of L'Abbaye.

As he looked out at the ships at anchor in the East River and the fishing boats coming home from the Sound, he wondered what he should do with himself. He had written a letter to Servien in Québec, which Champlain had promised to deliver; it might be on its way now, the first intelligence he had been able to provide. It might also have simply been discarded, or it might be lost en route. There were no doubt other agents who had not landed in the situation in which he found himself—thousands of miles from home, with no firm idea of what he should do and where he should go.

There were two choices. He could pursue the up-timers to Virginia or wherever they were going. They still clearly had a mission, and Servien would want to know what they learned and what they did. Or, he could find passage home to France, either by way of Holland or some other route, and present himself to Servien and report in person what he had learned.

The first course was also a leap in the dark. The size of the continent suggested that Virginia was very far away, just as Québec had been very far away. New Amsterdam was a fine place to hide in plain sight: as small as it was, there were men of every description speaking every conceivable language, making him yet another foreigner in a town full of foreigners.

The second course... was a leap in the dark. If his employer had written him off, dismissed him as lost or dead or run away, then his reception in Paris, if he ever got there, might be far less friendly. And what would he do? Present himself at the gates of the *Palais-Cardinal* and ask for an audience?

Marcel would have laughed.

When the sun went down he found his way into a tavern, seeking his first good meal in New Amsterdam. The tavern was located at the back of the West India Company Brewery, an ugly pile of a building that faced the market, directly opposite the fort. The front of the ordinary was on a muddy path beside a creek that ran from the dock northwestward into the middle of the island.

A tavern attached to a brewery had certain advantages—at least the beer was fresh. It was crowded: it seemed that men from every walk of life were present, from well-dressed *burghers* to laborers dressed as he was. Everyone's coin was equally good. Money and beer were great equalizers.

He was prepared to find a quiet corner where he could watch and listen. The patrons were still buzzing about the dirigible, spinning all kinds of fanciful stories about the up-timers and their wondrous inventions. He knew better—that the dirigible itself was made of materials from this century, that it could not fly fast or very far, and only carried a few men—usually the two up-timers. It was a toy: a clever toy, but no more. He could have told that to anyone present: but he wasn't interested in doing anything of the sort.

If things had been different, he would have spoken to no one, and he later wondered what had motivated him. Perhaps it was curiosity, or gallantry, or just a whim of fate: but as he stepped between two burghers amply overfilling their suits who faced away from each other, he spied a young woman sitting alone at a tiny table near a dirty window open to the early summer night, a meager plate of bread and cheese and a mug placed before her. She looked up and it seemed to Stephane as if she had picked him out of everyone in the room.

Stephane had never thought of himself as a ladies' man. That was a diversion that required time and money that he had never had. But he had no doubt that he was handsome, after a fashion: the little portrait that Captain Champlain had done was pleasant to look at.

She wants something, Stephane thought—*something that no one in this room has been able to offer.* It was time for him to walk away: to stay out of sight and draw no attention, to be *muet.* But he didn't walk away—he walked forward to stand at the table.

"Good evening," he said.

"Mynheer," she answered. Her accent was not Dutch: it was, he thought, Picard.

"May I sit?"

"Please." She gestured to another chair nearby, which was unoccupied. He sat; it was a bit warm—evidently it had been vacated.

He took a drink and set his mug on the table. "I should ask to what I owe the honor of your company, *goede dame.*"

"I . . ." She picked up a piece of the cheese, looked at it and set it back on the plate. "I needed to talk to someone."

"And you chose me."

"I did not mean to impose . . ." she looked away, then at him. "No, to be fair, I am imposing, but you had a kind face."

Stephane smiled. "Thank you. But there is something you want."

"You are very direct."

"I am interested in a good use of my time," he said quietly, and her face showed disappointment. "Are you offering something?"

She did not reply at once, nor did her posture or expression change.

Not the world's oldest profession, he thought. That was probably just as well. He had learned as soon as he came to New Amsterdam that the profession in question was largely under the control of a man named Van Vees, whom everyone called the Turk, and his wife, the keeper of a well-known and much more disreputable ordinary that was closer to the harbor. This young thing would not stand a chance if she went into competition with that sort.

"This place," she said at last, "is not as I imagined it. I had hoped that it would be more welcoming, more as it had been described to me."

"How was it described?"

"As a wonder, a new paradise. Like—home—but greater, sweeter. Instead it is a filthy, grubby place. A *tiny* place."

Stephane smiled, thinking of his recent experience.

"Are you mocking me?"

"No—I think you have not seen the land as I have seen it. The world is wider than just this little village. Not a day's walk from here are forests so vast that you might think there is no end to them. The river to the west of this island flows from a great wilderness, where men hunt for plentiful game."

"I have been told that the land is full of savage murderers. It is one of the reasons that I have not left here—there is nowhere safe to go."

"Why do you not return to your home?"

"I . . ."

She looked away from him, her chin held high, but her face set in a stony expression. He immediately understood the answer: there was no money to go home. For better or worse, she was here for good.

And he didn't even know her name.

"I am Stephane," he said. "Stephane der Hoefe."

"My name is Eugenie," she answered. "Forgive me, Mynheer der Hoefe. My Dutch is book-learned and almost at its limit. I . . . am almost at my limit." The words conveyed a world of meaning.

"Would you rather speak French?" he said.

"*Oui*," she answered eagerly. "That would be wonderful," she continued. "I am here in New Amsterdam, for better or worse. When I boarded the ship to take me here, I expected to come to a situation where I would have employment, a place to stay, a . . . a livelihood."

"You had a position awaiting you. But something happened, I presume."

"My patron is dead."

"And he made no provision . . ."

"No," she answered. "None. His family did not have use for me and—and turned me out."

The voice inside Stephane's head said, *This is none of your affair. You can offer her nothing; you cannot help her.*

He did not listen.

Eugenie was clearly in a difficult situation. She was alone, unescorted, in a foreign land whose inhabitants did not speak her native language, which was clearly French. But she had not resorted to tears, and had not offered the one commodity that women always had available.

"I am myself new to this town, Mademoiselle Eugenie. I am on my way from here to there—and I do not know anyone in New Amsterdam who could make use of your talents, which are..."

"Cooking and sewing, of course, and my father is...was... a dyer. I have some skill and knowledge, and I was originally to assist in a dyeworks."

"Surely this is a valuable professional skill. Why on earth would they turn you out?"

"The family—the younger brother and sister of the one who was to employ me—have no interest in the cost and work of setting up a dyeworks here in New Amsterdam. It is a profitable business, eventually. I was told that the natives, the savages, were fond of cloth in bright colors; this was why I came here."

She looked directly at him. "I am not a helpless woman, Monsieur der Hoefe. I do not wish charity. I did not leave my home and my family only to throw myself at the mercy of anyone who could provide me with a position. I thought that I would be treated with respect and fairness, but have found neither."

"What do you plan to do?"

"I have not decided." Her voice was tinged with vague despair, as if she saw her options narrowing and no solution in sight.

What can she do? Stephane thought. *New Amsterdam is too small, too provincial. It is no place for a single woman, even one with a valuable skill.*

She could not go home for lack of money, but she did not wish to go home in any event, he realized. Her father—the dyer—might be dead or infirm. Her family likely had some other plans for her, and she had walked away, or rather sailed away.

Then it came to him.

"You must leave New Amsterdam," he said. "This is no fit place. You must find a place where your skills will be prized."

"I cannot—I will not—go home."

"No," he said. "I do not counsel that. If I may offer advice... I realize that I have just made your acquaintance, so if I may be forward..."

"*S'il vous plait,*" she said, her voice firm.

"I recommend that you consider another colony—in fact, there is only one destination that is worthy of your attention. You should go to Virginia."

"Virginia? The English colony?"

"Yes." *Virginia*, Stephane thought. *That is where you should go. Where I should go as well. I could not decide my course—and it has been decided for me.*

"I speak very little English. My Dutch is far better, as poor as it is."

"I suspect that the wool that is spun, and cloth that is woven and dyed, speaks no language. Your talents transcend all such barriers, Mademoiselle; it is merely a matter of finding someone who will recognize it."

"How shall I find such a person?"

"Leave it to me."

"I shall be forever in your debt, Monsieur der Hoefe. I...I do not know how to thank you. My prayers are answered."

Stephane picked up his mug and gently touched it to Eugenie's.

Virginia, he thought. *My prayers answered as well.*

Chapter 28

Eugenie had taken a room in a small rooming house on Beaver-gracht, in sight of the marketplace. She told him that she had carefully managed her remaining money so that she had another week of room and board. He escorted her to the door of the house, where they parted with no more than a squeeze of the hand.

As he walked back to his even meaner lodgings at a sailor's doss, he wondered why he had jumped in with both feet. He could find no answer—but he felt that he had done the right thing, and that it was moving him in the right direction.

Among her meager possessions, Eugenie had pen and ink and a small supply of writing paper; and since she had been turned away from her expected employment she had sat down a number of times to write a letter home, describing her situation—how she was not properly professionally established, and how New Amsterdam had not turned out to be a Dutch Toulouse. It was no more than a grubby little town that seemed to be home to no one, just transients of all kinds on their way to somewhere else.

She had not even reached the point of putting pen to paper, even to summarize her thoughts. That would just be a waste of valuable paper, and she was unwilling to give in to the despair that she surely felt. It was as she had told the young French-man Stephane: she was almost at her limit, and did not truly know what she was going to do. Even his reassurance—*Leave it to me*—did not give her license, she thought, to permit hope to appear in her mind.

It was not supposed to be this way.

Eugenie had been trained with the skills of a dyer, carrying on a tradition that had been in her family for generations, and had made her home town famous for centuries. Toulouse was renowned for its skilled craftsmen, who were able to color fine fabrics with vibrant colors. In her kit she carried samples of her work that she had intended to show to her employer, as well as her own small kerchief that was tinted with the magnificent blue: not the flat, pale color imparted by indigo, or the indifferent hue provided by Brazilian dyewood, but the true, brilliant shade that could only come from the *coquagnes*, the balls of dye color that had been prepared for centuries by Toulousain *pastilleurs* for use in the dyeworks.

It was almost a lost art. The other, lesser but naturally cheaper substances, particularly indigo, had superseded the plant-based *coquagnes* that had been used by dyers for centuries. Her father told her stories of those times, when dyeing had made Toulouse wealthy; but the industry had been crushed by progress, despite an effort by the royal government to reestablish and support it in her great-grandfather's time. The industry was still popular in Toulouse, of course, but it was done not by a *teinteurier* but rather an untrained worker. Nowadays most customers didn't care: indigo blue was good enough and, she supposed, only a craftsman could tell the difference.

In Toulouse, in the last few years, some of the *teinteurier* blamed it on the arrival of the up-timers. It was an easy excuse, but Eugenie knew better; even before he was injured and disabled in an accident, her father made sure to pass on the secrets and tricks of the trade. No up-timer alchemy could take the place of skills honed over centuries.

The blue. It was always about the blue. When Monsieur—Mynheer—Ten Broeck had written to the dyers guild a year ago looking for a skilled craftsman to come to New Amsterdam, the letter had come into her father's hands, and he had written back, telling the Dutchman that he had just the craftsman.

You must go, Eugenie, he had said to her. *There is no future here: too many poseurs, too many unskilled men tramping on the prerogatives of the guild...*

You are much more capable, she had said. *It is you they want.*

I will not leave Toulouse, he had answered. *There is only one place I will go, and it is to sit at the right hand of the Father. The new world is for you, my dear girl. Go and bring the Dutchmen the blue, and they will make you rich and happy.*

But the blue was not enough motivation for Mynheer Ten Broeck's sons. They only wanted to drink and fight. The dyeworks project disappeared as if it had never been...leaving Eugenie with no position and no immediate prospects.

But maybe she would find both in Virginia.

For two days Stephane watched and listened, paying particular attention to ships as they came and went. New Amsterdam's resident population was fairly small, but its transient population was several times larger—pelt traders and hunters, traders from the Connecticut River, natives, and ships from Virginia and the Caribbean. It was these last to which he directed his closest notice, because any vessel coming from Virginia was likely going back there.

His patience was rewarded when a sailing vessel came to dock bearing a flag he did not recognize: a light-colored banner with a seal showing a queen with crown and orb, and a kneeling native bearing a sheaf of something. After a visit from the *schout*, dockhands began unloading bundles of what could only be cured tobacco.

Once he was satisfied that the unloading process was well in hand, the master-on-board and a New Amsterdammer—who looked to be the merchant who was taking charge of the cargo— made their way to the tavern where Stephane had met Eugenie a few nights earlier. Stephane followed, and when he came into the common room, he saw them sitting together, speaking about business. He found a place to sit where he could watch and listen.

"...Of course it's Orinoco, Piet. You know I would not cheat you."

"I know no such thing. It smelled right, though."

They touched mugs, a hollow metallic sound. "Tell me the news," the Virginian said. "I see the wall is coming along."

"It is a public project, so like all such things, it is one guilder for the wall and one guilder for the director-general. We make that fat man rich and beggar ourselves."

"Get rid of him."

"He's the nephew of the great *patroon*. We can't get rid of him. He'll be bleeding us dry as long as the city stands."

"City." The Virginian belched. "If this place ever becomes a city I'll dance naked in the public square. It's a damn good harbor, wasted on you Dutchmen."

"If you weren't making me wealthy I would knock you on your ass. But you know what I heard? According to the up-timers who were here, in *their* history New Amsterdam becomes an *English* place, and it becomes a great city. We're spared that. And as for it being wasted on the Dutch, Edward, we are the most skilled sailors in the world, I will have you know. So. What will you buy this trip?"

"Pelts, of course, but also beer from this fine establishment. And next time we come up I may have something other than tobacco to sell."

"Do tell."

"The Burgesses are admitting skilled workers of all kinds, Piet—they have so many projects and so many...what is the word? Undertakers—"

"*Entrepreneurs*," the Dutchman said. "That's what the up-timers call them."

"Sounds French," Edward sniffed. "I'll stick with a good English word. As I say, there are undertakers for every blessed thing under the sun. Down near Cape Charles one of the settlements is making a more serious effort at sericulture, of all things."

"What the hell is that?"

"*Silk*," the Virginian said. "Old King James of blessed memory was mad for silk, and the planters have been trying to make money at it since the starving time. Between silk growing, and glass, and potash, and weaving—every planter in the colony is bringing in any skilled labor he can find to get extra income."

"Where are you getting all the skilled workers? It must cost hundreds of guilders to bring them across the sea—and I daresay they don't come out from England anymore."

"I'd hoped to find some of them in this pesthole of yours, Piet. Every time I dock here I see men, arrived from every land, having every last *stuiver* pulled from their pockets. I will find work for them—and profit for their employers."

"Their owners?"

"Not *owners*. A work contract is not slavery: they sign on for a certain amount of time, work their trade, and then are free to make their own way. It's better than begging on the streets of New Amsterdam. Know of anyone looking for work?"

"Do you think I'd tell you if I did?"

The Virginian reached into his wallet and slapped several coins on the table. "If you're paid enough, you grubbing Dutchman. Find me some skilled workers looking to emigrate—and I'll make it worth your while."

Finally the Dutchman pleaded business and stood up, very slightly shaky on his feet, and made his way out of the tavern. The Virginian remained at his table for a little longer, perhaps enjoying a few rare moments of quiet before returning to the sounds—and smells—of dockside.

Stephane stood and walked to the man's table.

"I beg your pardon, Mynheer," he said in English. The man looked up, his eyes very slightly watery.

"What do *you* want?"

"I could not help but overhear your conversation," Stephane said. "I understand that you seek skilled workers for Virginia."

"That is true." He looked Stephane up and down. "What sort of skill do you possess, then?"

"I speak on behalf of a...friend," Stephane said. "An expert dyer, whose position here in New Amsterdam has not been all that was expected."

"You heard what I said about this town."

"Yes, Mynheer, I did."

"You are not offended?"

"I am merely passing through New Amsterdam myself," Stephane said. "I cannot help but admire your keen observation and wise insight."

The Virginian warmed to the compliment and smiled. "Your friend can read and write?"

"I believe so."

"And he...can present himself? I sail in two days, and am not disposed to wait. There is at least one other here in New Amsterdam, looking for workers for tobacco plantations."

"I can arrange it."

"And you expect to be paid for this service, I suppose."

"If you find my assistance useful, I would not turn it down. But I am content to wait."

✧   ✧   ✧

Stephane knew that his path now led to Virginia. He would escort Eugenie to meet with the Virginia merchant—and he would find his own way to go to the colony. If he was still in the employ of Monsieur Servien, there would be plenty enough to see that he could report on it.

Eugenie, for her part, was overjoyed. She was sure—and Stephane was confident—that she would convince the Virginian that her skills would be useful.

"Even if I must learn English," she added to him.

A few *stuivers* procured a pen and paper to compose a letter for his patron. He found a quiet place in the tavern to write, and as the wan afternoon light filtered through the open window, he set to work.

> *Most esteemed Monsieur:*
> *I now find myself in New Amsterdam, the Dutch colonial town. The up-timer ship has recently departed in the company of a Dutch vessel, the* Staat van Hoorn, *with their destination (I suspect) Virginia. It is certain that they are given authority by the government of the USE to treat with foreign colonies, as they were granted an interview by Director-General van Twiller—though I have heard that it was fruitless*

He paused; it was likely a true statement, but it wasn't certain. All he knew was that it had not resulted in any commitment from van Twiller. The Dutch colonists in New Amsterdam were not fearful of an invasion from New France: if anything, they were *indifferent* to any possible threat. He struck out *fruitless*, knowing that Monsieur Servien would still know that he had written it: but he was not about to copy out the entire letter again.

> *unsuccessful. I shall endeavor to make my way to Virginia by whatever means possible; there are coastal traders that travel between New Amsterdam and Jamestown, and it should be possible to find passage on one of them.*

He wondered if he should describe the encounter he had had with the up-timer Peter Chehab. Servien would want to know of it—but it would not redound to Stephane's credit, even if he had escaped a confrontation. Still, it would be wise to give some warning to his employer regarding the threat.

> *I must ask Monsieur to note that the capabilities of these up-timers must not be underestimated. We sometimes assume that they are dependent on superior technology or future knowledge; yet withal there are many among them who are simply capable—and therefore dangerous. Though the expedition of this vessel might have seemed at the outset to be amateur, it is possible that this is a far more sophisticated mission than I had originally suggested.*

Stephane paused. This was not what Monsieur Servien would like to hear: that his trusted observer had misjudged. He hedged his remark with conditionals: *might, possible, seemed . . .* but Servien would read right through it: *there is more here than expected, and Stephane did not see it.*

He wasn't sure *how* he could have seen it; but Servien's standards were high, and he might well be unforgiving. But there was no way to know. Indeed, there was no way to know whether Servien had heard a single thing from him since *Challenger* set sail from Hamburg six months ago.

> *I shall have a better sense of the situation when I reach Virginia, as the success of the mission of the up-timer ship will depend on the ability to make common cause with the planters. Indeed, this situation may have already been resolved, though there is no information here in New Amsterdam that anything of the sort has taken place.*
>
> *In any case I shall endeavor to provide whatever information I can obtain when I reach Jamestown, with the intention of finding passage home thereafter.*
>
>

I therefore remain
Your obedient servant
S. Hoff

In Stephane's reflections on his experiences over the last half year, he had wondered at the curious turns of fate that had brought him to where he now found himself. Things could have been more to his plan, and better to his liking. But, upon consideration, it could have been much worse.

It was clear to him, however, that there were times that his fate was in the hands of a merciful and just God. The encounter with Eugenie, the merest accident of chance, guided him now in the direction he knew to be right.

As he sat in the tavern, his finished letter in his pocket and ready to be sent by some means, the capability for the next part of his journey dropped into his hands.

A ceramic mug was suddenly placed in front of him, interrupting his thoughts. He looked up and saw the server moving across the crowded room, dispensing mugs to every patron.

"What..." he began, but one of the men at the next table gestured with his mug toward a young man near the center of the room. Numerous others were raising their mugs to him, and he was smiling and gesturing. He had obviously been imbibing for some time.

"A free one for all," the gesturing man said. "Drink up. Maybe there'll be more."

Stephane shrugged and drank, watching the proceedings. The young man was receiving congratulations and well-wishings from the others in the tavern; he looked to be a common laborer, not the sort that could afford to buy everyone in the house a drink.

Curious, Stephane took himself and his mug over to offer his own congratulations.

"Thank you for the drink," he said in Dutch. "What is the occasion?"

"Last night of freedom," the young man said, his eyes bright, his voice slightly slurred. "Might as well enjoy it."

"I do not understand."

He patted his vest. Stephane heard a crinkling sound, like paper. "I have my papers, friend."

Stephane sipped from his mug, carefully maneuvering out of the way of a reveler who had clearly been in the tavern far too long that night.

"Papers," the young man repeated. "*Leercontract*. Work and food. More than I'll find here."

A *leercontract*—a work contract. An indenture. What he would procure for Eugenie—except, no doubt, less prestigious than the sort offered to a dyer's daughter.

"How long must you work?"

"Ha ha," he answered. "From dawn till dusk." He laughed as if it was the greatest joke in the world. "Six years, and at the end I will receive my own grant of land. No land here: the great *patroons* have it all. No land for anyone but those *schoften*."

Clearly leaving town, Stephane thought. No one would use a term like *schoft*—bastard—to describe one of New Netherland's great landholders unless he was planning to depart the colony.

Last night of freedom, Stephane thought. "Where do you go, friend?"

"The place where any man can make his own fortune," he answered. "Virginia. They do not come to Virginia from England now, so they seek their indentures elsewhere." He patted his vest again. "Six years," he said. "And then I am free—and then I will be rich."

He raised his mug. "Virginia!" he shouted. "And freedom!"

His balance was none too steady; with a lurch he fell forward into Stephane's arms. He was young and whipcord-strong, at least twenty pounds heavier and four or five inches taller—but Stephane was ready for him and embraced him like a long-lost brother. After a moment he handed the young man off to another, as a dance developed in the middle of the tavern floor. It was not difficult for him to escape the revels and make his way out into the brisk early-summer evening.

The young man's name, according to the papers, was Andries Cuypers; he was twenty-one, in good health, in possession of all of his teeth, fingers and toes. The indenture was to a planter named Paulet; Cuypers was to board ship for Virginia the next morning.

It might require some footwork at the other end, but it would certainly do as a cover. Stephane had health and the requisite fingers and toes, and was not much older than twenty-one. All that remained was to make sure that the *real* Andries Cuypers did not appear on the dock tomorrow morning to claim his place.

Fortunately, everyone knew where to find the Turk; and fortunately, there was more than enough of Monsieur Servien's coin to obtain the services of one of his employees for a modest price, to help make a young man's last night of freedom pleasurable . . . and long-lasting.

Chapter 29

Maryland

As *Challenger* and *Staat van Hoorn* made their way up into Chesapeake Bay, it was obvious to Gordon that Captain John Smith had been right: it was as beautiful a place as any on earth, and as perfect as anywhere in North America to set up a colony.

And it had almost not happened at all.

Maryland had been settled only a few years earlier by English Catholics, by proprietary charter granted originally to George Calvert, the first Lord Baltimore. He had been ennobled first and become a Catholic second, while still a baron in Ireland. He had been a friend and staunch supporter of King James, but had resigned from public office when Charles became the king of England in 1625, partially to avoid embarrassing the young king by being an Irish Catholic close to the throne. He was already deeply involved in a scheme to take as many Catholics as possible away from England proper, and settle them in a colony he'd named Avalon—in Newfoundland. But the land was terribly unfertile, and the winters were terribly fierce, and using his continued influence and good will with the crown was able to swap his Newfoundland patent for a better one in a more hospitable land.

It was signed by the Privy Seal in March, 1632, but because of various objections—some of them coming from the existing

Virginia landholders and investors—it did not actually pass the
seals and receive its charter until the end of June. In the months
in between, Sir George Calvert, the first Lord Baltimore, had
unfortunately gone to an early grave at age fifty-two, leaving
the matter in the hands of his two sons Cecilius and Leonard.

It had been intended that the process of setting up the new
colony would be a slow and careful one. The Calvert brothers
set up an office in Bloomsbury, at the upper end of Holborn,
under the auspices of the Jesuit fathers in London, advertising
for skilled men of all professions to join the expedition (which
at the outset consisted mostly of Catholic gentlemen and their
households). The Calverts had seen what happened when a colony
was established without advance study, without preparation, and
without funds. Their father had seen to it that the charter had
many favorable terms and described a rich land, and they in turn
made every provision they could to equip the colony properly,
and a good-sized sum was poured into getting it ready.

In the up-time account of Maryland that Gordon had read,
they worked seventeen months on the project, during which
they had to deal with all sorts of intrigues—including attempts
by Virginia representatives to block the issuing and implementa-
tion of the charter, and even attempts to buy off their seamen to
prevent ships from being crewed. They also had to face a loyalty
oath, in which they would have to abjure the pope and swear
allegiance to the king—which was partially avoided by having
many of the would-be colonists embark secretly at a location
further down the English Channel. The two ships intended to
outfit the expedition—the *Ark* and the *Dove*—didn't set sail until
November 1633, and came to Maryland by way of the West Indies
in March of the following year.

From what he had been able to learn from intelligence gathered by Estuban Miro and Leopold Cavriani, Gordon knew that
the Maryland colony they were approaching had been settled by
a smaller, more hastily assembled expedition that had only just
barely escaped England at about the time that King Charles had
sold his rights in the New World to the French.

The second Lord Baltimore had gotten wind of the plan to
sell those rights and had obtained just one ship—the *Dove*, a
sixty-ton pinnace—with about a third of the number of settlers originally anticipated, but including both Calverts. After a

rough voyage to St. Kitts in the dead of winter of 1632, *Dove* had arrived at the Chesapeake about a year earlier than Gordon's history books recalled it. Sometime that summer a trading vessel from Jamestown brought the news that, like Virginia, Maryland colony was now on its own.

"De Vries says they've built a thriving colony," Gordon said to Pete as the ships moved steadily up the bay. "Apparently there are a lot of Protestants there—even among the households of the 'gentlemen.' In fact, they show tolerance for Christians of all stripes."

"Did you say tolerance?"

"Yeah. They have even taken in refugees that manage to make it across the ocean, or that haven't been welcome in other settlements."

"Like New England."

"Well—not so much like New England. Even the people who they don't tolerate turn out to be pretty intolerant. But there are a few New Englanders. There are also a few Jesuits, and they have their own ideas on what people should believe."

"What keeps people from believing that they'd welcome the French here with open arms?"

"Nothing. In fact, little bro, this is the one place we've visited—or plan to visit—where I wouldn't be surprised to see a French ship. I know that de Vries has his sails trimmed and is ready to cut and run if he sees a French flag—and we should be ready to do so as well."

There was no French ship in port.

In fact, there were no ships to speak of in the small, sheltered harbor of St. Mary's, in a narrow, shallow bay on the north side of the Potomac. If their ships had been ships of war, they'd have had no trouble taking the colony—forty or fifty little houses and a prominent church with a high steeple, framed against slightly rising hills behind, surrounded by a palisaded fort with mounted cannon. It was like a picture postcard: unlike most of the places in Europe, and even unlike most of the settlements they'd seen in the New World, St. Mary's looked clean and neat.

Challenger took the lead into the harbor, and to avoid any implication of threat, Gordon had Captain Maartens anchor out of what would have been broadside range, and lower away a boat. He, Pete and Captain Thomas James boarded and rowed to the dock. There was already a welcoming committee: two young, well-dressed men who were clearly brothers, and a middle-aged Catholic priest, complete with tonsure and pectoral. A half dozen armed men stood behind them, with no particular uniform: perhaps they were the closest guys to hand with muskets.

The three men looked worried.

Good, Gordon thought. *Maybe we can make an impressive entrance for a change.*

"Welcome to Maryland," one of the two brothers said as Gordon pulled the boat alongside. "I trust that you come in peace."

"Your trust is well founded," Gordon said. "My name is Gordon Chehab, and I'm here on a trade mission from the State of Thuringia-Franconia." He wanted to say, *take me to your leader,* but he thought he was already in the leader's presence.

"That is one of the provinces of the new country, is it not? The United States of Europe?"

"Yes, my lord," Gordon said, taking off his ball cap.

"Baltimore," he said. "Cecilius Calvert," he added. "My brother Leonard, and Father White."

"A pleasure to meet you, sir."

"Is my reputation so great?"

"I'm from up-time," Gordon said, not sure how to answer that. "My brother Peter," he said, gesturing to Pete. "And Captain Thomas James, who isn't, but he has a bit of a reputation as well."

"My Lord Baltimore," James said, making a leg; clearly he knew his business as a courtier.

"We do not stand on ceremony much here, Captain," Baltimore said. "And we welcome any who come to us in peace. I . . . am interested in knowing the reason for your visit."

"I am as well," Father White said. "This is my first chance to meet up-timers. I'm not sure what to say."

"We don't bite," Pete said. The two Calverts looked at him strangely; Pete gave a half-sincere smile.

Wiseass, Gordon thought. *That's going to get you in trouble someday, little bro, if it hasn't already.* But he kept silent.

"Perhaps we would be more comfortable in the rectory," Father White offered, gesturing toward the church.

"We seem to be drawing visitors from all points of the compass," Baltimore said.

They had arranged themselves around a trestle table in a large, airy room that smelled of dried herbs. The governor of Maryland was, indeed, not inclined toward ceremony: the two Calverts, the two Chehabs, the priest and Captain James sat with ceramic mugs in front of them, a wheel of cheese and a half loaf of bread on the table.

"Really," Gordon said. "Who else have you entertained?"

"We are often visited by our Virginia friends," Baltimore answered. "Most of those in our neighbor colony are friends, in any case. But we have become closer with them since our king determined that he had lost interest. And we see the occasional trading vessel from New Amsterdam. But earlier this spring we had...an ambassador, I suppose you might say."

"A Frenchman."

"Not quite," Leonard Calvert said. "A native, though one clearly accustomed to white man's ways. He gave his name as Savignon, and carried a letter of introduction from the Captain-General of New France, Monsieur Champlain."

"Samuel de Champlain?" Gordon said.

"The very one. He was polite and well spoken, this Savignon: a *courier de bois*, a sort of scout, who traveled alone but seemed quite capable of taking care of himself. He had made his way all the way down to St. Mary's merely to pay us a visit."

"I suspect there was more to it than merely a courtesy call. But do go on."

Baltimore wrapped his hands around his mug and stared into it for a moment, then placed them flat on the table. "Yes, good sir, you are quite correct: it was more than mere courtesy—or curiosity—that drew him to our settlement. He made us an offer."

"An offer you couldn't refuse?" Pete said. The down-timers all looked puzzled. "Forget it," he added.

"He intimated that the king of France was beginning to turn his attention to the New World, and that our little colony was of particular interest since we not only tolerated, but sought to expand the domain of the Holy Catholic Church. His Christian Majesty was most impressed with this, he said. Accordingly, he felt that we should consider the possible advantage of submitting to that monarch's authority at the soonest possible juncture, to obtain a favorable place when all of the Atlantic plantations were brought under French authority."

"I see. I can understand why they might take this approach."

"England is at present not a friendly place for Catholics, Mr. Chehab," Baltimore said. "Especially English Catholics. But for the love King Charles bore for my father, we might not have received enough advance notice of his intention to abandon the New World and we could well have ended up in the lap of the French king. But given the choice, I would like to think that I am still an Englishman, regardless of my king's decision—or the animosity of the average Englishman toward my faith."

"So you're not eager to line up in the new French world order."

"If...I understand you correctly, no. I am not. *We* are not. We did not leave England to become French, though I do not know how we could hold out against them. This Savignon suggested the same."

"I am glad to hear it, my lord," Gordon said. "We'd like to think that the English-speaking colonies here in the New World had common cause, and would want to work together to oppose the French. My country isn't at war with them at the moment, but...who knows when that could change again?"

"I believe that the French are your enemy in the long run," Baltimore answered. "The cardinal is your *particular* enemy."

"I don't think he has it in for me personally," Gordon said. "But yes, he's the one guy that we worry about."

"You should," Leonard Calvert said. "Savignon told us that you would be coming. The envoy told us that the cardinal knew of your mission," Leonard Calvert continued, "and that you would come and try to..."

"Try to *what*?"

"He wasn't clear. Get us to take your side, I suppose. Make common cause with you. Choose to resist the French authority, rather than follow the nation that shared our confession of faith."

"How does he know what we're doing?" Gordon asked. "How did he know we'd turn up at St. Mary's?"

Pete leaned back in his chair. "I think it's pretty obvious, big bro."

"Oh?"

"There's a spy. Someone who is in communication with Richelieu, telling him our every move."

"And how would anyone be doing *that*? By semaphore? By smoke signal? I don't see anyone carrying a radio. There's no way to keep anyone informed. Any intel that Richelieu has—assuming he has any, and this Savignon guy isn't bluffing—is two or three months out of date. Even if there is a spy, I'm not sure why it matters."

"He knows who we are, big bro. He knows our mission, where we're going, what we're doing in the New World. Don't you think it's a problem that the cardinal has that kind of intel?"

"I don't see how. If we were carrying some kind of secret weapon, yeah—if we were transporting troops or arms, if we could affect the balance of power in the New World...but we can't." Gordon looked at the two Calverts. "I'll tell you what we've told just about everyone on this side of the Atlantic. We're in no position to help you very much. This is a *trade* mission; we're trying to see the lay of the land, to learn who's on what side, to see what the French have done or might be doing."

"A trade mission is a convenient cover for your real purpose."

"I guess we don't look too much like traders."

"Commerce takes many forms, Mr. Chehab. You seem better disposed to engage in it than some."

"I guess that's a compliment." Gordon smiled. "My mission, and my country, is ready to extend the hand of friendship to anyone—any colony, any native tribe, anyone who might benefit from our friendship. Depending on where that goes, the USE might be able to help in the future."

"It is not clear that there is much of a future," Leonard Calvert said. "We retain friendship with Virginia—but England has abandoned us, and the French wish for us to give up without a fight."

"Where did he go when he left here?"

The two Calverts looked at each other. "We cannot be sure," Baltimore said at last. "But we have our suspicions."

"I'd like to know what they are."

"We have a...neighbor," Leonard Calvert said. "No: an *intruder*. Four years ago—before your Ring of Fire, before King Charles made his decision, before our father was even given our charter to settle Maryland—a Virginian adventurer named Claiborne established a trading post on Kent Island in the Chesapeake. My brother directed us to request him to depart, which he refused. The matter was brought before the Privy Council in England, but no decision was rendered. And it then became irrelevant when the rights to English settlements were transferred to France."

"But not irrelevant to *us*," Baltimore continued. "William Claiborne was, and remains, an intruder, a trespasser, and worse. He has sought to incite the natives against our colony, though our close neighbors have spurned his advances. A year ago one of my subordinates, Captain Cornwaleys, seized his ship on the Patuxent River and exchanged cannon fire with another. Our neighbors in Virginia Colony have repudiated him—they would rather have friendly relations with Maryland, now that England has abandoned us—but still he remains."

"You think this Savignon might have gone there?"

"I cannot discount the possibility." Baltimore placed his hands on the table, palms down, and made a study of them. "Claiborne has every reason to welcome any envoy who would offer to aid him against us."

"Even if it meant making an alliance with the king of France?"

Baltimore looked up at Gordon. "I do not think he views it that way. Indeed, sir, I do not think most people of his sort give such matters any consideration. Adventurers, explorers, soldiers of fortune all pledge allegiance to foreign flags at times. It is perhaps black and white when one bears a coronet and a grant of arms from one's king; but for an average man, even a gentleman, allegiance comes cloaked in shades of gray."

"And even your black and white is a little unclear, my lord," James said. "Do your loyalties still lie with the king who abandoned you?"

"My loyalty is still to England, Captain," Baltimore said. "King Charles, and King James before him, were friends to our late father. Fear drives the king now: fear and greed. Until the French arrive and the battle is joined, I shall retain the fig leaf of hope that England—*my* England—will come to its senses and restore our status as a colony."

There was quiet for a time. Gordon didn't know what to say, and was grateful that Pete didn't find anything to say.

"Did Savignon tell you what the consequences might be if you did not agree to cooperate with him?" Gordon asked at last.

Lord Baltimore and his brother exchanged glances, as if they were considering whether the answer was something they truly wanted to share.

"Mr. Chehab," Baltimore said. "Have you ever visited London?"

"Can't say that I have, not here or up-time. Why do you ask?"

"London is a huge city, sir, with many shops and factories; they are vulnerable to depredations by both natural and man-made causes. In particular, there is a peculiar species of criminal who preys upon the weakest shop owners and proprietors by informing him that, without his protection, some calamity will surely befall them. Usually those that refuse suffer that result—and usually it happens at his hands."

"I know the type," Gordon said. "It's not peculiar to this century—or to London. We call it the 'protection racket.'"

"Pretty standard stuff," Pete said. "'Nice little colony you've got here,'" he added in his best wiseguy accent. "'Would be an awful shame if something were to happen to it.' So Savignon offered you . . . protection?"

"He allowed as how if we were resistant to his offer, there were natives not very far away whose . . . passions would be unrestrained."

"Nice," Pete said. "He can't be responsible for their actions if you give the wrong answer."

"Something very similar," Baltimore said. "We are ready to defend ourselves, but we are not a nation under arms: we must farm our crops, herd our livestock, conduct business, and attend to any number of other things. There is no way of knowing if he is telling the truth—and if he is, there is no way of knowing where these natives lie in wait."

Zwaanendael crossed Gordon's mind: the overgrown ruins, the field of crosses. Men cut down in the fields as they tilled crops, killed by natives from whom they had no reason to expect hostility.

This could be the same—at the instigation of the French king.

Make an offer they can't refuse, he thought.

He looked at Pete, who shrugged—as if to say, *your play, big bro.*

"What you need is information," Gordon said at last. "If the threat is real, you need to know it. Now *there*," he added, "I think we can help you."

Chapter 30

Jan de Vries picked up a set of dividers and examined it carefully, then set it back down on the chart, its points spreading across the Chesapeake.

"You want to take on the defense of this colony?" he asked, turning his attention to Gordon.

"No," Gordon answered, with a side glance at Pete. "This is reconnaissance only."

"Until the shooting begins."

"Shooting doesn't *need* to begin," Gordon said. "If we're careful."

"Involving yourself—involving us—in a ground operation means that shooting can begin whether you are careful or not. Ask a soldier," de Vries said, looking at Pete.

"What the hell does that mean?"

"It means what it says."

"I am offering them the opportunity to get a look at what they might face. We're going to launch *John Wayne*; Pete will be with the ground force and I'll be in the air. We'll sail up the Chesapeake and see what we can see."

"I still advise against it," de Vries said. "And I expect that Captain Maartens will do the same. Neither my ship nor *Challenger* is built for river sailing. Either or both vessels could founder, run aground, or worse."

He tapped the chart table, which held copies of maps from

the Grantville libraries. By now, a number of down-time artists made a living copying maps, graphs, illustrations—whatever could conceivably be of use—from the various libraries in Grantville, public or private. The precious originals, of course, were rarely allowed to be taken out of the town.

"As excellent as these maps are, they are more than three centuries out of date. After that much time, rivers change their courses. And they certainly change their depths—even if these maps provided depths in the first place, which they don't. They're maps, not nautical charts."

Pete was still focused on the beginning of de Vries' little speech. "What would be worse than foundering or running aground?"

"These savages you expect to find. What if they find *us*? If we are becalmed, or close to shore, or imperiled in any way as we go up into this unknown land, we can come under attack. You are willing...you are *eager* to risk all of that for a handful of colonists?"

"Yes," Gordon said, crossing his arms across his chest. "I am. I don't want to shrug and sail away and see St. Mary's become another *Zwaanendael*. Is that what *you* want, Commander de Vries?"

Challenger made its way slowly upriver. On the second day, they unloaded the dirigible on a stretch of flat river bank and Gordon and Leonard Calvert prepared to take to the air in *John Wayne*, heading across the wooded and hilly lands west of the upper Potomac, while Pete accompanied a scouting party moving inland.

"Don't take any unnecessary chances, little bro," Gordon said when the dirigible was ready to launch. "This isn't cowboys and Indians."

"I'm not a cowboy," Pete said. "And I know. Learned to duck, remember? And *you* better not take any chances."

"I'm in a dirigible."

"You're not immune to attack, when you come low enough—and sooner or later, you have to." Pete squinted at the early-afternoon sun. "Nobody knows what's waiting out there. The French might have an army up in the hills."

"They don't."

"You don't *know* that. We're here to find out."

Gordon looked beyond Pete at the little group of Marylanders waiting for him to join them: half a dozen Englishmen, and an Indian in buckskins who had accompanied them on *Challenger*.

"Just be careful, Pete. There are any number of ways for this to go Charlie Foxtrot. An arrow kills you just as dead as a bullet from a high-powered rifle."

Pete didn't answer. He put his hands on Gordon's shoulders and gave them a little squeeze, then turned and walked away, looking back for just a moment as if to acknowledge.

Just as *John Wayne* was ready for launch, Gordon saw Ingrid Skoglund approaching across the open field where it had been inflated.

Gordon waited for her to reach him. She was alone—Sofia was, presumably, still back aboard *Challenger*—and had a determined look on her face to which he had become accustomed.

"What can I do for you?"

Ingrid looked up at the dirigible and then back at Gordon. "You are going to launch your airship shortly, I see."

"Yes. Leonard Calvert and I will be doing some exploration."

"I see. I...should like to accompany you."

Her voice was completely level, but Gordon saw fear in her eyes; it was something he'd seen back in Albuquerque, years ago—usually the first time someone decided they wanted to go up in a balloon.

"I can't promise it will be comfortable. It's a pretty spartan setup."

"I am not concerned about *comfort*, Gordon. I merely wish to—"

"Yeah. Go for a ride. Where's Sofia? I'm pretty sure I can't carry both of you along with Mr. Calvert, not for any distance, anyway..."

She smiled. "Sofia does not have any desire to go up in your ship. She does not like the sea, but is terrified of the idea of flying."

"And you aren't?"

"Of course I am. But that should not prevent me from accompanying you. Even unescorted by Sofia."

"I hadn't considered inviting you. Is that an oversight on my part?"

"An assumption."

"Oh?"

"That I would not be interested, or that I would be too frightened. Either way, the assumption is false; if this expedition someday requires me as its medical professional to travel in the airship, I should be accustomed to the experience. Since this is not an emergency, I shall have time to do so."

"Very matter of fact."

"Thank you."

"So you are not frightened."

"I didn't say that, Gordon." She looked up at the side of *John Wayne* again, as if affirming its existence. "I said that I would not be *too* frightened."

The plan, as Gordon and Pete had sketched it out, was to sail up the Potomac River as far as practical and then use *John Wayne* to scout inland for signs that the Indians were on the warpath. They'd chosen to go up the Potomac rather than further up Chesapeake Bay, in part because Lord Baltimore had suggested that the local natives were not numerous and were by and large a peaceful lot—and in any case, the threat, if there was one, would be coming from tribes allied with the French. An attack of the sort that had destroyed *Zwaanendael*—which could presumably be launched by the same Nanticoke Indians—would be repulsed by the strength that St. Mary's had available; it would take something bigger.

De Vries was unable to provide any information on that, and Gordon had frustratingly little information at his disposal. The French had allies among the Iroquois Confederacy: he'd learned that much at New Amsterdam. But their native lands were two hundred miles away. On the other hand, this Savignon character was an Iroquois of some stripe, so that suggested a tribe allied with the confederacy.

All Gordon had to go on was a half dozen books he'd brought with him, and a B- from high school history.

It wasn't enough—and it wasn't clear how much of it applied any more.

Less than half an hour after *John Wayne* lifted off, Gordon caught sight of the largest cross he had ever seen—and he'd seen plenty of them; back in West Virginia, every fourth hillside and every other hay field seemed to have three crosses arranged in a line, the middle one taller than the others. But this one cross was massive. The upright appeared to be hewn from the bole of one single tree, with another massive trunk arranged as the crosspiece, completely whitewashed. It was set up in a clearing on a small island on the starboard side of the boat, with a little altar of white stones placed in front of it.

"What's that?" he asked of Leonard Calvert. The younger man's reaction to flying reminded Gordon very much of his own; instead of being afraid of the height or overawed by the technology, the Marylander was obviously enthralled by the rush of being aloft— the impression given by the vistas and the change of perspective seemed to overwhelm any other emotion. He stood beside Gordon at the controls. Ingrid had found a seat near the center of the car.

"That marks where we first landed," Calvert said. "When we came ashore in our own chartered land, we erected that cross and held a Mass of thanksgiving that the Lord had brought us safely here."

"A noble deed," Ingrid said.

"Yes," Gordon agreed.

"But you didn't build your colony there."

"We did at first. We laid out three houses and a barn—but it was clear that the island was far too small. So we took *Dove* and explored until we found our present location."

"But you didn't move the cross."

"It's a monument, Gordon, not a public building," said Ingrid. "It marks an event."

"That's right," Calvert said. He looked away from Gordon and out at the cross, his face radiant in the afternoon sun. "Why would we?"

"Well, it's . . . I don't know. It seems untended, vulnerable."

"You mean to say that we should move it to our colony to protect it."

"Yes. It looks like the sort of thing that someone might come and just knock down for the hell of it."

Calvert frowned, as if he were considering the proposition. "No one from our colony would do that, and I don't think that the Indians care much about it one way or the other. Father White goes there from time to time to say a Mass to commemorate our voyage here, but otherwise it's left alone.

"Is that something that up-timers do, knock things down . . . 'for the hell of it'?"

"Apparently they do sometimes," Ingrid said.

"*I* don't," Gordon said, glancing at Ingrid. "But yes, that sort of thing happened all the time. Vandalism, you know."

"I do not know," Calvert said. "'Vandalism.' An interesting choice of words. You mean like the Vandals, who pillaged ancient Rome."

More like a biker gang, Gordon thought. In his mind's eye, he imagined Pete—a heavier-set, shaggier Pete with a beard and a leather jacket with a Harley and a group of his fellow delinquents, committing some random act of violence or destruction...for the hell of it. The image almost made him laugh out loud.

Except that Pete, like him, like all of Grantville, got moved three centuries closer to ancient Rome, where there were no biker gangs—just mercenary companies and well-meaning religious refugees.

"Like that," Gordon agreed.

"That makes no sense," Calvert said, watching the cross as they passed by; he casually crossed himself, as if by afterthought. "No one would destroy something just to pass the time—and anyone who did it by intention, at least in Maryland, would wind up in the stocks, or in gaol, or would be sent away. We have far better uses for our time."

When the two ships reached the bend in the Potomac near the place where Aquia Creek emptied into the wider river, *Staat van Hoorn* found an anchorage some distance from the bank while *Challenger* continued to follow the river. They traveled very cautiously—the river might be deep enough for the Dutch vessel, but the water was muddy and had plenty of floating debris. The copies of up-time maps in their possession were useless for this sort of navigation and de Vries wasn't taking any chances. As for Maartens, he didn't want to go on either, but Gordon was determined. Despite his polite (and not-so-polite) opinions, *Challenger* went on alone.

The scouting party was led by a Yaocomico Indian. He dressed in buckskins like the Marylanders, but his long, dark hair was pulled back in a greased queue and he wore a braided bead necklace that he would occasionally touch as he mouthed inaudible syllables—a prayer or a charm, Pete had no idea which. He had a beautiful bow strapped across his back.

The half dozen Marylanders didn't seem too happy to be along on this expedition, with the exception of their senior man, a big, rough-hewn blacksmith named Tyler. He didn't talk much, and seemed to trust the Indian scout implicitly. As they set off into the woods he gave Pete a once-over glance and without a word nodded as if he approved. Pete returned as good as he got: he wasn't looking for approval, but he did want to have some trust among the group.

The scout led them inland along a trail that Pete couldn't even pick out. The land near shore was damp and swampy, but the Yaocomico was very skilled at avoiding sinkholes and other traps. They moved single file without stopping, the Indian in the lead, Pete just behind, and Tyler bringing up the rear behind his more reluctant comrades. The ground cover got ever more rough and the tree canopy ever more dense, so that it felt that they were marching into a forest cave.

They paused after an hour in a clearing heavy with shade. A small creek wandered through the clearing. After the Indian tasted the water the men set to filling their canteens, while he remained erect and alert, as if there might be some interruption to the pastoral scene. Pete leaned against a tree nearby, while the Marylanders seemed oblivious to any danger.

The Indian glanced at Pete and said, "Not thirsty, stranger?"

His English was quite good. Pete didn't know what he had expected, exactly—maybe some sort of *F Troop* parody speech— but this wasn't that.

"No. Not much. Rather keep my eyes open."

"You have been in the woods before."

"Been out in the field." *But yes*, he thought. *Lots of time in the woods when I was young. Not woods like this, but...* "What's your name?"

"I am called Paul."

"That's not a native name."

"No," he said, touching his necklace for a moment. "No one wants to know my real name, even if I chose to share it. 'Paul' is the name I was given when I accepted the sky-father god."

"Christening name. Got it. Are you the first to take on Christianity? From your, uh, tribe, I mean."

"Among the first. Our sachem thought it wise to send one of our people to live with the Marylanders, and they taught me the ways of their god along with many other things."

"And what they call you back among your people—"

"Only matters to my people," Paul said. "Most whites never even ask, stranger."

"Peter. Pete to my friends."

"Peter. Peter and Paul." He fingered his necklace again. "The sky-father god has a sense of humor, bringing us together."

Pete smiled. "Well, no one's going to build a church on me. Did you have a road to Damascus moment?"

Paul thought about that for a moment. "I don't think so."

"Well, no matter. You seem to know your business. Have you been a scout all your life?"

"I am a mere youth. There are many more skilled than I."

"But they could spare you."

"I asked to come," Paul answered. "I wanted to see the men from another time."

"Not much to look at." Pete spread his hands. "I'm a man just like you."

"Like me?" The Indian let out a laugh that rang off the trees and the stones by the creek. Tyler and some of the others looked up. "You have come from the time to come, and you say we are *the same*. How can this be? Answer me a question, Peter from the future: Why are you here? Why did you come here?"

"You mean, why did I come from the future, or why am I on this continent?"

"The first. But I would like to hear your answer to the other as well."

"I haven't the faintest idea," Pete answered. "I come from—" Pete squatted down and picked up a small branch from the forest floor and twirled it between his fingers. "Look. Let me put it this way. For some of the folks from Grantville, the Ring of Fire gave them a second chance."

"What do you mean?"

"A second chance. Well, imagine you're hunting in the woods and you see a deer down there, right near the creek, and you get it in your sights—but a twig snaps under your foot and it's spooked and bounds away. But instead of running out of sight, it stops over there"—he gestured toward the tall grass on the other side of the clearing—"and you get another opportunity to shoot it.

"But I don't see it that way. I think the Ring of Fire was a *first* chance for me. Before we came here I was nowhere and I was going nowhere, and now I'm in a whole other world. I don't know if what I'm doing now makes a difference to anyone but me, but it makes a difference to *me*, and that's what matters."

Paul mulled over the comment for some time, watching the Marylanders finish refilling their canteens and get ready to move again. Then he said, "You are right. You *are* like the rest of these men."

"Oh?"

"You are always thinking about what has gone and what is to come. In the meanwhile the *now* is passing you by. You think about where your life is going, and about the path you have already taken. There is never a thought for the life you are living *now*."

Chapter 31

"You seem preoccupied," Ingrid said.

The Potomac River, too narrow for *Challenger* to navigate, snaked below *John Wayne*, passing through lightly forested lowland. It was the second day of scouting; while the ground force made forays in various directions, the dirigible made sweeps above them.

"I'm worried about Pete."

"Your brother?" Leonard Calvert said.

"My *kid* brother."

"Your 'kid brother' is a soldier, Gordon," Ingrid said. "He has faced danger before. He seems drawn to it."

"I worried about him then too. But this is a whole new world." He glanced at the map clipped to the wall near the dirigible's steering yoke. *We're passing over Washington, D.C.,* he thought. *The White House and the Capitol Building and the Washington Monument should all be there—instead it's nothing but a swamp.*

"He's with Paul," Calvert said. "The Yaocomico scout. He knows his business and will protect the party he leads."

"There," Ingrid said. She had stood and was walking gingerly back and forth, as if she did not trust the floor of the dirigible's car. "I'm reassured. Aren't you?"

"That's the Indian we saw before we took off this morning?"

"Yes," said Calvert. "He lives in St. Mary's. He's converted to the true faith—he doesn't even paint his face anymore."

"I guess that's progress. Are there a lot of—" Gordon couldn't quite wrap his tongue around the Indian name. "Natives living in your community?"

"Very few. There was a Yaocomico village where St. Mary's is now located. They accepted payment to relocate so that we would have access to the deep harbor. We first met them when our ship made landfall. They hunt and fish and grow crops all along both banks of the river. They are a peaceful people, resourceful and slow to anger."

"I know what my brother would say about a tribe like that."

"Indeed. What would he say?"

"In the long run, they're screwed."

"He means that they have no future, my lord," Ingrid said. "Peter Chehab is known for his insights. But he should know—he is an up-timer, after all."

Calvert's brow furrowed as he thought about it, then he realized what Gordon meant. "Not from our colony, surely. We mean them no harm—indeed, we have lived in harmony with them for some years."

"Yeah. They said that up north too. But if history takes its course, this peaceful and resourceful and primitive people will be in the way of the next colony, or the next better harbor, or the road you want to build. Their forests will be the place you want to plant.

"Sooner or later they'll be the ones to move, because you're staying for good. When you told me the name of the tribe— Yow . . ."

"Yaocomico."

"I didn't recognize it." Gordon swept a stray hair out of his face. "I'm willing to bet that's because in the time I come from they're all gone. Their peaceful ways caused them to give it up to some tribe, or some colony, or some invading army."

"We have promised them that we will live in harmony," Calvert said, anger touching his voice. "What would you have us do?"

"I don't know. Make that promise binding on your children and grandchildren." Gordon looked down at the Potomac again, at the Washington D.C. that would never be.

We made promises like that, didn't we? We promised the Wampanoags, and the Iroquois, and the Cherokee, and the Apaches.

Until it was their turn to get out of the way.

What would Mike Stearns say about it? If the USE made a treaty with natives here in America, would it be any more likely to keep the terms, knowing what was done to them in our past?

Gordon wished he had an answer for that, something he could tell Leonard Calvert. The man was perfectly sincere—the Yaocomico were their *friends*, like the Indians who sat down to Thanksgiving dinner in Plymouth side by side with the guys in the Pilgrim hats. *Look how that turned out.*

"The only problem," Ingrid said, "is that, as with all such assurances, you have no way to actually make it binding. The history of Europe is full of princes who made promises that were broken—sometimes by them, sometimes by their heirs."

"We plan to keep the promise," Calvert said. "With no more help coming from England, we will have to be even better friends to our native neighbors. Our sovereign lord the king might not care about them—but we do."

Maybe there's hope after all, Gordon thought. *Just maybe.*

Paul held up his hand, halting the march. Pete had come to respect his sure feet and keen eyesight: he'd clearly seen something up ahead.

At a gesture, the Marylanders took cover. Pete unslung his rifle and found a tree; Paul crept forward, giving a backward glance to the up-timer, who nodded, tracking him with the sight of his weapon.

Thirty feet away Paul stood upright, gesturing again to the party. They moved forward to gather around him.

The Indian held up a strip of material caught on a bramble. It was about three inches long and had a bit of fur on one end, as if it had been part of a cloak. A small shell bead was sewn into a seam. Paul smelled it and tasted the end of it, then examined the stitching before looking up, a frown on his face.

"Susquehannock," he said. "They are very far from their hunting grounds."

"Tell me more," Pete said.

"They have been enemies of my people for a generation," he said. "They are pressed by tribes further north, beyond the mountains, and they would like to hunt in our forests and fish in our rivers. But they do not want to give up their walled villages." He spat. "And they fear our arrows."

"As well they should," Tyler said.

"There are two hands of them for every one of us, friend," Paul said to the Marylander. "There are only so many arrows."

"I don't know much about these Susquehannocks," Pete said. "But up-time there was a river called the *Susquehanna*. It was in Pennsylvania, which is a big state—province—north of where we are. If their villages are up there, then Paul's right—they're a long way from home.

"That means one of two things, or maybe both. Either they're invading, or this is a scouting party working for Savignon. Regardless, they might be our enemy."

"And they outnumber the Yaocomico ten to one," Tyler said. "Which means they outnumber both Englishmen and Yaocomico five to one."

"Only if they're all migrating down here," Pete answered. "They can't have that many warriors."

One of the other Marylanders spoke up—Ferson, the cobbler. "Captain Smith said that they had six hundred warriors. But that was twenty years ago. There might be fewer now."

"Or there might be more," Pete said. "Especially if they've been offered a nice prize. Paul, where do these Susquehannocks stand with the French? Do you know?"

"I do not," the Indian answered. "But they are enemies of the Five Nations, who want them as subjects. That means that they might make good allies for the French."

"And since they're already the enemies of your people..."

"Good enemies for Maryland as well," Paul said. He tucked the strip of material into his satchel.

Finding the scrap of leather and fur was a lucky break. By examining the ground nearby, the scout was able to pick up a lot of information—including the direction the Susquehannocks must have been traveling and how long it had been since they passed by. They were moving south by east, and had been in the clearing no more than half a day earlier.

"We need to report this back to *Challenger*," Pete had said at once. Paul had looked at him curiously, as if he'd insulted him.

"We will lose the track," the scout said.

"We have a general idea of where they're going. And we have

a dirigible to track them," Pete answered, gesturing upward with his thumb.

"Your dirigible did not find their track in the first place."

"That's true. But I don't want us to get too close to them without air support. What's south and east of us?" He set down his pack and pulled out an up-time road map. It was next to useless for terrain features other than rivers, but it was something. Based on where they were currently standing—somewhere north of where the Capitol Building would have been—traveling east would bring them to the Anacostia River.

"The trees extend at least a mile," Paul said. "We come out of cover near a river that leads down to the big water where the ship is anchored."

"So what's your plan?"

"Find the Susquehannocks. That *is* our mission."

"How big is this war party, do you think?"

"I am not sure," Paul answered. He squatted down and looked at the grass and dirt, the track that led away from the clearing. "Fifteen or twenty."

"So two to three times our number. I hope you weren't planning a frontal assault."

Tyler grunted. Paul frowned. "Do you feel that I am not leading properly?"

"I don't want us to get too close, like I said."

"I see. How close *do* you want to get? They will continue to move, up-timer. If we do not pursue them closely, they will get far ahead of us."

"They can't get too far. We have a freakin' *airship*," Pete said. "Remember? We need to report back, meet up with *Challenger*, and let them know what we've found."

"We have found nothing yet." Paul turned on his heel and walked away, following the track. Without a word, the Marylanders began to follow, as if to say, *we're not getting out without him.*

Pete cursed under his breath and fell into line.

As *John Wayne* came in sight of *Challenger*, Gordon prepared the dirigible for landing on the near shore. For the past day and a half he'd seen Pete waving to him from the deck as he approached, but he wasn't there.

As the dirigible made its slow approach, he pulled a megaphone from a hook near the control yoke.

"*Challenger*, this is *John Wayne*," he said through the speaker, though that was, he realized, pretty obvious.

"What news?" It was Maartens' voice.

"Nothing on the current sweep," he said. "Where's Pete?"

"No sign yet."

Gordon exchanged glances with Leonard Calvert and Ingrid. The scouting party was supposed to be back before sundown and the sun was already pretty far gone in the west.

"I'm going to take a look around."

"What is your fuel situation?"

"I've got two hours or so left," Gordon answered, looking at the gauge. Even without fuel for the burner, he could keep aloft for some time after dark—but it wouldn't be an easy landing.

There was a long pause, as if Maartens was considering what he thought of the idea.

"*Ja.* Be careful," the Dutchman said at last.

They came out of the deep woods onto a wide, flat riverbank. Paul paused, fearless, kneeling down to look at the footprints in the soft soil.

Pete scanned the area. He already had his rifle in hand, and gestured to the Marylanders to crouch down: but they seemed oblivious to any danger. Whatever sixth sense he had learned from a few years soldiering made him suspicious.

When he heard the crack of a gunshot and watched Tyler, the blacksmith, spin and fall into the muddy grass, he knew that he'd been right. The Marylanders dropped low then—except for two damn fools, who took off running, as if they would be safer that way.

He cursed under his breath. Paul, ever unperturbed, gestured toward the tree line, a few dozen yards away, and began creeping toward it, as another few shots rang out.

"What about—" Pete nodded toward the two colonists, their light vests and blouses showing up against the reeds and grass.

"If we follow them, we all die," Paul answered. "What would you choose, up-timer?"

"I'd choose to avoid this firefight entirely. We should have headed back."

The little group of colonists looked frightened. Tyler lay bleeding, a wound in his left shoulder. He tried to get to his feet, but Paul held him down below the level of the grass.

"Planning on leaving him behind too?" Pete said angrily.

"His wound is in his shoulder, not his leg," Paul answered. "He can walk—or crawl—if he wants to live."

Pete looked across the open field, trying to figure where the shot had come from. Whoever had scored a hit on Tyler was a pretty fair marksman at this distance. Any return fire, even with a superior weapon, would need a stroke of luck to hit.

Fifteen or twenty, he thought. *And they can shoot.*

You're an arrogant bastard, he wanted to say to their Indian scout. *Unless you* led *us into this...*

He shook the idea out of his head. One of the Marylanders was working on trying to stanch the flow of blood from Tyler's shoulder; Paul was already moving away, crablike, keeping low.

Pete squatted down beside the big blacksmith. "We need to get back to the trees. Can you make it?"

"Have I a choice?"

"Probably not."

Tyler grunted, and got to his knees, gritting his teeth. With the help of a friend, he began to move forward, as more shots went overhead. Every few feet, Tyler said something under his breath that didn't bear repeating.

"Is there some up-time means for locating them?" Leonard Calvert asked, lowering his spyglass.

"I wish," Gordon said. "No, I don't have any magic at my disposal. I'm just looking for some sign of them." He squinted toward the sun, which was well down near the horizon. "They could be anywhere down there."

"Our chances of locating them are..."

"Minimal."

"Then why—"

"Because I can't just sit back on *Challenger* twiddling my thumbs. And if there's something wrong—"

"Then it's a good thing you have your doctor on board," Ingrid said. "With Peter, I suspect, *something wrong* means someone is injured. Or worse."

"How much fuel do you have left?"

"Maybe an hour. And an hour of daylight." Gordon looked over the side at the forest cover below.

Pete, he thought. *Where are you?*

Calvert lifted the spyglass and scanned the middle distance. "Do you see anything?"

"Nothing," Calvert said. "Nothing but trees and... wait."

"What?"

"Someone. There's someone down there."

Gordon took three quick strides to where Calvert stood. "Is it Pete?"

"No," Calvert said. "It's Ferson. He's running, and he keeps looking over his shoulder."

"Is he being chased?"

"Not from the look of it."

"And he's the only one? Where's Pete—where are the others?"

"Perhaps," Calvert said, lowering the glass and looking at Gordon, "we should ask him."

Gordon knew that altitude he gave up he might never be able to get back; but the rope ladder was only a hundred feet long. They had one additional coil of rope aboard, letting him remain almost a hundred additional feet in the air.

It was obvious how scared the cobbler was; it was enough that he was willing to climb two hundred feet of rope in mid-air, while Gordon tried to minimize *John Wayne*'s drift. When Calvert pulled him aboard, he lay gasping for several moments. Ingrid knelt next to him, examining bruises.

"He is not wounded," she said after a moment.

"What happened?" Gordon asked.

"Shots," he managed. "We got shot at."

"Where?"

"Up... upriver. Garrett and I ran."

"You ran?"

"Shooting. Indians," Ferson said.

"*Where is my brother?*"

"I... I don't know. There was shooting. I—"

Gordon crouched next to the cobbler and grabbed him by the shirt collar. Ingrid put her hand on his arm, but he didn't seem to notice. "Where is my brother? *Where's Pete?* Why did you run?"

"Where *is* he?" Gordon repeated.

Ferson was terrified and speechless.

"Gordon," she said. "Let him go."

Gordon looked from Ferson to Ingrid and back. He let go of the man, who remained sitting up. The doctor stood, looking alarmed. "He ran because he is not a soldier, Gordon. Where is his musket? Where is his pike? He ran because he was scared."

"Where is John Garrett, William?" Calvert asked. "What happened to him?"

"I don't know," Ferson said. He looked close to tears. "He was with me, but I lost track of him."

"William," Calvert said to the cobbler, "can you help guide us back to where the shots happened?"

"I think so, my lord," he managed. "I will try."

Chapter 32

Under the canopy of the trees it was hard to read facial expressions. The sun was below the treetops and little of it was filtering through; they were huddled behind a group of trees shrouded in underbrush, watching for an approach.

"We're in deep trouble, Paul," Pete said. "I don't know what the hell you thought you were doing, but we are well and truly in the crapper now."

"We will wait until dark," the guide replied, not looking at Pete.

"That doesn't give us any advantage."

"It gives us the cover of night," Paul said. "Their numbers will not matter as much."

"But their stealth will matter a hell of a lot more. If we wait until dark they kill us. Not with gunshots, like they killed Ferson and Garrett—"

"We do not know that they are dead."

"A couple of unarmed farmers running for their lives? I wouldn't bet on them," Pete said. "They won't kill us with guns, Paul. They'll kill us with hatchets, or pointy sticks, or their bare hands. They're used to the woods. We've mostly got civilians, and one of them is wounded. You might be able to evade a hunting party; I might. But Tyler, and the rest of your Marylander friends?

"We have to think of something, or we are *dead*."

✧   ✧   ✧

The river was visible in the gathering darkness, snaking a few hundred feet below the dirigible. Ferson stared intently down, looking for some landmark he might recognize.

"We'd see signs of them if they'd been killed," Calvert said. "They must have retreated into the trees."

"Won't the attackers come after them?" the cobbler asked.

"You said that the shots came from in front of you," Gordon said. "You were traveling east...so they were near the river, or across it. And if they're really after Pete and the others, they'll have to come over open ground."

Calvert put his hand on Ferson's shoulder. "How good a shot are you, William?"

"I have a fowling piece at home, my lord," Ferson answered. "I can shoot at game—but I'm not a crack shot."

"You'll do," Gordon said. "These natives have probably never seen a balloon before." *It is balloon*, he thought, remembering *F Troop* again: it was one of those anachronistic things that they'd laugh about later, something down-timers would never understand.

God, Gordon thought, *I hope we get to laugh about this later.* It was a chilling thought he didn't really want to entertain: that something had happened to Pete, that he'd walked into some kind of trouble that killed him.

An arrow, a bullet, a poison snakebite...it didn't matter that Pete was an up-timer. It could kill him just as dead.

My kid brother, Gordon thought. *My kid brother.*

"What do you want me to do?" Ferson said.

"What do you have in mind, Mr. Chehab?" Calvert asked.

"If we see the attackers crossing open ground," Gordon said, "we're going to scare the hell out of them."

"So you don't intend that we should kill anyone we see."

"That's up to you," Gordon said. "I'm just driving."

"They are coming," Paul said quietly, pointing toward the edge of the woods.

Pete looked toward where the Indian scout indicated. He couldn't see much in the dim light, but he thought he might have picked out something moving through the high grass.

"How many have you seen?" he whispered.

"Six," Paul said. "But I expect that there are several more behind them."

"Susquehannocks?"

"We all look alike from this distance, do we not?" Paul asked, smiling thinly. "I expect they are Susquehannocks. They take pleasure in torturing their prisoners," he added. "Best not to be captured."

"That's reassuring. Look, if I fire at anyone incoming, they'll know exactly where the rest of you are. I'm going to find a different blind to shoot from."

"Can you hit them at this distance?"

"I can scare them, at least," Pete said. *I don't know*, he thought. *But I might as well try.*

He slung his rifle over his shoulder and began to move. His plan was simple: pick a hiding place—underbrush, or a tree, or a rock—and move to it, as quickly and as quietly as possible. Then do it again, and again, until he was close enough to cover the others and far enough away to distract the incoming hostiles.

Hopefully he could take enough of them with him before...

Before what? He asked himself. *Before they kill you? Is this why you came along on this little scouting mission? On this adventure with Gord?*

Is this why I'm back in the seventeenth century? To die by being tomahawked, some unknown up-timer killed by some unknown down-timer?

Curiously, for the first time during the adventure to the New World, he felt his thoughts drift to Penny and to his little daughter Karen, whom he'd not seen for months.

They'd married two summers ago, when he was in Suhl and Karen was already on the way. Penny was sweet, but could stand on her own: which was good, since he wasn't going to be there much while still on active duty. There were others who would've just walked away—just paid child support and left the rest of it behind—but it didn't strike Pete as right. So they married in Grantville while he was on leave, with all of his family and all of her family together in the church. Karen came along enough months later at the clinic in Suhl, and no one was particularly scandalized.

He carried a picture of each of them in his wallet; he might have taken them out now to look at them, but there wasn't light enough to make them out.

But it was all right. He knew what they looked like.

Penny had a picture of him, too. If he didn't come back from this little American vacation, that would be all she had. As for Karen...maybe she deserved to have a Daddy.

He thought about that for a moment, as if it was a new thought that had never crossed his mind before.

And maybe, you dumb ass, he added to himself, *it never has*.

"They'll have to get to me first," he said, crouching behind a fallen log, squinting into the dusk over his rifle.

"There," Calvert said, pointing at the ground. He and Ferson aimed their weapons at a pair of figures moving through the rushes on the west side of the river, muskets in their hands. The two men apparently hadn't heard the sound of the engines driving the dirigible. That wasn't surprising, given the way the wind was blowing.

Then, in the gathering dark, they both fired, a bright flash. Gordon had turned the dirigible end-on so that it was making scarcely any headway; he hoped that he could keep it in place long enough for the other two to manage multiple shots.

Ferson was already reloading. "I don't think I hit him, my lord," he said to Calvert, who had raised his spyglass to look.

"It may not matter," Gordon said. "They're not expecting to be attacked from above."

Pete saw movement a few hundred yards away, and was training his rifle on an incoming Susquehannock warrior. Suddenly, he heard the crack of two shots somewhere out in the open ground.

His target heard it too and turned, standing erect: he had his musket slung and was carrying something—a hatchet, Pete thought—in his hand.

He was in Pete's sights, but his back was turned away. He'd stopped advancing and he probably hadn't specifically seen Pete. It was as clear a shot as he was going to have, but he hesitated. It bothered him to shoot a man in the back.

He'll kill you *if he can*, Pete thought.

They take pleasure in torturing their prisoners, he heard Paul's voice say.

He pulled the trigger and watched the man spin and fall.

"They're in the woods," Gordon said. "Hear that?"

A wildly aimed shot came from below, but the shooter hadn't correctly determined the location of the dirigible and it went wide.

"Time for some psych warfare," Gordon said. He took the bullhorn from under the control yoke and raised it.

"Call off your attack," he said into the bullhorn, and it echoed across the riverbank below. "Run away now, and you will be spared. Remain, and I will rain down death on you." He covered the speaking end with his hand. "Fire again," he said to the others, and they took aim at targets and fired.

Thank God for big brothers.

Pete wasn't sure whether the attackers understood English, but it had to spook them to hear a loud voice from the sky threatening to rain death on them.

There were more gunshots. Pete wasn't sure if they came from the Indians on the ground or from the dirigible; but he wasn't budging until it all died down. The cavalry had come to the rescue.

John Wayne took Tyler aboard by rigging a sling, though he managed to pull himself up the last twenty feet with one arm. Bringing the three remaining Marylanders, Pete, and the Indian guide aboard would have made the dirigible almost impossible to fly back, so they'd need to make it to *Challenger* on foot. They were six or seven miles from the head of the Chesapeake. Assuming they weren't attacked again, and *John Wayne* maintained a slow drift, it was likely that everyone could get back safely.

In the morning, with *John Wayne* reinflated and refueled, Gordon and Pete took Will Ferson aloft to look for the missing man, but the search was fruitless. Either he had fallen somewhere they didn't see, or he was still wandering around the wilderness, or he had been captured by the Susquehannock raiders.

There was no outcome that favored John Garrett.

"What now, Chehab?" Maartens asked.

"We go back to St. Mary's," Gordon answered, looking at Pete and then back at *Challenger*'s captain. "There isn't much more we can do here."

They were standing on the quarterdeck, the captain's private domain. *John Wayne* had been deflated and stowed; *Challenger* remained at anchor at the head of the Chesapeake.

"I don't see as we've done *anything* here."

"What did you think we were going to do? Stop an invasion? That was never going to happen."

"So the rest of these damn savages are still out there, on the loose."

"Except that the Marylanders know that the Susquehannocks are out there, Captain."

"There are a hell of a lot of them, *ja*? What are they going to do when they all arrive?"

"They'll have to do the best they can."

Maartens grunted. "Huh. Seems as if you're giving that advice to every colony you meet, Chehab. The Danish miners, you can't protect—and they seem to be handling matters well enough on their own anyway. The Puritans don't want your help and New Amsterdam doesn't care. And now Maryland. What will you tell the merchants in Virginia? '*Na*, no help here, terribly sorry'?"

"What do you want me to tell them? I don't have a damn thing I can do." Gordon ran a hand through his hair and walked to the rail, looking down at the gentle waves below.

"Don't listen to him—" Pete began, but Gordon turned around, anger in his eyes.

"*Shut up*, little bro. You damn near got *killed* out there playing Great White Hunter. This isn't Triple-A—this is the major leagues, and there are people throwing at your head. I don't know what would have been worse—if you'd gotten shot, like Tyler, or worse, or if you'd gotten captured by those bastards and tortured. What the hell would I actually tell everyone? Penny, our parents, David, Lucas, Terri, Caleb? What would they tell Karen when she was old enough to understand it?"

"Gordon—"

"I'm not done. I've read about what they do to people. They want to see how much they can take. Sometimes I wonder if de Vries is right about the natives—that they're just not like us. They're a whole different species. I didn't sign up to watch my brother get tortured."

"Didn't happen, big bro. The cavalry came to the rescue. I knew you would."

"Liar."

"You'll never know."

The two brothers stared at each other, both angry, both waiting for the other to look away.

"Family reunions are so nice," Maartens said, and spit over the side.

Pete looked at his big brother. "Do you think we'll get court martialed if we pitch him into the bay?"

"Probably."

"Damn," Pete said. "Because I'd really, really like to do it."

"Like to see you try," Maartens said.

"Don't tempt me."

"So what are your orders?" he asked Gordon sardonically.

"We have a wounded man," Gordon said. "Ingrid is attending to him now. We have a death to report, and we need to brief Lord Baltimore on what we've seen. It's time to go back to St. Mary's."

Chapter 33

Paris

Cardinal Tremblay's servant bowed his way out of the private study as the gentleman swept past him, paying no attention to the man. Tremblay sat behind his patron's desk, and looked up as his guest came up to stand opposite.

He removed his spectacles and laid them carefully on the table beside the opened letter. Once again he marveled at the glass-grinding ability of the Americans, whose handiwork had presented him with glasses that saw at distance *and* for close work as well. These lenses had actually been made by a French grinder here in Paris, but the man had learned the techniques from studying in Grantville. Here as in most areas, the up-timers made no effort to keep their knowledge and methods secret. Cardinal Richelieu had always marveled at that, but he was glad to take advantage of it.

"Esteemed Monsieur," he said. "To what do I owe the pleasure of your company?"

"I am not here for social purpose, Eminence."

"Of that I am sure," Tremblay answered. "Our new king keeps his keeper of the seals quite busy. Very well, Monsieur Séguier: how may I serve you?"

"I am told that you are receiving correspondence—*state* correspondence—originally intended for your late patron."

"Many of His Eminence's allies and friends reside far from Paris," Tremblay answered. "They have not heard of the sad events." *And I am curious who in the Palais-Cardinal has a wagging tongue*, he thought, filing that idea away for future consideration.

"So you *are* still receiving letters."

"There is no point in denying it."

"I require that you turn them over to me. My master needs to be informed of all of your master's ... intrigues."

"Not all of the correspondence sent here deals with affairs of state."

"Spare me your dissembling," Séguier said. "*Everything* in which Cardinal Richelieu involved himself constituted affairs of state. Do you not think that referring these things to the royal court was your duty?"

"Ah. Duty." Tremblay rose from his seat and leaned forward on the desk. "I did not realize that the keeper of the seals busied himself with going from place to place in Paris, demanding that every letter writer in the kingdom turn over his correspondence to our new king out of some sense of duty."

"Richelieu is—was—no ordinary letter writer."

"No, indeed. But that explains why you are here, rather than having me summoned to your presence in the Louvre, which would, I daresay, be more public."

"Cardinal Tremblay," Séguier said, clearly leashing his anger, "you have the opportunity to help your king or become his enemy. I assure you, Monsieur, it is critical is it that you make the right decision."

"Your relationship with the Cardinal was quite cordial when he sat in this chair; your daughter is married to his nephew, *n'est-ce pas*? I realize that you must affirm your loyalty to our new monarch, but there is something to be said for personal loyalty as well. What exactly do you want of me, Monsieur?"

Séguier and Tremblay stared at each other for several moments; perhaps the keeper of the seals realized that intimidation and bluster would come to no good outcome, and at last his expression softened.

"Let me be more specific, Eminence. It has come to the attention of the *Conseil* that a military expedition has been prepared, with a destination in the New World. In order to properly inform His Highness of its nature, I should like to know of its purpose and objectives."

"There is no secret to that," Tremblay answered. "Three years ago, the king of England conveyed all of his claims in the Atlantic plantations to the king of France, in exchange for certain considerations. This expedition is intended to enforce France's hegemony there. All of this was discussed in the *Conseil* months ago."

"And only *now*, after three years, it is being undertaken? Why the long delay?"

"I cannot answer that question. It is not for me to say what the cardinal, or our late king, had in mind with respect to the disposition. Obviously, other matters took priority."

"I ask again—why now? Is there some particular item of correspondence that occasions it?"

"What makes you think so?"

"I have my sources."

That much is clear, Tremblay thought. *And when I find them, they will be in need of new employment.*

"There is no letter that has recently arrived that is of sufficient moment for an expedition to be fitted out. That matter has been in train for months: one does not suddenly order four warships to sail across the Ocean Sea."

"Two."

"I believe that the expedition consists of four vessels."

"It has been decided that if it is to be undertaken at all, two ships will be sufficient."

"Ah, so you *do* know about it. Were you just checking to see if I was well informed, or is there some more subtle strategy I do not discern?"

"I wanted to see if there was something more to it than we had been told. So—tell me. What is the import of the letter you have just received?"

"Why don't you just ask your sources?"

"They were not privy to its contents. If you please, Eminence." Séguier extended his hand expectantly.

Tremblay thought a moment, weighing what harm it would do to show him the latest letter from Servien's agent; he considered what good it might do, but was at a loss. On balance, he concluded that he did not need another enemy, and the Alsatian would probably not be harmed if Séguier—and thus King Gaston—knew of his existence or his mission.

He handed the letter from the Alsatian spy to Séguier, and

gestured him to an armchair. He sat behind the desk and watched as the keeper of the seals read through the document, written in a careful, tiny hand. Tremblay easily read the nobleman's lips as he worked his way through it.

> *Most esteemed Monsieur,*
>
> *I should expect that the arrival of this letter surprises you, as you have had no communication with me for some time. It was not my intention to keep you thus uninformed, but circumstances beyond my control made it impossible for me to send any messages before* Challenger *set sail for the New World.*
>
> *It is now clear why the expedition included the up-timer Gordon Chehab. He is an expert aéronaute—he had up-time experience piloting lighter-than-air vessels— which to the unaided eye appear to be no more than a large canvas sack that can be filled with hot air and flown a distance, perhaps as much as a hundred miles.*
>
> *I need not tell your esteemed self that the ability to fly* any *distance makes* Challenger's *mission dangerous to His Majesty's possessions in the New World, as it provides the ability to both perform surveillance and carry out attacks from the air. The captain-general here in Québec, the esteemed Monsieur de Champlain, concurs with this assessment and has promised to provide every assistance, as well as to make sure that this missive reaches your hands.*
>
> *Regrettably the whereabouts of* Challenger *and its airship are presently unknown, as I departed at the earliest possible convenient time to be able to reach an officer in His Majesty's service so that I might update your intelligence. I know that it was intended to sail for Massachusetts-Bay and New Amsterdam, but I have no further information.*
>
> *It is my intention to travel to the Dutch settlement, from which I may have further opportunity to communicate.*

"Who is this correspondent?"

"An operative. He was sent aboard the up-timer vessel that crossed the ocean at the end of last year. He has been able to keep us informed—intermittently—with intelligence about goings-on in the New World."

"And what is going on?"

"Our relayed information is very scarce. Apparently the up-timer radio was destroyed in an accident during the ocean crossing. We have no facility in New France. All that we know is based on the letters we receive from this operative."

"How many of these"—he waved the letter—"have you received?"

"Two. This is the second one. There was a confirming letter from the Sieur de Champlain confirming Hoff's visit and asking for further instructions."

"What did you tell him?"

"Nothing yet. In the absence of the cardinal, there is no policy."

"At least you have been wise in that. It is unfortunate that the *Conseil*—"

"It is *unfortunate*," Tremblay interrupted, "that my esteemed patron was murdered on a king's high road along with my sovereign lord. If he was alive, this uncomfortable conversation would not be necessary. The government of the realm would be in safe hands and our king and queen would be safely in the Louvre Palace with the newborn heir to the throne of France.

"But that is not where we are, Monsieur. We are in a different place and time. If you wish to have the *Conseil*—or your esteemed self—or His Highness King Gaston kept informed of this correspondence in future, I shall make an effort to do so. The author of the note does not know of the news of the realm, so he does not know that the man with whom he corresponds is no longer picking up the post."

Séguier did not respond at once. Clearly the keeper of the seals was unaccustomed to outbursts of this sort from cardinals, even *in pectore* ones. But at last he stepped away from the desk, still holding the letter from the Alsatian spy.

"I will inform His Highness that there is an operative in the New World, from whom we expect to receive further intelligence. I will expect that any correspondence will be presented at once. Am I understood, Eminence?"

"Of course, Monsieur."

Without a further word, Séguier walked out of the study, still holding the Alsatian's last letter.

Chapter 34

Atlantic Ocean
West of the Azores

Captain Léonidas Dansin slowly ascended the ladder from airless and dark into stiflingly hot and bright daylight. The officer of the watch stood to attention and offered a salute, to which he responded with a cursory nod; the man's expression never changed.

From amidships he made his way to the quarterdeck, glancing briefly at the glass as he passed. Nothing had changed: the barometer showed no difference from when he had last examined it.

There was still no wind, not even a cursory breeze, the afterthought of a gust that might fill the sails of *Royaume Henri*. It was enough to make a less patient man irate: becalmed, drifting, awaiting more favorable weather to permit the ship and its sister vessel to be on their way.

Fortunately, Dansin was a patient man. More patient, in any case, than the *grand-maître de la navigation*, the young lord of Maillé-Brézé, who stood with his back to the rest of the ship, alone in what would otherwise be Dansin's private demesne.

He was also more patient than Father Jean-Baptiste, the admiral's spiritual advisor and confessor, who had been praying fervently for wind to drive the ships toward the New World shore where he would take personal charge of the congregation of the faithful that awaited him. The good father had been offering masses thrice daily to importune the Father, Son, Holy Ghost and any saints with whom he remained on speaking terms to give them back the means to continue their mission. Under his breath, his remarks had been less pious and less charitable.

It might have tried his patience: but Léon Dansin was a patient man.

"Good morning to Your Grace," he said, remaining at a respectful distance.

The young man turned to face him. The admiral had been showing some amount of strain in the current circumstances, but had in any case been nothing but courteous to his senior captain—while berating and venting his anger on nearly everyone else.

"And good morrow to you, Monsieur," Maillé-Brézé said. "I hope that your barometer glass is not broken, for its reading never seems to change."

"I believe that it is in good working order, Your Grace," Dansin said. "It is not the instrument that is at fault, but the heavens."

"Father Jean-Baptiste would assign you two score *Aves* for such an utterance. Or worse."

"Worse, I fear," Dansin said. "But it would not make the wind pick up. I have already tried that."

"I believe that you have."

"It is, in any case, beyond our control, Your Grace," Dansin continued. "We have no choice but to wait for a favorable wind."

"We had been making excellent time, Dansin, on our former course. And time is very much of the essence . . . three days becalmed! It erases all of our former gains."

"We are still afloat, Your Grace," Dansin answered. "We suffer from no maladies, and there is no dissent among the crew." *And if you had followed my suggested course*, he thought, *we would be most of the way to Saint-Christophe by now, rather than dallying on the southern verge of the Sargasso.*

All this because Monsieur assumed that the most rapid crossing of the Atlantic Ocean would be on a straight line.

"If we remain adrift much longer . . ."

"There will be wind," Dansin assured him. "There is always wind . . . eventually."

Please God, he added to himself. *Father, Son, Holy Ghost, and any saints with whom I remain on speaking terms.*

✧   ✧   ✧

The expedition had, indeed, begun auspiciously. Weighing anchor at Brest, the two ships had moved briskly westward across the Atlantic, taking advantage of favorable trade winds. To Jean Armand de Maillé-Brézé, it must have seemed no more complex than a boating trip in the Mediterranean.

Dansin had advised at the outset that their course be south by southwest, with the objective of gaining landfall on one of the French islands in the Caribbean. The winds and currents favored such a passage, and he had made it several times before. That was the primary reason that the Prince of Condé had suggested him for this expedition.

Maillé-Brézé was a sailor, *oui, certainement*—but not one familiar with the storm-tossed Atlantic: rather, he was accustomed to the shelter of the Bay of Biscay or the more bucolic tides of the Mediterranean. His careful examination of a globe of the world, along with some smuggled up-timer maps, made him confident that the most direct route was *north* of the Azores and then directly west, rather than south and southwest as Dansin had politely suggested.

Time is of the essence, Captain, Maillé-Brézé had said. *We must do what is expedient. You are experienced with these matters,* n'est-ce pas?

He was experienced. Fatalistic, but experienced.

They went north of the Azores into the doldrums: and there, in the horse latitudes, the ships hit an unfortunate patch of calm.

Dansin set a good table: it was obligatory, with someone so close to the king and cardinal aboard his vessel. He had stocked the hold of *Royaume Henri* with the delicacies and gastronomic comforts that would stand up well to an Atlantic voyage. He was, therefore, the host for any gathering in which the two ships' captains sat together at a meal with their admiral.

On the evening of the third day of calm, François Vielle, his junior captain—a skillful sailor but of lesser birth, yet possessed of some esteemed patron of whom Dansin himself was unaware—was rowed from *Saint-Christophe* to *Royaume Henri* to join them.

"If only we had some up-time wizardry to save us," Maillé-Brézé said, examining his wineglass as if considering the vintage of the contents by sight.

"I do not know if there was ever any up-time technology to

call up the wind, Your Grace," Dansin told him. "But they say that their ships carried great engines, like those in their land carriages."

The young admiral nodded. "I understand that both floating and flying carriages were made of *metal*, can you imagine it? Metal ships I can see—they displace water with air; though it seems like a devilishly expensive material. But how could airships made of metal even *fly*?"

"The American aircraft can clearly fly, Monsieur."

"I am sure that your esteemed uncle had insight into that, Your Grace," Vielle put in. "Someday France too will have such airships."

Maillé-Brézé smiled at the thought. "And within their sailing vessels, who can know what other"—the admiral gestured vaguely toward the open port and the ocean beyond—"wizardry is taking place within?"

Dansin sighed. It was well known that the American ships used principles and technology that was not "wizardry," but rather elaborations of those he had known since he was first learning his craft. Wooden vessels were far cheaper than those made of metal, but the idea of a metal ship was not hard to accept, as the principle of buoyancy had been understood by Archimedes. Indeed, from what he had read, even wooden ships in the up-timers' history were eventually given metal sheaths on their hulls to protect against rot and shipworm. The up-timers seemed casual, almost indifferent, about military secrets. Anything they knew, others—such as his own people—would soon know also.

Surely Maillé-Brézé knew of this as well . . . but perhaps he had been too busy with his societal commitments. Dansin himself was from Saintonge, like Captain Champlain—gently born, but from far outside the elevated society of Île-de-France.

"The Americans like to keep their secrets," Vielle said, in blithe disregard of fact. He poured more wine into his glass. "They may have to be taken by force."

"I think we have already tried that," Dansin said.

"We shall have to try *again*," Vielle answered quickly. Dansin watched him glance quickly at Maillé-Brézé, as if looking for approval.

And meet the same fate, Dansin told himself. Vielle was at least five years his junior, and whatever his nautical prowess, was no soldier. Dansin had been present at the siege of La Rochelle several years earlier—one of the things that had attracted Cardinal

Richelieu's attention, and which no doubt contributed to his present assignment.

"I cannot say what His Majesty may or may not do," Dansin said. "Nor can I speak to His Grace's esteemed uncle's intentions on the matter. But attempting to wrest anything by force from the up-timers seems to have met with little success."

"What do you suggest instead, Captain Dansin?" the admiral asked, shifting attention from wineglass to ship captain and giving him the same scrutiny that he had applied to the vintage.

"I daresay that we will continue to meet with success by pursuing more...subtle means. The Americans keep some secrets, yes, but not all of them—nor even most of them. They bring changes to light, and they spread to all of us."

"You seem uncommonly well informed," Vielle said, his tone of voice implying that he believed exactly the opposite. Once again, Dansin noticed him looking sidelong at Maillé-Brézé to gauge his reaction.

"I am sure," Dansin said carefully, "that your many visits to Grantville make you much better informed, Captain Vielle."

Maillé-Brézé raised one eyebrow. "I did not know that you had visited the American city," he said to Vielle. "Pray tell us more."

"I—I did not say that I had visited Grantville, Your Grace," Vielle said after a moment, reddening slightly. "I think Captain Dansin engages in a jest."

Vielle gave Dansin a murderous look; Dansin kept his expression impassive.

"A jest," Dansin said. "Of course. It could not be otherwise."

That night, clouds gathered in the north, a sudden summer storm that was further evidence of the unpredictability of the Ocean Sea. Vielle's attempts at toadying were largely ignored in the wake of a freshening wind, rewarding Dansin's patience.

In deepening night the sails were filled with a steady breeze pushing them southward—and westward toward their destination. From his post on his own quarterdeck, Léonidas Dansin could hear the fervent chant of Father Jean-Baptiste, offering thanks to the Divine Trinity for their deliverance.

You have no idea, Dansin thought, *of the perils from which God the Father might be asked to deliver us.*

But he did not tempt fate by speaking of it.

Chapter 35

Atlantic Ocean
Near Chesapeake Bay

Thomas James found the sailing master of *Challenger* at the taffrail, taking a sounding of the waning moon. The night was clear, the wind brisk; off in the distance there was the sound of gulls near shore.

He waited for Claes Maartens to lower his instrument and make a notation on a slate, then stepped forward to stand beside him.

"Beautiful night."

Maartens grunted. "Were you never taught never to praise good weather, for it would then change for the worse?"

"I find that I cannot carry all of the superstitions of sailors in my head, Captain," he said. "Besides, they so often conflict with each other."

"I suppose they do. Sail with Dutchmen, you get one set; with Englishmen another. As for the up-timers..."

"I thought they had no superstitions at all."

"There is something about passing under ladders. And I recall that Peter Chehab was put off because the ship's cat was all black. But they are not as bedeviled with such things as most."

"The up-timers seem upset," James said.

"With each other," Maartens agreed. "They've hardly spoken since we left St. Mary's. That was a near thing, that ambush on shore."

245

"They should be drinking to their good fortune, don't you think?"

"It's what *I* would do," Maartens said. "Life is too short to worry about dangers yesterday. It's dangers today and tomorrow that should concern them. But Master Gordon seems fond of what he calls 'the long view.' Something to do with the reason they're here in the first place."

"Aboard *Challenger*?"

"*Na*, more complicated than that. It's the never-ending question of why the Americans are here in our century. After five years it's *their* century as well—whatever purpose God has for bringing them back, He will reveal in His good time. Or not."

"Or not," James said.

Maartens picked up the slate and squinted at what he'd written down. He scowled, as if the notation somehow offended him. "*Ja*, well, at least the moon is still behaving as it should. I wonder if it was different in the world of up-time."

"I can't imagine how."

"Didn't they say that men from their world—from their own nation, in fact—actually walked on it? That might have changed it."

James shrugged.

"I wonder how many of the things they tell us about the future are actually true."

"I don't see as they would have any reason to lie, do you?"

"I suppose not," Maartens said. "But it's a simpler question to ask whether any of it still matters."

"May I come in?"

Gordon looked up from his book—a boring, badly written history that told him less about Virginia than he needed to know—to see Ingrid Skoglund at the door of his little cabin. It was past dark, and the only light was from his lantern, which rolled very slightly on gimbals that kept it steady with the pitch of the ship. Pete was on deck somewhere, avoiding him as he had done since Maryland.

He felt as if he was in one of those little Dutch portraits, where it was all dark except for the light from something in the center of the picture.

"Please." He shifted on his hammock, and moved a cloth bag off his locker so she and Sofia had a place to sit—except, to his surprise, Sofia was not with her. Ingrid stepped into the cabin, her head bent, and took the offered seat.

"I'd better keep the hatch open," he said. "People will talk."

"You mean that I am unescorted. Sofia was tired; I have kept her quite busy organizing the supplies from Maryland."

"I...yes. I am unaccustomed to talking to you in my cabin."

"Let them talk, Gordon. I do not care."

He marked his place in the book and set it in a little wooden box with others he needed to read. "What can I do for you?"

"I need to talk to you about your fight with your brother."

"Whatever it is, it's over. He'll be fine, he's just sulking. He'll get over it."

"No," she said. She folded her hands in her lap and fixed Gordon with her gaze. "You underestimate the problem, Gordon, just as you underestimate your brother."

"I don't—"

"Oh, yes. Yes, you do. You are the elder brother, more worldly, more...diplomatic, more compassionate. To your eyes Peter is a headstrong adolescent, prone to violence and irreverence. You must be on constant lookout that he does not do anything, nor say anything, from which you must rescue him."

"Sounds about right."

"But it is *not* right. It is inaccurate, misleading, and it will lead you to the sort of fight that now separates you. I heard your argument, your dispute, when you returned from the battle on the river—and he was correct: he cannot be protected at all times; he is no longer a child."

"This is the man who tried to hit on you. Uh, he sought a—"

"I lived in Grantville for a year, Gordon. I know what the expression means. Yes, this is the same man. You told me that you were going to find him and talk to him. Did you?"

"I told him off."

"I do not need to be protected," she said. "I can protect myself. I bear no hostility to him; to be honest, I suppose I should be complimented." She smiled. "He found me attractive."

"You *are* attractive. It doesn't mean that you should have to deal with—"

She held up her hand; he let the sentence drift away, and neither of them spoke for some time.

"You chose your brother for this expedition," Ingrid said

at last, "because you needed someone whom you could trust. But there is no one aboard *Challenger*, or, I suppose, Captain de Vries' ship, who is superfluous: he is also here for a reason. There are skills that Peter possesses that are valuable to you and to the expedition. When you determined that he and the others should go into the wilderness, you did not put him in danger: the *situation* put him in danger. If he had been killed, it would not be *you* that killed him."

Gordon didn't answer. It was what Pete had said: but it was not how he had said it.

"Do you understand what I am trying to say, Gordon?"

"If he had died, some of me would have died with him."

"Yes. Of course, of course it would have been thus. Can I tell you something? A doctor's existence is life in the midst of death. A little of me has died on many, many occasions; yet I am still a doctor, and wish to be nothing other than a doctor.

"Losing a father is painful. To lose a brother would be difficult. No, worse than difficult. But it did not happen, Gordon. He survived the event; he is still here, still aboard *Challenger*, still necessary to the success of this voyage. You still need him."

"I know."

"Then act on that knowledge," she said.

"You should go tell Pete all this."

Ingrid stood up, keeping her head slightly bowed; Gordon stood up as well, just missing the beam above his head.

"What makes you think I haven't done so already?"

Eight bells woke Gordon. He lay awake in his hammock, feeling it swing gently with the lapping tide against the hull below. There was a time early in the voyage when he would awaken and wonder where he was and what the hell was going on: but months along, that didn't happen anymore. He knew where he was.

He just wasn't always sure what was going on.

"Pete."

"Mmph."

"Pete, are you awake?"

There were several seconds of silence and then: "No. I'm asleep. It's the middle of the night, and I'm asleep."

"We need to talk."

"I need to sleep. Go talk to the officer of the watch."

"I need to talk to you."

"Can't it wait? Sleep, remember? I'm asleep."

"You've spent the last five days avoiding me. You're here; you're awake now."

"No, I'm not."

"And I'm here. You and I need to talk."

Another several seconds of silence; then Gordon heard a hand move to a louvered panel and open it; moonlight filtered in, so he could make out the rough outlines of Pete's face.

"Go ahead, big bro. I'm listening."

"I didn't do you any favors back in Maryland, Pete. I didn't do myself any favors either. I'm sorry if I embarrassed you."

"It takes more than that to embarrass me. But thanks. No hard feelings."

"Really?"

"No. Not really." Pete shifted in his hammock. "Look, big bro. This is the cross-country trip you promised me years ago, but I'm not sixteen anymore. You can't treat me like I am. You didn't bring me along to protect me—and even if you did, you can't. If we wind up fighting the French somewhere, there's a chance that I'll take a bullet or a sword or something—"

"Pete—"

"Let me finish. I might get hurt; I might get killed. You'll have to figure out what to tell Penny and Mom and Dad and Grampa and everyone else—but they'll know that it's part of the wonderful world we live in. People die all the time, and more so in our brave old world. This isn't happy adventure time; it's what we get for real life, and there are dangers. You can't protect me from everything we meet."

"I can see that you don't walk into traps."

"Like hell you can. You can't prevent any of us from anything, not really. Not even with your big bad dirigible."

"That big bad dirigible saved your ass."

"Yes. Yes, it did. And I appreciate it, and I hope that if my ass needs saving again you'll be there to do it. But if it isn't and something happens, and it's not your fault, you *can't act like it is your fault*. You can't be waiting to feel guilty because your kid brother bought the farm."

"Don't talk like that."

"Don't tell me how to talk."

Gordon let the silence stretch out this time. He watched Pete swing gently back and forth in his hammock, the moonlight chiseling out his features.

Pete was a long way from the kid he'd left behind. He was right: he wasn't sixteen anymore. Gordon was the oldest, but all of his brothers and sisters were grown up now, making their own way. Any of them could have something happen to them. He'd been away from Grantville for a year: anything could have happened and he'd never know.

Don't talk like that, he thought.

Don't tell me how to talk, he added right afterward.

"'Billy, don't be a hero,'" Gordon sang—off-key, of course. "You have to keep your head low, little bro."

He expected an angry reply—or at least a sarcastic one. But his brother surprised him.

"I'm not looking to have a nice tombstone, Gord, not yet at least. I want to stay alive and not play the hero unless absolutely necessary. I have people to go back to."

"Nice of you to mention it."

"Just because I don't talk about it, big bro, doesn't mean I don't think about it. And when I do, I realize that I...don't want to die in some stupid place for some stupid reason."

"I don't want that for either of us."

"Good. I'm glad we agree. And...I'll try to keep my head down. I'd hate for you to have to bring that kind of news home."

In the moonlight, Pete extended his hand, and Gordon took it.

"So, tell me," Gordon said. "What should we expect in Virginia?"

"It has changed a great deal since the withdrawal of the English," Thomas James said. "A *great* deal."

"I don't know much about Virginia before the withdrawal. I've got Pocahontas and John Smith and, I don't know, Hiawatha. But not much on what it was actually like."

James looked puzzled for a few moments, then shrugged. "Virginia has the distinction of being the oldest still-extant colony settled by the English. They survived a native massacre that killed a third of them in 1622, and they made enough mistakes in their early years that they should have been long since extinct. But perhaps the Lord of Hosts watches out for them, though they not be servants of some harsher God.

"In 1624, King James of blessed memory established the charter under which they were authorized to operate. This instrument replaced a series of corporate agreements which had all failed for one reason or another—usually avarice or pride; they seem to be the favorite deadly sins for the rich burghers of Virginia.

"Even before the 1624 charter, though, these fine gentlemen had begun to meet in legislative assembly to discuss matters of concern to their polity. This was ... not, however, with explicit permission of king and Parliament. I understand that both King James and King Charles were aware of the practice—and apparently they saw no reason to forbid it."

"Or endorse it, I would guess."

"I should say not. Especially since the dismissal of Parliament eight years ago. King Charles has left them in a sort of limbo, neither granting nor denying the authority of the burgesses to meet. In the meanwhile they have approved their resolutions and duly sent them on to London so that they could be examined by the Privy Council."

"Which they never did, I guess."

"No. Never. And when the king transferred his rights to the king of France, the message was dispatched by a courier with no apology, no approval, no denial and no direction for the colonists."

"Sounds like a familiar story. But how is this different from any other colony, Captain? Didn't King Charles set the New Englanders and the Marylanders adrift as well?"

"Ah, well, there's the difference." Captain James drew out his pipe and tobacco pouch, filled the bowl of the pipe and tucked the pouch back into his pocket. Then he drew out a little wooden box of matches, slid it open and took out a match.

He looked at the match for a few moments; it was a product of some enterprising Grantville inventor, a worthy successor to all the spent Bic lighters that had run out of fuel years ago. He struck it against a rough surface on the side of the box and lit his pipe, then quickly blew it out. "Wonderful invention, these things," he added, putting box and spent match into the same pocket, as if the used one might be useful again.

He puffed on the pipe and then continued. "The Marylanders are Catholic exiles, most of them. As for the colonists in New England ... the king and his archbishop felt that they'd seen the back of them once and for all. But the Virginians, the gentlemen who paid their twelve pounds ten or twenty-five sterling for that grant of land, they were not *exiles*—they were not religious dissenters. Many of them had friends and allies and brothers and uncles back in England. It was not a difficult decision for many of them to sell their portion and sail for home."

"They abandoned their plantations?"

"Not the ones with plantations," James said. "Mostly the middling sort, the ones who had something to go back to and not too much to lose. A lot of the little planters went back, the ones who had bought a small spread, enough to grow their tobacco and maybe a little corn. I would guess that one in three or one in four found it better to return home."

He took his pipe from his mouth and examined it, as if he wanted to make sure it was properly shaped. "But this"—he pointed with the pipestem at Gordon—"this is a powerful inducement, Mr. Chehab. The Virginians sought to do all sorts of things: at divers times they set up an iron works, a glass factory, a potash factory, silk...but it all comes down to tobacco. Tobacco is gold—and anyone who has remained to cultivate it has decided it is worth the risk from the French."

"I gave it up."

"I'm sorry?"

"Smoking," Gordon said. "I gave it up. Mostly because of the lung cancer thing. I smoked in high school, but the Ring of Fire pretty much put an end to going back to it. A few years away and I don't want to go back."

"Huh." James put the pipe back in his mouth and inhaled. The aroma of tobacco smoke swirled out of the bowl; it was a tender, warm smell, a long way from unfiltered Marlboros. It almost made Gordon want a puff of it. "The men of England—and, I must say, many of the women—are over the moon for tobacco. It is a cash crop, like sugar, except that any fool who will work moderately hard can grow it. And so they do.

"When King Charles issued his proclamation five years ago, before the Ring of Fire, he made it illegal to grow the noisome weed anywhere in England and Wales. He caused shipments of tobacco to be carried only in English hulls, to be stored in English warehouses and to be taxed by English tax collectors. Now, to be fair, there were still many farmers in England and Wales growing tobacco despite sheriffs and other officials—and there were thousands of hogsheads of tobacco making their way to Holland and France, free of English duty. If they weren't caught.

"But if any wastrel can grow tobacco, and there are thousands of willing customers, why wouldn't they stay here in Virginia?"

"You're throwing me a soft pitch," Gordon said. "They would leave because of the French."

"Mr. Chehab," James said, "I am not certain what a 'soft pitch' might be—but if you mean an easy answer, I cannot help but disagree. Most of the rascals in Virginia believe one of two things. First, that the French might never come—that there is nothing to fear from that quarter."

"And what's the second thing?"

"Aye, that one is even easier," James answered. "In the absence of any loyalty to the land of their birth, there are men who would do the same as their king has done to them: turn their backs and swear allegiance to another. The leaf does not care about the flag it was grown under—and the French king will no doubt be happy to take all of the silver that the English one has left on the table."

Chapter 36

Virginia

Cape Henry was in sight when they picked out a ship in the distance. It was bearing north by northwest. Soon after they came in sight, the other ship hove to and sent a boat across. De Vries came over as well, joining them on *Challenger*'s main deck.

The boat held an officer and two crewmen in civilian dress. When it came alongside the three men climbed up the rope ladder to the main deck. They made to greet Maartens, but he gestured toward Gordon.

"You're the captain?" the officer said. It was an English accent with a twang that Gordon didn't recognize.

"I represent my government," Gordon said. "I don't recognize your flag."

"Nor I yours. You aren't a Frenchman, and don't sound like an Englishman or a Spaniard."

"I represent the United States of Europe," Gordon said. "My name is Gordon Chehab."

"Michael Corthell," the man answered, touching his hat. "Second officer of *Vigilance*, out of St. George's Town in the Summer Islands."

"Bermuda," de Vries said. "Cut adrift like the rest of the English colonies."

"We travel up and down the coast," Corthell said. "We're nineteen days out of St. Kitts, and we have some news."

"Eight weeks ago a French fleet set sail from Brest," Corthell said, "bound for Virginia. The king sent his *grand-maître de la navigation* to command it, with the goal of sweeping the colony from the continent."

"What exactly does that mean?" Gordon asked.

"It means that the king of France has chosen to take action at last," the Bermudan officer said. "It's not clear whether this is the orders of the late king or the new king."

"Wait. New king?"

"Yes, of course. Gaston d'Orleans has been crowned king of France after the death of his brother. Some sort of ambush—he and the Red Cardinal were killed. Had you not heard?"

"We've been out of touch. Jesus." Gordon took off his ball cap and ran his hand through his hair. "Wow, that changes everything. What do you think this new king will do? I mean, Richelieu was ruthless and wasn't likely to show any mercy. But I don't know what to expect now."

"I would still expect no mercy."

"But this new king isn't going to burn the colony to the ground, is he? What would be the point of that?"

"Vengeance is a powerful motivation, Mr. Chehab."

"Profit is much more powerful," Gordon said. "Surely the king of France understands how valuable Virginia could be. So... just how big is this fleet?"

"Big enough to have an admiral to command it."

"Wait a minute," Pete said. "You said that you were nineteen days from St. Cat—"

"Kitts. St. Christopher," Corthell said.

"Yeah. In the Caribbean, I guess?" The Bermudan nodded. "And you just told us that *three weeks ago* you got word that a French fleet was on the way."

"That's right."

"So I have a question for you. *How do you know?*"

"I'm sorry?"

"What I asked you. When did you hear that a French fleet had left for Virginia?"

"Just before we weighed anchor."

"It takes twelve weeks—maybe ten with a strong wind—to cross the Atlantic Ocean. How could you possibly have word about something that happened *weeks* before that?"

Lieutenant Corthell stood to his full height, no easy trick in the pilot house. "You are not calling me a liar, I trust."

Pete didn't answer for a moment. "I just wondered if you got your addition wrong."

"No," he answered, looking at Pete. "I did not. And I can assure you that my information is accurate and correct."

"I don't see how."

"I do," de Vries said.

Pete looked at him curiously. De Vries kept his eyes on Peter Chehab without answering.

"A word with you," de Vries said. "Both of you," he added, gesturing toward Gordon. The three men walked across the deck, far enough away for what passed for privacy aboard a sailing ship.

"You've got something to say," Gordon said. "Let's hear it."

"He's telling the truth," de Vries said. "There is a facility established on St. Eustatius—one that I saw in action, using the code that you use to communicate between *John Wayne* and this ship. When I first encountered you in New Amsterdam, I assumed you were aware of it—but it has become obvious that you are not."

"What sort of facility?"

"A tower that lets people on that island communicate with stations in Europe."

"Wait," Gordon said. "Hold on. There's a *radio tower* on St. Eustatius?"

"Yes. It was built last winter; it survived an attack by the French, seeking to drive the Dutch off the island. It has been in operation for three or four months."

Pete put his hands on his hips and appeared ready to let loose on the Dutch captain, but he didn't seem to have the right words. Gordon stepped in. "You have known about this since before we met you."

"*Ja*," de Vries said.

"And just when were you planning to tell us?"

"When I thought it right. I am telling you now," de Vries said, as if it was the most reasonable answer in the world. "I do not see why you find this a problem."

"The problem is that we have no way of trusting you."

"Why?" de Vries answered. "I have given you valuable information, have I not? You two, of all people, should understand why this is of critical importance. While the Dutch and Spanish fight over sovereignty in the south, the Dutch—and your government—have the advantage of up-to-the-minute intelligence about the situation in Europe. The Spanish are ignorant of the existence of the tower, and even if they knew would be unlikely to make good use of the information."

"I could have used that valuable information a month ago."

"To do what?"

Gordon didn't answer.

"You said that the French attacked St...." Pete began.

"Eustatius," de Vries offered.

"Yeah. That place. You say that the French attacked there. Were they after the tower?"

"No, not as far as we could tell."

Gordon wondered who 'we' was, but asked, "So do the French know that there's a radio tower in the Caribbean?"

"I do not believe so," de Vries answered. "There is no way to be sure, of course, but they will deduce it sooner or later because it will be obvious that intelligence is reaching the Caribbean at a pace no ship can match."

"So the new king of France is at least as smart as my brother," Gordon said.

"I daresay he is," de Vries said.

Pete looked as if he wanted to deck de Vries, but he and Gordon exchanged a glance and Pete seemed to stand down.

The port of Jamestown was unusually crowded, not just with foreign ships. There was a trading vessel from New Amsterdam, *Koppig*, which was being loaded with hogsheads of tobacco; the Bermudan they'd met near the Capes; and another two-master that was flying the Union Jack and looked considerably worse for wear. There were also numerous smaller vessels, clearly not capable of open-ocean sailing.

The arrival of the *Staat van Hoorn* caused only a small stir. De Vries was known here, and there were merchants ready to receive goods he had carried from New Netherland. But the presence of *Challenger*, flying the USE flag, attracted considerable attention.

De Vries seemed unsurprised by it all. Gordon was more taken aback: he hadn't expected things to be this busy. His view of Jamestown was of a tiny settlement, like the national park he'd visited when he was in grade school. The town was perhaps three times the size of New Amsterdam and much of its works and many of its buildings looked freshly built. Of all the settlements they'd seen in the New World, Virginia's was by far the largest and busiest.

"And King Charles is giving all of this to the French," Gordon said to James as they waited for *Challenger* to be made fast to the dock.

"*This* is partly due to the king's action," James said. "When Virginia was left on its own, trade opened up with the Dutch—both in New Amsterdam and the Caribbean. Virginia has lots of land to cultivate, particularly in the outer shires."

"How many 'shires' are there?"

"Eight, if I recall. Most are near Jamestown, but Virginia's claim extends all the way to the mountains. West of here there is a great range of peaks, and beyond is the South Sea, and their claim extends all the way there."

"There's a lot of 'there' between the mountains and the sea," Gordon said. "I think you've confused the Appalachians with the Rockies. Remember, I'm from *West* Virginia up-time—not all that far from here. But to get back to the subject, why are all the locals here?"

"I assume that the House of Burgesses is in session," James said. "It seems a little late, though. Trinity term should have ended a few weeks ago. They must be meeting in extraordinary session."

"Because..."

"They must have heard rumors that will now be confirmed: that the French are coming at last."

Chapter 37

The House of Burgesses was not the United States Congress. Gordon and Pete were able to walk into the assembly hall, where a large number of Virginians had gathered; at the moment, there didn't seem to be much distinction between spectators and participants. To be honest, other than themselves, Gordon was having a tough time telling the two groups apart. Since anyone who could pay a pound of tobacco could participate, there were a fair number of backwoodsy-looking men who looked as if they'd put on their "best clothes" to be a part of this session. They stood in groups of two or three, glancing at the up-timers and at the more elegantly dressed grandees who were also present.

"This is like a freakin' state fair," Pete said. "It's like they're going to judge a prize pig or something."

"Democracy in action," Gordon said.

Pete smiled. "You watch, though. When they get settled, those guys"—he gestured toward three well-dressed Virginians standing on the platform at one end of the hall—"will be telling the rest of them what's going on."

"One man, one vote."

"But some votes probably count more than others."

"Captain James told me that the House of Burgesses these days is a free-for-all. The loss of connection with the home country means that aristocracy isn't worth what it used to be worth."

"Oh, you think so?" Pete said. A bailiff—a man named Peirse, with a tall rod and a sash of some sort—was gesturing for them and others to take seats in the rear of the hall. They walked toward the indicated place. "I still go with the idea that people don't change much. Look at what's happened in Europe since we arrived here with our newfangled ideas of the equality of man. People still tip their hats to guys with titles. People still bow to kings and kiss the rings of bishops. There may not be any connection with the nobility of England here—and I'm not so sure of that, even—but the bumpkins will still listen to their betters."

"You're sure of that?" Gordon asked.

"Yeah," Pete said. "Just watch."

One of the grandees rapped a large mallet on a block of wood on the platform.

"Hear ye, hear ye," said Peirse the bailiff from somewhere near the front, "the Honorable Court and Assembly of the Burgesses of the Free Colony of Virginia is now in session. Be upstanding and uncover."

Everyone in the hall removed their hats. A black-robed cleric arose and intoned a prayer for the safekeeping and blessing of the assembly, its members, and the colony in general.

Hats returned to heads, and everyone resumed their seats. The man who had rapped the mallet stood to address the assembly.

"We are met in a time of ill news, sirs," he began. "Intelligence has confirmed the rumor that we have already heard: that the French king, who claims dominion over us—"

There were shouts of "Foul, foul!" and "Never!" from the crowd—both in the ranks of seats near the front, and among the gallery in which Gordon and Pete sat. Peirse stamped the floor with his rod; the speaker waited for quiet to ensue, and continued.

"The French king, who *falsely* claims dominion over us, has dispatched a fleet to subdue the colony of Virginia...or destroy it."

There was more shouting, and more stamping.

"All men in Virginia know me," the man said. "My plantation of Bellefield is prosperous as the result of hard work and careful management. No one can accuse John West of indolence or ignorance. And the same is true of you—all of you: from the great reeves to the smallest landholder. We are true to our calling and faithful to our trust. We have not abandoned England: our king has abandoned us."

Through further calls of "Shame, shame!" and the like, West continued to speak, his tone strident, his voice rising above the responses from the audience. "That we do not have the protection of His Majesty's navy makes us vulnerable—and we know that the French king has friends among the savages.

"In recent years the men of the outer parishes have renewed and extended the palisades beyond Martin's Hundred, but a concerted attack at the same time as a naval invasion could be our undoing. Withal, I do not believe that the French king would pass an opportunity to acquire so rich a land or so hardworking a people as his servants will find in this colony. We are not defenseless—indeed, we may have new assets to assist us."

Gordon looked at Pete and whispered, "Did de Vries promise something to these guys?"

"I don't know," Pete said. "But *we* sure as hell haven't. Unless you're planning to save the world. Again."

"I want to know what I'm getting into."

"It never stopped you before."

A neighbor in the gallery hushed them as West continued to speak.

"—without the means to resist them, especially if there are many ships. I believe—and the other members of the council aver as well—that we must make our intentions clear from the outset.

"So I ask you, gentlemen of the House. How should we respond when the French come to call? What are we prepared to do?"

There was a murmur in the hall. No one appeared prepared to answer at once. Suddenly, a man somewhere forward of where Gordon and Pete sat rose to his feet and said, "I call for a point of order, Governor."

John West looked down from the platform. "Speak your mind, Paulet."

"No fear but that I shall."

The man turned to face the audience. Paulet was a tall, heavyset man whom Gordon guessed to be at least fifty. He wore a respectable suit of clothes that appeared somewhat antiquated, as if it had been taken out of the closet and donned for the first time in a long time.

He squinted, and his gaze seemed to fall upon the Chehab

brothers. "Governor West spoke to this House at Hilary," Paulet began. "You should all remember and mark his words. The French, he told us, had *lawful* possession of this land of Virginia, but were not truly interested in *physical* possession. Too many things clouded their minds: their alliances, their disputes, their intrigues.

"And despite this it seems that they have cleared their calendar of these things: what is more, there is news—very accurate and timely news, I venture to add—that they have launched a fleet against us. That certainly portends a desire for physical possession. Where the Frenchman comes, also come priests and tax collectors. I have interest in neither: I have been here in Virginia, a free man and land holder, for eighteen years, by headright granted by King James of England. What that great monarch has granted, I defy his son to put aside.

"We are Englishmen, gentlemen. We are as much Englishmen as the members of the House of Commons to whom this *king*"—he spat the word out—"refuses the right to assemble. He has fallen under the sway of bad advisors, mayhap, or his French queen."

"Not anymore!" someone shouted out. The queen of England had died in a carriage accident two years earlier.

"She *was* his queen when he made his devil's bargain with the king of France," Paulet continued, his voice strident now.

West, from the platform, rapped his gavel. "Does the gentleman seek to inquire on his point of order, or just make a speech?"

Paulet turned to face the rostrum. "Mind your words, *Governor*," he said. "But yes—I inquire upon my point. You did not think this day would come, when we would face this threat; yet it descends upon us now. You speak of *new assets*. Before we make any decision, perhaps you should elaborate on exactly what you mean."

"We have visitors in Virginia," West said, not rising to Paulet's obvious anger. "They are said to be emissaries from the new nation in the Germanies."

"That bastard de Vries," Pete hissed under his breath.

"They are . . . up-timers, I believe it is called?"

"Yes," West said, gesturing to Peirse, who began to make his way toward where Pete and Gordon sat. "They have come back to this time because of the Ring of Fire. They come to our shores on a sailing vessel, but who can know what wonders it contains?"

Peirse had reached the brothers, who stood among murmurs from the audience and the members of the House of Burgesses.

"Come forward," West said. "We would hear from you, up-timers."

"They are not members of this House," Paulet said. "There is no precedent—"

"There is no precedent for anything we are experiencing, Thomas," said another member of the House, rising in his place. "I say we should hear what they would say."

"And I object to it," Paulet said.

"I call for the yeas and nays," the other man said.

Over Thomas Paulet's complaint, Governor West said loudly, "Those who would grant the floor to the up-timers shall say 'Yea.' Those who would deny them the right to speak, shall say 'Nay.'

"Which of you says 'Yea'?"

There was a resounding shout in the hall.

"And who would say 'Nay?'"

Paulet, still standing, and a handful of others, spoke their defiance.

Peirse gestured with his bailiff's rod toward the front of the hall, and Gordon began to walk forward, his brother just behind.

Chapter 38

As he passed through the center of the House of Burgesses—several dozen men of varying ages and social classes, all watching him advance toward the rostrum—Gordon wondered what he was going to say. For more than three months he had spoken to colonial leaders and Indian chiefs, *patroons* and ship's captains—and all the time he had been focused on one mission: information gathering.

And now he was about to address the largest gathering of the richest colony in North America—and he was probably going to tell them what he'd told everyone else: *no*, *Challenger* didn't have a load of whiz-bang toys; *no*, the USE wasn't going to provide up-time tech and weapons—at least not in time to fend off the French fleet heading this way. But *yes*, there was ultimately something in it for them if they made common cause with the rest of the colonies and, possibly, with the natives.

This was a colony that could make a difference in that war.

What was more—the thought crossed his mind as he reached the front of the room—the presence of a radio tower in St. Eustatius had changed the nature of his mission, and might give him an opportunity to give President Piazza and Estuban Miro an update of where things stood in North America without having to sail all the way back to Germany.

But what would it mean for a French fleet to descend on the colony, and what would it look like if *Challenger* (and *Staat van Hoorn*, for that matter) turned and ran?

"My name," he began, "is Gordon Chehab. I am a citizen of the United States of Europe and the State of Thuringia-Franconia, and I was born in 1976. I am an up-timer, and until five years ago I lived in a small town in West Virginia—a place not very far from here. To you, I am a stranger to your land, just as the Ring of Fire made us all intruders on this century.

"But this century is *my* century now. If I live out three score and ten years, which is what the Bible grants a man, I will die in 1680 or so—three hundred years before I was born. I have trouble getting accustomed to the idea but it is a fact of life.

"Several months ago, *Challenger*—the name of the ship lying at your dock with our flag flying over it—set sail from Europe to visit North America. Ours was a mission of exploration and trade: a peaceful mission, intended to investigate the state of the colonies along the Atlantic. We have been to Newfoundland, to Massachusetts Bay and the mouth of the Connecticut, to New Amsterdam, and to Maryland. We always intended to come here—to learn where you stood relative to the French, whom we consider our rivals, if not our enemies. We have been forced into this—this other fact of life, I suppose I would say—because we pose a threat to them, and because they pose a threat to us. We have made much of our technical knowledge public, even to the French; we have made alliances, not to make common cause against enemies but to strengthen bonds between friends. We truly seek to live in peace, and wish to create more and better relationships with others who seek the same."

The room was silent now: the Burgesses were listening carefully and watching intently. They wanted to know what Gordon was about, and were waiting to hear what he would say next.

"*Challenger* has no single weapon that will help you defeat the French fleet that is said to be headed for Virginia. You may have heard about battles we have fought and won since the Ring of Fire, of technology and tactics we possess...back in the USE. You may also have read, or been told, about things we had up-time: things that we might have a few of, or we might no longer have at all. As we accustom ourselves to the seventeenth century, we lose more and more of the twentieth century. Grantville was not a community of expert soldiers, master craftsmen, top-notch scholars or wealthy philanthropists. Five years ago we were a small town filled with ordinary people. The Ring of Fire has forced us into an extraordinary position.

"Today I stand before you as a representative of the State of Thuringia-Franconia, the greatest and richest of the USE's provinces. I know very little about you; your names are not names I know...and that is my fault, not yours. Most of us know very little about Virginia, and this is the first opportunity we have had to visit it...at least in this century.

"In some places we have visited, they do not view the French as a threat. I do not need to convince you here. Your king has abandoned you, and will not protect you against the fleet that is on its way. In a way, he has endorsed its action, washing his hands of his valuable plantation, like—"

"Like Pontius Pilate," Pete whispered to him.

Gordon glanced at his younger brother, who stood beside him letting Gordon do the talking.

"Like Pontius Pilate," Gordon repeated. "From what I have been told, he gave you a better deal than some of his colonies, letting those who wanted to do so come home to England. Other colonies weren't so lucky. But if you stayed he has told you, in as firm a voice as he could, that he didn't care what happened to you.

"I only know of one thing that I can definitely offer by way of help. *Challenger* is carrying a dirigible: a lighter-than-air craft that we can use to try and get a look at what's coming. I don't know if we can help you fight off this French fleet, but I can at least help you see what you're going to face."

He heard Pete curse under his breath. *It doesn't matter*, Gordon thought: *if De Vries told them about us, he told them about the dirigible too.*

"If Virginia survives this attack, there may be the possibility of assistance—if I receive approval from my superiors. I wish I could offer more, but that's all I can do for now."

Jan de Vries was waiting for them on the steps of the assembly building. He was smoking his pipe; the smell of good Virginia tobacco swirled in the air around him.

Before Pete could take charge of the situation, Gordon grabbed de Vries by the elbow and steered him off the steps and out of the way of the departing Burgesses.

"You have a lot of damn nerve," he said. "What did you tell them we were going to do?"

De Vries took his pipe from his mouth and tapped it against the heel of his boot.

"I don't know what you mean."

"You're talking to the reasonable brother," Pete said. "Don't let me get involved in this little discussion."

The Dutchman looked from Gordon to Pete and back. "I told them you were here to make an alliance."

"You know we're not able to do that."

"Please spare me," de Vries said. "Of course you are. You as much as offered an alliance to Van Twiller; I am told that you wanted to be an honest broker between the Puritan fanatics and the Indian savages. Why else are you here in Virginia?"

"What do they expect us to do? We can't fight an armada of French warships."

"*Armada?*" de Vries laughed. "How many ships do you think they can spare?"

"Enough to spare an admiral to command them."

"Do you know who the *admiral* of the French fleet is? He's Richelieu's nephew. He's seventeen years old. How many ships do you think they trust him to command?"

"I don't know," Gordon said. "I would have thought that if the French would bother to send a fleet, it would be a substantial one. Are you telling me you believe differently? Or do you know something *else* you're not revealing?"

"You sound like you don't trust me, Chehab," de Vries said.

"I don't trust you, de Vries," Gordon answered.

"I never trusted you," Pete said.

The Dutchman looked from one Chehab brother to the other. Without responding, he took his pipe—which he still held in his hand—and tucked it into an inner pocket.

"Now, that's a fine way to treat an ally," de Vries said. "The Virginians will be expecting your help—you and your dirigible. I assume you will not be running for open ocean instead of staying and helping to fend off the menace—and that you'd like my assistance as well. Or is it a matter of trust?"

"I'd feel better if I knew what your actual motive was," Gordon said. "I'm not sure. You showed us *Zwaanendael* and told me, in words of one syllable, that the Indians were no fit allies. You told me that New Amsterdam wasn't going to support any sort of alliance against the French because they didn't believe there was a threat.

"And within a day I learn that you knew there was communication capability between the Caribbean and Europe and didn't tell me, and I get pushed to the front of the class to give an inspiring talk to a group of tobacco planters that are now all expecting me to save them from a French war fleet? I don't know how many ships a seventeen-year-old admiral gets to command. But based on the armament of my own ship—which is a single four-pound stern chaser—I'm inclined to believe that *one* warship is probably enough to put *Challenger* at the bottom of James Bay. Your ship is pretty lightly armed too. Do you think you're going to have any better luck?"

"You miss the point."

"Oh? What's the point, then?"

"The dirigible gives you all the advantages, Chehab," de Vries said. "You will see the French fleet's strength days before it arrives. If it is weak, we have the advantage of surprise—they are likely expecting little resistance, I would guess. The French will not know the waters or the territory, will not know when to attack.

"And if it is strong, *Challenger* and *Staat van Hoorn* can weigh anchor and be well clear of the Capes long before our ships could be trapped. *Ja*, you can say; *terribly sorry, Mynheeren, but all I have is this four-pound stern chaser. Must go, good luck.*"

"You want to make us look like complete bastards," Pete said.

"Typical soldier," de Vries said. "Reducing everything to a matter of *honor.*"

By the time they returned to *Challenger* Gordon had shrugged it off. He was trying to sort out everything he knew about de Vries, everything that the man had said and done. In the lens of what he had learned in the last day or so, he wanted to reevaluate their relationship.

Pete, however, was still fuming. He was ready to cut all ties with the Dutchman. He muttered about going aboard *Staat van Hoorn* and punching out de Vries. He wanted *Challenger* to set sail immediately, to go down to St. Eustatius so they could report back to Piazza and Miro.

"Good thing that you're not in command," Gordon said. They stood leaning on the rail, looking out at the dock. The scene was lit by a late-summer sunset; the air was thick with humidity and the odor of drying tobacco and animal manure, and there was not the merest breath of breeze.

"I can't believe you're going to let him get away with this."

"With what?"

"Twisting us around his finger," Pete said. "Look, from the time we met him in New Amsterdam, de Vries knew *exactly* what was going on—far more than we did. He knew that the king and cardinal had been killed. He knew that there was a war going on in the Caribbean between an alliance of English and Dutch and our guys against the Spanish—because he already knew at the time that there was a radio tower down there in touch with Europe. Don't you think that we would have set sail for there right away if we'd known that?"

"I imagine we would."

"But he obviously had another agenda in mind. He wanted to show us the swan place—"

"*Zwaanendael.*"

"The graveyard. That place. He wanted us to see what had happened there. He must have wanted to go along with the adventure up in the Chesapeake."

"Why, do you suppose?"

"Maybe to delay us. I don't know. I'm not sure if we can trust him at all anymore. We—"

Pete stopped in mid-sentence. They had been watching people come and go on the dock. There was a boat not too far away that was loading tobacco leaf for shipment, probably to the Caribbean; a couple of merchant types haggling over the price or quantity of something or just exchanging pleasantries in Virginian mercantile fashion; and others just passing by.

"What—?"

"Wait here," Pete said, and made his way down toward the gangplank, without explanation and without looking away from the dock. Gordon tried to follow where he was looking, but didn't see anything out of the ordinary—but Pete clearly did: he had a look in his eye of a sharpshooter who had picked out the target and was just waiting for the moment at which he would pull the trigger.

Gordon followed him. Pete was intent on something and seemed to be ignoring his older brother. When he reached the gangplank he broke into a run.

On the dock, someone else began to run as well, and disappeared before Gordon could identify him.

Chapter 39

Jamestown

It had been a few months since Stephane had been at sea, but the tang of the salt air and the sights and smells of an ocean-going vessel were welcome after the grit and stink of New Amsterdam. There were a dozen men traveling to Virginia to take up indenture to one or another Virginia planter. None of them asked any questions. Most were still feeling the effects of the sort of celebration that the actual Andries Cuypers had enjoyed. Most, also, were unused to the rolling of the sea and were messily seasick before the ship cleared the New Amsterdam harbor.

The ship captain, an Englishman from Virginia named Bullock, seemed a good sort; the indentures were fed no less and no worse than the sailors got. Two days out, one of the crew suffered a fall and couldn't get about. Stephane offered to serve, and for the rest of the voyage earned a few extra coins going up in the rigging—largesse he shared with his fellow passengers.

The coast of North America was beautiful and largely unsettled, like most of the interior that he had seen. From time to time there was smoke from a campfire, or evidence of some native settlement. But for five days they traced the contours of His Christian Majesty's New World lands and scarcely saw another soul.

The land here was largely untouched by man. Europeans—particularly the French—would have lots of opportunities to make their fortune. From what his fellow indentures told him, tobacco was making the Virginians rich. The English were still mad for it, the Dutch and French and Spanish not far behind. Apparently anyone willing to work could grow the stuff. All of the indentures were making the bet that they could survive long enough to get their own plots to make their own fortunes. In this respect, at least, the New World was exactly what the up-timer histories said it would be—a place where ordinary men could accomplish what the Old World denied them: a route to independent wealth.

During the Atlantic crossing, the up-timers had talked very little about their homeland. Stephane knew that they had grown up in the mountains somewhere inland, where Grantville had once been situated. They seemed to have little of what the Germans quaintly called *Sehnsucht*.

Stephane had met a few up-timers, and some of them seemed adrift in their new time, uncomfortable with what they had because they yearned for all they had lost. Not so Gordon and Peter Chehab: they seemed comfortable with the current century, though Gordon had some curious ideas in his dealings with strangers. Peter, in that respect, was a much better fit, and easier to understand. If Stephane had been following Gordon in New Amsterdam, that up-timer would have wanted to *talk* to him, or *reason* with him, or some such. Pete was no doubt interested in talking, but would not hesitate to be as violent as needed once the talking was done.

No. No *Sehnsucht* for "West Virginia." Peter Chehab belonged here and now. It made things much more clear.

On the dock in Jamestown, the planters had sent their hired men to meet the ship that brought newcomers. The indentures did not arrive like convicts, though. When the ship docked, they were free to disembark with whatever possessions they might have.

He wondered how Eugenie found it. She had been taken on by the Virginia planter. Stephane had been paid, and he had in turn paid for a servant girl to accompany her on her voyage. He did not see her when his vessel docked...and he wondered how he might see her again.

Stephane knew that someone would be waiting for Andries Cuypers: someone expecting a young man of twenty-one years, in good health, with all fingers and toes. But, like the *actual*

Cuypers, left behind in New Amsterdam, the man sent by the planter Thomas Paulet was going to be disappointed.

Stephane Hoff, adventurer and Monsieur Servien's eyes and ears, walked away from the busy Jamestown dock and into the town, setting aside his identity just as he secreted the indenture papers in an inseam in his vest—gone, but perhaps ready to be used again.

Stephane had expected Jamestown to be much like New Amsterdam: a small, isolated town carved from the wilderness, a frontier place full of strangers.

It was certainly a frontier place. The buildings were made of rough-hewn timbers, and the outside palisade was wood as well—hardly the sort of thing that would withstand a siege, or an attack from a warship. There were no grand avenues, no statues of kings or generals...but no sign of sacking or marauding, either.

It had grown beyond its original walls. At the head of the peninsula where Jamestown was located there was a slight rise with an old, crumbling fort called the Block House. Beyond, a cobbled path led past a large glassworks and then on into the swampy interior. The creek that separated the peninsula from the mainland was being drained, but still seemed to Stephane to be no more than a filthy marsh. A brickworks and a clay pit were in full operation, with a lime kiln nearby. North of the inland path was the newer part of the town. If the oldest structures of the town looked recent, the ones in the expanded part appeared as if they had been built only a few months ago. In the pleasant, almost sultry, late-spring weather there were work crews building more. There was further settlement across the James River, which had docks of its own and a handsome church visible from the main town.

There were plenty of places to observe without being observed. Truly, he needed to do that. Now that he was in Virginia—the most prosperous of the English colonies, and a likely place for France to begin its takeover of its new domains—he was not sure where his path might lead.

From the time he had left *Challenger* he had been on his own, sending letters to Monsieur Servien that, he hoped, had reached his patron's hands. There was no way of knowing whether that had happened, nor had there been the possibility of any response.

If his letters had not reached Servien then he was likely given up for dead. The one he had sent from Québec was most likely to have gotten through, while his letter from New Amsterdam—placed in the hands of a Dutch merchant captain—could well have been dropped in the ocean.

It would not be fair to say that Jamestown was not preparing for the eventual arrival of the French. There was a new ironworks on the northern outskirts of the town, clearly in use. Muskets were being stacked on a bench outside the door of the factory, loaded into crates, and carried into the magazine: another new building located nearby. Stephane wondered who might be designated to carry those weapons, but that was quickly answered—a ship had limped in a few weeks earlier after an encounter with a privateer off the Sommer Islands, and Governor West had put them in the colony's employ: he saw them swaggering about in the taverns and on the dirty streets of the town.

There was still no way to defend against attacks from warships.

Because of the number of strangers in town—the stranded sailors and others who were new to the colony—accommodations were hard to find, and not very comfortable, at least for those accustomed to comfort. He was indifferent to that, so long as it kept him out of the rain. Two days after the boat arrived in Jamestown the skies opened up and the town and bay were lashed with wind and soaked with precipitation that made the air thick and hazy. The boarding house turned its residents out of doors in the morning, to go to their work or to look for it. He found refuge in a livery stable near the town center, in view of the great church and the assembly hall.

The master of the stable told him at once that he didn't tolerate idlers. Stephane accordingly picked up a pitchfork and began to work on the pile of hay, which earned him an approving grunt and no further complaints.

The stable was busier than he would have expected. The reason was quickly explained as he listened to the conversations of grooms and servants bringing their masters' mounts to be stabled.

"...don't know what he *expected*," said a servant, leading a beautiful riding palfrey out of the rain. "Half the planters in the Tidewater are already here, with the other half due shortly. There are scarcely enough beds for the people who actually live in this benighted place, let alone all the visitors."

"Don't think he even considered it, Matt," another man said. "I don't think he considers much, other than tobacco and—" He made a rude gesture, in the universal language of impolite men. Both laughed. "It's a wonder he even thought about coming."

"He'll want his voice to be heard, Martin. Edward Warrington is a man of opinions, if you please."

"Other people's."

"All the same. They're all here to see and be seen, Martin. They don't care much about speaking and listening."

"Aye, I suppose so." They had led the horse to a stall now, and the groom—Matt—had gotten to work taking out his currycomb and a towel. The palfrey snorted and shook its head, spraying droplets of rain all around. Stephane had all he could do not to laugh, as the two servants shied out of the way of the water.

"But even so . . . I don't know what anyone is going to say, or hear, that will make much difference."

"What do you mean?"

"I mean that they'll all have to come to terms with the bloody French, won't they? That's what this is about—to decide when they're going to kiss arse, and who's going to line up first to do it."

"I don't see any French around, do you?"

"Not right *now*." The groom began to work on his charge. He seemed a skilled lad; the horse began to gradually become more placid as he whispered quietly to it, running the comb carefully through its mane. "But it's a tale that reached Master Warrington's ears that they're on their way, and will be here any day."

Martin snorted, leaning back against the rail at the far end of the stall. Stephane wondered whether he had any work at all— he and Matt clearly knew each other, but Martin wasn't doing anything with the horse, merely watching Matt work.

"They've been 'on their way' for three years, isn't it? Every week there's a new rumor of a great fleet of warships, stuffed with soldiers and cannons, ready to come conquer poor Virginia. I've been 'prentice here four years, since before the colony passed to the French, and I expect to make my six-year term without seeing a single Frenchy on Virginia's fair soil. It's just an excuse, Hilary court for the Burgesses, to come and talk and drink other people's wine."

"Gives me a chance to visit Jamestown. And listen to you."

"And you should count that a privilege, my rustic friend. Else you'd get no schooling at all."

"*Schooling*? From a lazy brewer's apprentice like you? You'd best be getting back to your work, Martin, before your master finds out you've been *schooling* me and beats you for putting on airs."

"He's scarcely risen from his bed," Martin answered. "The young lads will be working the mash tun this morning; there's not much for me to do for a while yet."

"Suit yourself. But I have work to do."

"Are you sending me off then?"

"Stay or go as you please. But I'll come to your master's tavern tonight and I'll have a thirst on me."

Martin took his friend's indifference as an indication that it was time to leave. But as he walked to the door of the stable he added, "You mark my words, bumpkin. You'll be leading that horse back to your master's plantation when this grand meeting is over, just as you led it here. Nothing will change."

"When we're both done with our terms," Matt answered without looking up, "things will change plenty."

"We'll all be rich," Martin said derisively, turning his collar and walking out into the rain.

The groom had spoken the truth: planters and their entourages were arriving in Jamestown, to attend an assembly—the House of Burgesses, a gathering of all of the landholders from this vast colony.

Some were quite grand, but it was clear to Stephane that, in some bizarrely English twist of egalitarianism, that *all* of the planters, from high to low, were permitted to participate in this affair—and always had done, even before the arrival of up-timers and their exalted notions of democracy and free speech. He did not understand in the least how rustics could imagine that there was anything that their betters would want to hear from them on any subject—but the price of admission to the House of Burgesses was a pound of tobacco, paid into the colony's magazine, or storehouse.

Like most people in Jamestown who had nothing better to do, Stephane found himself watching the spectacle of the Burgesses' gathering. He knew that sooner or later he would have to find himself a secure position, something that would keep him going.

And find Eugenie, he told himself; but another part of him knew that he should not be distracted thus. She had nothing to do with his mission for Monsieur Servien. Yet he could not get her out of his mind.

It distracted him; it made him less careful.

And when he found himself walking along Jamestown dock and came in sight of *Challenger*, he realized, suddenly, that it had made him *much* less careful. He looked up at the main deck and saw Peter Chehab looking right at him.

A moment later, the up-timer was running for the gangway. A moment after that, Stephane was running back toward the town square, knowing that this time he'd need to get away—and there might be nowhere to run.

Chapter 40

Virginians on Jamestown dock were not prepared for a muscular up-timer putting on a burst of speed, running down *Challenger*'s gangplank and out among them, dodging and changing direction like a fullback in traffic. He was clearly after something—and most people concluded that it was the better part of wisdom to simply get out of the way of the lunatic.

Up-timers, they thought, shrugging their shoulders.

Pete was determined that this time he was not going to lose track of the little Frenchman. Alsatian. *Whatever*, he thought. *Spy*. Jamestown was much bigger than New Amsterdam—but the Dutch had built that as if it was a cramped little town in Holland, with the buildings close together and the alleys narrow and dark. Jamestown, on the other hand, had wide-open areas, broad streets, and there was plenty of construction going on. His quarry had fewer places to disappear.

The older part of Jamestown lay on a peninsula, really an island connected to the mainland by a narrow bridge of land. Pete knew—and he suspected that the little spy knew as well— that if he got across he would be able to disappear anywhere. But it wasn't certain that the spy would think far enough ahead to realize that Pete had figured it out.

Instead of trying to pursue him along the dock, Pete cut across the plaza in front of the Burgesses' assembly hall, down along the cart path, and along the street of workshops behind it. Keeping the neck in sight, he ran until he saw a wide alley that would take him directly toward it. Then, as if he was rounding second and stretching for a triple, he cut left and ran as hard as he could, his boots squishing in mud and who knew what else. The entire exercise took no more than two or three minutes. He came out from between two buildings and stopped in time to see the little spy moving directly for him.

As he had done in New Amsterdam, Pete ran right at him, and this time was able to grab him by his vest and push him up against the brick wall of a building.

"All right, now," Pete said. "Let's have some answers."

"*Je ne parle pas l'Anglais,*" the man said, obviously out of breath. Pete was too—he was a little more out of shape than he would have liked—but he was doing his best not to show it.

"Yeah, tell it to the judge. You didn't have any trouble speaking English when you were aboard *Challenger.*"

The man didn't answer. Whether that was defiance or just fear Pete wasn't sure—and it didn't matter.

"Wonder how you'll look with one eye," Pete said, shifting his grip so he had a hand free. He moved it, thumb first, toward the other's face.

It was good to know that he had some intimidator genes; that did the trick.

"Please, Monsieur," the man said. "I mean you no harm."

"And I don't consider you a threat. But you've been following me—us—at least since you jumped ship. I want to know who you're working for, and right now, or I may be obliged to do harm to *you. Comprendez-vous?*"

"*Oui,*" he said. "Yes."

"So answer the damn question."

"I... report to a man in Paris."

"Paris as in France." *That sounds pretty stupid*, Pete thought as soon as he said it. *What other Paris is there?*

"Yes. But—I have lost touch. I do not know if he knows where I am."

"Didn't he send you here?"

"It was never my intention to go across the ocean," the man answered. "When you set sail I was aboard and had no way of escaping."

"As opposed to when you went overboard in Newfoundland."
The man shrugged. "A nice little swim."

"So why did you come aboard in the first place? To see what
we were doing, no doubt. And what did your man in Paris want
you to do about it?"

"Report only," he answered. "Just information. If any action
was to be taken, it would not be by me. I told you, Monsieur, I
am no threat to you."

"Except that your 'man in Paris' must be Cardinal Richelieu.
Isn't that right?" He lifted the man up and gave him a hard shove
against the wall. "Isn't that *right*?"

"No one so grand," the man said. "His Eminence the cardinal
employs a far better sort of person than me."

"Well, here's some news for you: his Eminence is apparently
worm food right now, along with the king. There's a new king
now. Just heard."

The other man looked stunned, as if he didn't know how to
respond. After a moment he said, "I have already *gone missing*,
Monsieur. Now if you are to gouge out my eye or break my neck,
please do so—or tell me what I can do for you."

They began to walk back toward the dock at a leisurely pace,
Pete firmly holding one of the Alsatian's arms. Pete knew his
strengths, and he knew Gordon's—and determining what to do
with a spy was clearly one of Gordon's.

"We're going to take a nice stroll, Frenchy," he said. "Don't
try anything."

"I am not French," the other man said. "And what would I
try?"

"Escaping."

"I am more valuable than I thought," he added. "You are not
in the ideal situation to deal with prisoners."

"I can always kill you afterward. And what do you mean
you're not French?"

"I am Alsatian, up-timer. Alsace does not belong to France.
It belongs to the Hapsburg dynasty."

"Anyone who was working for Cardinal Richelieu is a Frenchy,
as far as I'm concerned."

"What makes you think I am—I was—working for the cardinal?"

"A shot in the dark."

The other man seemed to be considering the meaning of the expression as they walked slowly along the lane beside the House of Burgesses building. "Ah," he said. "You are guessing."

"It seems logical. And if it's not true, then you'll tell us who you *are* working for—even if we have to—"

The Alsatian held his hand up. "I know, even if you must hurt me or threaten to kill me. But I don't think you'll do that."

"Really? Why not?"

He sighed. "You are a soldier, Monsieur Chehab. Capable of killing someone, I'm sure, and possibly you have already done so. No small thing—but done in the heat of battle. I do not think you will kill in cold blood. Back there, just now, you might have, but that time is past. You will not now kill me when you are done with me."

"I would not be so sure of that."

"I am quite sure of it," he said. "It is what stands between me and the end of my life."

They emerged into the great open plaza; Pete could see the masts of *Challenger* at the dock beyond. It was a simple matter of walking that far and handing him over to Gordon for whatever questions he might ask.

Then things became complicated. As they crossed the square, he saw a man—a ship's captain, from the cut and style of his clothes—pointing in their direction, and talking to a constable. The two began walking quickly toward Pete and the Alsatian.

"Cuypers!" the ship's captain said. "Hold it right there, you!"

Pete stopped, looking from the captain to the Alsatian and back. His charge looked baffled.

"Yes, *you*!" the captain said, pointing at the Alsatian. "You've cost me no end of trouble! Mynheer Paulet is here in Jamestown, and he's not a man who likes to be cheated."

"*Je ne parle pas l'Anglais,*" the Alsatian said.

The captain had reached them, the constable behind him. "Oh, don't give me any of that. Your English—and your Dutch, for that matter—was perfectly good aboard ship."

"I said the same thing," Pete said.

"What have *you* to do with this? Are you working with him? You're one of those up-timers, aren't you?"

"No. And yes," Pete said. "What do *you* have to do with it?"

"This man is Andries Cuypers," the captain answered. "He's got a signed indenture to the planter Thomas Paulet, for which Master Paulet has paid a goodly sum. He did not attend his new master, and until he does, I don't get paid. So he'll be coming with me." He reached out and grabbed the Alsatian's arm—only to find that Pete still had hold of the other one.

"I don't think so," Pete said.

"Obstructing the law, are you? We'll see about that," the captain said. "Constable, arrest this man."

"I don't think this is your man Kipper—"

"Cuypers," the captain said.

Pete shook his head. "Whatever. This isn't your guy. He's a Frenchman, and he was aboard *Challenger* until he jumped ship."

"In Jamestown?"

"Well, no. In Newfoundland."

The captain looked at Pete and burst out laughing. "In Newfoundland? What, did he *swim* all this way? No, I think you've been staring at the sun too long, friend. This is Andries Cuypers."

He grabbed the Alsatian's vest with his free hand; there was a crinkling sound. He reached inside and pulled out a folded parchment, which he opened and waved in Pete's face.

"Do you know what this is, up-timer? I daresay you do not. This is his indenture."

"Stolen."

"Mayhap that's true, but he took passage here from New Amsterdam using this *stolen* document, and so now he's Andries Cuypers, like it or not. For the next six years. After that, he can take whatever name he likes."

The Alsatian—or whatever he was—disengaged his arm from Pete's grasp. Pete knew at that moment that if he fought it, there would likely be violence, and the outcome would not necessarily work out in his favor.

"You should mind your own affairs, American," the captain said, a self-satisfied smile on his face.

With that, the three of them—the captain, the constable, and the spy—walked away, leaving Pete standing in the middle of the square, his fists balled as if he was looking for something to punch.

✧　　✧　　✧

"What do you mean, you lost him?" Gordon asked.

"I had him," Pete said. He clenched a fist and looked for something to slam it against. Ingrid put a hand on it; Pete looked at the doctor for just a moment, then let his fist drop to his side.

"I have some questions for him," Gordon said. "I need to talk to this guy. He left *Challenger* in Thomasville; you saw him, or thought you saw him, in New Amsterdam—"

"It was him."

"All right. Fine. You saw him in New Amsterdam. Now he turns up here. It explains a lot," he added, rubbing his forehead.

They had gathered in Gordon and Pete's cabin when Pete came back on board, looking like his hair was on fire. Ingrid had been right behind him when Pete came in and slumped into his hammock, ignoring whatever manners their mother had taught him to use in the presence of ladies.

Ingrid, for her part, was paying no attention.

"What does it explain, Gordon?"

"We knew we had a spy," Gordon said. "Somehow, our movements were being tracked. It explains that native envoy in Maryland. It explains why there's a fleet on its way." He rubbed his forehead again, as if he was expecting a genie to pop out and give him three wishes. "Christ."

"I don't get it," Pete said.

"You don't get what?"

"How *anyone* knows *anything*. Remember how we used to laugh at those old TV shows from the sixties? How every one of those plots would be blown to hell if the spies or secret agents or whatever just had cell phones?"

"Pete, what—"

"Look. This little bastard—excuse me, Doctor," he said to Ingrid; she rolled her eyes. "This little spy doesn't have a cell phone. He doesn't have access to a radio. He may know what we're doing; he may know where we're going. But who is he going to tell? *And how is he going to tell him*? Maybe he sent a postcard or something, but it takes weeks—sometimes, even months—to get across the ocean.

"Whatever Richelieu knew, or the new king of France knows, it's not much more than we know. It explains nothing. Nothing at all."

"But if he's a spy—"

"Then he's one of many. It's like a chessboard, and the French have all these pieces on it. Our op sec is blown, but we're still ahead of him."

"And his admiral?"

"Yes. And his little dog too."

Ingrid had been watching the exchange, trying to follow the up-time references, non sequiturs, and verbal sleight of hand. She crossed her arms in front of her chest. "What is our situation?"

"I—I'm not sure."

"What are you going to do?"

"I don't know. Get the dirigible aloft and take a look. Past that—I don't know."

"What does 'op sec' mean?" she asked. "Is that some sort of Latin expression? I do not know it."

"Operational security," Pete said. "This isn't a secret mission anymore, if it ever was."

"Well then. You have your work to do, and I have mine." She stepped past Gordon and headed toward the doorway of the cabin.

"What do you plan to do?"

"I'm going to try and get some of your answers," she said. "I am going into Jamestown, and I am going to tell a lie."

Chapter 41

Ingrid was prepared to go ashore by herself, but relented when Sofia insisted on accompanying her. Gordon wanted to go as well—"I'll wear a slouchy hat and walk funny," he said—but she insisted he stay behind. Instead, she consented to have Captain Thomas James accompany her as a manservant. He set aside his highly fashionable beaver hat, took up a position behind her, and the three of them made their way onto Jamestown dock.

The mission was simple—and duplicitous. According to Peter Chehab, the authorities had not believed anything he had said regarding Stephane Hoff's identity. They had claimed (and he had produced papers to prove) that he was a young indentured servant named Cuypers. The Lord God only knew how he had managed the deception; but Ingrid had no trouble imagining him capable of doing so.

Once she had rejected the idea of Gordon accompanying her, sub rosa, in order to make contact with Hoff, he had provided her—and James—with questions to ask him, if she was able to find him alone.

"How are you planning to do that, by the way?"

"Deception," she answered. "I shall tell them something they do not wish to hear."

"Such as—"

"That Peter is sick with fever, and that his brief contact with Stephane has made him sick as well."

"Huh. I better keep him out of sight."

"That would be best," she said, one eyebrow lifting. The expression made him smile for some reason, and he made some incomprehensible up-timer remark about mystery spooks.

All of her professional life, she had been accustomed to being bold and assertive. It was a requirement in a men's society, in her time. And from what she had learned of the up-time world, even despite the vaunted statements of equality, women there still had to fight for recognition.

Thus, to James' surprise, she walked briskly and without hesitation toward the triangular fort at the end of the dock. Two soldiers, muskets in hand, were in front of the open gate. As she approached, they came alert, weapons ready—but not aimed at her.

"I am looking for the planter Thomas Paulet," she said, not breaking her stride. One of the soldiers stood in her way, but seemed taken aback by her determination.

"He is not here, lady," the man said.

"Then you will direct me to him," she said, stopping before him. She looked past the guard into the fort, as if she was looking for him.

"I—I am obliged not to leave my post—"

"Then you will find someone to guide me."

"I don't know..."

"It is a matter of the greatest importance," she said. "I am a doctor, and there is someone who is ill. *Dangerously* ill."

"Dangerously ill?"

"Yes. A man in service to Master Paulet. A certain"—she looked over her shoulder at James—"Cuypers. Isn't that right, Thomas?"

"Yes, ma'am," Thomas said. "That is the name that we were given."

"Cuypers. He is lately arrived from New Amsterdam."

A look of recognition came across the man's face. "Little man? Foreign?"

"Yes. That's the one."

"Aye. Well. He's in the stockade here, awaiting Master Paulet's pleasure." He gestured over his shoulder. "And you say he's sick?"

"If not now, he soon will be. And so will all of you, unless I am permitted to examine him."

"All of us? What ails him?"

She looked about her. "I do not wish to speak of it here," she said quietly. "I do not want to cause a panic. He recently came in contact with a member of our crew—I come from *Challenger*, the up-timer ship. The crewman is ill."

"Terribly ill," James said.

"Best let her in, Benjamin," the other guard said. He looked as if he was trying his best not to breathe the same air Ingrid was using. "If he's really sick—"

"I should check with the chief," the first guard answered. "He'll have me in the stocks if I let someone pass who's not qualified."

"She's a doctor," James said. "And you have someone who's ill," he added. "One sick man...in a fort...at close quarters..."

"How long will it take?" Benjamin asked.

"Just a few minutes. Half an hour at most. You can post a guard if you wish."

"You could act on Master Shakespeare's stage," James said quietly as they crossed the fort courtyard.

"I did not require your embellishments," she whispered back. "I had convinced them that I needed to examine him."

"They were not convinced."

"Because I am a woman and you are a man? You think they were more disposed to listen to *you*?"

"In part," he answered, and when he saw her face fill with anger, "but also because you needed to make a better case. Such men are not accustomed to making decisions except as it affects *them*. It is easier to turn you away. But when they became convinced that if the prisoner was sick, *they* might become sick as well...they are simple. They make simple choices."

"Especially when a man tells them what choice to make."

He bowed his head, as if giving up the argument. "As you wish."

The stockade was no more than a sectioned-off area of the courtyard, like a horse stall, with a lattice of stout poles secured at the door. Stephane sat on a hay bale inside, looking a bit dejected. When he saw Ingrid Skoglund walking toward him, he looked surprised—and then did his best to mask it.

Their guard escort did not notice; he unbarred the gate and admitted the three visitors, then barred it again and turned to face outward.

"Andries Cuypers?" she said. "I am Doctor Skoglund, from *Challenger*. You had an altercation this afternoon with a member of our crew."

"I . . . might have," he said.

Ingrid gestured to Thomas James, who positioned himself in front of Stephane, between the little Alsatian and the gate, so that the guard—should he turn—would not see him.

"I have very little time, Stephane," she whispered in German. "I have some questions for you. If you answer them, I may be able to help you."

"I do not require your help, Doctor," he answered.

"Our crewmember has contracted McHale's Fever," she said in English, loud enough for the guard to hear. It was a ridiculous name, one provided by Gordon. "I fear, young man, that you may have been afflicted."

"Is it serious?"

"Serious enough." She opened her medical bag and drew out several instruments, including a scalpel, and handed them to Sofia. Stephane looked from Ingrid to Thomas James, who nodded at him, as if to say, *watch your step.*

"Were you in the employ of the late cardinal?" she asked quietly in German.

"No," he answered.

"What is your mission? Why are you in Virginia?"

"I am looking after a friend," he answered. "No more. Your up-timer friend has the wrong impression."

"Does he." She tugged on his shirt. "Pull up your sleeve, young man," she said in English.

"What are you going to do?"

"Test your blood," she said. Sofia handed her the scalpel, which she carefully wiped on a piece of linen. Stephane's eyes grew wide as he looked at it.

"Are you trying to scare me?" he asked Ingrid in German.

"I don't think she needs to," James said quietly in the same language. "You're already scared, aren't you, little man?"

"What do you want?" Stephane asked Ingrid in a whisper.

"Do the French know of our activity, of our movements?"

He looked from the scalpel to Ingrid's face, and then back at the instrument. "Yes," he said. "If my employer has received my letters, then he knows."

"When was the last letter?"

"I sent one from New Amsterdam."

"And the others?"

"I sent one...from New France."

"What do you know of the fleet that has been sent?"

"I know nothing of any fleet."

"I think I see signs of the fever, ma'am," James said in English. "Shall I hold him down before he becomes wild?"

"*I know nothing of any fleet,*" Stephane repeated, his voice urgent. "This is the first I have heard of it."

She looked at the scalpel for several seconds. It was clear that Stephane was unnerved by the doctor; it was also clear that he was outnumbered and vulnerable.

"I swear by the Blessed Virgin and the saints," he said.

Ingrid placed the scalpel back in her bag. "I believe you," she answered. "Very good, Thomas," she said. "I think our young man is not ill after all."

"And you believed him."

"Yes," Ingrid said. "Yes, Gordon, I did. He was frightened. I think our Captain James was even frightened. He did not know what I might do."

"What might you have done?"

"I am not disposed to discuss my professional secrets," Ingrid answered, smiling. It was dark now; the warm day had given way to a pleasant evening, with a fresh breeze blowing through Hampton Roads. "In the event, I did not need to do anything."

"You're a cool customer."

"Is that meant as a compliment?"

"Certainly, yes."

"It is accepted, then."

"What about Hoff's friend? Do you believe him about that?"

"I see no reason not to. When examining a set of facts, the simplest explanation is the most likely to be true. He offered that explanation right away, without dissembling. I therefore accept it on its face."

"I'm surprised he has any friends in Jamestown."

Ingrid did not respond to this comment; she could see that Gordon was frustrated and unsure. After all that had happened, after all the disappointments and dangers, Gordon Chehab was uncertain how matters were to be resolved, and what his part would be in their resolution.

"Thank you," Gordon said at last, "for getting information that we couldn't. I hope that this guy is no longer a threat... but I feel as if I'm turning my back on something dangerous."

"Regrettably," she answered, "that is true no matter what direction you face."

Stephane was more relieved than he would like to admit when Doctor Skoglund left his little stockade cell and made her way out of the fort. She had been prepared to...

Well, you don't really know, do you? he thought.

He had revealed more than he had intended: that he had been in New France; that he had sent letters to an employer in France, though not the cardinal—but he knew that this was a distinction that they would see as making no difference, especially if the cardinal was indeed dead. But they had told him something as well: that there was a French fleet on the way to Virginia.

All he had to do was to hold on until then. His new employer, Master Thomas Paulet, had his plantation in Charles City shire, upriver and inland from Jamestown. The gathering of planters in the House of Burgesses was likely to take a few more days, and then he—and whomever else had chosen to sign on with this particular planter—would be off to grow tobacco, or corn, or shovel horse dung. Explaining his present predicament was simple: the up-timer had mistaken him for someone else, chased and assaulted him, and had then been proved to be mistaken. Stephane—Andries—was sincerely sorry to have caused any embarrassment to his new employer, and would work doubly hard to make it up to him.

When the French fleet arrived, there would be nothing to keep it from attacking the settlements, or landing its troops. There would be a place for him on the return trip. He would find a way.

And as for Eugenie...he had not seen her and did not expect to see her again. A pity, that.

C'est la vie, he thought. *La vie d'un espion.*

Chapter 42

Gordon did not worry about the possibility that the good citizens of Jamestown would seize his dirigible as he had in Boston: but almost every square foot of Jamestown was occupied, particularly with the Burgesses meeting. He therefore had *Challenger* move across the wide part of the James River to the sandy stretch opposite—"Surry side"—where there was more space among the newer parts of the James City shire; upriver there was an open area where they could lay out the dirigible and inflate it.

Within an hour there were several boats of various sizes watching the operation, as well as a considerable number of citizens observing the process from shore.

When it was ready, *John Wayne* fairly leapt into the air, as if it had missed the experience. Gordon knew that *he* had missed it: the exhilaration of being aloft, of seeing the land and water laid out like a relief map beneath him, reminded him once again of why he had been eager to come on this expedition in the first place.

There was a pleasant following breeze and a low cloud cover, not quite ready to deposit rain on the plantations below. It afforded a nice gray background for *John Wayne*, in case anyone was actually looking for it. At low altitude, the farmers could make him out clearly, and waved their hats as he passed over; but once he reached the broad stretch of Hampton Roads at the end of the peninsula, he took the craft up over a thousand feet, blending *John Wayne* with the gray of the clouds.

"Just how we like it," he said to Pete. "Lots better than a sunny day for recon."

"It's not like they could really lob anything at us."

"We're all about tactical advantage. They don't know that *we* know they're coming. And they don't know we have a dirigible."

"I bet they do. Depends on whether the little bastard's letters got through."

"It can't have gone air mail."

They laughed together; it was strangely relaxed, as if this was a pleasure cruise, and not a recon mission to see if there was an enemy fleet off Virginia's shores.

It's like the balloon festival, Gordon thought. *Except Pete's here. And, oh yeah, it's the seventeenth century.*

Pete picked up the binoculars and held them loosely in his hands; there wasn't really anything yet to look at. "Ingrid said he told her he got into New France. That means Québec, right? Or is it Montréal?"

"Québec. There is no Montréal yet. I think there's a trading post on the island, but Québec is the main town up there. That must have been a hell of a swim."

"He must have gotten a ride. And he must have gotten some help to reach New Amsterdam. If I hadn't seen him there I wouldn't have believed it. But more officers get into trouble by saying 'that can't happen' ... it's like an idiot's last words."

"Which are?"

"'Hey, guys, watch this!'"

"Funny. Well, all right—they know we have a dirigible. But we've only taken it out when we were in New England, and then we launched it from New Amsterdam. Do you think they have any idea of its range, or its speed or anything?"

"No. All they know is that we can fly. You know, de Vries is right about one thing: if there's a big fleet coming toward Virginia, we'll have time to pull anchor and head for St. Eustatius. We'll know before anyone, and we can use the exercise bike"—he pointed toward the crate holding the pedal-operated transmitter—"to let *Challenger* know."

"And let de Vries know too."

"I still don't trust him."

"I don't either. But I think we're stuck with him. So . . . I'm going to take the *Duke* up to two thousand feet. If anyone sees us it's because they're specifically looking for us. Otherwise—"

"Tactical advantage."

"Damn straight."

Beyond Cape Henry the wind freshened and began to blow from the southwest, pushing *John Wayne* toward the mouth of the Chesapeake. Gordon once again had the chance to admire the engineering that had gone into the dirigible's design. With a set of guide wires near the steering yoke he could adjust every control surface.

It was a great application of twentieth-century ingenuity to seventeenth-century materials. It made him feel more at home in the time where the Ring of Fire had dropped him.

"What's so funny?" Pete said, lowering the binoculars. There was nothing to see—the coastal waters were, thankfully, devoid of French armadas.

"I was thinking about something de Vries told me about you."

Pete frowned. "What did he say?"

"He told me you were a better fit for this time. Your mindset was more suited to the seventeenth century—that you belonged here and I really didn't."

"I guess I should take that as a compliment."

"I think he meant it that way, but it was more a way of insulting *me*, telling me I was too soft, that this time would eventually eat me up and spit me out. That I wasn't adapting."

"You've adapted. Look at you. Look at *this*." He waved at the dirigible above their heads. "You're, what's the expression? 'Master of all you survey.' De Vries gets to watch while you get to fly."

"I think he meant my temperament, my up-timer outlook. How I still want to save the whales. And the Indians."

"Do you?"

"Yes."

"Still my idealistic big brother. We've already had this argument, haven't we? There isn't any way to save all the whales, or all the Indians . . . but yeah, we can save some of them. You're right: these people, all of them, don't have to make the same mistakes. They can learn from the history that might never happen. But in the meanwhile too damn many of them are trying to kill us."

"Because they think we're weak?"

"Because they want our *stuff*. The French can probably build a dirigible like the *Duke* already. It won't be too long before they can build an airplane or an ironclad. Our technical advantage has a lifespan, big bro, and when it's over we had better have built the next thing or the French, or the Turks, or whoever, are going to come and kick our ass. This is how we've all had to adapt to this world, by understanding where real power comes from."

"It comes from the barrel of a gun, you're going to say."

"Or it's death from above. We may not save the world, Gordon, but we're making the world over in our own image."

Gordon checked the fuel gauge on the propane tank and did a calculation to confirm it. They were at turnaround, the point at which they would need to turn back in order to manage powered flight all the way back. There was some leeway in the timing, since they could coast without fuel for some time, as long as they had some altitude. But it would put them completely at the mercy of the wind.

They were eighty miles east of Hampton Roads and a trifle north. Assuming that the French ships would be taking the usual course south toward Jamaica and then turn north, their ability to see them at a distance was hampered by the way in which the wind had pushed them.

"We're going to have to head for the barn, Pete," Gordon said. "If they're out there, we can't see them yet."

Pete was looking eastward with the binoculars; he didn't answer.

"Look, I know both of us would like to know for sure, but—"

"I think I see something."

"Are you sure?"

"No," he said. "I'm not sure. Give me a minute."

Gordon squinted at the horizon; it was unlikely that there would be anything out there. Any experienced commander knew to stay south for most of the passage. Navigators avoided the direct route because it was so easy to wind up becalmed.

Of course, *Challenger* had avoided the usual path as well to reach Newfoundland. Maartens had wanted to go by way of the Caribbean, until Gordon had overruled him.

Pete lowered the glasses. "Come here. Take a look at this."

Gordon stepped over to where his brother was standing. Pete handed him the binoculars and he raised them to his eyes.

In the distance, almost at the limit of his vision, he saw something above the swell: the upper part of a mast. There was a pennant at the top, but he couldn't make it out.

"It's a ship."

"And a big one. There are three masts; it just changed course. And there's another one behind it, I think, not as big."

Gordon handed the binoculars back to Pete. "Is that them, you think?"

Pete's face was serious. "I think so. If it's the vanguard of the French fleet, it's about fifty miles away, so it's, what, a hundred fifty miles from Virginia? At four knots that puts them a couple of days away. Maybe three or four, if they wait to make sure all the ships are together."

"We need to get back to report this."

"We need to get a closer look, big bro. All we know is that there's something."

"I don't think we can get much further from home. There's no guarantee we can make it back to land—"

"We need to *get a closer look*." Pete looked out over the ocean, and then back at his older brother. "At the very least we need to know what's coming, and how many. Grab some altitude; we can coast home."

"We may not—"

"This is seventeenth-century risk-taking, big bro. We can contact *Challenger* to go pick us up. If we drift too far north we can land in Maryland. This is why we're out here, right?"

Gordon was able to gain five hundred feet or so, using some extra fuel to do it, now he knew he'd be riding back without power. He forced *John Wayne* southward, so that the prevailing wind would keep them in range of the Virginia coast, and turned the dirigible east and out over the ocean. Pete kept an eye on the masts he'd sighted.

"There's a three-master and a two-master," he said. "I think it's a French pennon, but that's just a guess. The three-master must be a couple of hundred tons—it's definitely a warship."

"It's either French or Spanish, then."

"Yeah. Not a lot of choices, are there."

"Can you see the rest of the fleet?"

Pete slowly scanned the horizon, starting northeastward and

moving slowly south. A few times he paused, then moved on, shaking his head.

"No. No sign of them."

"There might have been a storm that separated them."

"They'd have slackened up, Gordon. These two have put on full sail: they're coming at speed, close to the wind, headed for Cape Charles."

"Maybe—"

Pete turned to his brother, the binoculars still in his hands. "Maybe what? Maybe, big bro, this is *all they sent*. Their seventeen-year-old admiral got trusted with two—count 'em, two—ships, to conquer all of Virginia."

"That might be enough, you know," Gordon said. "There are a couple of little cannon on the fort, and I know that the colony has a single ship with some armaments... but we have nothing to fight that."

"Nothing except American ingenuity," Pete answered, grinning. "Come on, big bro. Let's just get a little closer."

"Pete..."

"Just a *little*. We can coast home, Gordon. Let's see what we're dealing with."

The topman on the *Royaume Henri* shouted something down to the foredeck; the able seaman thought he'd seen something up in the clouds—a shape, something unusual that he couldn't make out.

Topmen were supposed to be sharp-eyed. They were also usually the youngest and most nimble—and not to be trusted with an expensive item like a spyglass. It might be dropped to the deck and shattered, it might be lost overboard, or it might be stolen and sold.

On the foredeck, the officer of the watch, who was equipped with a fine glass that his honored uncle had bought him just before the ship weighed anchor at Brest, looked skyward... and saw nothing but the angry clouds that might let loose a storm at any moment.

He thought it best not to trouble Captain Dansin or the *maître de la navigation* with a topman's mirage.

Pete took the controls while Gordon stretched the antenna along the edges of the cart and the under surface of the dirigible, attaching it to metal hooks. Then he unpacked the pedals and the black box, attaching the extension cord to the outlet and placing the earphones on his head. He moved the switch to TRANSMIT.

"Found it," Pete said. "Got a westward current at this altitude."

"Good. Let's try not to drop the *Duke* into the drink." He began to pedal.

"You just made that up, didn't you."

"Yeah. I can't sing but I can quip." He watched the dial move slowly up into the range where he could begin to send.

CQ, CQ, CQ, he sent on the telegraph key. There was only one recipient in range as far as he knew: *Challenger.*

He moved the switch to RECEIVE.

C'mon, he thought. *Let's be paying attention now. Got some news for you boys.*

CH1 DE JW2 JW2 KN, he heard at last.

"Got 'em?"

Gordon waved at him and moved the switch. *RST 577 E OF CAPE CHARLES. 5X5*; the last code, as before, was an assurance that they were safe. *CONTACT POSITIVE.*

RPT MSG.

CONTACT POSITIVE. 2 SHIPS ONLY. RPT 2 ONLY.

He waited for a response for several seconds.

"What did they say?"

"I'm waiting," Gordon said.

"Did you tell them there were only two ships?"

"Yeah. First thing."

RPT MSG. ENQ 2 SHIPS ONLY?

ACK.

"What did they say?"

"Well, you know, this medium doesn't really lend itself to nuance, little bro. But I get the impression that they're a little surprised."

EST TO BASE?

3 TO 4 HR. UNDERWAY NOW.

"You told them we're on our way, right?"

"Yeah. Do you want to do this?"

"No, I like to watch you pedal."

"Okay. Shut up and let me finish."

WILL BE WAITING.

ALL GOOD. SK.

✧   ✧   ✧

John Wayne's propane tanks gave out with Cape Charles in sight. They drifted over a lonely plantation south of the James River with hundreds and hundreds of mulberry trees. In the fading, gray afternoon light they could see a large central building, a long, glass-roofed structure and a number of cottages, as well as a church conspicuously lacking a cross on its steeple.

"Puritans, you think?" Pete said.

"Maybe," Gordon answered. "Puritans trying to grow silkworms. Man, there's something new every place you turn."

By the time they came in sight of Jamestown and their landing site it was almost fully dark. Maartens and James were out on deck, along with a man Gordon recognized from the House of Burgesses: John West, the governor of the colony. He apparently wasn't standing on ceremony. When they'd brought *John Wayne* to rest, the three of them had come ashore to help. Soon the bundle was being secured to be loaded back aboard *Challenger*.

"There are only two ships," West said. "You're sure?"

"That's what I told you. They're headed this way," Gordon said. "It's a hundred and thirty miles, perhaps a little more, east of the Virginia coast."

"Two ships too many," West said, frowning. "But...why did the French king not send a larger force?"

"I assume that he thought it would be enough. It might be."

"What is your estimation?" West looked from Gordon to Maartens, and then at Thomas James.

"I think, Governor, that their confidence is high. With the proper preparation...for which we have very little time...we may be able to surprise them."

West considered this for a moment, then nodded.

"Very well," he said. "We'd best get to work."

Chapter 43

Atlantic Ocean
East of Cape Charles

The *grand-maître de la navigation* was not pleased.

Even Father Jean-Baptiste, usually welcome on the quarterdeck, had been dismissed. He had retreated belowdecks, and Dansin thought he might have heard a sob as he went past.

The captain of *Royaume Henri* sighed as he climbed up to join his admiral. He took a glance at the barometer and squinted at the sky. The clouds were low, and the visibility was poor.

He cleared his throat.

"Your Grace requested my presence," he said.

"I do not like this, Dansin. I informed the good Father that I was displeased that he could not bring me good weather through his intercession with Our Lady."

"That did not sit well with him, I note."

"No." Maillé-Brézé turned to face Dansin. There might have been a hint of a smile, but it was no more than a hint. He clearly was displeased, and not just about the weather. "This is taking too long. This has *already* taken too long."

Dansin did not answer. He was reasonably certain that there was no response that would do anything but anger the young nobleman.

"Do you have nothing to say?"

"I am at your service, Your Grace," Dansin said. "If you believe that there is something I can do right now—about the weather, or anything else—then I pray you command me."

"Are you mocking me, Dansin?"

"Mocking you, Your Grace? I would not dream of such an insult. I merely have need of instruction. But I do have my limits."

"The weather, for example."

"I am a trifle concerned about that. Bad visibility favors the defenders."

"I would have thought it would favor no one. Surely they cannot see us coming."

"That is true," Dansin answered. "Even if they could, there is little that these Englishmen can do in opposition to our ships or our troops. Despite Your Grace's desire to make a quick end to this campaign, they cannot oppose us if we are able to get close to their settlements. But bad weather—bad visibility, in particular—can play unpleasant tricks on even the most superior naval forces. That's even more true when you're operating in an estuary instead of the open sea. It is for this reason that I propose that we should land at the nearest settlement: the one named for their queen, Elizabeth. It is where the James River is widest, at a place called Hampton Roads."

"I thought we had decided that our destination was Jamestown, Dansin. The chief town."

"By seizing the first we can easily advance upon the second, Your Grace, without risking shallower waters. I should think—"

"Shallow waters? The James River is deep draught—so we have been told. Jamestown is undefended, particularly against a foe such as *Royaume Henri* and its companion."

"That is true, Your Gra—"

"We strike at the *head*, Dansin. Take the most important settlement, and the rest will fall without a blow being struck. This—this *Elizabeth* place." He waved his hand, as if dismissing a waiter in a Paris restaurant. "It is of no moment. We can safely ignore it. What is more, we shall position all of our troops on this vessel, so that we may strike all at once."

Dansin looked his young admiral directly in the eye. He had been twenty years on the decks of ships, longer than Maillé-Brézé had been *alive*. He knew, or inferred, all that needed to be known about the handling of ships—particularly against stationary, land-based targets.

His watchword, as ever, was caution. The logic of the situation suggested that they proceed carefully. Troops from his and Vielle's ships, once landed, would be irresistible when backed by the ordnance aboard. With nothing ashore, and in shallow waters—even if the James River was deep draught as Maillé-Brézé suggested—there were a fair number of ways that the expedition could place its foot wrong. All the more so when visibility was so bad.

There were any number of things that could harm his ship, and put the entire expedition in jeopardy. Who would take the blame? Who would suffer? Not the Cardinal's nephew.

"I shall endeavor to carry out Your Grace's commands," he said. "If I may have leave to withdraw?"

"Yes, yes, of course." Dansin, without letting his resentment reflect in his face, bowed his way away and out of the admiral's sight.

On the James River
Virginia

At the north end of Warrosqueake Bay, where the James River was narrow and shallow, the crew of the two-master *Cecelia* was finishing the job of scuttling their vessel. Water was up to the cross-spars of the masts; the hull, which had been barely seaworthy enough to get them across the ocean from Bermuda, was already settling toward the muddy bottom of the channel.

With *Cecelia* in place, navigation was going to be hazardous at best.

Under the eaves of the pilothouse, Gordon and Pete stood and watched the operation, out of the dripping rain. It was a grimy, gray day, with enough humidity to make their shirts stick to their backs. The ladies were sensibly underdecks, staying out of the damp.

"Tell me how anyone isn't going to notice that."

"I'd be surprised if they didn't—even in bad weather," Gordon said. "But it makes the navigation more difficult. That goes double for a sailing vessel in unfamiliar waters. *Cecelia's* men were only too happy to oblige."

"Why?"

"De Vries and I talked to them. In exchange for scuttling their ship, if they're able to board and seize one of the French ones they'll get to keep it."

"They get to be pirates?"

"Privateers. With the Virginia flag and a letter of marque, little bro."

"What I said."

"Well, yes. But it's all legal. They get to be legitimate. Based on what I described to de Vries, both of the French ships are bigger and better than that hulk. Especially now."

"How'd it get all beat up like that?"

"Pirates, apparently. Without the Royal Navy to protect Bermuda, it's attracted the wrong sort of folks."

"So what goes around, comes around. And meanwhile they take this enormous risk."

"They're taking a risk, that's for sure. But that's something that sailors know how to do—and we don't, and these planters in Virginia don't."

"Meanwhile..."

"Meanwhile, we set them up for the other part of the surprise."

They went below to their cabin. The day was overcast, making it gloomy belowdecks. Pete sat on a trunk and began to strip his rifle, as a way to keep his hands occupied. Gordon leaned back in his bunk.

"Why are there only two ships?" Pete asked at last. "If this is an invasion, then why didn't they send something substantial?"

"I don't know."

"Huh." Pete lay the stock of his rifle on his lap. "No guessing? No thoughts?"

"I have plenty of them. But I'm not ready to jump to any conclusions. If I do, and I'm wrong, we're—well, prisoners at best. Along with *Challenger*."

"So maybe we should bug out."

Gordon looked across at Pete, half-visible in the dimness of the room.

"Are you ready to do that? Tell Governor West, tell the planters that we're going to cut and run?"

"It's what de Vries wants to do."

"I don't look to him for guidance on how to behave. Do you?"

"No. Of course not. And I'm not saying we should run. But all of this... doesn't feel quite right. We know that of all the colonies the French now claim, Virginia's the most valuable. So why in hell aren't they hitting it hard now?"

"I assume they're stretched pretty thin."

"By what? They're not at war now."

"Well, true, but—"

"They're *not at war*. They made peace with us. They wanted to have the American colonies so they could have oil, or tobacco, or whatever—they looked up-time and saw that this was the future. So why aren't they hitting us hard?"

"They must have assumed that two ships was enough."

"It's clearly not."

"Oh, no?" Gordon sat up. "We got a quick look at them from up in the air in *John Wayne*. They don't know we could do that. They don't know that *we* know they're coming. If they assumed that they could just show up off Jamestown with two heavily armed warships, lob a couple of cannon balls and then land some soldiers, they'd catch the Virginians with their pants down and it would be over quickly.

"Since we have a little time to prepare, they're going to meet with resistance. It still might not be enough, but it's more than they were expecting."

Pete returned to working on his rifle. "I don't know. It doesn't sound like Richelieu."

"And according to what we've been told, he's dead. Maybe someone else sent this expedition—someone who isn't as smart as the cardinal. Funny, I didn't know you were an expert."

"I'm not. But everyone treated him as, I don't know, the evil genius—the smartest guy in France, whatever. But even if he's gone, why isn't there a Plan B?"

"Is there something we're not considering?"

"Such as?"

"No clue. It just seems so unlikely that the French would send so little unless they were damn sure that they could win with it. I suppose it's possible that when he died someone changed the plan, but even so."

"You think there's some secret weapon aboard one of those French ships?"

"Wouldn't you make sure that this was a sure win? If that meant some sort of force multiplication, then you could send a *smaller* expedition. Like, oh, say, one with only two ships."

Gordon thought about it for a long time; in the background, he could hear the sound of the rain on the deck and in the river.

"If you were in charge of our expedition, little bro, what would you do?"

"I wouldn't just run. I think you're right: it sends the Virginians, and probably everyone else in the New World, the wrong message. Even though we don't officially represent our country, it would tell them that we weren't reliable or honorable. But I would sure as hell come up with a Plan B in case this whole thing goes sideways."

"Go on."

"We should make sure that *Challenger* and *Staat van Hoorn* are downriver, and can get away if we need to. We should get *John Wayne* up in the air and help out wherever we can. If Jamestown falls, both ships and the dirigible should meet up somewhere south of here, and we should make for St. Eustatius to send a radio message. We want the Virginians to win, but we're not here to do that—our greatest mission is to survive and report."

"You've been saying that for a few months."

"Yeah, and now it's come to this. Who knows, maybe the French know that we're in the New World. They may even know we're here in Virginia." Pete held his hand up. "No, I don't know how, big bro—Richelieu had his spy, maybe he got word of us back to France."

"And what does that mean?"

"That the French haven't sent a fleet to take Virginia, regardless of what the Dutch have heard. They've sent some ships for a different sort of prize. They want *us*."

Jamestown

Stephane did not know how long he might spend in the stockade, but his confinement was ended within a day. A pair of men called for him: one, a wizened, thin elderly man with a sour look on his face; and a large, burly one with a nasty scar on his bald head and a missing right ear. The older man carried a small satchel; the other one was armed, and had a whip tucked into his belt. Stephane stood at their approach.

"You are Cuypers?" the older one said from outside the cell.

"I am," Stephane replied.

"And you are not sick, I see. The up-timer doctor was satisfied with that."

"Yes."

"Good. Then you will come with us. Your new master should like to see what sort of servant he has engaged."

Stephane looked from the older man to the larger, younger one.

"He is here to assure your good behavior. I trust that you are intelligent enough not to attempt escape, and to realize that it will only add to your punishment."

"I do not know what I have done to merit punishment," Stephane answered. "A madman up-timer chased me through the streets of Jamestown—"

"Silence," the old man said. "I did not ask your opinion on the matter; Master Paulet does not take kindly to insolence from his indentures, and neither do I. I am sure that you merit punishment. You are just the sort: I can tell at once." He hooked a bony thumb in his belt and turned to the guard. "Release this man into my custody, if you please."

The guard seemed only too ready to comply; there was something about the old man that was intimidating. Stephane was not sure what it was, but he knew that he'd better find out, and quickly for his own sake.

"May I have the honor to know to whom I speak?" he asked, not looking the older man in the eye.

"A courtly request. I am Josiah Dawson. Master Paulet has engaged my services to manage his indentures. To manage such as *you*, Cuypers, or whatever your name might actually be."

"I—" Stephane began, as the barred gate was opened and he walked out, suspecting that he was only moving from one sort of prison into another. Dawson raised his hand, and Stephane let the sentence drop.

"I do not care who you are. You speak with an accent that sounds French to me. If you are a Frenchman, then God help you. Our master, like most of the gentleman planters, takes a low view of those who would be our lords and masters."

"I am not a subject of the French king," Stephane said.

"Good. That is the last I wish to hear of it. Do you understand?"

"Completely."

"Completely, *Mr. Dawson*," he said.

"Completely," Stephane repeated, "Mr. Dawson."

Dawson gestured across the yard toward the gate of the fortress. "After you...Cuypers."

Chapter 44

Hampton Roads

From the foredeck of *Royaume Henri*, Dansin could see the buildings of the Virginian settlement etched in the cloud-shrouded moonlight. Even at the discreet distance where his ship lay, he could see that Elizabeth City—scarcely a city by any definition— was undefended and, most likely, unaware. If it had been his choice, troops would be on shore now, under the protecting fire of his two ships' guns.

But it was not his choice. It was the decision of his young admiral that they go for the head—that they move directly on Jamestown.

It had been Maillé-Brézé's wish to sail up the James at night, but without sounding charts it was the height of folly and Dansin had firmly refused. For just a moment he had thought that the admiral would dismiss him and direct Vielle to take charge of the expedition and carry out that order—but giving Vielle the command was, if not the height of folly, at least on the upper slopes.

The weather was not going to favor them in any case. If the breeze that blew over the Spanish Armada half a century earlier had been a Protestant wind, the low clouds and fog looked like a Protestant storm. Dansin had an uneasy feeling about what lay before them.

✧　　✧　　✧

A thousand feet up, Pete took a close look at the French ship through his spyglass. The two ships had hove to, almost as if, having reached Hampton Roads, they were unwilling to continue. But it wasn't to be expected that they'd try to sneak up the James at night.

Too bad, he thought. *That would make it easier for the guys from* Cecelia.

But no one sailed in close waters at night in this century. It was just too dangerous. Too many things could go wrong, no matter what the possibility for surprise.

The lead ship was clearly the most dangerous. It was a two-decker; Pete guessed it to have sixteen guns on each of the two decks, culverins on the bottom and demi-culverins on the top, and light guns fore and aft. That was a lot more guns than *Challenger* carried. The other one had only about twenty guns. It was a single-decker, but there were enough gunports that it was likely to do a fair amount of damage to anything in its range.

John Wayne might be able to provide some annoyance, but not very much. They could drop something over the side; incendiary bombs would work best. But...

They probably wouldn't work all that well, given how crude they'd be. Ships were not stationary targets. Unless they brought the *John Wayne* down low—which might expose them to gunfire— they'd be likely to miss their target. True, wooden ships burned easily, but these were warships with large crews. They were prepared for the danger and had enough men to put out fires quickly.

And if they tried any such attack, they'd obviously give up the advantage of stealth. Gordon didn't want the French to know that they were being observed until the last minute, and maybe not even then.

Whatever the French ships were here for, whatever they wanted to do, would become clear tomorrow. *Challenger* and *Staat van Hoorn* were well downriver, in a narrow cove at the southern end of Surry side. If things went wrong, the two ships should be able to slip by and out into open ocean.

With a radio connection between *John Wayne* and *Challenger*, they'd know at once whether or not things were going wrong.

All they could do was wait.

✧   ✧   ✧

Morning came dim and foggy. Maillé-Brézé heard Mass on the quarterdeck and then ordered the ships to make sail. It was almost as if the crew had been waiting for the order: they snapped into action, preparing to go upriver. The admiral himself was in good spirits. He had chosen his most elaborate uniform and was taking note of everything happening aboard *Royaume Henri*.

"Today," Maillé-Brézé said. "Today we shall strike a blow for His Most Christian Majesty. *En avant!*"

His uniform included a decorated dress sword. He had it out and raised, and waved it in the air to the cheers of the crew of *Royaume Henri*. It was the sort of image that was intended to be memorable; and so it was.

The fog made it difficult to navigate, and Dansin kept the ship close-hauled with the smallest amount of sail that permitted them to make any headway. The broad bay narrowed into a river that grew progressively more constricted. The coasts were largely unsettled, with forests and marshy areas—and it was eerily silent.

Dansin had read what he could about Virginia. There had been an English colonial presence here for nearly three decades, with mixed success. The first settlements had nearly starved to death, and they had unsafely spread themselves too wide and suffered a terrible massacre a few years later at the hands of native savages—who were still out there.

When His Most Christian Majesty's flag flew over Jamestown, or the remains of Jamestown, something would need to be done about that. Dansin's fellow *Saintongeux*, the Sieur de Champlain, had been very successful with natives up in the north. No doubt he, or someone he trained, would be effective in eliminating the threat here as well.

Now here they were; complacent, unaware, ready to submit. These Virginians were not fanatics, like the heretic New Englanders. They were, he understood, mostly interested in making money. The king and the cardinal would find no fault with that. Profitable ventures by French subjects were a positive good for society—particularly when there would be profit for the crown. It was money that some king should receive—and if the English king had spurned it, then the French king would gladly accept.

Suddenly, Dansin's reverie was interrupted by a shout from the topmast. He opened his spyglass and looked ahead.

"What is it?" Maillé-Brézé asked.

"Debris," he said. "It looks like the top of a mast. It is even flying a banner."

"Really?" The admiral opened his own spyglass and placed it to his eye. "Why, you are right, Dansin. It is the banner of Saint George—an English ship. It appears to have heeled over to port, out of the channel."

"Not necessarily," Dansin said. "The mast is tilted away, Your Grace, but that means that the hull has probably slid further into the channel. We must give it a wide berth."

There was plenty of maneuvering room, but Dansin was still wary of the further shore, which was shrouded in fog. One uncooperative current; one stray gust of wind...

"Signal *Saint-Christophe*," he shouted to the topman. "Obstacle to port."

Royaume Henri crept along through the fog. The coast to port jutted out as the course of the river turned almost directly north. Dansin had a leadsman taking soundings. The admiral fretted, as if all of the precautions that Dansin was taking were unnecessary.

The next noise that came out of the fog, downriver from them, was a scraping sound.

Dansin uttered an oath that would cost him many *Aves* when he took the time to say them. Despite his warning—despite everything that any prudent sailor would do to avoid obstacles and take care in an unfamiliar channel, under difficult circumstances—François Vielle had managed to locate the hull of the sunken ship.

Maillé-Brézé heard it too, though he did not identify it at first, frowning at Dansin's oath.

"Was that—?"

"I fear that it was, Your Grace," Dansin said. "*Saint-Christophe* has found the hazard."

"They should deal with it themselves."

"Your Grace—"

"We have *business* to attend to, Dansin. Jamestown cannot be far away, and—"

Then, drifting indistinctly through the fog, he heard shots being fired, and shouts.

"What is...?"

Dansin peered downriver. The fog made visibility poor at best, but it could only be one thing. A boarding operation was underway—and with all of the soldiers located aboard *Royaume Henri* per his admiral's orders, *Saint-Christophe* had been left scarcely defended.

Most sailors in their expedition were excellent shots across water; it was something that distinguished the French from their English or Spanish counterpart.

But not in this fog.

"Hard about!" he ordered, and ran to the pilothouse. Maillé-Brézé, who seemed to realize something was amiss only seconds after, ran after him. *Royaume Henri*, unaccustomed to maneuvering in such shallow waters, came into the wind, its sails flapping.

There was only one crystal receiver, and Gordon had not wanted to take it off of *Challenger* and place it ashore at Jamestown. To put the rest of the plan into action required more primitive means. From *John Wayne*, a few hundred feet up, Gordon watched the action as best he could through the drifting fog. He saw the smaller ship fetch up against the hull of the sunken *Cecelia*. That was a bit of luck—it made the boarding action easier than it might have been.

Then he saw the larger one put about, fighting the current around the point of land that, someday, would be Hog Island.

It had taken some effort to keep *John Wayne* far enough downriver to witness the action; with a few adjustments he had it drifting slowly up toward Jamestown.

As soon as he came in sight of the town, he took out his bullhorn and shouted, "Call to the bullpen!"

Pete heard "Call to the bullpen!" and looked up to see *John Wayne*'s nose peeking through the fog a few hundred feet up. He waved—he wasn't sure whether Gordon saw him or not—but it didn't matter.

With the help of several stout Virginians, small clay pots from the wooden box at the bottom of his canoe were tossed into the boats strung out along the river. As each pot struck and shattered, it burst into flame. He hadn't thrown a baseball in quite a while, but it came back to him easily.

Some of the other men looked like they could throw strikes as well.

When the boats were all aflame, he waved to shore, and a man standing by un-looped the stout rope that had anchored them all to Jamestown's pier. As soon as he'd done so, the man ran as fast as he could.

"Damn," Pete said.

As they watched, the boats—loosely tied together—began to drift downriver on the rapid current of the James.

"What is it?" Maillé-Brézé said. "What is going on?"

"That damn fool Vielle fouled his ship on the English hulk. When I catch hold of him I'm going to throttle him," Dansin said. "But something else is happening."

"What?"

"I do not know, Your Grace," Dansin said. "I think..."

Royaume Henri had managed to turn downriver and was slowly making headway, aided by the river current. Dansin took out his spyglass once more. The fog was making it difficult to see anything, and he did not want to drift past *Saint-Christophe*—or, worse yet, collide with it.

He took a speaking trumpet from beside the whipstaff and put it to his lips. "Vielle!" he shouted. "What is your status?"

There was no answer—but he could hear something else: not just shouting, but a grating sound, like...like...

"On my mark," he heard in English. "*Fire!*"

And suddenly, speeding through the air, he could see—and hear—a barrage headed for his ship.

As it neared, he dove for the deck, taking the *grand-maître de la navigation* with him.

If it had not been so foggy...

If the channel had been wider...

If François Vielle had been even mildly competent...

If his admiral had not shifted troops to *Royaume Henri*...

Those were the first four things Dansin thought, as he got to his knees. The results of *Saint-Christophe*'s broadside had ripped into *Royaume Henri*, shredding sails and pockmarking the hull. Two of his men nearby lay dead; they probably never saw it coming.

Maillé-Brézé was alive and unharmed, though he looked stunned and surprised—perhaps merely at the effrontery of Dansin throwing him to the deck.

He looked at *Saint-Christophe*, only a few hundred yards away. There were men on deck—unfamiliar men—and the guns that had fired, not all of them, but enough—had been run back in and were likely being loaded again. He needed to bring *Royaume Henri* about and prepare a broadside.

Then he looked upriver, and from around the point of land he saw fire: drifting on the rapid current, headed directly for his ship.

According to the plan, *Saint-Christophe*, once in the control of the Englishmen, should have put on sail and gone downriver. The sound of its guns came as a surprise to Gordon, who could hear them from a quarter mile away.

But *Saint-Christophe* was well and truly grounded, its keel stuck against the concealed upper hull of *Cecelia*. The captain of *Cecelia* realized that, if *Royaume Henri* decided to reply with a broadside of its own, they would be a prime target. But before he had an opportunity to react, he saw the bigger ship maneuver with the wind, passing *Saint-Christophe* and heading for open water. The flotilla of fireships swept slowly past.

The Englishmen aboard *Saint-Christophe* whooped and hollered as the French ship dwindled into the fog.

Chapter 45

Jamestown

Under the direction of Dawson, Stephane and other servants and employees of Thomas Paulet were employed in preparing clay pots full of a volatile liquid. A mechanic of some sort had come to the dock with a cart, and he and two others clad in heavy coveralls and wearing thick gloves carefully offloaded large stoppered jugs. Then, as they lined up, the liquid was poured into them and—on stern instructions from Dawson—they immediately covered the opening with a round cork. The reason for this became obvious when one of the servants, a young lad whose name Stephane never learned, managed to drop the cork he was holding and the contents of the pot abruptly burst into flame. One of the coverall-clad men immediately grabbed a bucket full of sand and doused it, while everyone else jumped back.

They were filling clay pots with *flame*—with some up-timer hellfire—and it would be used against the incoming French fleet. It made him frightened...and angry.

The pots, once they were properly sealed, were stacked carefully on straw padding in wooden crates. It was slow work, and after the first accident everyone was even more careful—the men in overalls as well as those like himself who had no protection whatsoever. He was more sure-handed than some of the others, but he paid particular attention to handling the pots and the

312

corks. He even made sure to hold his breath whenever he could, in case the vapors from the hellfire liquid were noxious.

When all of the pots were filled and stoppered, the workers were permitted a short break. Stephane, along with the others, made their way to a water pump where they drank their fill and washed off their hands and faces.

It was then that he saw Eugenie.

She was standing alone, near a group of women who appeared to be studiously ignoring her. Even from a hundred yards away he could see that she was upset and had been crying. Almost as if she could feel his eyes upon her she looked up and met them.

Her glance was earnest, almost pleading.

Without hesitating he walked away from the group at the pump and toward her. He heard Dawson's voice say something, but he ignored him. It had something to do with punishment—he would face that when it came.

When he reached her, it was clear that she was very upset and was making every attempt to hide it.

"Mynheer der Hoefe," she said quietly in Dutch. "Monsieur," she added in a whisper in French, "it is not safe—"

"No," he replied. "It is particularly not safe to converse in French. Madame Eugenie, what is wrong?"

"My...employer," she began in Dutch. "He has—"

"He has not *harmed* you, I trust."

"He has...left no mark. Yet. But he warns me that I shall be arrested as a French spy if I do not comply with his wishes. A spy! I am no such thing—you know, you assisted me in New Amsterdam...but..."

"I assisted you," Stephane said. "I arranged for you to come to this place. I have done you a great wrong, Madame."

"It is not your fault, Mynheer. I would have faced this, or worse, if I had remained in New Amsterdam."

"Still—I feel that I am at fault. I must make it right."

Eugenie looked past Stephane, her eyes widening. He turned around to see Dawson's overseer approaching. The hulking man with the scar and the whip had a leering smile on his face.

"I cannot let you endanger yourself or jeopardize your situation," she said.

"I will assume the risk." He turned back to her, opened his palm and pointed to it, using it as an impromptu map. "Here is the House of Burgesses. Along the side there is a narrow path. Meet me there when the moon rises and I will attend to this."

"Mynheer der Hoefe. This is..."

"Moonrise," he whispered, then turned to walk toward the overseer.

Paulet had quartered his new employees and servants in the upper level of a stable. From there they saw how their handiwork was employed. The pots of hellfire were tossed onto boats that quickly burst into flame, and were then cast adrift to float downstream. Sometime during the morning they heard cannon fire, a broadside from a ship; the men speculated on what it could mean.

Then a warship bearing the name *Saint-Christophe* came into view and anchored near Jamestown dock. The men aboard seemed to be jubilant, and when a group of them rowed ashore, they were singing—in English. Stephane recognized them as members of the crew of an English trader that had been in port until a few days earlier.

Where was the French fleet that Doctor Skoglund had so greatly feared? What had happened to this French warship? Where were its sisters?

I shall be arrested as a spy, Eugenie had said to him.

It would be no safer for Stephane—who was no Dutchman. The Englishmen new in the service of Thomas Paulet knew no better, but the two other Dutchmen would realize, sooner or later, that he was not Andries Cuypers. Dawson had already seen through the facade, and no doubt was looking for a way to use that information against him.

All of Jamestown seemed to be celebrating the victory over the French, however it had happened. *Saint-Christophe* appeared to be a prize ship, and its captain and other officers were being paraded through the main street. The men in the loft were not permitted to depart. They were given a meager supper, and then the stable was closed and barred from the outside. Paulet apparently feared that one or another of his new servants would seek to leave his service.

After most of them settled down to sleep, Stephane found his way to an upper window at the end of the loft. It was slightly ajar, and gave onto a narrow alley twenty feet below. For an Alsatian hill climber, or a topman, it was no challenge.

✧　　✧　　✧

Staying clear of the night watch, even in a small town like Jamestown, was no challenge either. While he hovered in the shadows waiting for Eugenie, he wondered why he was there—and what he might do next.

This was where I would be finding a ship to take me home, he thought. *To report. Of course, that's not home—even if there was a home in Paris, it would be one where Monsieur Servien, if he bothered with me at all, would always be able to find me. But if the cardinal was dead, perhaps Monsieur Servien was dead as well. My mission is nothing now.*

Alsace, he thought. *Home is Alsace ... but that was a place I left behind long ago.*

As for his mission ... His reports seemed insignificant now. Greater things were in train, plans to which he was not a party. The king had sent a fleet of some sort, and it had somehow been reduced by one ship. There were no French soldiers on the streets of Jamestown now.

And even if there were ... what would he say?

Bon soir, mes amis. I am in the service of the king of France and desire an audience with your commander.

He almost laughed at the thought. That sort of bluster had been successful with the Sieur de Champlain, yet as he considered the event he wondered that the captain had taken him at all at his word.

His reverie was interrupted by a soft voice. "Mynheer den Hoefe."

Eugenie.

Why am I here—not just in Jamestown? he thought. *Here. Now.*

He crept close and then stepped out of the shadows. Eugenie was standing there, a basket over her arm. "Come," he whispered. "We must go."

"Where?"

"It doesn't matter. Away from here."

"The gate is closed—"

"Yes, yes," he said. He took her gently by the arm; she flinched for a moment, then relaxed and let him guide her. "But the dock is not."

"You plan—"

"Hush. Do you trust me?"

"I ... suppose I must," she said. "I have trusted you thus far, though I do not know why you are risking yourself."

"We will discuss it later."

"Mynheer der Hoefe—"

"Stephane," he said. "Call me Stephane, and I shall call you Eugenie. But we will speak when we are away from here."

At the dock, the guard was light, almost indifferent. The moonlight was dim, still shrouded in cloud. Away from the fortress there were small *kanos*—*canoes*, as they were called in Virginia. Boarding one and assisting Eugenie, letting the tie rope loose, and carefully and quietly paddling out into the river was a simple task.

"There are other plantations upriver," he said in French, when they were out of sight of Jamestown. He continued to paddle, but slowly. Eugenie sat opposite, hunched down, her expression scarcely visible. "We will find employment there."

"I ... see."

"There is something you must know," he continued. "You are no spy, and it is a cruel thing for you to suffer under the imputation. But I am."

"A spy?"

"Yes. I was sent to spy on the up-timers, and wound up accompanying them to the New World. We ... parted company, and I have found my way here. But for a set of indenture papers, they would have custody of me now."

"You signed an indenture?"

"Not precisely." He described in no particular detail how he had acquired the signed papers of Andries Cuypers. "But I do not find the situation to my liking."

"Nor did I."

"I am sure of that. I refused to let it stand and have thus rescued you from it, since I trapped you in it in the first place. I am sorry, Eugenie. I suppose that is why I am here—why we are here."

"I do not know what you expect of me in return. And even if there is another plantation, or some other place, that would employ us—there is an appearance of great impropriety. Unless you wish me to pose as your—"

"Cousin," Stephane said. "Our fathers, brothers, died in a shipwreck. Now we must make our way as best we can."

"So you do not..."

"No," Stephane said. He let the oar drag in the water. "No. I do not."

"You do not find me attractive?"

"On the contrary. In another place, at another time, there might be other arrangements. But I do not wish to complicate matters now."

"That is an interesting way to put it."

Stephane took a deep breath. "Eugenie. Mademoiselle. I am, of course, attracted to you. I am a healthy young man in the prime of life; you are an attractive, handsome woman—an intelligent, skilled craftswoman—who, unfortunately, requires if not a protector, a friend and guide. But it is not being attracted to you that motivates me to help you."

"Then what? Is this part of your . . . professional engagements?"

"You mean my espionage activity?"

"Yes. Is this part of that?"

"No. It was not so in New Amsterdam, and it is not so here in Virginia."

"Then why?"

He laughed. "To be quite honest, I have been asking myself that question. I lack an answer. But here we are, a woman from Flanders and a man from Alsace, far from home."

"Cousins."

"Yes. Cousins. And I am moved to assist you because there are few indeed on this continent whom we can trust. Perhaps we can find our way to a French settlement, though they are far away. Perhaps we can find some safe spot far from Jamestown, and if the French fleet truly arrives we can take our place."

"I see."

"But Jamestown has become unsafe for either of us, right now. I would wish to offer you more assurance; but regrettably I cannot."

They traveled along in silence for some time, then Eugenie said, "Stephane."

"Yes?"

"I shall be glad to be your cousin."

Though she could not see it, Stephane smiled. Wherever the river took him, he felt that he was moving in the right direction. The smile became a grin, and stayed on his face for quite some time. In the darkness, of course, there was no one to see. Oddly, that made him more cheerful than ever.

Chapter 46

Chesapeake Bay

The fireships ran ashore against the swampy beaches on the south side of the bay where the hulk was grounded. The current of the river aided *Royaume Henri*, keeping her ahead of them until they were no longer a threat.

The unexpected, short-range broadside from *Saint-Christophe* had done more damage than Dansin originally thought: the foremast had been struck almost dead-on, the hull had a pair of holes just above the waterline aft of amidships, and he had six dead and as many wounded crewmen.

But, thank God, Jean-Armand Maillé-Brézé was not among the dead or wounded; and neither was Father Jean-Baptiste, who was attending to those whom the attack had claimed—freeing Dansin to deal with other things.

His young admiral seemed stunned by the turn of events. Dansin found an anchorage across the wide bay in the lee of a small island. Maillé-Brézé, by that time, had gone below decks with the priest to visit the wounded. It was the best thing he could have done.

When they returned to France, it was very likely that Dansin's career was over. He assumed that, whatever the report, the blame would fall on his shoulders rather than on those of Maillé-Brézé. That was the way of things with those of gentle birth. If things had been different...

If the young man of gentle birth had taken his advice and drawn on his experience...

If, if, if. But "if" did not repair the masts or sew together the sails, it did not patch holes in the hull or bail water from below decks or change the weather or bring back the dead. It solved none of those problems. It merely made him angry.

In the meanwhile, he would have to address these things himself to make *Royaume Henri* seaworthy. The *grand-maître de la navigation* might wish to launch another attack on the Virginia colony. Dansin could imagine such a desire and such an ambition; he even shared it himself. But they had lost the element of surprise, they had lost a ship, and it would take time to ready the ship that remained for such an attack.

And every failure would fall on his shoulders. It would be Maillé-Brézé's disappointment; but it would be Dansin's *fault*. That was just a fact of life in aristocratic nations. *Bien sûr*. To be sure; of course; it was the very nature of things.

Jamestown

John Wayne and *Challenger* returned to Jamestown near sunset. *Staat van Hoorn* had gone out past Point Comfort to keep a closer watch on the remaining French ship. Gordon would have preferred otherwise, but de Vries didn't appear to want to argue the point.

Gordon reasoned that he was as likely to set sail for the Caribbean, or New Amsterdam, or someplace else as provide surveillance. But it was clear that the Dutch captain had his own agenda, and had had it all along.

Gordon received a hero's welcome when he came across the river from where *John Wayne* had landed. Most of the town hadn't gotten the full details of the day's events, and there was a rumor that somehow the dirigible had brought about the retreat of the French warship—some up-timer magic.

"They'll figure it out," Pete told him as they stood on the main deck of *Challenger*. "Once our ship sets sail, there'll be lots to do here. I don't think the French are going to take no for an answer."

"I think you're right. We've got to get word back home. I think our best move is to sail for St. Eustatius and make use of that radio tower."

"That's a good idea." Pete looked off across the town, not at his brother.

"Something bothering you, little bro?"

"Unfinished business."

"What kind?"

"Oh, different things. That little bastard Hoff is in this town somewhere. I still want to find out what he knows."

"I thought Ingrid settled that for us."

"Yeah, well, she didn't. I still have some questions."

"There won't be much time to ask them. I want us to be underway tomorrow or the day after—the sooner the better."

"About that." Pete turned to face Gordon then, his face serious. "I think there's some preparation needed here, big bro. And I think I'm the guy to do it."

"There's not much time—"

"There's plenty of time. At least a month. It'll take you that long to sail down to St. Houston."

"Eustatius."

"Whatever. To sail there and come back. In the meanwhile, I can show these guys how to make minié balls. They're mostly hunters here, not soldiers, so they've already got a lot of rifled muskets. Once they can load with minié balls they'll have better firearms than anything the French will bring."

He hesitated a moment. "Well. Probably. I suppose the French might send over some of those Sharps-style breechloaders that Turenne's cavalry used in the war. But I doubt it, since I don't think they have that many of them yet. Either way, having the Virginians armed with rifled muskets will even the odds quite a bit."

"You . . . want to stay in Jamestown?"

"Yeah, Gord. That's what I want to do. After all the chasing around we did after we got to North America, we finally found someone here in Virginia willing to put up a fight. So I figure we owe them. You go run the errand down south, and then you come back and pick me up."

"I'm pretty sure I don't like the sound of that."

"I'm pretty sure I don't need your permission to do it. I talked it over with Governor West, and he thought it was a good idea too. I'm staying here; you're leaving town."

Pete seemed determined. Gordon thought about it; he considered what it would mean to not have Pete aboard.

I finally take you on a trip, little bro, he thought. *And you ditch me.*

"We'd be coming back here after St. Eustatius. We could lay over for a while then."

"And they'd have lost a month. No, this is better—I'm a spare wheel on board *Challenger*, and you're probably not going to do much shooting."

"I wouldn't bet on that."

"I'll take that bet, big bro. Go down, use the pay phone, and come back. I'll be here—not planning on going anywhere, and the French probably don't have another invasion planned in the next month."

"I wouldn't bet on that either."

"I can take care of myself. Just—go. I'll be all right."

"You've already gone through this argument in your head, haven't you, Pete? You've figured out what you'll say, and what I'm going to say, and what you're going to say to that."

"Pretty much."

Gordon leaned on the rail, looking away from Pete and concentrating on something, anything—his hands, the grain of the wood, the slant of the sun and the long shadows they cast as they stood there, two up-timers out of time.

"Look, I'm sorry to spring this on you. But you're right. I've gone over this for the last few days—ever since we decided to stay and fight. I actually thought we might wind up headed for the Shenandoah with a pack and a rifle—"

"Yeah, and our banjos. We'd fit right in."

"Not in this century. I figured that if we lost, we'd want to be nowhere near Jamestown. We could make it across country to St. Mary's and hide out there if we had to. But if *Challenger* survived, I'd send you off and I'd stay. It's why I'm here, I think, to help get these boys ready for war."

Jamestown

In the end Gordon couldn't watch as *Challenger* slipped downstream. There was Pete on the dock, standing beside Governor John West—he was broader in the shoulders and six, maybe eight inches taller. There was Pete making a pitching motion like he was on the mound in the World Series; and then Jamestown was out of sight.

Gordon had no set place on deck and was just as happy to go down to his bunk and try to concentrate on something else while the sun filtered in through the louver on the cabin window.

"Am I disturbing you, Gordon?"

He sat up in the hammock and looked across at the doorway; Ingrid stood there, half smiling.

"No, not really." He stood and beckoned her to the trunk on which she usually sat. "Is there something I can do for you?"

"I believe that I am to ask that question," she said, sitting down and spreading her skirts. "It is part of my 'bedside manner.' Is there something I can do for *you*?"

"No. I just—no. We aren't half an hour away from Jamestown and I'm worried about leaving Pete behind."

"You did not leave him *behind*. He chose to remain in Virginia for the purpose he told you. And me."

"He discussed it with you?"

"Of course he did. I am *his* friend too. You knew that, didn't you?"

"I guess I knew. So—what did he say to you?"

"We talked about all sorts of things while you were off on your trip. He has more depth than I originally thought. Like you, he dwells on the meaning of things—why the Ring of Fire, why he is here."

Gordon smiled. "He talks about how this is his first chance to do something important. We were just regular folks, and then we were thrust into this—all of this. Three and a half thousand up-time Americans, fewer every day. Most of us are still regular folks, Ingrid, trying to do our best."

"I know that. I have watched you, Gordon—both of you—as you have dealt with native chiefs and Puritan commanders, Dutch officials and Virginia planters. Always—perhaps not always Peter, but certainly you—trying to do what was right. To correct as much as possible here in your new world the mistakes and evils you committed in the one you came from. I think that's very impressive. It's certainly not common. And I think, in the end, your efforts will not be useless."

"Can I tell you a little secret, doctor-patient confidential?"

"Very well."

"I've been scared to death of screwing up. I mean, I've worried about Pete doing stupid things, and I've worried that we'd run into some problem that a simple 'trade mission' couldn't handle. But I've worried most that I'd take some step I shouldn't or say some words I couldn't take back. I've worried about that from the time we left Hamburg."

"I can believe that."

"You can? Did it show?"

It was Ingrid's turn to smile. "Not in the way you mean. You may have been uncertain, but you were also conscientious, caring, and honorable. I do not think that your patrons in government could ask any more of you. When we return and report what we have found, you should expect to be rewarded for your accomplishment. I doubt they could have found a better leader."

"I don't believe that."

"I know you don't. It is one of the reasons I know it to be true. It is also one of the reasons I wish to work alongside you. I not only have freedom I would not find in many other places, but I have honorable work that I can trust you not to squander."

"And Pete—"

"Will have his 'first chance' to do something important. When we return from St. Eustatius, you will see it as he does."

"I hope you're right."

"Of course I am. It is the duty of the doctor to reassure her patient. This will all work out, Gordon. I believe that the Divine Creator caused the Ring of Fire for His own reasons—and someday we may learn why. In the meanwhile we must do the best we can."

They fell into companionable silence for a minute or so. Then Gordon rose from the hammock and went to sit beside Ingrid on the trunk. After a few seconds, they started holding hands. By now, after all that had passed, it seemed a very natural thing for the two of them to do.

James River

In the morning Stephane woke before Eugenie and tended to the little fire, adding brush and kindling enough to bring it back to life. He had set a few snares and caught a rabbit, which he made quick work of dressing so that they would have something for breakfast.

Yesterday's fog had been burned off by bright sunlight. Eugenie was not stunningly beautiful, but in the morning light she was very attractive. If he was another sort of man, that might have led to something else right then; but Stephane, whatever he was, was not that sort. He felt protective of her, and while he did not know where he, or they, should be, he knew where they should *not* be—in Jamestown.

From where they had brought the canoe up on land, there were two plantations relatively close by. One of them should need two honest workers. This was the New World. In the Old World there were many laborers and little land, but here there was much land and few laborers.

In the meanwhile, he had other duties to perform. Personal ones. He felt free—more so than he'd ever been. Since he was a child, decisions had generally been made for him. Now, faced with what was perhaps the greatest decision in his life, he had made it himself.

So, now, he made another decision. Whatever happened, however things ended up for him and Eugenie, he would have no regrets. Feel no remorse, wish for no different course of action. What was, was; what would be, would be.

Was this what the Americans meant by "liberty"? Somehow, he doubted it. They seemed as bound to duty as any people; at times, even more so.

He had never felt any animosity toward them, although he had been working to thwart their purpose. The Americans had been simply adversaries, not enemies. Now, for the first time, he felt a kinship toward them. When they had arrived in their new world, cast adrift like no people in history, what had they felt?

Fear, hesitation, uncertainty—no doubt. But as time went on, he thought they were coming to feel much as he did on this glorious and beautiful morning.

Free. Free to choose; free to decide.

Free.

Epilogue

Magdeburg, capital of United States of Europe

"Still no word from the Chehab expedition?"

"I'm afraid not, Mr. President," said Estuban Miro. "I think by now, after months of silence, we must conclude that they suffered some sort of disaster."

Ed Piazza rose from his chair and went to the window in his office. Since he'd moved to Magdeburg, one of the things he missed was his office in Bamberg that overlooked the Regnitz river. He'd always liked the view from that window, especially the sight of the Altes Rathaus—the city's town hall—that straddled the river. When the capital of the State of Thuringia-Franconia had been moved there from Grantville, he'd been sorely tempted to take over the town hall for the state government. But that would have stirred up hard feelings on the part of the town's officials; and, besides, it would have been impractical. Push came to shove, as picturesque as it might be, the Altes Rathaus was a medieval structure. The new building that had been built specifically for the purpose of housing the SoTF's government was plain—some said, downright ugly—but it had running water, electricity and toilets.

The same was true of the office he'd moved into since arriving in the USE's capital. Running water, electricity, modern plumbing. None of that was much comfort today, though. The Americans who came through the Ring of Fire had been forced to make

325

many hard choices, these past five years. Most of them good, but some bad. And whether good or bad, far too many of them had proven to be costly.

And so again.

Two more gone. Brothers. Another family with a gaping wound torn in its side.

"Well, hell," he said.

Cast of Characters

Bogaert, Harmen van den. Trader and surgeon. Former Dutch ambassador to the Iroquois.

Bradstreet, Simon. Magistrate of the colony.

Calvert, Cecilius, Lord Baltimore. Governor of Maryland

Calvert, Leonard. Brother of Cecelius, resident of Maryland.

Cavriani, Leopold. Spymaster for Ed Piazza.

Champlain, Samuel de. Captain-General of New France.

Chehab, Gordon. Balloonist; head of the North American expedition.

Chehab, Peter. Gordon's younger brother. Soldier. (Married to **Penny**; his daughter is **Karen**.)

Claiborne, William. A Maryland colonist who has established a rival colony on Kent Island.

Corthell, Michael. Second officer of Bermudan ship *Vigilance*.

Cuypers, Andries. An indentured servant; Stephane steals his papers.

Dansin, Léonidas. Captain of *Royaume Henri*.

Dawson, Josiah. Manager of indentures for Thomas Paulet in Virginia.

De la Marche, Philippe. Courtier, a favorite of Jean-Armand de Maillé-Brézé.

De Vries, Jan. Commander, master of *Staat Van Hoorn*.

Dudley, Thomas. Deputy Governor of Massachusetts Bay Colony.

Endecott, John. Soldier and citizen of the colony. "Puritan John."

Ferson, William. A Maryland cobbler.

Garrett, John. A Maryland farmer.

Gustav, Karol, Lukas, Ole, coal shovelers, and **Jens**, the supervisor.

Hoff, Stephane. Alsatian, spy working for Étienne Servien.

Jaeschke, Ulrich. Radio operator aboard *Challenger*, originally from Magdeburg.

James, Thomas. Explorer and author. Second in command at Thomasville.

Jean-Baptiste, Honoré de. Chaplain of *Royaume Henri*.

Johanssen, Lars. Captain of *Kristina*.

Laurent, Eugenie. A French dyer, befriended by Stephane.

Lykke, Goodwife. Owner of a rooming house in Nye-Alborg.

Maartens, Claes. Sailing-Master of *Challenger*.

Maillé-Brézé, Jean-Armand. Admiral of France and nephew of Richelieu.

Maillé-Brézé, Urbain. Jean-Armand's uncle. Marshal of France.

Marcel. Leader of a street gang in Paris in Stephane's youth.

Martin, a brewer's apprentice, and **Matt**, a groom, in Virginia.

Miro, Estuban. Chief of Intelligence in the State of Thuringia-Franconia (SoTF).

Montségur, Père. A Dominican priest who taught Stephane during his training.

Nasi, Francisco. Former Chief of Intelligence.

Nilsson, Sofia. Companion to Doctor Ingrid Skoglund.

Paul. A Yaocomico Indian scout in Maryland.

Paulet, Thomas. Virginia planter; his plantation is in Charles City shire.

Peirse, Nicholas. Bailiff of the Virginia House of Burgesses.

Piazza, Ed. President of the SoTF.

Richelieu, Cardinal (Armand-Jean du Plessis, Cardinal-Duke). Chief minister of France.

Roe, Thomas. Governor of the Danish colony.

Savignon. A native coureur de bois in New France.

Seguiér, Pierre. Keeper of the Seals for King Gaston.

Servien, Étienne. Créature (client) of Cardinal Richelieu and Stephane's handler.

Skoglund, Ingrid. Doctor, Grantville-trained. Originally from Jansköping, Sweden.

Tremblay, Cardinal (Père Joseph). The "eminence grise" to Richelieu.

Tyler, James. A Maryland blacksmith.

Van der Glinde, Jan. Representative of Kilaen van Renssalaer.

Van Twiller, Wouter van. Governor of New Amsterdam. Nephew of van Renssalaer.

Vielle, François. Captain of *Saint-Christophe*.

Walks-In-Deep-Woods. Iroquois shaman and outcast.

West, John. Governor of Virginia; his plantation is Bellefield.

White, Father James. Priest of the St. Mary's colony.

Winthrop, John. Governor of Massachusetts Bay Colony.